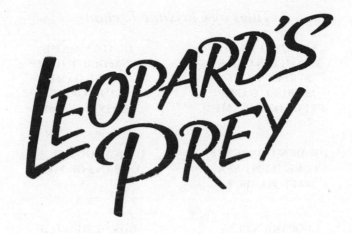

Titles by Christine Feehan

Anthologies

DARKEST AT DAWN
(includes DARK HUNGER *and* DARK SECRET*)*

SEA STORM
(includes MAGIC IN THE WIND *and* OCEANS OF FIRE*)*

FEVER
(includes THE AWAKENING *and* WILD RAIN*)*

FANTASY
(with Emma Holly, Sabrina Jeffries, and Elda Minger)

LOVER BEWARE
(with Fiona Brand, Katherine Sutcliffe, and Eileen Wilks)

HOT BLOODED
(with Maggie Shayne, Emma Holly, and Angela Knight)

Specials

DARK HUNGER
THE AWAKENING

CHRISTINE FEEHAN

JOVE BOOKS, NEW YORK

THE BERKLEY PUBLISHING GROUP
Published by the Penguin Group
Penguin Group (USA) Inc.
375 Hudson Street, New York, New York 10014, USA

USA | Canada | UK | Ireland | Australia | New Zealand | India | South Africa | China

Penguin Books Ltd., Registered Offices: 80 Strand, London WC2R 0RL, England

LEOPARD'S PREY

A Jove Book / published by arrangement with the author

Jove Books are published by The Berkley Publishing Group.
JOVE® is a registered trademark of Penguin Group (USA) Inc.
The "J" design is a trademark of Penguin Group (USA) Inc.

ISBN: 978-1-62490-533-9

PRINTED IN THE UNITED STATES OF AMERICA

Cover art by Dan O'Leary.
Cover handlettering by Ron Zinn.
Cover design by George Long.

For Erin Galloway, with love

For My Readers

Be sure to go to http://www.christinefeehan.com/ members/ to sign up for my PRIVATE book announcement list and download the FREE ebook of *Dark Desserts*, a collection of wonderful desserts sent in by readers all over the world. Join my community and get firsthand news, enter the book discussions, ask your questions and chat with me. Please feel free to email me at Christine@christinefeehan.com. I would love to hear from you.

Acknowledgments

As always when writing a book, I have several people to thank. Melisa Long, for information on the bayou and the Cajun people. Thanks so much for taking the time to talk with me. Brian Feehan, who always drops everything to work out tough fight scenes and discuss difficult scenarios and give me pep talks when I need them most. Domini, as always, you make the book so much better! I appreciate you all so much!

1

THE bayou was no place for the faint of heart—especially at night. Alligators, snakes, even the occasional large cat preyed upon the unwary. Strange lights and mysterious sightings of everything from ghosts to vengeful creatures haunted the bayou at night. It was easy to get turned around, to get lost in the endless sea of grasses and the mist-covered cypress trees. One misstep and a man could sink below the ground and never find his way to the surface.

Remy Boudreaux loved the bayou. Night. Day. It didn't matter. It was home, and it always would be. He loved the superstitions, the healers and the magic. The food. The swamps. Even the damn alligators. He loved the sultry heat and the golden sunset pouring into the water.

There was New Orleans. A city he was proud of. No matter how many times nature—or man—slammed it, the city rose over and over, each time better and stronger. It was his city. His bayou. His swamp. And his people.

The people in the bayous and swamps went about their

business every day without asking for a handout. They fished and hunted, shrimped and pulled in crabs for their families. If there was trouble, they preferred to handle it on their own. They carved out lives for themselves and their families in mosquito-infested swamps and waterways. They didn't ask permission or give apologies. They lived life as it came and they lived it large. Most had big noisy families, and celebrated every chance they got. They were your best friend or your worst nightmare, quick to anger and just as quick to give you the shirt off their backs.

Remy had traveled all over the world and he'd come back time and again to the bayou—and to his people. He loved each of them as fiercely and as passionately as only a Cajun could—or a leopard protecting its lair. What he didn't love was murder. These were his people and no one was going to come into his world, take lives and get away with it.

Remy was a big man, tall, broad-shouldered with the signature heavy roped muscles of his kind. His hair was a bit shaggy, and midnight black. His eyes were either a striking cobalt blue or, if the situation called for it, glacier blue. Unless his cat was close, and then his gaze went watchful, serious, focused and very green. His face was tough, strong jawed, the lines carved deep. He had a serious shadow going nearly all the time, and the scar running down the side of his neck could have been from a knife—or a claw.

Remy Boudreaux was not a man anyone crossed. He was as Cajun as they came, born and raised in the bayou. He was more animal than man, the instincts of his leopard aiding him as a homicide detective. He had a reputation, well deserved, as a man not to trifle with. He took murder in his city or his bayou or swamp personally.

There was little moon and the water appeared black and shiny as the airboat skimmed over it. Tall grassy reeds rose in columns on either side of them, forming a narrow canal. The grasses were thick and impenetrable, making it impossible to see over, around or through them. Gage, Remy's brother, handled the airboat easily, guiding it through the treacherous waters without hesitation.

"You sure about this, Gage? The same killer? When we are absolutely certain, we are going to have to inform the FBI," Remy said. His gut already gave him the answer. Gage didn't make mistakes, not when it came to murder.

Gage Boudreaux was sheriff of the parish. He and his men were responsible for bayous as well as the outlying areas. Right now, he was running the airboat with a grim look on his face. He felt exactly the same way about murder as Remy did.

"The body was found at one of the camps on the edge of the swamp, on the other side of Fenton's Marsh."

Remy swore under his breath. "Saria found the body, didn't she? She's still creepin' around the swamp at night taking photographs. I was hopin' Drake would get that girl under control."

Gage snorted. "Our sister has never been under anyone's control, Remy, and you know it. Her husband is wrapped around her little finger. He's no help. In any case, she knew better than to disturb a crime scene. She took pictures just in case someone or something came along when she went for help."

"There's no cell phone service out in the swamp. She has no business out there without backup. Anythin' could happen. And this is not the first dead body she's discovered out there. You'd think Drake would have enough sense to know she isn't safe alone in the swamp at night," Remy snapped.

Sometimes his much younger sister made him crazy. She was a law unto herself, and she had been since she was a toddler. Their drunken father forgot her half the time and most of the boys were off doing their own thing, so she ran wild—and was still running wild even married to a man like Drake Donovan, who was certainly no pushover around anyone but her.

Saria had no problem going into the swamp at night for

her photography. Granted, she made a lot of money on her photos and her reputation as a wildlife photographer was growing, but the things she did were dangerous and she had to stop. That was all there was to it.

"Whoa, bro," Gage said. "I see the storm clouds gatherin'. Gettin' into it with Saria is useless. You'd be talkin' to the wind. She'd go all silent, nod her head as if she understood completely and then she'd just do whatever the hell she wanted to do." Gage shrugged. "Although, if she listens to anyone, it's you."

"I wasn't plannin' on confrontin' Saria," Remy stated. He had long ago given up confronting her directly unless the circumstances were dire. She always seemed to know if he was willing to back up his threat with action or not. Locking her up was the only—and extremely dangerous—solution. Saria tended to retaliate as any self-respecting leopard would.

He didn't want any more details on the crime scene. He liked to make his own first impressions, so he didn't want to talk about what Saria found in the swamp. The serial killer from four years earlier had hit New Orleans hard, leaving behind four dead bodies over a period of two months, and then he was gone. If this was the same killer, Remy feared this wouldn't be the only body found, and no one would be safe until he was caught. The swamps and bayous were lonely and took in a lot of territory. The killer would have a big playing field.

Remy was Cajun, born and raised, but he was also leopard—a shifter. A small clan of leopards had made their homes along the bayous. He didn't just take the form of a big cat—he was leopard with all the traits of a beast. The wildness in him was always close to the surface. Passion ran just as hot as tempers. Jealousy and fury were every bit as strong as love and loyalty. There was no way to fully submerge their animal natures. They lived by a different set of rules and answered to their lair leader—Drake Donovan. Theirs was a ruthless, brutal set of laws, but necessary to keep their people under control. Some married leopards, others married outsiders who usually had no idea and never would. It was necessary to keep their ability to shift absolutely secret—even from family who were unable to shift.

"Drake and Saria have a guest stayin' at their bed-and-breakfast," Gage ventured. "A friend of Saria's. They went to school together."

That cool, matter-of-fact tone didn't fool Remy for a moment. There was a hint of excitement, a definite I've-got-a-secret-that-will-blow-your-mind underlying all that cool.

Remy remained silent. The easiest way to get someone to tell something they were eager to spill was to not be interested. He kept his eyes on the black water ahead.

Gage growled, a rumble of annoyance. "You'll never change, Remy. Bijou Breaux, the daughter of the most famous rock star in history. She's finally come back. Her daddy's been dead for four years. You'd have thought she'd come back a long time ago."

Remy remembered enormous, wild cornflower blue eyes, so haunted that there'd been times he'd wanted to sweep that child up in his arms and take her somewhere safe. She had inherited her father's ability to sing the angels right out of heaven. He ought to know—he'd followed her career.

"It couldn't have been easy bein' the only daughter of a man that famous. He died of an overdose, Gage. The drugs and women goin' through that house must have been horrific for a child. Every time we turned around, the cops were at that estate and somethin' bad was goin' on."

"Poor little rich girl?" Gage asked, a teasing note in his voice.

Remy turned cool eyes on him, and the grin faded from Gage's face. "I wouldn't put it like that, although the kids in school certainly taunted her day and night. I believe the proper line was, 'born with a silver spoon.'"

"She inherited millions. And the money's still pouring in," Gage pointed out. "Just sayin', bro. Money can make up for a lot."

"Trauma and neglect? I don' think so," Remy said. "Her daddy was crazy. Everyone in the bayou and in New Orleans knew it, but he got away with it. He had everyone in his pocket. The cops, the teachers, everyone said she was a problem child with no talent, and moody as hell."

"Maybe she *was* a problem child," Gage argued.

Remy sent him a steely glance, the sliver of moon lighting his face for one brief second so that the lines etched deep seemed carved into stone. "Or maybe her father paid them off, like he did the cops and judges and everyone else he came into contact with. Maybe you're just a little too young to remember what Bodrie Breaux was really like."

"Aren't all rock stars into women and drugs?" Gage gave a little shrug. "His music was awesome. It couldn't have been that bad bein' the daughter of someone who is a legend."

"Really? I heard the kids taunting her on the street more than once. And her best friend slept with her father in high school and then tried to blackmail him, at least that's what Saria said, and I believe he did sleep with the girl, even though Bodrie denied it and accused both Bijou and the girl of lying. With a father that famous, how was it possible to tell a real friend from someone who just wanted to use you to meet your daddy?"

Gage sent him a look over his shoulder—one that made Remy uncomfortable—but he wasn't certain why. He felt sorry for the child, he always had. She was all eyes and thick, wild hair, a sullen expression, moody and ready to fight at the drop of a hat.

"You seem to know a lot about this girl."

Remy gave a casual shrug. "I helped her out a time or two. And sometimes Saria would talk about her when I came home." Twice he'd pulled Bijou and Saria out of a party when things got out of hand. Both times the girls had been sober, but a few of the very drunk boys thought they had easy targets. Well, they were lucky to have walked away intact. Bijou Breaux was no easy mark and neither was

Saria. They'd had to fight for themselves almost from the moment they were born. Each had a soft heart, one that could get her in trouble if the wrong man came along. It was no surprise that Saria and Bijou had become friends. Both were loners and had to grow up fast.

"When she was young," Gage, said, "I'll admit I didn't care much for her. She always had such an attitude. I never saw her smile, not one time."

Remy remembered her small, tentative smile, as if she feared with one smile she might be giving too much of herself away. She'd held both arms tight around herself, her long hair hanging in her face, drawing his attention to her eyes and her feathery, impossibly long lashes. Her bow of a mouth curved reluctantly, and for one moment his heart had stuttered. He'd seen a glimpse of a young girl, already far too old for her years, holding on by a thread.

"She smiled. Maybe you were just too much like everyone else, judging her for how you thought she should be. I'll bet you thought she was stuck-up."

Gage kept his eyes on the black, shiny water, maneuvering the airboat around a bend and through a narrow opening in the tall grass to the canal that veered off toward the swamp.

"She *was* stuck-up."

Remy shook his head, watching the water ahead of them for alligators. Bijou Breaux had been a mixed-up kid, born into a rotten situation. All the money in the world didn't fix what went on in that mansion. Just once he'd caught her with drugs and he'd been ice-cold, his reaction so ferocious he couldn't comprehend his own emotions. He dumped the drugs, not caring who they belonged to. His leopard wanted to be unleashed on the others in that upscale, expensive hotel room, and he'd barely managed to keep the animal under control while he beat the three men to a bloody pulp and then yanked Bijou out of the room and out into the night.

He'd done the unforgivable, shocking himself. His anger had to go somewhere and, God forgive him, he didn't know what to do with her. He sure as hell wasn't going to put her in the system. He gripped her shoulders with hard fingers and shook her like a rag doll until her head lolled on her shoulders and tears filled her eyes. She didn't blink them away, and she didn't stop staring at him. He knew he couldn't hide his fury. Worse, he knew he was angry at her father, at her situation, at the corrupt department he worked for at the time, not at such a young, mixed-up little girl. He was frustrated by his helplessness and was taking it out on her.

She'd been eight years old and should have told her daddy on him or had him brought up on criminal charges. He'd never struck a woman in his life, let alone a child. He would have beaten a man for shaking a child so hard had he caught him doing it. She'd endured it stoically.

He'd put her back on her feet hard enough to rock her. She didn't utter a sound, just looked at him, puzzled. She should have threatened him. Talked back. Done any number of things a smart-ass child with too much money would do or say, especially one whose daddy could buy and sell them all without noticing the cost. He expected it. He waited for her reprimand.

She'd studied his face for a long time. Serious. Sober. "Why did you do that?" There was true curiosity in her voice.

"What the hell's wrong with you, Bijou?" He'd turned away from her, restless, his leopard on the prowl, fury still holding on to him with both fists. Those getting ready to party with her had all been older—eighteen to twenty-five—all friends of her father and, ominously, all men. He'd wanted to unleash the leopard on them, not just beat them. "You aren't like him." He knew she was aware exactly who he was talking about. Her rock star father, a legend revered by everyone—everyone but him. "You're like your mother, not him. What the hell were you thinkin'? Are you lookin' to let him completely destroy you? Is that what you want?"

She frowned, pressing her lips together tightly for one moment and then taking a small breath before answering. "No one gives a damn."

"I do. I give a damn. And you should too. Do you have any idea what could have happened here tonight if I hadn't come along?"

"I expected to die." She sounded old—too old. Oh so weary and very honest. She wrapped both arms around her middle and held on tightly.

His heart had nearly ceased beating. Worse, his eyes burned. How could her father expose her to the kind of people who surrounded her day and night? It was the very first time he thought of his own young sister, running wild in the swamp, home alone, caring for their drunken father while he and his brothers lived life.

He wanted to shake her all over again, and he wanted to pick her up and carry her somewhere safe. But where? There was nowhere he could take her that her father wouldn't come after her and buy his way out of trouble.

"I ought to beat you within an inch of your life for even suggestin' such a thing. You're not a coward, Bijou, and don' you ever act like one again." His hands did settle on her thin shoulders. Hard. But he stayed still, resisting the urge to make her a target for his rage all over again. She looked at him without wincing. "Do you understand me? This will never happen again. Will it?"

Her eyes on his, she shook her head.

"Say it. I want to hear you say it. You're done with drugs, alcohol and anything else that father of yours has to offer."

"I'm done with drugs and alcohol," she had repeated in a low, steady voice.

"I'm takin' you home and havin' a word with your daddy." He planned to beat the man within an inch of his life, just as he'd promised her he'd do to her if he caught her with drugs again.

That's when she'd given him that smile. That so small, tentative smile, as if she knew what he wanted to do. "It won't do any good, but thank you all the same."

The child was standing there thanking him and he'd just committed an unpardonable sin, shaking her hard enough to injure her. And she was right, which only infuriated him more. Even his chief wouldn't back him up. He would have to take her back to that mansion with its swimming pools, home theater, bowling alley and all the drugs and alcohol and blatant corruption and immorality that went on there.

She didn't say a word as they made the journey from the hotel to her home. The gates were manned by a guard who waved them through and frantically called up to the house. He stopped her as they approached the door to the ten-thousand-square-foot mansion.

"You know what I did, layin' my hands on you like that, was wrong. No one, law enforcement or not, has the right to ever touch you, especially in anger."

She nodded solemnly, her gaze steady on his, a rather disconcerting stare for one so young.

"Are you sorry?" she asked.

There was nothing in her voice or on her face to give away her feelings on the matter.

He frowned, thinking it over. She deserved the truth, but he wasn't certain he knew the truth. His gut had reacted. His leopard, snarling. Raging. But, no, it wasn't right, yet . . .

"I don't know the answer to that, Bijou," he said, brutally honest with her, with himself. "I don't know what else I could have done to get your attention or to . . ." He faded off, knowing he'd been frustrated, not having any idea what to do with an eight-year-old child who was already an adult and heading down a path of destruction he couldn't stop.

He wasn't a fool. Good people often took bribes. They had families and needed the money. Cops had extra work when Bijou's father was in town, hiring out as bodyguards and security. Often the extra perks included young, good-looking women. Bodrie Breaux was never going to have to answer for his deeds, unless there was truly a judgment day. Neither were the others whose job it was to protect this child, but took his money instead.

He could arrest Bodrie, but he'd lose his job, just as Bijou said. He couldn't argue with her, and he couldn't explain why the sight of her in that hotel room was so disturbing, surrounded by drugs and men who surely would have taken advantage of her had not another guest become upset at seeing a child with three older men going into a hotel room.

He reached past Bijou and opened the front door, indicating for her to precede him. She straightened her shoulders and her chin went up. A sulky, sullen expression crept over her delicate features as she shook her wild mane of hair to let it settle in her eyes. She marched in with Remy behind her.

There were needles lying around the marble floors; a bowl filled with pills and lines of cocaine lay out on a mahogany coffee table. Empty bottles of various strong alcoholic beverages along with empty wine bottles were scattered around the room. Several band members in different states of undress lay huddled on pillows, or on couches with one and sometimes two young women. Boxes of unused condoms were scattered around the room and used condoms were on the floor and the expensive rugs. Bodrie Breaux sprawled naked in a stupor between two naked women.

Bijou didn't look at any of them. She kept her too-old eyes on him. There was no doubt she could read the distaste on his face. "Don't do it. If you arrest him, he'll be out in an hour and you'll lose your badge. Don't bother. I'd rather have you around."

"Who are they?" He nodded toward the two women with Bodrie. One had lipstick smeared across her face. Someone had drawn on her breasts with lipstick, and cocaine still clung to her belly.

"One is my tutor and the other is my governess. They get paid a fortune for something that has nothing at all to do with me." There was no bitterness in her voice, only weariness, and acceptance. "When he gets tired of them, he'll fire them and hire new ones."

"Can I take you somewhere else?"

She shrugged. "Where? I have no other relatives. I have no idea who my mother's people are. There's me and

Bodrie." She shrugged a second time. "I've got this. This is a nightly occurrence."

"I can't leave you here." Remy shook his head. He'd shoot himself first. He'd never ever sleep again if he left a child in such an environment. He could sort it all out at the station once he got her out of harm's way. "Get out to the car. I'm taking you to Pauline Lafont. She owns the Lafont Inn."

"I know her," Bijou responded. She looked around the room, and for the very first time, she looked like the child she was. Her shoulders sagged, and for one moment, tears swam in her eyes. She blinked them away and nodded, bolting past him for the door.

Once in the patrol car, he scribbled his private number on a piece of paper and handed it to her. "You get into trouble, call me."

Pauline had taken her in for the night, just as he'd known she would. He'd gone back and talked to his supervisor and then, on suggestion of the captain, took a leave of absence. It took a long while for the sick feeling to leave his gut and an even longer time to forgive himself for the way he'd handled the situation. Bijou needed someone to treat her with a little caring, not shake her until her teeth rattled. And he damn well should have stood up to the department, even if it did cost him his job. He'd been so disgusted with them, himself, and especially Bodrie Breaux.

The encounter with Bijou had changed his life. He'd left New Orleans and joined the service. He traveled as often as he could, to see if more of his kind were in the world and, if so, how they handled the savage nature of their leopards. He had resolved to be more in control and to come back home and change things, make more of a difference. He'd run into Bijou a couple of times after he'd returned home, mostly when she was in some kind of trouble, but she avoided his eyes. To his knowledge, she didn't drink or do drugs, although she was often at the parties.

"She's just a little kid, Gage," Remy murmured aloud. "Cut her some slack."

Gage laughed, a taunting, annoying sound that made Remy wish he wasn't always striving for control. He had the urge to shove his brother out of the airboat.

"Well, Bijou is no little girl anymore. She's stop-traffic, drop-dead gorgeous."

Remy's heart stuttered and, deep inside, his leopard snarled and unsheathed his claws at the note of interest in Gage's voice. He still felt protective over that child and he was damn well going to look at her like she was a child, even though he knew Gage was right about the way she'd grown up. Something in Gage's smug, secretive attitude raised an alarm. He was missing something. His head went up and he fixed eyes that had gone a cobalt blue on his brother.

"Saria didn't bring that girl out here, did she?" He knew the answer before his brother answered. A snarl escaped, a low sound that set the swamp into a frenzy of warning calls. "She's not home two minutes and they're already in trouble together."

Gage shot him a look and then hastily turned his attention to picking his way around a cypress grove. He cut the speed of the boat and maneuvered around the large broken knobs sticking up in the water. "They found a dead body, bro. They didn't actually kill the guy."

"Fils de putain," Remy snapped, swearing under his breath. "It's bad enough to have Saria runnin' the swamp at night, but draggin' Bijou with her is ridiculous. Don' think for a minute those two aren't goin' to get into trouble. Damn Drake anyway."

"Well, you can take it up with him," Gage said. "He's guardin' the vic, keepin' the gators and other creatures off the corpse."

Bright lights lit up the swamp just ahead as the boat eased its way around the bend. The sound of a generator matched the steady drone of insects. Alligators bellowed disapproval from various directions, reminding them that every step they took on solid ground or in the water was dangerous.

Cypress trees rose out of the water, long tails of moss hanging from nearly every limb, draping the branches and swaying with the slight wind.

Remy stepped off the airboat onto the semisolid ground. His boots sank a few inches and he hastily moved to firmer ground. The swamp smelled of decay and death. The scent of blood was strong. Drake Donovan greeted him with a firm handshake.

His brother-in-law always surprised him with his strength. He was rugged-looking, with his permanent five-o'clock shadow and his wide shoulders and thick chest. It wasn't that Drake didn't look strong, it was that his grip was crushing, and Remy was an extremely strong man himself.

There was something steady and enduring about Drake, a calm most leopards couldn't quite achieve. Drake not only had the hot passion and temper of the leopard under control, but he could lead a lair of alpha males and keep them loyal and working together. Remy considered Drake a fair man, as did the other leopards, which went a long way when the law of the jungle prevailed.

"Saria okay?" Remy asked.

Those cool green eyes went a little gold. "She's just fine, thanks. Finding the body was a bit of a shock, but Saria doesn't spook easily."

That was Drake's way of saying Saria was his and no one else was going to tell her what to do. A definite back-off warning.

Remy met those glittering eyes with a stare of his own. "She's your responsibility, Drake, as is her guest." His chin nodded toward the vomit on the ground a few feet from him. "That's not Saria, so I'd say it was Bijou. Neither should have been out here without an escort, and you know it. That body could have been either of them. I don' want my sister or any other woman seein' this kind of thing." Remy refused to drop his stare, something that could be construed as a challenge to the leader of the lair. Damn it all, Saria and Bijou had no business in the middle of a gruesome murder scene.

Drake didn't blink. "Saria is Saria, Remy. You and your family are responsible for the way she is. I don't beat my wife because she was allowed to go her own way from the time she was in the cradle, nor will I ask her to change. I fell in love with an independent woman."

Remy shrugged, refusing to take the blame for his sister's shenanigans now that she was married. "Perhaps you should accompany her into the swamp at night, at least until this killer is caught."

A slow grin softened the hard lines in Drake's face. Laughter lit the green eyes, so that the gold was nearly gone in an instant.

"You're trying to get me killed, because you know if your sister thought for one moment I was protecting her in her precious swamp she'd probably stick a knife in me. If you want leadership that bad, Remy, say the word. It's all yours. You tricked me into it in the first place, you and your hell-raising brothers."

Drake's ability to defuse escalating tension was one of the traits Remy most admired in his brother-in-law—and what was most needed in a leader. Remy had never been able to keep Saria under control, and neither could her husband. She went her own way. When it was needed, Remy had no doubt that Drake would put his foot down and Saria, being sensible about most things, would listen—he hoped. He couldn't imagine Saria defying her husband over her safety.

He nodded, allowing a small grin to escape. "It's not happenin', bro. I'm not takin' on the lair for you."

"I took on your sister for you," Drake pointed out.

Remy shook his head and turned his attention to the crime scene. They were all waiting for him and he needed to get on with it, but even after all the years on the force, he had to steel himself if it was the same serial killer from before.

The body hung from the limb of a cypress tree, and just like the others he'd found in the courtyards of New Orleans four years earlier, death had been both gruesome and brutal. Blood ran in rivers, pooled in dark, dank puddles. Insects clung to every inch of the body. Sprays of blood soaked the nearby trees and brush, indicating the victim was alive when the killer had cut into him. The body had been hacked open, and the killer had harvested the rib and chest bones. The left hand had been hacked off.

He closed his eyes for a moment. It was impossible not to recognize the victim, even with the swarm of insects clouding his face and body. The face was distorted in death and covered in bugs, but everyone in the bayou had seen that particular red plaid shirt many times on a shrimper named Pete Morgan.

Pete was as good as they came. Fiercely loyal to his wife, family and friends. He'd been in the bayous all of his life. Born and raised. That red plaid shirt had been his trademark. He owned several of them and didn't wear anything else unless it was Sunday. Remy had gone to school with him, fished with him, stood for him when he got married. Got drunk with him when his firstborn had died a week after birth. Rejoiced with him when a healthy son was born two years later.

Remy made the sign of the cross, uncaring that anyone saw him. It was always difficult to see a gruesome murder, but to know the victim made it ten times tougher. He took a deep breath and forced himself to look around the crime scene, giving himself time to assimilate that his friend was dead and his end had been brutal.

He knew why Gage hadn't said a word to him. Of course he'd recognized Pete. So had Saria. It was even possible that Bijou had. Gage needed a fresh pair of eyes, completely absorbing the crime scene. Gage believed in Remy and his abilities so he'd allowed him to be just as shocked as the rest of them.

"He isn't shy, this killer." Remy tested his voice, found it professional and steady. "Any boat comin' through the swamp could have seen him, but he still took his time." He turned and looked at Drake. "The vic hasn't been dead that long." Which meant Saria and Bijou just missed the killer. He might even have heard them coming.

Drake nodded as cool as ever. "Saria was very aware of that."

Remy didn't care if Saria was aware of it or not. He wanted Drake to be aware of it. He had no doubt this was the same killer. The signatures were all there. The killer didn't bother to try to hide them—or maybe he wasn't aware he signed his work. The first kill site Remy had seen of this man's work had been in the vaunted Garden District in a historic bed-and-breakfast, with the victim hanging in the middle of the courtyard right beside the fountain. Just as this one was gruesome and messy, that scene had been horrendously nightmarish.

Arterial blood had sprayed everywhere. The body swung grotesquely from the hangman's noose, and the left hand had been cut off, dipped in oil with candles tied around the fingers and displayed obscenely on a very precise and clean altar. The altar had been in sharp contrast to the messy scene.

Remy turned to survey the altar erected there in the swamp a few feet from the body, precisely, he knew, four and a half feet to the inch, just as it was in the last four murders, four years earlier. There was no doubt this was the same killer. If he repeated the same pattern as he'd followed four years ago, there would be at least three more bodies before he was done. Each body would have different bones removed from it, all while the victim was alive and hanging. Sometimes they died of shock and blood loss first, other times of asphyxiation.

The killer was bold and always prepared. He took his time, and often the crime was committed in an area where anyone could happen upon him. Still, he never seemed to hurry. The altar, so meticulous and precise, was at such odds with the haphazard kill site. If Remy hadn't known better, he would think there were two perpetrators at the scene, but he'd studied the photographs and committed the scenes to memory. There was one murderer, and he cared nothing for the victim.

Clearly, the murder victim wasn't human to him. The only thing he wanted was the bones; the rest was a personal ritual of some sort. He just got the job done of harvesting the bones as quickly as possible, hacking up the victim without seemingly noticing the mess, or the fact that the donor was still alive. Only then did he slow down and take his time over the preparation of the altar. Whatever he was doing seemed to catch him up in some kind of weird enthrallment—unless there were two of them—which Remy had considered more than once.

"Voodoo?" Gage asked.

Remy frowned and shrugged. He didn't believe it was a voodoo altar, although certainly it appeared to be one. There were objects found in voodoo practice, but when he'd consulted Eulalie Chachere, a legitimate voodoo priestess, she had told him that the altar wasn't right even for a black magic practitioner. Still, he would consult her again. She was an expert and if anyone could figure out what that altar meant, it would probably be her. Remy knew her and trusted her. "You'll have to consult Eulalie. She worked with me before so she's familiar with the crime scenes. She won't disclose details. She can be trusted."

"I was hoping you'd work this case with me, Remy," Gage admitted. "You're the murder expert, not me. He's not finished."

No, he wasn't. Remy had an extra sense for such things even if he hadn't seen the murderer's work before. He would kill again and soon.

Remy nodded. "I'll talk to Eulalie. She'll help us. I'll need to talk to Saria and Bijou as well." He sighed. The last thing he wanted to do was talk to Bijou about anything unpleasant. It had taken years to forgive himself for the way he'd handled her ugly childhood, and he'd hoped that if they crossed paths as adults they could both put it behind them.

He forced himself to look at the body of his childhood friend. As long as he'd been the "vic" Remy could push the reality away for a time so he could get the job done, but grief was pushing close. "Have you notified next of kin?"

"I'm going to do that now," Gage said.

Remy inhaled. He should be the one to do it. He'd been best man. When he opened his mouth to suggest it, Gage shook his head.

"I was friends with him as well," Gage said. "And I went to school with his wife. You have enough to do. You always get the short end of the stick, and I'm askin' you to take lead on this. The least I can do is spare you talkin' to Amy."

"Thanks, Gage," Remy said. "Tell her I'll stop by later."

"The photographer has already taken pictures and forensics is waiting. I wanted you to see everything first before anything could be disturbed. Saria took photographs as well. She documented everything she saw and had Bijou do the same. Saria has an eye for detail. I told her you'd want a word with her. They're both waiting at the Inn."

Remy nodded as he skirted the crime scene. Somewhere close would be the stash of a bloodstained, hooded plastic suit, homemade, stitched together with meticulous, even stitches, plastic gloves and coverings for boots. He found what he was looking for the required four and a half feet from the body on the opposite side of the altar. This time, the discarded, bloody suit was half in the mud, as the killer had chosen a cypress tree near the water's edge, not giving himself enough room to put the clothing in a safer place. A mistake?

Remy frowned. That was unlike the killer. He didn't make mistakes, but the ritual of the altar and discarding of the kill suit was part of his rigid routine. He had never deviated. The plastic clothing should have been set safely away from the water, which meant the tree chosen should have been over by several feet. Remy turned back, and studied the grove of cypress trees. There were plenty of others trees the killer could have hung the body on.

He studied the grasses and the directions they were bent. Trails led around various trees and always back to the one the killer had used to hang Pete. "Are you certain the integrity of the crime scene was preserved? Saria and Bijou didn't walk around? None of you did?"

Drake shook his head. "We know better."

Remy nodded and made his way carefully around the area to the back of the tree where Pete's body hung. The old cypress had several letters carved into it, obviously over several years. The letters *P* and *M* had a fresh line drawn through them. His leopard gave a leap of recognition. This particular spot had been a favorite of those living up and down the bayous or close to the marshes and swamps, to meet and party. He remembered it from his youth. *His* initials were carved into the trunk, along with his brothers' and even Saria's.

"He didn't choose this location randomly," Remy said. "He wanted to use this specific tree. Gage, take a look at this. Have the photographer photograph the entire trunk."

He studied the old carvings. The spot was easy to access from two different canals and a good place to meet where parents weren't going to find you. Lovers had carved their initials into the trunk surrounded by hearts. Others had simply put their initials in. *S* and *B* definitely stood for his sister, Saria. He wondered if the bold *B* and *B* were Bijou's initials, although he couldn't imagine her ever coming to the swamp to party. He wanted a list of all initials and a confirmation of just who those initials belonged to and said as much to Gage. If the killer was choosing victims by those who had partied here, had this gone from random killings to actual targeted prey? Or had it been that all along?

2

REMY stood outside of the Lafont Inn staring up at the grand Victorian-inspired chateau. The Inn was old-style elegance, an era long gone by, but well loved. The chateau was a hidden jewel set back from the edge of the lake where cypress trees had given way to groves of white pine and oak. Marsh, swamp and lazy bayous all were within easy reach. Visitors could lie in the hammocks set in the shade of the trees a few feet from the water, staying cool in the trees while the breeze off the lake fanned them.

White with pale blue trim helped to veil the house when the fog poured in from the lake and bayous. A wraparound porch and large balconies on the second story invited guests to view all kinds of birds and wildlife in the comfort of intricately carved and spacious rocking chairs.

The Lafont Inn had been in the Lafont family for over a hundred years. Miss Pauline Lafont had inherited the house from her grandmother, who had married a Dubois. The name of the estate had changed at that time, but Pauline had returned the original name to the family property when she decided to modernize the house and turn it into a bed-and-breakfast some years earlier. On Saria and Drake's wedding day, she'd given the Inn to Saria as she had no children and considered Remy's little sister the daughter she'd never had. Pauline had then married the man of her dreams, the one man she'd loved always—Amos Jeanmard.

Remy rubbed his aching eyes. He didn't want to be like Amos, sacrificing his personal happiness in order to preserve the leopard species. Amos had married the wrong woman, a leopard, and stayed with her for years. Only after she died did he marry Pauline, the woman he truly loved. A part of him understood, but he was tired of being alone. He wanted a family, a woman to come home to. He'd traveled the world looking in the rain forests in the hopes of meeting someone who not only attracted him physically, but who could live with a man like him. He had all but given up hope of finding a female that not only suited him, but who he could love.

Leopards were lethal cats, wild and savage and wanting a mate as well. A man couldn't just bring home anyone, because if their cat became edgy and dangerous, so did the man. Sex could get rough and his temper could be short. He had great control, but lately his leopard had been displaying every negative trait a leopard had.

He sighed and forced himself to move through the trees toward the chateau. He'd been on for nearly seventy-two hours gathering evidence for a murder in the French Quarter and had been on his way home when Gage had called him.

He was edgy. Restless. His body hard and hurting. His mind a little chaotic. Not a good sign in the middle of a murder investigation and never good when he was going to see his wild sister. He didn't need to say a word to her about going to the swamp at night, she'd know what he thought and she'd be on the defensive. If he was honest with himself, he couldn't blame her.

His leopard needed to run. Leopards didn't do well cooped up. If they weren't let out every now and then, the human side became every bit as dangerous as the animal side and he'd never felt so edgy in all his life, not even when he was in the jungle.

"Saria," Remy raised his voice. "Where are you, honey?" He walked farther into the darkened entryway. As always, his heightened animal senses took over. He could see easily even with the lack of lighting. He inhaled, taking scents into his lungs.

It always smelled good at the Inn. There was always a seemingly endless supply of fresh coffee and he could count on his sister to have a large pot of stew or meatballs and gravy simmering on the stove. Saria and Drake managed to give the old place a welcome feel of home from the fireplaces to the fresh-baked bread and home-style cooking. Besides the rich aroma of coffee and spices, he smelled the faint scent of lavender. Without thought, he followed that drifting, inviting scent through the hallway toward the kitchen.

"Saria? I'm lookin' for a cup of coffee. Where the hell are you?" he called out again. She should have known he'd be coming no matter how late it was, if for no other reason than just to make certain she was all right.

"Saria is in her darkroom developin' her photographs. I can get you a cup of coffee if you like." The voice came from the kitchen. Smoky. Suggesting dark nights and silken sheets. Sex and Sin. Velvet like a neat whiskey so smooth, yet burning all the way down.

Remy closed his eyes. His body tightened, a savage, urgent reaction to that amazing voice. No woman should be allowed to sound like that. That candlelight and "come take me to bed" tone gave her unfair advantages over a man.

He turned slowly. No one could possibly live up to that sultry, southern drawl so erotic and sensual, an invitation to wild nights and temptation. She stood draped against the wall, one hand on her hip, her enormous eyes on his face. He would never forget those eyes. Before, they'd taken up her face, a wild cornflower blue fringed with impossibly long, thick feathery lashes, as dark as the cloud of hair tumbling around her face. Now, her eyes drew attention to her remarkable skin and the perfection of her bone structure.

As if her inviting skin and the wealth of thick black hair cascading down her back weren't enough to bring a man to his knees, her body was all soft inviting curves, and firm defined muscle. Her legs were long and slender and she had a small waist, emphasizing her breasts and hips. Her generous mouth had full, curved lips, bringing on enough fantasies to last a lifetime. His breath caught in his throat and need slammed low and mean into his body.

His reaction to her shocked him. His leopard raked and clawed for supremacy. His body hurt, a deep savage ache, every muscle tense, his cock thick and hard, demanding to be sated *now*. He'd never had such a visceral, intense sexual reaction to a woman in his life. He wasn't a gentle man, his cat was too aggressive, but he'd learned control and kept a tight grip on both the man and the leopard. What the hell was it about Bijou Breaux that sent him spinning out of control?

Remy was grateful for his ability to keep his features expressionless. Bijou was sixteen years younger than him— a damned baby—and his body had no business reacting to hers no matter how sexy she was. It was wrong in every way.

She pressed her lips together, the tiniest movement. Her lashes fluttered, veiling her eyes, but not before he caught a glimmer of hurt. "You probably don' remember me. I went to school with Saria."

She stepped forward—into his space. His leopard ripped at him. His body tightened until he almost felt sick with need. He actually flexed his fingers, his palms itching to run over all that glorious skin. Lavender engulfed him, nearly drove him out of his mind. She extended her hand.

"Bijou Breaux."

Self-preservation or white knight? He detested hurting her. She'd been hurt by enough people. Silently he cursed. He couldn't stand seeing that small flash of hurt, not associated with him. He was going to race to the rescue and let her know he hadn't forgotten her.

"I don' forget faces, Bijou," he admitted. Or eyes like hers. What the hell had happened to her in the growing phase? Her mouth should be outlawed. "Of course I remember you." He took her outstretched hand and knew instantly it was a mistake to make physical contact. "It's nice to see you again." Damn. How absolutely mundane was that? He couldn't take a step, his body hurting like hell, his leopard roaring at him.

Her hand was small, fingers slender, slightly trembling as she shook his hand—or attempted to. He placed his other hand over hers, holding her still, locking her to him while his eyes searched hers. Her lashes came down immediately, hiding her thoughts from him. She definitely had trust issues.

"Are you visitin', or back with us?" He didn't let go of her hand, waiting for her answer. His body went still, watchful, his cat coiled, every muscle locked and ready.

"I bought a club in the French Quarter. I'm home for good." She smiled at him, a brief flash of perfect white teeth. "It's difficult to stay away. I think the bayou gets in our blood and just doesn't let go."

Her voice stroked his body with caressing fingers. He felt her touch right through his veins so that his blood surged hotly and his cock jerked hard. He let her go to keep from pressing her palm on that throbbing, burning hard-on that wasn't going away anytime soon.

"But you're not stayin' at the Breaux estate?" Hell. He had to keep the conversation going because he couldn't move. He was grateful there were no lights on.

"I'd rather burn that place down then ever set foot in it again."

That smoky velvet tone didn't go with the words at all. It took him a moment to assimilate what she'd actually said, he was too busy trying to tame his wild craving for her. He told himself she was a baby. A kid. He was a damned pervert even thinking about her, let alone losing control and nearly throwing her up against a wall.

His cat had a vicious temper, a powerful, passionate

animal he worked at keeping in check at all times. If his cat was influencing him sexually, it would be the first time—and it was a hell of a time to choose. He forced his chaotic mind to get a grip. Bijou would rather burn down a mansion than set foot in it again, and what did that say about her child-hood? The sad part was, he was probably the only one who would ever understand.

"Are you puttin' the estate on the market?" Reluctantly he allowed her hand to slip away. His heart ached for her. She was all woman on the outside, but there was still a small part of her that was that child who had never had a childhood.

Bijou turned and moved away from him, a graceful sway of her hips, her long hair a waterfall of living silk tumbling past her waist, the ends caressing the curve of her buttocks. She crossed the floor to the counter where the coffeepot waited.

"I don' know. Bodrie was so famous, and so loved by everyone."

Her voice remained soft and sultry, without a hint of bitterness, but he noticed immediately she didn't call Bodrie Breaux *dad* or *daddy*.

"Not everyone," Remy disputed as he tested his ability to walk. Sympathy for her helped ease the terrible need raging through him. He managed to make it over to the table where he toed a chair around, dropped into it and stretched his legs out in front of him to ease the pressure in his jeans.

She turned her head to look at him through her long feathery lashes and clouds of black silk. "Be careful, Remy, you can get death threats if you don' give him his due adu-lation."

Before he could read her expression, she'd turned back to pouring his coffee as if she hadn't just dropped a bomb in the room.

He took a breath to calm the explosive reaction deep in his gut to her announcement. Swearing under his breath, he exhaled, and shifted again to ease the muscles coiling and the adrenaline flooding his body. "What threats, Blue? Have you been gettin' threats?" His nickname for her slipped out. He'd never called her Blue to her face, but mostly referred to her as Blue when he talked with Saria about her in the old days.

For some reason the moment he was around her he heard the song, "Blue Bayou." More than that, when the sun shone on her thick, black hair, blue lights played through the strands, and then there were her striking blue eyes.

"Do you take your coffee black?"

"Of course." He sent her a little smirk. "I'm Cajun, honey."

A brief flash of a smile lit her eyes for a moment. "A manly man. How could I have forgotten? You were always scary."

"Was I?" Remy asked. His eyebrow shot up. He was quite certain he had the ability to scare the hell out of anyone.

Bijou nodded slowly and took the chair across the table from him. She wasn't safe. She might think she was, but she was well within striking distance, and somewhere in the back of his mind, that same fantasy was playing—throwing her up against the wall and ripping her clothes away from all that beautiful, soft skin.

"You still are," she conceded. She glanced toward the door, clearly hoping Saria would appear suddenly to rescue her.

The sexual tension in the room was nearly as acute as their awareness of one another.

"That's a good thing," he said with a small grin, trying to ease the rising tension between them. "You were about to tell me about death threats."

She sighed and took a cautious sip of the coffee she'd poured for herself. "I suppose I did bring it up so I can't very well pretend I didn't." She ducked her head and thick strands of hair covered her face.

Remy leaned across the table and tucked the wild cloud behind her ear. Startled, her lashes flew up and her gaze collided with his. The tip of her tongue moistened her lower lip. He caught the rise and fall of her breasts beneath her shirt. It was interesting to him that she hadn't turned on the lights.

His leopard roared at him, rising like a tidal wave, fighting him for supremacy. His leopard was difficult, but not like this, savage and feral and so determined. Remy fought the cat into submission, although it snarled and prowled, not settling at all. All the while he studied Bijou's face. Never before had his cat responded to a woman. Was it possible she was leopard? Little was known about Bijou's mother. It was nearly impossible to tell if a woman was leopard. Only when the woman entered the Han Vol Dan—a period of time when the female cat came into heat at the same time a woman ovulated—did male cats react. Sometimes, the two periods of fertility never synced, and the cat never emerged.

"Has your life been threatened?" Remy pursued. He wasn't about to let it go, not even with his body screaming at him. He let his hand fall away from all that silky hair and satin skin.

Bijou shrugged. "Just about every day. There's been so many it's impossible to take them seriously. Fans of my father don' believe I have the right to his money; after all, I wasn't there when he died. It was no secret that we didn't get along. The tabloids had a field day. Bodrie liked to read about himself so he fed the stories and kept our so-called feud goin' in the magazines."

Remy drummed his fingers on the table beside his coffee cup. His leopard was more agitated than ever and he needed an outlet for the restless energy. She was sitting across the table from him, but damn it all, he wasn't that big of a pervert. He had to stop thinking of her as a woman and think of her as a victim. Someone in need of a policeman. There were threats against her life, of course he'd be upset on her behalf. As an officer of the law, it was his duty to make inquiries and ask her questions. She was his sister's friend, staying at Saria's Inn. If Bijou was in danger, so was Saria. He had every reason to be disturbed over the threats.

Sadly, he was too damn old to listen to anyone's bullshit—especially his own. "This has been goin' on since Bodrie's death?"

Bijou nodded. "Yes. Apparently his home should be made into a sacred shrine to him."

"If you didn't inherit, who would have?"

"I'm his only proven heir and he named me specifically. There were plenty of children who came forward to claim they were his, but DNA disputed it."

"How much money are we talkin'?"

Bijou's gaze met his. "You don' listen to the news, do you?"

"Too depressin'. All those murders. Gives me a bad outlook on life."

Her answering smile was faint. "Hundreds of millions and growing every day."

He went still inside. She dismissed death threats she received, and she was worth hundreds of millions of dollars? People killed for a pair of shoes, let alone that kind of money. "Did the threats come in the form of letters?"

Bijou shook her head. "Remy, you've got a real murder to solve. This is silly stuff. Some of Bodrie's fans were crazy. They worshipped him and apparently still do. I've lived with it all of my life. I've come home, bought a club and intend to live out my life in the place I love. Bodrie isn't goin' to dictate my life to me, not anymore."

She had all the money in the world and she wanted to come home to the bayous. Something wild and feral deep inside him settled. He could breathe again, his body once more his own, his cat relaxing, stretching lazily. He took another long, satisfying drink of coffee, regarding her over the rim of the mug.

"Nevertheless, I want to see those letters, Bijou. If you

don' have them, give me the name of your lawyer, or your contact at the FBI and I'll take it from there." He wasn't a man who took no for an answer and his tone said it all.

"If you insist."

Now that he knew he was getting his way, he relaxed even more. "How long have you been home?" Because if it was longer than a couple of days, he was going to drown his sister.

Bijou looked around the large, homey kitchen. "Isn't it funny what makes a place a home? Miss Pauline was so good to me. I used to come here or go to Saria when I couldn't stand bein' in that house. Neither ever ratted me out, no matter how much money Bodrie offered around the bayous and swamps for my location."

She was painfully beautiful, with her skin and tumbling hair, that drawling, sexy voice and perfectly kissable lips, and hearing her use the term *ratted out* made him want to come across the table and find out just how kissable her lips really were.

"I traveled for several years," Remy said, deciding it would be far more prudent to converse with her rather than assault her. "And I knew this would always be my home. The heat, the mosquitoes, all of it—is home."

"I agree." She leaned her chin into her palm, her gaze steady on his. "Why did you call me Blue? You did that once before, a long time ago."

"I did? I think I have a good memory, and I don' recall makin' that mistake when you were a child." And he'd better start convincing himself she was still a child. Her eyes were too old, held too much knowledge for her age.

"I didn't mind," she admitted. "You were one of the few people who ever seemed to give a damn about me. Callin' me Blue just meant you'd given me a nickname. People do that when they care, at least that's what I thought at the time."

She was breaking his heart and clearly she wasn't trying to. She gave him her little smile that never quite reached her eyes and spoke in that smoky, matter-of-fact tone. She wasn't looking for sympathy and would be upset if she got it.

He forced a casual shrug, resisting the urge to yank her into his arms and hold her close to his heart. She certainly brought out the white knight in him. He had a protective streak a mile wide when she was around. "That song, 'Blue Bayou.'" He wasn't going to tell her that every time he heard it instead of "bayou," he heard "bijou."

"Since I love the bayou," Bijou said, sweeping her hair back over her shoulder in an unintentional sexy gesture, "I'm fine with your nickname for me."

How old was Saria? Maybe she was older than he thought. "What the hell were you doin' runnin' the swamp at night with my crazy sister?"

He looked up as Saria came through the doorway, grinning at him. He had known she was there. She was leopard and moved in silence, but he was leopard and he'd scented her the moment she'd come out of her darkroom and entered the main part of the house.

Saria laughed at him. "You're not goin' to think I'm crazy when you see these pictures, Remy. I had Bijou write down everythin' she could remember, her impressions and even sounds she heard, and I did the same. We didn't discuss the crime scene so we wouldn't taint each other's memory."

"Good thinkin', Saria," Remy admitted.

"Comes from havin' brothers in law enforcement," she said cheerfully.

Saria set the pictures she'd developed on the table in front of him. For the first time she seemed to notice the lights were off. "What are you two doin' sittin' in the dark?"

"Visitin'," Remy answered. "Waitin' for you to get out of that room so I could give you a lecture on safety, which you clearly won't listen to, and drinkin' your very fine coffee."

Saria put her arm around Remy's neck and dropped a kiss on his cheek, a rare gesture of affection for his younger sister, and one that told him she'd been shaken by finding the murdered man. He patted her arm gently.

"It was Pete Morgan, wasn't it?" Saria asked, stepping back.

She wasn't fast enough. Remy caught the faint scent of fear and felt her body tremble. His sister was a tough little thing, but finding the body of a friend, one murdered in such a vicious, gruesome way, had to have been distressing. She flipped on the light and crossed to the counter to get a glass of water.

"Yes. I'm sorry, Saria. It must have been horrible for you."

She turned and faced him, leaning back against the counter. "How do you do it? Gage and the others break up fights most of the time and go after idiots, but you have to look at murders all the time."

He was very aware of Bijou across from him blinking rapidly as if the light bothered her. He knew better. She'd always acted tough, as if she didn't care, but she had a soft heart. "Most murders around here are pretty straightforward. Stupid arguments, revenge. That sort of thing, not a serial killer who rips apart people I know."

"I don' think I'll get that image out of my head for a long time, if ever," Bijou admitted.

Remy's gaze jumped to her face. He didn't need the light on to see that her eyes were haunted. He cursed his sister silently. "What exactly *were* you doing in the swamp tonight?"

"I was showing Bijou a nest I've been taking a series of photographs of. I landed a really big contract with a company that provides stock photos and they wanted the swamp at all hours along with the wildlife and plants," Saria answered. "I'm supposed to capture the feel of the swamp throughout all seasons."

Remy swallowed his sarcastic reply. Sending in the pictures of the murder would certainly show the company that gave his baby sister the contract what kind of danger they put her in, but Saria would ignore his bad humor and good advice. She went her own way and made her own decisions. He couldn't blame her. Maybe it was guilt that made him so overprotective of her now. When she was a child running wild and free in the swamp, he hadn't paid attention. Like Bijou, she hadn't had supervision and she'd been the adult in the home, not her drunken father.

"Remy." Saria sounded loving.

He looked up at her. She looked so young, but so adult. Just like Bijou. Of course they'd gravitated toward one another and been secretive about it. For good reason. He sighed.

"I had a good childhood," she said. "Stop beating yourself up. I love that you want to protect me, but I'm all grown up now. You can't take care of all of us."

"I can damn well try," Remy replied. His gaze jumped to Bijou's face.

She sent him a faint smile. "I see why you were so insistent on me explainin' the threats. You have a strong protective instinct, but really, Remy, you have enough family to look after without addin' me to the mix."

He wished that was all it was. "Don' kid yourself, Blue," he snapped without thinking.

Color swept into her face and she frowned at him. The hell with it. Let her figure it out on her own. Clearly, no matter how often he told himself she was a baby, his body said other things. He was leopard enough to know there was more going on than he could see. Instincts were strong in leopards and never once had he found himself in such a predicament.

Saria stared at him in shock. She looked from Bijou to Remy and shook her head, dropping into a chair.

"Tell me about your mother, Bijou," Remy ordered, slipping the photographs into an envelope without more than a cursory inspection. He had no doubt they were excellent. Saria's skills were known throughout the country, her reputation building fast. He didn't want to distress Bijou any further.

"My mother?" she echoed, her voice even softer, taking on more of that smoky, sultry flavor. "I don' know anythin' at all about her. Well, just what Bodrie told me. He met her backstage at a concert and she was strikin'. He couldn't take his eyes off of her. But honestly, Bodrie couldn't take his eyes off of most women."

Remy was aware of Saria's sharp glance from him to Bijou and back. She was smart, and she knew Remy didn't bother with small talk. He interrogated people for a reason. He was good at it, sounding conversational and interested, putting whoever he was interrogating at ease and slipping in questions so easily no one knew how much information they actually gave up. If he was bringing up the uncomfortable question of Bijou's mother, he was doing it for a reason.

He flicked one look at his sister, and she pressed her lips together, getting the message to keep her mouth closed.

"Did he ever talk about her family? Where she was from?"

Bijou shrugged. "He mentioned they came from someplace near Borneo. He always said she was exotic, but he never talked about her family. I got the impression they were dead."

"You have a lot of money, Blue," Remy pointed out. "Hire a PI and find out."

"Why?" Bijou regarded him steadily over the rim of her coffee mug. "Why would I want to do that now? It isn't as if Bodrie wasn't known around the world. He went on world tours all the time. I ought to know. He dragged me along on most of them." She took another drink of the aromatic coffee and gave another shrug. "I needed them when I was a child. Even knowing someone was out there fightin' for me would have helped, but they didn'. They left me with him."

Again, he couldn't detect bitterness in her voice. Just resignation. She accepted that most people loved, even revered her father and thought he could do no wrong. She went her own way, made her life and made no apologies for it.

"I think it would be difficult," Saria said to Remy, "if I was Bijou and I inherited all that money, to trust anyone comin' out of the woodwork and claimin' they were related. Money makes people do crazy things."

"It comes with the territory, Saria," Bijou said. "I learned that in school. Real friendship is a treasure and that's why I always appreciated you. I knew if I came home, nothin' would have changed between us."

Remy was prouder in that moment of Saria than he'd ever been, and she was pretty extraordinary in his book. The fact that someone as wary as Bijou would have complete confidence in his sister when they hadn't seen one another in several years, made him respect Saria all the more.

Saria laughed, dispelling some of the tension. "I'm definitely that wild girl runnin' the swamps. I love it here. I don' need a lot of money to be happy here, Bijou."

Bijou's smile was faint. "I bought my little club with the hopes that I can draw a crowd. I'm renovatin' the little apartment above it."

"You're planning on livin' above the club?" Remy nearly came out of his chair, but managed to force himself to stay outwardly calm. Was she insane? Bijou had more money than most in the world, in her own right she was huge in the entertainment business, she'd admitted to death threats and she was going to reside with no security right above the club where she sang.

"I thought it was a good idea," Saria said, a little frown forming. She knew her brother's tone. His voice went low and soft and drawled more than ever. "What's wrong?" She looked from Bijou to Remy for an explanation.

"It's nothin', Remy," Bijou said. "I told you."

"Just a little matter of death threats," Remy explained to Saria. "You know, nothin' serious at all."

"I don' appreciate the sarcasm," Bijou said, her eyes widening. "I don' recall you bein' so sarcastic."

"That's because you hero-worshipped him when he didn' deserve it," Saria pointed out, laughing all over again. "He has a bossy attitude and never lets you forget he's the one runnin' the show."

Color crept up Bijou's neck into her face. "I did *not* hero-worship him," she denied. "He was bossy back then too."

"There's a difference between bein' bossy, which I wasn't, and bein' the boss, which I am," Remy said, in his mild voice. "In any case, worshippin' me is a good idea. I'm all for it."

Saria rolled her eyes and laughed, the sound joyful. Remy hadn't seen Saria for a couple of weeks and he forgot how he felt in her company. She seemed relaxed and happy, her home always open and her smile ready. When had his sister become so different than the wild child he remembered? Sure, she still went her own way, but she was confident, not defiant. He liked being in her company. Her happiness radiated from her, surrounding everyone close to her. Her joy lifted those around her. She was definitely a woman, all grown up, married to a man closer to his age than hers. And she was happy.

"You know you'll have to stay with me." Saria turned to Bijou, all serious, her mercurial nature showing. "At least until Remy checks everythin' out and we know you're safe. It will be fun," she added. "I've missed you."

"That's a good idea," Remy said. "Make certain I get all of the threats, Blue, anything you have, paper, recordin's— all of it."

Bijou shook her head. "I feel like I'm being railroaded. I don' recall anyone ever bein' able to do that to me, not since I turned thirteen."

"Someone needs to look after you," Remy said. "Especially if you're goin' to run wild with my sister."

Saria kicked him under the table. "I don' run wild anymore, Remy. I'm a workin' girl these days. I spend so much time takin' pictures I barely have time to run this place properly or do guidin'."

"Guidin'?" Bijou echoed. "You take tourists out in the swamp and bayous?"

"That's how I met Drake," Saria said. "I was his guide. Maybe you should take over my business. You could meet . . ."

Remy slammed his coffee mug onto the table. "Okay,

that's it. I'm drownin' you in the bayou, Saria. I should have done it when you were born. I knew you were goin' to be giving me trouble. Blue is *not* takin' strangers into the swamp. I'd be shootin' someone before nightfall."

Saria leaned across the table and mouthed *Bossy* at Bijou.

"Clearly you don' have enough to do, Remy," Bijou observed. "Or you've been deprived of shootin' someone for a long while now."

"A little of both," Remy said. "But now that I've got your sassy ass back in New Orleans no doubt I'll have my hands full."

"No doubt."

"You're really goin' to make your home here?" Remy asked. "For good?"

Bijou nodded, her vivid blue eyes meeting his. "I'm tired of fightin', Remy. I've made so many mistakes trying to be someone I'm not. I just plain don' like the life, traveling, living in hotels, the bodyguards and constant paparazzi and crowds. I think for a while there, I felt as if I had to compete with Bodrie, which, of course, was impossible."

"You have a beautiful voice," he said, drumming his fingers on the table. Once more that restless, dangerous feeling was building. He could feel his muscles coiling, his body going still, as if at any moment he would leap on his prey. He was very aware of Saria sending him an uneasy glance. She was leopard and her senses would pick up the shift in his body instantly, going on alert herself.

"Thank you. The thing is, I have to sing. I have to write music. It's there in me and I have to get it out. I don' expect anyone to understand. I just have this personal need. I'm done with the big tours and singing rock and roll all the time. I'm not Bodrie, nor do I want to be. I love the blues, and jazz. I play the piano, not a guitar. I love the saxophone. I can rock with the best of them, but that's not my real dream. Everyone says if I switch from rock and roll to what I prefer, I can't make it. My fan base won't follow me, but this is something I have to do. My manager said I didn't have

the talent for blues and jazz, but I love it so much and I want
to try."

"That's bullshit, Blue, you've got talent." Remy felt the
clawing at his gut. His cat needed to run, and he'd better get
out of there soon. He had no idea why he was so reluctant
to leave. Saria just made the place too comfortable.

"We'll see, won't we?" Bijou flashed one of her small
smiles. "I'm singin' occasionally in my own club, so we'll
see if I can draw anyone in."

Saria shot him a look that clearly said, "What the hell is
wrong with you?" He couldn't very well tell his baby sister
that *everything* about Bijou Breaux set his leopard off.

"Oh, no doubt you'll do fine," Remy said, meaning it. Her
voice was special, sultry and filled with sex and sin. She'd
have all the local single men flocking to her club. Every male
tourist in town wanting to get laid would be there as well.
Just the thought made him want to grind his teeth. His leopard flexed his claws and raked at him, adding to his dete-
riorating mood.

His skin itched. Every joint ached. His jaw hurt. Every
sense heightened. Lavender drifted through the room into
his lungs, and he took the scent deep. He could find Bijou
Breaux on the darkest night, no matter how faint the trail.

"Did you know, Remy, when the light hits your eyes a
certain way, they change color?" Bijou observed. "You have
the darkest blue eyes and they suddenly go green or sometimes, they glow, like a cat in the dark. I remember a couple
of times when I was a little girl, I fixated on your eyes. I
used to dream about them."

Saria's frown deepened. "Did his eyes scare you?"

"I suppose they should have, but no. I found the change
sort of comforting." Bijou gave Remy another tentative smile
that sent another hot surge of blood rushing through his
body, straight to his groin. "For all his bossy ways, your
brother can be rather comfortin'."

Remy eased the painful ache by stretching out his legs,
taking a moment to breathe, rather pleased that she wasn't

afraid of his cat. She didn't know the glowing eyes signaled his cat was close, but that didn't matter. He didn't want her afraid of him—well, maybe that wasn't altogether true. One of them had to have good sense, and clearly his leopard was reaching for supremacy.

He gathered up the photographs and the two sealed statements. "Gage will be askin' you questions later so expect him. Tell him I have the pictures you took and your written statements. He's asked me to consult on this one so I might be back askin' questions as well." He stood up and pinned his sister with cool eyes. "Stay the hell out of the swamp until this nutcase is caught. He's dangerous." He waited. Still. His leopard coiled and ready.

Saria sighed. "I'm not quite the idiot you think I am, Remy. I have no intention of runnin' around in the swamp while a vicious serial killer is out there."

"I've never considered you to be an idiot, just very adventurous," he corrected.

Now that he had his sister's agreement he allowed himself to focus on Bijou. The moment he centered his attention on her, he knew it was a mistake. She looked up at him with her impossibly blue eyes and all those long lashes, the cloud of silky hair tumbling around her face and that mouth that needed to be outlawed and he knew he was lost. It wasn't going to matter that she was his sister's age. Hell, nothing was going to matter. Bijou Breaux was going to be seeing a lot of him.

"I want *everythin'* you have on those death threats, Bijou. Bring them by my office tomorrow around noon. And don' give me any trouble over it."

She sent him a faint smile and gave a small salute. He didn't wait for sass. He turned abruptly on his heel and got the hell out of there before he—or his leopard—did something disgraceful.

3

REMY stared down at the photographs Saria took of the crime scene. The forensic photographer's photos were scattered across his desk along with those of his sister. He kept frowning at them, because they damn well didn't add up. Saria was a pro. She didn't make mistakes. She'd used her zoom lens to record each section of the crime scene. She'd been methodical, so much so that if he'd put the pictures together, they would form a very accurate and detailed replica of the crime scene. And that was the trouble.

He sighed and ran both hands through his hair for the tenth time. Evidence bags lay on top of each of the pictures of an object that had been on the altar. A bag corresponded with each of the forensic photographs, but not with Saria's. The difference was put down to Saria being an amateur at a crime scene, but he knew better. Nothing rattled Saria for long, and she was surrounded by her brothers and Drake, who were all methodical when it came to solving crimes. Her work was impeccable—which meant someone had added an object between the time Saria took the pictures and the forensic photographer had taken them.

He studied the pictures of the altar as a whole. Rocks formed a rectangle on the ground. Not just any rocks. Each rock was somewhat flat, oval in shape, and had been placed precisely one inch from the next. He knew because he'd measured the distance several times. How could a killer be so absolutely precise? Did he carry a damned ruler along to the murder? Was he just that good that his measurements weren't off at all, not by so much as a hair?

The macabre hand of the dead man was soaked in oil and set upright in the exact middle of the altar, but in the front. Remy was certain, if the same held true from the last murders, they would find out the oil was baby oil. He even knew the brand. Trying to track that down had been a dead end. The murderer had chosen the most popular brand of baby oil. A black candle was tied to each of the fingers of the hand and had been burned.

Three inches directly behind the hand and in the exact center of the altar was a bowl of the victim's blood. The bowl was plastic—again, untraceable, although of course they'd try. Unfortunately, anyone could buy that particular brand of picnic supply at any store. The bowl was always filled with precisely one pint of blood. How did the killer get the amount so exact? Another big question.

Behind the bowl, again three inches exactly, was the victim's heart, offered up like some damned sacrifice. Scattered around the altar were objects clearly taken from the swamp. Spanish moss, a leaf from the hanged man's tree, a shell, three different types of feathers as well as leaves from various plants, all objects found right there at the crime scene. None of it had been carried in by the killer and not one thing on the altar held a print.

But there was the length of the candles in Saria's picture. They had burned an inch, if he judged it correctly, and there was only the bowl of blood. In the forensic photographer's photograph, the candles appeared to have burned a little longer, not that precise inch, although it was difficult to tell. A knotted string lying half in, half out of the bowl of blood was not in Saria's picture. Not in the ones of the entire altar and not in the ones of just the bowl of blood that she had taken. There were close-ups. Perfectly clear pictures. Nowhere was that small seven-knotted string until the forensic photographer took the pictures several hours after her.

How long had it taken Saria and Bijou to make their way back to the Inn and tell Drake? Drake had brought a generator and lights to the crime scene. He'd had to retrieve those items and make his way back. Had the killer been there all along? Had he watched Saria taking pictures of the crime scene and then finished his ceremony? Bijou had been there as well. How close to both women had he been?

Saria and Bijou had to have interrupted the ritual ceremony the killer was compelled to conduct after each murder. The compulsion was so strong that he'd stayed concealed in the swamp and then, after the women left, he'd finished his ritual. That was the only answer to the discrepancy between the photographs.

His heart reacted to his conclusions, going a little crazy at the thought of either Saria or Bijou so close to a vicious serial killer. He wiped his hand over his suddenly dry mouth. He was going to have to try to talk to Saria whether she liked it or not and try to point out that not only had her life been in danger, but her friend had been in jeopardy as well.

The killer had balls. He'd proved that enough times. He murdered his victim, taking his time harvesting the bones and then conducting his bizarre ritual where others could come up on him at any time. The fact that he could be discovered didn't seem to faze the killer at all.

Remy picked up Saria's photograph of the entire altar, comparing it with the forensic photographer's picture. The most interesting thing of all was the altar contained no blood spatter whatsoever. Not on any of the objects, so Remy was certain the altar was constructed after the murder and harvesting of bones took place. But . . . Remy studied the pictures. There wasn't a single drop of blood on the ground inside the altar. The scene was messy, all around the altar and beyond it, but not the ground where the altar had been constructed.

"He covered it," he said aloud. "He had to have covered the ground where he was going to make his altar. He didn't want any blood spatter on his precious altar."

Remy sighed again. He wasn't getting any closer to understanding the killer. Even the photos and the files that the FBI had sent from the previous murders weren't helping. He had no idea if anything on the altar was significant. It appeared to be a voodoo ritual, but if it was, it was like none he'd come across in all his years there in the bayous. Voodoo was a part of his community and he respected it and those who practiced it. Whatever the killer was doing had nothing to do with the voodoo he knew.

He smelled lavender and almost before the scent could compute he heard the low murmur sweeping through the bull pen. A low wolf whistle had him turning his head, his heart giving a quick leap and his cock jerking at that now familiar scent.

Bijou walked through the bull pen, turning heads as she made her way toward him. She was dressed in a pair of jeans that hugged her curves lovingly and a simple rose-colored shirt that looked as elegant as she was. Her thick cloud of hair was pulled back in a long intricate braid, but tendrils had escaped and curled around her face, drawing attention to her bone structure, flawless skin, beautiful eyes and fantasy mouth.

Remy swore under his breath. Did she have to be so damned sexy? Couldn't she walk like a normal woman? She had to be aware she was surrounded by men leering at her, but her hips swayed and she had that little smile fixed on her face that made him crazy. His leopard jumped right along with his heart. She was truly breathtaking. He couldn't blame the other men for gawking, but he didn't have to like it—and his leopard hated it. The beast raked and clawed and snarled. Bijou Breaux certainly brought out the animal in him every time she got close.

He shook his head and stood up. He knew that little smile that never quite reached her eyes. She looked like money, a little haughty, elusive and completely unattainable. She also had her gaze glued to him, making him feel as if he were the only man in the room. Her white knight charging to the rescue when she didn't even know she needed rescuing.

His heart did a crazy dance in his chest. Bijou could get up in front of thousands of people on a stage and sing her heart out—he knew—he'd watched a few of her concert performances on YouTube. She detested being Bijou Breaux in person. She looked relaxed, but he knew better. He knew her. He could read her, and sweeping through the bull pen was difficult for her with so many staring at her. She had her eyes on him because he was getting her through it. She was pretending no one else was around. No one but him.

Remy covered the distance between them with long, purposeful strides, his eyes holding hers. The moment he reached her, one hand circled the nape of her neck while he leaned in to brush a kiss on her temple, staking his claim, as well as indicating she was under his protection by drawing her in close to the shelter of his body. When he lifted his head, his formidable gaze swept the bull pen, putting everyone back to work instantly.

His leopard was close to the surface, the itch under his skin, his jaw aching and his teeth feeling sharper to his tongue. He had a feeling his eyes had gone cat, glowing as they changed color. He breathed her in, uncaring that his coworkers had never seen him act this way toward a woman. He wanted them to see and understand the warning he was giving them.

"Blue." He deliberately called her by his nickname for her, making it intimate. Connecting them. "You brought the letters to me."

"You gave me an order." She didn't look left or right, but kept her gaze on his face.

Her sultry voice sent heat through his body. It obviously didn't take much for her to ensnare him or his leopard. "That's a fact," he agreed, wrapping his arm around her waist and turning her back toward the door. "Let's do this over lunch. I've been here all night and I forgot to eat this mornin'."

The moment he touched her skin, electricity arced between them. He felt the current rushing through his body and jumping back to hers. The beat of her heart echoed through his. His leopard pushed at him hard. He pushed back, taking control quickly.

"That's not good for you, Remy," she said, her frown drawing his attention to her full lower lip. "You need a keeper."

"Are you applyin' for the job?"

Her blue eyes darkened and her lashes swept down, veiling her expression. "I've heard you're quite bossy. I'm afraid I wouldn't do very well under those circumstances. I've been told I have problems with authority figures."

He found himself laughing. He remembered saying that very thing to her when she had been about thirteen and he'd dragged Saria and Bijou out of a party at his own father's bar. He'd been home for a brief visit and he'd caught the two of them in the bar. She'd been sassy, and he'd given her a lecture as he'd driven her to Pauline's Inn. He'd taken both girls there, certain they'd behave for Pauline when they wouldn't for anyone else.

"It's the truth."

"I just have never recognized anyone that could be a real authority figure," Bijou contradicted in her smoky, sexy, melt-a-man-in-his-tracks voice.

He wrapped a length of her long, thick braid around his fist and pulled to keep from kissing that tempting mouth of hers. "You aren't lookin' in the right place, Blue. Open your eyes."

She laughed, a soft, sensual sound that went straight to his groin. Laughing was so unexpected and so unlike Bijou, but just as sexy as her voice.

"I'm afraid to do that, Remy, especially if you're applyin' for the job. You'd be . . . *bossy*." She laughed again, soft and low, sending hot blood pounding through his body.

"You've spent too much time with my sister," Remy pointed out, and stopped in front of the door to the small café just down from the police station.

Bijou stiffened and halted abruptly. "You want to eat out? In a restaurant? In public?"

"Where else?" He tightened his hold on her. "You're safe with me."

Bijou shrugged. "If that's what you want, but I'm not so certain you're safe with me."

Remy opened the door and she slipped inside, immediately stepping to one side waiting for him as heads swung around and a low murmur started up in the café. People recognized her. How could they not? Her face had been plastered on every tabloid for years and now, she was famous in her own right. Her face went still, composed. She wore that slightly haughty, don't-touch-me expression she'd worn as she moved through the bull pen.

Remy glided close, and she tucked her body into his, beneath his shoulder, almost without conscious thought. He wrapped his arm around her, aware everyone in the room who knew him—and it was most of the customers—would consider that gesture one of proprietorship. Bijou obviously considered it a casual gesture and she relaxed against him.

"Booth or table, Remy?"

Remy smiled affectionately at the dark-skinned waitress with bright eyes and a ready smile. "Give us a booth if you can, Thereze, somewhere we can sit where no one will notice us."

Thereze burst out laughing. "I think it's a little too late for that, Remy."

He looked around, and dozens of cell phones were up in the air, snapping pictures. He heaved a sigh as many of those in the café began texting furiously.

"Follow me, and I'll do my best." Thereze tossed Bijou

a smile over her shoulder as she led them through the café toward the back. "Before you leave, you'll have to autograph somethin', even if it's a napkin, for my husband, Emile. He's the cook here and trust me, honey, he's your biggest fan."

Bijou nodded. "Of course. I'd be happy to do that."

"Maybe a picture with him to put up on the wall," Thereze added. "We own this place, and he'd be over the moon if you did that for him."

Bijou's body brushed against his. Remy looked down at her. Her smile was fixed in place and genuine, but the tension in her body belied her expression.

"No problem," she agreed, but her smoky voice had dropped another octave.

Remy waited until they were seated, had menus and Thereze had bustled off to get them water and bread. "Will it really bother you to have your picture taken with Emile? I've known him for nearly my entire life and he's a good man."

Bijou shrugged, avoiding his eyes by looking at the menu. "Of course not. I said I would, didn' I?"

She sounded casual and sweet, even to his highly trained ears. Still, he didn't believe her. He reached across the table, pushing down the menu with one hand and tipping up her chin with the other, forcing her head up, forcing her vivid blue eyes to meet his.

"Tell me. I'm okay with you bullshittin' anyone else you feel you need to, but not me. What is it?"

Her gaze drifted over his face, taking him in. Deciding. There was a moment of hesitation but he refused to release her. He simply waited.

"I don' mind takin' a picture with anyone," she said, her accent thickening, "but you have no idea what one picture will start." She gave a little shrug. "No matter. If the food is good, it'll be well worth it."

That little half smile, so secretive, told him she wasn't exaggerating. Something was going to happen once she took a picture with Emile.

"I'm not goin' to leave you here alone, Blue," he assured. "Whatever it is, you won' be alone."

"Tell me that after I'm here a few hours."

"Hours?"

She nodded her head. "The nice people come first, askin' for an autograph. Then the more bold ones askin' for a picture. And then the ones who believe I owe them somethin' because they listened to Bodrie's music, or mine. In the middle of all of that, will be the really ugly ones who want to give me lectures and tell me I've never had talent and I'm skatin' on my daddy's fame." She shrugged again.

He let go of her chin, scowling. "If that really happens, why the hell are you runnin' around without a damned bodyguard?"

Her long lashes fluttered for a moment, and then lifted. Her blue eyes laughed at him. "I thought I *was* runnin' around with a bodyguard."

"I'm bein' serious."

Thereze put two glasses of water in front of them and poured a cup of coffee for Remy as she lifted an eyebrow at Bijou in inquiry.

Bijou smiled at her as she nodded. "I'd forgotten how strong the coffee is in New Orleans," she admitted. "The heat and the coffee."

"And mosquitoes," Thereze added.

Bijou nodded again in agreement. "The mosquitoes, although I've noticed they don' bother me quite as much as other people. It's rare for me to get even a single bite. Something to do with my blood, or my scent. Whatever it is, I'm happy about that."

"Somethin' else?" Thereze asked.

"I'm fine, thank you."

Remy waited until the waitress moved away. "Blue, why would you go around without a bodyguard if people do you that way?" He wasn't about to let it drop. She couldn't tease her way out of the question. He wanted an answer. She was as elusive as the wind, but not to him. Never to him. He refused to accept her evasions.

Bijou sighed. "I forgot how relentless you are when you want something."

She was silent, absently stirring her coffee with a spoon. Remy waited. He had the patience of a leopard on the hunt and it had always stood him in good stead when interrogating a suspect. Bijou was like a wild, wary animal, not certain who to trust. He was going to be that man.

She finally looked up at him, her gaze once again moving over his face as if looking for something. "I'm coming home, Remy. I want a home and this is it, my last stand. I've been battling uphill for so long and I'm just plain tired. I'm not makin' records or doin' concerts anymore. I want to have a quiet, peaceful life. I need to sing, so that's why I purchased the club, but I need a home. I'm done with travelin'."

"You're very successful as a singer."

She sent him a brief smile. "Yes. I can't say the business wasn't good to me. Nothin' on the scale of Bodrie, but certainly more than most and I'm grateful. I truly am. I think I had to prove to myself I could do it, and I've done that. I just want to come home now."

He didn't blink. Didn't take his eyes from hers, forcing her to hold his gaze. "Why? I'm not buyin' into the quiet peaceful life, Blue. Not for a moment."

Color crept into her face and for a moment her blue eyes shifted away from his, feathery lashes veiling her expression. "It's partly true, Remy. I don' know what else to tell you. I spent far too long fightin' a losin' battle, tryin' to outrun Bodrie. I learned it was foolish to even try. What was the point? He's my father. He wasn't the monster I thought him, or the god others did. I'm not ten anymore, desperate for my daddy's love."

"Everyone needs love and family, Bijou," Remy said.

She pressed her lips together. "I need peace. And a home. I'm not him. I have a voice, but I *choose* not to be a rocker.

I don' have to make excuses, or be angry. I don' have to try to please anyone else. It's been a long road to learn things Miss Pauline tried to teach me so long ago. To be honest, I don' like the life. I want a different one."

"Miss Pauline tried to teach us all things we took forever to learn," Remy said. "The bodyguard," he prompted gently.

She was hiding something from him. She'd even admitted it, but she wasn't going to reveal anything else, not so soon. He couldn't blame her. She hadn't seen him in years. The strange connection he felt toward her when she was young had been his need to protect a child. Now, she was all grown up and his feelings were so intense he could barely control them.

"If I look like a regular person, everyone local will accept me that way. Eventually no one will think a thing about me walkin' around town on my own, and I'll have my life back." Bijou picked up the menu, clearly finished with the conversation. "What's good here?"

He let her get away with it even if he didn't altogether agree with her. "Everything. Emile has turned this little café into the premiere place to eat." Remy took a sip of coffee and allowed himself to really look at her. "You're really beautiful, Blue." It was the simple, raw truth and he saw no reason to pretend otherwise.

Looking at her was painful, and not just because she made his body ache. He was very aware of the other men in the room and the way people were gawking at her. The leopard in him snarled and raked at his gut. He found it necessary to breathe deep to keep the animal calm while he drank her in.

"Thank you, Remy. I do appreciate you sayin' so, but you're starin'."

"I'm well aware of that. I'm thinkin' you're goin' to need to get used to it."

They both waited until Thereze took their orders. Once the waitress was gone, Bijou opened her mouth to respond, but Remy gave a small shake of his head and without asking a single question, she halted. His leopard had gone still. Coiled. Ready. The great spine flexed. Remy smelled mint and soda pop. He turned his head and watched two young girls approach. Teenagers. Both were nervous, their fear and excitement coming off of them in waves.

Remy was well aware of the deep breath Bijou took as she turned her head toward the girls, a welcoming smile curving her soft lips.

"Can we have your autograph?" one asked while the other looked as if she might faint.

"Of course," Bijou answered readily. She took the proffered pen and tablet. "What's your name? Do you live here in New Orleans?"

"I'm Nancy, Nancy Smart, and this is my cousin, Alexandria. We both live here," Nancy volunteered. "We went to your concert in Lafayette. It was so much fun."

"That was fun for me too," Bijou said as she wrote on the tablet. "The Lafayette concert was like comin' home and bein' with people I know after travelin' so much."

"I heard you bought a place here. Are you goin' to be singin'?" Nancy ventured as she took the tablets and hugged them to her. "Can underage get in?"

"That's a good question. I should think about how we can do a few special nights for everyone," Bijou said. "Thanks for mentionin' that."

Nancy beamed. "I hope you do."

The two girls nearly tripped over one another, giggling as they hurried back to their booth. Bijou twisted her fingers together and sent him a small smile. "I'm sorry."

"Don' apologize. That comes with the territory."

"I hope I can still keep the younger crowd listening to me," she said. "The kind of music I love isn't always the most popular with them."

Her voice when speaking was amazing. The blend of smoke and sultry heat slipped under his skin and stroked like caressing fingers.

"Did you bring the threats against you?"

She nodded and drew a packet out of her tote bag. The stack of letters was at least an inch and a half thick and was in a plastic bag. "These are the ones I'm mostly concerned about. There's a lot more, but these are the worst. My manager told me to keep them inside somethin' to keep fingerprints off of them." She pushed the packet across the table with one finger. "They're all yours. I hope you have fun readin' them. You'll need a really good sense of humor."

Her fingers fiddled with the water glass, idly turning it in circles.

"Bijou." Remy used his lowest, most commanding voice. "Look at me."

Her lashes lifted and the impact of those vivid cornflower blue eyes hit him hard. "Has someone or something scared you?" She didn't respond, but he saw the answer in her eyes. "You can tell me. Just say it."

Her hand went defensively to her throat, to the thin silver chain that dipped into the neckline of the shirt she wore, almost as if that chain was a talisman. "It's silly really. I'm becomin' a little paranoid. I thought if I stayed with a friend—with Saria—I could sort things out. She's very grounded."

He resisted the urge to snort his opinion of that. The truth was, for all her wild ways, Saria was grounded and she made a loyal friend.

"I used to get a few threats before Bodrie's death, nothin' really scary, just that I didn' know what a good daughter should be like to her daddy and I was goin' to learn a few hard lessons." She nodded toward the packet. "I could recognize his patterns. He's been writing me a very long time. When I started singin' on my own, a new theme started. I had no talent. I shouldn't be tryin' to capitalize on my daddy's good name and if I didn' stop, I was goin' to find myself in a dangerous position."

She closed her mouth abruptly, pressing her lips together tightly as Remy swung his head toward two more people approaching. This time it was a couple. They looked to be in their sixties.

"Ma'am. Miss Breaux?" The man held out a napkin. "Would you mind autographin' this for us? Mr. and Mrs. Chambridge."

The woman smiled hesitantly. "We try to go to all your concerts."

"We've got all your music," Mr. Chambridge added.

"Of course," Bijou said, "I'd be more than happy to give you an autograph. I can't believe you're so kind as to come to my concerts and support me."

As if she'd thrown open the gates to a fancy mansion and invited everyone in, the others in the café quickly rose and pressed close, thrusting paper, shirts, napkins and even a backpack at Bijou to sign. She didn't hesitate, but was gracious and sweet to every single person jarring the table and crowding around them. The temperature went up fast. Remy found himself wanting to shove everyone back away from her, especially those that touched her arms and shoulders, or "accidentally" brushed her hair.

It was as if the floodgates had opened, and there was no going back. Remy began to feel uneasy. His leopard snarled and raked at him, so close his skin itched and he could feel fur rippling beneath the surface. The closer the crowd pushed on Bijou, the edgier he became. Anyone wishing her harm could easily slip up behind her and plunge a knife into her back or shoot her.

His jaw ached and he rubbed it, trying to soothe the tense muscles developing so quickly. Bijou continued to sign autographs and talk briefly with each person, and just as she predicted, individuals became bolder, asking for pictures with her. Bijou posed with that same soft smile on her face. Over and over.

More people poured into the café, brought, no doubt, by the text messages of friends. Two men pushed their way through the crowd. Thereze protested as she tried to get through the mass of people to deliver the food. The men pushing at Bijou were obnoxious, pressing for her phone number, where she was staying, and when she simply smiled and shook her head, one swore and called her *bitch*.

Remy stood up so fast he knew his cat was closer to the surface than he'd even imagined. His reflexes were lightning. He caught the man by the back of his neck and slammed him down on the table, holding him there.

"I'm done with this. Everyone go back to your tables. And you can apologize for your mouth," he added to his prisoner. His voice was deceptively low. His eyes definitely glowed cat—he was seeing with a cat's vision. His aggression was doubly so. He knew his strength reflected his leopard's closeness.

The man muttered an apology as the crowd hastily dispersed. Remy let him up but retained possession of his arm. "I know you. Ryan Cooper. You came down here a couple years ago and you work at the strip bar. I know where you live. If you give Miss Breaux any trouble, any at all, you'll be gettin' a visit from me and it won't be pleasant. Have I made myself understood?"

"Yes," Cooper said, and glanced at his friend. Remy recognized the man as Brent Underwood. He only knew Underwood because the man hung out with one of the shifters, Robert Lanoux. Underwood quickly looked away.

Remy let go of Cooper abruptly. Cooper staggered back a couple of steps and turned, nearly sprinting from the café. Remy watched him go, following his progress out on the street, ready for anything. Cooper was a mean bouncer. He provided drugs for the patrons and sometimes allowed underage boys into the bar, getting them hooked early on the after-hours sex and drugs. Remy made a mental note to talk with Robert about Cooper and Underwood.

Thereze set the food on the table.

"I'm so sorry," Bijou said. "Sometimes it happens and disrupts everythin'."

"I suggest exitin' through the kitchen when you're ready to leave," the waitress said. "Those people are crazy."

Remy sank down into his seat, grateful he could keep a straight face. Thereze had been the first person asking for both an autograph and picture.

"If you were my official bodyguard, Remy, I'd be sued every ten minutes or so," Bijou said, and then flashed a genuine smile, one that lit her eyes. "Just sayin'."

"He had it comin'," Remy all but snarled. "He can keep his opinions to himself."

"The problem is this, my friend"—Bijou leaned across the table and put her hand over his—"people were probably recordin' your every move, just because you were with me. You're a policeman. You can't do people that way. You'll be very lucky if you don' end up on YouTube."

"Tell me again your harebrained reasoning for not havin' a bodyguard." His leopard wasn't settling fast enough. He had the urge to throw her over his shoulder and carry her out of the café. What would happen after that he didn't dare admit, even to himself.

"You haven't changed much," Bijou said, and pushed the food on her plate around.

"Don' kid yourself, Blue." He pinned her with his eyes. Leopard's eyes, staring straight and completely focused on prey. "I've changed. If I took you home to your daddy, I'd beat the shit out of him and have him thrown in jail for child endangerment. I'd call the feds and have them clean up the department like I should have done all those years ago. So don' you for one minute believe I'm that same idiot that let you down. It was the act of a coward to leave you with him."

Her lips, so full and tempting, frowned. "Is that what you think, Remy? That you were a coward? First, you didn't leave me with him, you took me to Pauline that night. You saved my life. That's what you did. You saved me. Never for one minute believe that I'd be here without you, because I wouldn't."

She didn't flinch when he bunched her shirt in his fist, fury rising all over again at the thought that a child would want to take her own life.

"I wouldn't be here without you, Remy," she repeated, honesty in her voice.

"Damn it to hell, Blue, you're goin' to get us into trouble if you keep this up. Why the hell aren't you afraid of me? You don' have good sense."

"Who says I'm not afraid of you? You're a very scary man. Even I can see that. Eat. You skipped breakfast."

He forced himself to loosen his grip on her. What was he going to do? Yank her across the table, lay her out and devour her? It might be what he wanted, but he had learned control. He just needed a break from that faint temptation of lavender.

"I am hungry," he admitted, meaning it. Not caring if she read his true meaning.

Evidently she had no problems translating. Color tinged her flawless skin. "Just eat, Remy. Everyone is starin' at us."

He sighed and took a bite. The food was spicy and every bit as good as he remembered. Emile was an extraordinary chef. "His dinners are even better. You can't make a reservation here, and people wait for hours for one of his meals."

"The food is outstandin'," Bijou agreed. She sent him a little grin. "I have to admit, I love to eat good food."

"That's one of the hazards of bein' from New Orleans. We love great food, music and fun."

"Which means I have to work out daily," Bijou said, "but if I can eat this kind of food, it's well worth it."

Remy's gaze dropped to the package of threats. "You were tellin' me why you suddenly, after all this time, became uneasy with these threats."

Bijou made a face at him over her fork. "You're like a pit bull."

He nodded his head solemnly. "Proud of it too."

"Bodrie owned several properties beside the mansion and I inherited those along with the copyrights to his music, his record label and everything else. One of the properties was a camp he liked to go to party." She lifted her lashes and there was faint humor in her eyes. "Because, you know, he didn't party enough at any of the hotels, his home or anywhere else."

"Poor man. I can't imagine Bodrie Breaux stayin' for very long at a camp, even if he has every luxury. One swarm of mosquitoes and he'd be out of there."

"So true. That was his number one complaint. But he liked to play up his Cajun heritage. He almost always took a camera crew out with him, to document his need to go back to his roots." She ate another forkful of food, chewing thoughtfully while she looked at Remy. "I went to the camp a few days ago and there was a huge eye painted on the walls inside. The first few times I came across that eye, I thought it was a childish prank. Like, 'I'm watchin' you,' but each of the properties had the eye painted on a wall, includin' the mansion. I haven't gone there, but the caretakers said someone broke in and ruined the wall in the entryway."

"And?" Remy prompted when she fell silent.

"At the cabin, someone left a dead animal, killed inside the house, right by the eye. It was all very dramatic with *'You're next'* written in the animal's blood. I took photographs just in case it was a real threat and not some idiot trying to make the tabloids."

He swore under his breath. "Bijou, what the hell were you thinkin' waitin' so long to come to me about this?"

"I didn't want to be rescued again," she admitted reluctantly. "I hate that you saw me like that, in need of rescue."

He resisted the urge to swear again. She did bring out his protective instincts, there was no denying that, but damn it all, she'd been eight years old. "Tell me the rest."

She blew out her breath as she glared at him. Remy couldn't help laughing. "Now that's the girl I remember. No one can duplicate that exact look. I'm sorry I'm annoying you, Blue . . ."

"You certainly don' sound like it," she contradicted, putting down her fork to study his face.

Her hand went to the fine silver chain she wore, fingers curling around it. She twisted the links absently, drawing the pendant up out of the neckline of her shirt, giving him a glimpse now and then of the artsy piece. It looked expensive—and it looked like a piece of jewelry a man very interested in her would give as a gift.

"You could be right. Just tell me everythin' right now because I'm goin' to get it out of you eventually." He reached across the table, unable to stop himself—another loss of control *she* caused—and pulled the silver chain until the pendant was completely exposed.

The piece was round, three-dimensional and beautiful. He recognized the work of Arnaud Lefevre, a renowned sculptor who made rare jewelry pieces as well. His work went for tens of thousands for the jewelry and hundreds of thousands for his sculptures. One of the most prestigious galleries in New Orleans carried his work. Occasionally, Arnaud visited the various galleries around the world displaying his art and it was always a huge gala event.

"Where'd you get this piece?"

"Arnaud gave it to me," Bijou said. "Isn't it beautiful?"

"You two goin' out?" He asked the question casually, but he wasn't feeling casual.

She frowned at him and carefully put down her fork. "I thought we were talkin' about the threats to me."

"We were. Now we're talkin' about you steppin' out with Arnaud Lefevre."

4

BIJOU studied Remy's completely expressionless face. His eyes had gone strange, from a brilliant cobalt blue to a deeper shade of green that almost glowed. He looked—dangerous. His gaze was focused on her, unblinking, mesmerizing and a little exhilarating. She found herself staring at him, unable to look away. Remy had a commanding presence. He exuded absolute confidence. There was no back up in him. He was even more of a steady rock than she remembered.

Remy truly fascinated her. For most of her life she'd thought of him. With her every adversity he'd been there, forcing her to do her best, believing in her, even if it had been a child's imagination. He had become her white knight, the man who had come charging in and saved her in her darkest hour. She'd clung to his belief in her. The words he'd said to her became her mantra to live by. He believed she was strong—wasn't a coward—and she'd done her best as a child to live up to his confidence in her. She'd never broken her promise to him. Not once, no matter how tempted she'd been.

He was so beautiful—in a very masculine way. There was nothing feminine about Remy other than maybe his eyelashes. His shoulders were wide and ropes of defined muscles rippled every time he moved. She'd flirted—how could she help it—and he'd flirted back. Strangely, she was more at ease with him than she ever was with anyone.

"Arnaud is a friend. I've admired his work and bought one of his sculptures several years ago at a gallery in New York. He was having a show there and I met him. He apparently enjoys my music."

"Everyone enjoys your music."

"If you're thinkin' he's a stalker, or makin' death threats, you can think again. He has my private number and can call me anytime. I have to change the number every couple of months and I send it to him." The thought of elegant Arnaud Lefevre as a man going into the swamps and painting eyes on the walls of buildings was laughable.

Remy frowned. "I don' have your number. Why is that?"

Laughter bubbled up. She rarely felt like laughing, but for some reason when she was with Remy, she felt happy. "Do you want my private number?"

A tiny thrill swept through her at his nod. She tried hard to suppress it as she held out her hand for his phone. He looked so serious. Her hand trembled as she took his cell phone and entered her number before handing it back.

Remy glanced down and then smiled at her. "Blue?"

"My code name if anyone ever gets ahold of your phone." She sent him a faint grin.

Bijou was used to false adulation. People liked her and wanted to be around her because of who she was—Bodrie's daughter or because she was a wildly popular singer. She didn't want that from Remy, and he wasn't that kind of man. Remy made her feel as if he knew her—as if he could see inside her where no one else had ever looked.

She'd come home for the reasons she'd told him, but it was more than that. She'd never been able to connect with a man, to trust a man enough to get close to him. There was always Remy, and no one ever quite came up to her childhood image of him. He was the larger than life hero who she compared every man she met with. She knew she had trust issues. She didn't always like men, her lessons in their behavior and lack of loyalty had been hammered into her very early. But there was Remy . . . He was the only man who had ever stood for her—the only man who cared enough to lose his temper when she'd done something so very, very stupid.

Why did he have to be so freakin' beautiful? She hadn't been prepared for that.

"Havin' money or fame, or both, doesn't guarantee a man is good, Blue," Remy said. "Of all people, you should know that."

She caught at the slender chain and held on. What was that supposed to mean? Did he think she was still eight and not so bright? She'd learned that lesson years ago. Before she could think of a reply Remy picked up the stack of letters protected by the plastic sleeve she'd put them in and turned the package over and over.

"What's in here that scared you so much you came home?"

He made her sound like a little rabbit. "Your sister said you have a one track mind and it's most annoyin'. I'm beginnin' to believe her."

He leaned across the table, his cobalt blue eyes holding her gaze captive. He was absolutely mesmerizing. "No, you don'. You find me charmin'."

Her heart stuttered. A million butterflies took flight in her stomach. She had been so certain she could come back to New Orleans and find that her childhood hero was really a figment of her imagination. The real Remy was far more potent and sexy than she had ever conceived. He was larger than life. Protective. Funny. Intelligent. Everything she could ever want in a man, and that was totally unexpected.

"I suppose one could call you charmin'," she agreed in a slow, grudging voice. All the while laughter bubbled close to the surface. She liked spending time in his company.

More, he made her feel safe, and she hadn't felt safe in a long time. It occurred to her that she was in over her head.

"Blue." Remy's voice went very low, a stroke of velvet over skin. "I do enjoy the way you're lookin' at me, but I want an answer. What has you scared?"

She forced her mind to focus on his question rather than his sexy tone. That meant not looking directly at him. She found she really loved his face, the strong jaw with the darker shadow and his strange, almost cat eyes. Bijou pulled herself up short. She felt a little like a teenager with her first crush. She hadn't really experienced that stage of development and it was disconcerting to find she was entering into it at this late date.

"Twice, when I was a teenager, living in the mansion with Bodrie, I had a huge fight with him. A giant eye was sprayed on my bedroom wall with a can of red spray paint. A few months after Bodrie died, I found that eye drawn on the ground in my front yard with the same red spray paint. It was disturbing, but not at all frightening." She shoved both hands through her hair and sat back in her chair.

How did one explain to those probing eyes why she hadn't been more proactive about death threats? She'd grown up around them. Stalkers were part of her childhood. As a teenager and while she attended college, she'd dealt with both threats and stalkers on a regular basis. Nine times out of ten, the threats ended up being someone trying to scare her because she'd turned them down when they'd asked her out on a date.

"Threats and stalkers are commonplace with bein' Bodrie's only child. I wanted to live a normal life . . ."

Remy growled. There was no other word for it. The sound was frightening. Her gaze jumped to his.

"How the hell did you expect to live a normal life, Blue? You're worth a fuckin' fortune. You're the daughter of one of the most infamous men on the planet and you sing for a living. A little protection might have been an intelligent decision."

She pressed a hand to her suddenly churning stomach.

"If you're goin' to insist on insultin' me, Remy, then screw this. I'm not tellin' you a thing." She'd never discussed her life with anyone. It wasn't easy, especially with him. Damn him anyway. She was all caught up in his good looks and dark sensual nature, and forgot he thought of her as twelve. "Thanks for lunch, but I've got a few things to do." She reached for the packet of letters.

His fingers shackled her wrist, pinning her hand to the table. "I'm sure you're very aware I have no problem with public confrontation. I don' mind throwin' you over my shoulder and takin' you somewhere more private to discuss this. Can you imagine the number of videos and pictures that will be put up on YouTube?"

She glared at him, afraid to say anything. They stared at one another for a long while. He didn't blink once. Not once. She became aware of his thumb sliding back and forth over her wrist. It felt like a caress to her and after a couple of minutes, she couldn't think of anything else she was so aware of that small motion. His touch sent a rush of heat through her entire body.

"I shouldn't have implied you aren't intelligent," he relented. "I read the newspapers and more than once your name has come up for the business decisions you've made. It's just that I know a lot more about human nature than you do. I've seen just about everythin' ugly one human can do to another. I don' want to take chances with your life."

She was in *way* over her head. For all of her money and sophistication, the life she'd led, she'd never been really attracted to a man before and she was falling fast for Remy. She kept reminding herself the attraction was leftover hero worship of a man who had cared enough to be angry at her. He clearly still thought of her as a child.

"It's all right." She experimented with moving her wrist subtly, hoping he'd get the hint and release her so she wasn't so aware of him physically.

"No, it isn't," he contradicted. "We both can't be hotheads, Blue. You're goin' to have to mellow out and learn to stay calm. Stalkers and anyone puttin' you in danger are always goin' to be a trigger for me."

The way he looked at her with those deep blue eyes, so focused on her, mesmerizing her, the way his thumb moved over her bare skin, sent her tumbling straight off a cliff. There was that note of humor combined with his lazy drawl that added somersaults and dizzy spins to her fall. How could she possibly ever hope to be sensible when he was so sexy without even trying?

"I refuse to believe I'm a hothead," she said. "Now you, on the other hand, have a certain reputation."

He nodded. "I've earned it, so believe it, *chere*. Tell me the rest."

"Then don' be interruptin' me," she said.

Bijou had the feeling the only way to save herself from her reaction to his Cajun charm was to run for her life. She must have unconsciously started to pull away from him because his fingers tightened like a shackle around her wrist, holding her still.

"Then don' be distractin' me," he admonished.

It was impossible not to laugh. "I can see why Saria says you always get your way. You're very persistent and charming at the same time."

"Thank you."

She shook her head. "That was not a compliment."

He tapped the letters.

Bijou sighed. "It was the progression more than anythin' else that scared me. I was in LA when I found the first one. Then when I moved to be closer to the university I was attendin', I found the same thing in my underwear drawer."

Remy sat up straighter. "He was in your house? In your bedroom?"

She nodded. It was rather humiliating to have to admit any of it. "On my underwear. The eye was drawn on a pair of lacy boy shorts with spray paint." She felt the color creeping up her neck. There was no way to stop it.

"And you didn't go to the police?"

His voice had gone very soft. She went still, the hair on the back of her neck raising in response to his tone. Her body recognized danger.

"The point is," she said hastily, "in the beginning, whoever was stalkin' me just left his silly eye in spray paint and that was the end of it. About a year ago he started addin' messages about me sinnin' and how I was goin' to pay for it."

When he started to say something she held up her hand. "This is difficult for me, Remy, so let me just get on with it. He started breakin' into Bodrie's properties and then those last three letters were sent by the same man, I'm certain of it. They aren't very nice. This has been goin' on for years with no sight of him, just that stupid eye starin' at me. But those letters . . ." She trailed off, glancing at his set jaw.

She was trembling and knew he could feel it because his hand was wrapped around her wrist. There was nowhere to hide. "Hopefully when you read them, you'll understand. They're fairly graphic, and he's definitely been watchin' me. Everywhere I go, even in my own home. He has to be gettin' in the house and finding a way to watch me."

Remy's gaze moved past her to the street and then back to her. "I want you to turn slightly to your left and look across the street. There's a man standing on the grass over there, back behind the tree. He's watchin' us and has been since we entered the café. Tell me if you've seen him before."

Remy had sat there, all calm and composed, never letting on, yet he'd noticed someone outside the café watching them. She'd been so wrapped up in Remy, she wouldn't have noticed if the man had stood over her. Even now, she could barely pull her gaze from his. His eyes and voice were hypnotic. There was something feral about his unblinking stare, and she was trapped in his dangerous spell and her own hero worship.

Her heart kicked into high gear in anticipation of the possibility of uncovering the identity of her stalker. Her mouth went dry. Remy's fingers stroked comfort along her wrist. "If he sees me looking, won't he run?"

"I have the advantage of havin' a cell phone and four brothers. Take a look. If he notices and takes off, the boys will shadow him."

Remy and his brothers were always an impressive sight when they were together. She had always wanted to be part of a big, noisy family. Not waiting, Bijou turned her head and looked straight across the street.

The man looked to be about forty, with shaggy hair and a beard. He was a good distance away, but he was definitely looking through the window at her. Their eyes met. He looked away quickly and turned on his heel and walked briskly away.

Bijou frowned. "I've seen him around, Remy. I've been in so many clubs and given so many concerts, it's impossible to tell for certain, but I think Rob knows him, Rob Butterfield, my manager."

"He's not the only one watching you, Blue. That idiot Ryan Cooper is hangin' out by his car, but his attention is on you."

"I didn't actually autograph anything for him," Bijou reminded. "He got ugly and you read him the riot act. He probably wants an autograph and is waitin' for me to leave without you."

"That's not going to happen. I'm headin' down to the voodoo shop to talk to Eulalie Chachere. You can go with me."

She blinked, sitting up straight. He almost sounded as if he was giving her an order instead of an invitation, but maybe she was just being sensitive. She had fallen too far under his spell and needed to pull back. "I have a few things to do this afternoon." She had planned to walk around and get reacquainted with the French Quarter before returning to the Inn. It wasn't pressing but it was self-preservation. If she spent too much more time in Remy's company she would be well and truly lost.

He smiled at her and her heart nearly stopped. His mouth curved, bringing his lips to her instant attention. His teeth flashed white and strong. The bottom dropped out of her stomach.

"I'm askin' you to accompany me. I like your company

even if you are a bit of a hothead." The humor faded from his eyes. "I am going to be talkin' to her about the altar the killer left behind and that might be upsetting to you."

Her temper kicked into high gear. He *did* think she was a baby. He would never have even considered that Saria would be upset by the discussion of the details of a murder. Again color swept up her face. She'd thrown up. The evidence had been left behind, messing up the crime scene.

"I wouldn't mind comin' along and hearing what the voodoo lady has to say," Bijou snapped. "Let's go right now." She knew she sounded annoyed and challenging, but she couldn't help it. Lately she'd been restless and moody. She'd always been edgy anyway, and now it seemed so much worse. She was driven, but didn't know to what. Sometimes she spent nights just pacing, trying to get rid of the edgy darkness that seemed to be spreading through her.

His slow grin sent a million butterflies winging their way through her stomach. "You *are* a little hothead, Blue." He gave a mock sigh that made her heart skip a few beats. "I guess I'll be the one to rein in the temper."

She deliberately rolled her eyes. "I have way more control."

His gaze jumped to hers, held her captive. There was something very hot and sexy in his eyes. "I'm takin' that as a challenge, *chere*. I'm certain, if I put my mind to it, I'll find a way to make you lose control."

His drawl was quite frankly sinful, his voice implying things she didn't dare think about. Lately she'd had too many nights when being celibate seemed impossible. Her body out of the blue would suddenly grow hot and tight and needy. She knew the moment that happened again, she would be thinking of Remy Boudreaux and fantasizing like crazy. If she wasn't already, she was going to turn into a lobster, terrified he could read her mind.

"Let's go before those people in that booth over there work up their courage and come ask for your autograph," Remy suggested.

"I promised your friend I'd sign something and have my picture taken with her husband," Bijou said. "I need to do that before we go."

"We're goin' out of here through the kitchen," Remy decided. "And you're goin' to get it done fast or you'll be starting another riot."

She frowned at him. It was that or throw herself at him. He was so darned mesmerizing. "I certainly didn't start a riot. But you're right," she had to concede with a quick, nervous glance toward the little group in the booth eyeing her. "If we don' get movin', we're goin' to be here for a long while."

Remy threw money on the table, glided to his feet as silent and as fluid as any cat she'd ever seen. There was something feral about the way he moved, muscles playing subtly beneath his clothes. Every movement was graceful, and yet masculine.

Bijou knew she was falling further under his spell. He'd been the only man in her life that had ever counted for anything and she'd allowed him to grow into a fantasy hero. He was sixteen years older than she was and he saw her as that broken child. He had no way of knowing she'd always been too old for her age—she'd had to grow up fast and learn to be responsible.

Remy's body shielded hers as she rose from the seat, his roped muscles and wide shoulders blocking her from the view of the others in the café. He took her hand and her heart sang. There was nothing she could do about her reaction to him. Her pulse raced, and he had to have known, but he simply moved against her, guiding her without words, just with his body, back toward the kitchen, away from the others.

She allowed herself to indulge her fantasy for just a little while. Remy made her feel safe and cared about, when she'd never had that, not once in her life since that moment when she was eight and he'd come for her and saved her from herself. She fit beneath his shoulder and when he moved her in front of him, his hands on her hips, she was never so conscious of a human being as she was of him.

Bijou inhaled. She should have taken in all the smells of the kitchen, but instead, there was only the scent of Remy drawn deep into her lungs. She swore she'd be able to pick him out of a crowd by scent alone. He seemed to invade every part of her, rushing through her bloodstream like a firestorm.

Thereze held the door for them as they hurried through. Emile was waiting, his smile eager, gaze on Bijou.

"I hope you enjoyed your meal," he greeted.

"The food was fantastic," Bijou said. "You're an amazin' chef. In all honesty, and I've eaten in some really great restaurants, clearly you are a master at what you do."

It was easy to sound sincere, because she really meant it. He didn't seem like the prima donna chefs she'd met, although she noticed his kitchen staff didn't make a move toward her, not even when he handed her his apron to sign. Someone had gotten a special pen to write on the material with and clearly that was brand-new. Emile had made certain he was prepared.

Bijou took the pen and carefully wrote a short note, praising his café and the amazing food, adding that it was wonderful to meet him and then scrawling her name under the message.

"I hope you'll come back," Emile said, nearly glowing.

"We need a picture," Thereze insisted, holding up a camera.

"No, no need. I don' want to bother you," Emile said, but he stepped up to Bijou's side and wrapped a long arm around her shoulders.

Bijou glanced toward the kitchen door. Thankfully no one could see them, and the flood of people asking for pictures wouldn't come. She looked up at Remy's face. His eyes had gone from a deep blue to a strange, startling green, almost glowing. His eyes were fixed on Emile, and he looked . . . dangerous. There was no other word for it. He looked as if he might tear Emile limb from limb.

She was suddenly afraid. He looked more animal than man, his face and body utterly still, his entire being focused on Emile. The hair on her neck stood up and something wild deep inside unfurled and stretched. She could feel the languid stretch and that same steady focus on Remy as he had on Emile. She blinked and the strange wildness in her faded, gone as if it had never been. Sometimes she felt she had faulty wiring, that elusive feeling blinking on and off.

Remy's gaze jumped to her face. His expression softened. His eyes grew warm and he winked at her.

Her heart went into double time. There it was—the perfect reason not to trust Remy or be charmed by him. She didn't know what just happened, but she knew what she'd seen. She was a great observer of humans, and Remy was extremely dangerous. Hidden beneath that very charming and sexy and—so okay, it had to be said—attractive, magnetic, and every other word for just plain a woman's fantasy, was something else. She'd had her warning. It couldn't be denied no matter how much she wanted to do it. Under the surface of her childhood hero was something dark and scary.

Damn it all. She was going to be one of *those* women. She smiled for the camera as she acknowledged to herself that flash of truth wasn't going to get in her way of dreaming about him. All it took was that smile, the warmth in his eyes, that focus on her making her feel as if Remy saw only her, not everything and everyone around him, which was far closer to the truth.

Remy held out his hand to her and she put hers into his without even hesitating, without even reprimanding herself for being an idiot and not running for the hills when she had the chance.

Remy leaned close, his mouth against her ear, his warm breath stirring her blood into a surging wave of pure heat rushing through her body. "Stop thinkin' so much," he admonished.

Who was thinking? Certainly not her, especially when he brought her hand to his mouth and brushed a kiss along the back of it, and then pulled her hand against his chest and trapped it there—right over his beating heart. She was well and truly lost. A certified idiot when it came to romance and men, because she didn't care what that look had been all about. She cared that Remy was holding her hand so close to him that she could feel that steady beat of his heart.

He hurried her out of the café through the back entrance and maneuvered his way down the block toward the voodoo shop. She went with him willingly, enjoying the feel of his body moving against hers as they walked together.

"I don' like men very much," Bijou admitted, compelled to confess.

"I know," he said, in no way perturbed.

"I'm just sayin'," she insisted. "You need to hear me, Remy." She didn't care if she was making a fool of herself. It had to be said. She looked good, she wasn't going to pretend she didn't know that, but she was broken. She didn't relate to men. She didn't let them close to her. She couldn't have a physical relationship because she couldn't ever let herself get that intimate.

Maybe she was reading Remy all wrong, but she wasn't going to lead him on. She knew she was flirtatious with him, and she was so attracted physically she wanted to rub herself up against him like a cat, but she also knew she wouldn't get past the initial first base. She'd rather make a fool of herself than have him think they could have any kind of physical relationship.

"I hear you, Blue. It's just that you're not makin' any sense right now. Keep it up and I'll have to show you what I mean and then you're going to go all rabbit on me and try runnin'." There was amusement in his voice.

Once again she had no idea what he meant. Remy could be quite cryptic when he wanted.

"It's not that," she said. "I'm not a coward. I may throw up when I see a brutal murder, but I don' run, not even from stalkers."

"That's a good thing, because you're about to get another one."

"Very funny." She was through trying to tell him she

wasn't going to sleep with him no matter how charming he was. She wasn't built for one-night stands and she didn't trust anyone enough to actually sleep in a bed with them, so she was sorry, out of luck, even if the man was fine like Remy. He wouldn't listen to her, so that was on his shoulders.

His soft laughter brushed against the insides of her mind, curling her toes and sending alarms shrieking through her entire body. She was lost when she was in his presence—so consumed by childhood hero worship she couldn't think straight.

Remy's fingers tightened around hers and he stopped abruptly right in front of the stairs to the voodoo shop. She was so close to him she felt the heat pouring off his body and tiny electrical charges seemed to arc between them. Bijou stared at the buttons of his shirt. Self-preservation was an absolute must. He had other ideas. He lifted her chin with one finger, forcing her gaze to jump to his.

There was an invitation to laughter there and something more. It was that dark, rising lust mixed with genuine affection that fascinated her. He bent his head slowly toward hers even as he gathered her closer, shifting his body just slightly. His lips whispered against hers, the merest of brushes, but the feel of his mouth against hers was too exquisite to just pull away.

"I'm goin' to kiss you, Blue. So don' do anythin' rash."

She blinked at him. "Why?"

"Because I know a thing or two about makin' a public statement." His hand slipped to her throat, and he lowered his head that scant few millimeters to her mouth.

Time stopped for her. The ground under her feet shifted. His mouth came down on hers, his lips moving, teasing, teeth nipping at her bottom lip so that she gasped. Instantly his tongue swept inside, tangling with hers, taking command. He led her right over a cliff where there was no way back. Lights danced at the back of her eyes and her body seemed to melt against his. He was the one who broke the kiss, slowly easing back, kissing the corners of her mouth before lifting his head.

She blinked rapidly, trying to come back down to earth when she'd been soaring across the sky just moments earlier. Taking a breath, Remy's hands steadying her, she glanced around, hoping for a rescue. Her body didn't feel her own anymore. He'd laid claim to her and all he'd done was kiss her.

Blinking again, she focused on the buildings across the street. Two cars were parked close together and both had cameras sticking out of the windows. A man stood in the street with a professional camera. She recognized him as one of the men who often followed her and took candid shots for tabloids. His name was Bob Carson and he often made her life miserable. Ryan Cooper had draped himself against a tree and he glared at her.

"Remy," she hissed, stiffening. "You're goin' to be in the tabloids and on the Internet and everywhere else. Are you crazy?"

"It's called making a statement, and I think I just did that. In a matter of minutes gossip and rumors will be spreadin' like wildfire not just through New Orleans, but everywhere. I'm countin' on those videos going up."

He looked so self-satisfied she wanted to smack him. "You have no idea what you've done. People are goin' to think . . ." She trailed off, pressing a hand to her mouth. He had no idea the firestorm he just brought down on himself.

"Exactly." Smug satisfaction and male amusement.

Bijou shook her head. "Remy, you don' want the tabloids comin' after you. They'll follow you everywhere and say horrible things about us—and you. They could put your job in jeopardy. They'll try hacking your phone and bugging your house. Nothin' in your life will be sacred or off limits. I don' want that for you."

He took her hand, ignoring her. "Let's go inside."

"Remy, you aren't listenin' to me. I've consulted professionals about stalkers and you could have just set yourself up as a target . . ." She trailed off, understanding flooding her chaotic mind. He'd kissed her, not because he'd wanted to, but because he knew the paparazzi was there and would publish a picture of the two of them. He'd deliberately set himself up and made a complete fool of her in the process.

She stiffened. "I'm leavin'."

"You're goin' inside where cameras aren't going to catch that foul little temper of yours," Remy said, reaching past her to open the door. He thrust her inside. "We can talk about this when we're alone."

Bijou glared at him, waiting until he had closed the door. "I don' need savin', Remy. I'm not that eight-year-old child anymore, just in case you hadn't noticed. You can quit being the white knight chargin' around trying to save me."

He grinned at her. "I noticed, Blue. I wouldn't have been kissing that eight-year-old like I just kissed you." He looked past her, his smile widening. "Eulalie, so good to see you."

Bijou let out her breath and turned around to face the owner of the store. Eulalie Chachere was absolutely beautiful with flawless, dark skin and chocolate eyes with feathery lashes. She was tall, with an amazing figure and made Bijou feel like the little kid Remy had just reduced her to.

"Have you come for a love potion, Remy?" Eulalie teased and wrapped her arms around his neck, kissing him on first one cheekbone and then the other.

Bijou's breath hissed out of her. Her fingers flexed. Ached. Her nail beds hurt. Her jaw felt as if someone had punched her. Eulalie's form swam in front of her eyes, shimmering like a heat wave, red and yellow images.

Remy kissed Eulalie's cheek and then firmly put her to one side, keeping his body between Bijou's and the voodoo priestess. He reached for Bijou's hand, his fingers soothing the aches running down the back of her hand to her fingers. He rubbed her knuckles gently, although he didn't look at her, which, she decided, was a good thing. Fury burned through her for no apparent reason. She had a visceral reaction to Eulalie so intimately and blatantly touching Remy as if they were old friends—or lovers.

"I don' think a love potion will be necessary . . . yet," Remy said. "We'll see. I may come beggin' later."

Bijou ran her tongue over her teeth. Remy sounded like such a flirt. Clearly he flirted with every woman he came near. Unexpectedly she wanted to claw and rake at him—or Eulalie. She couldn't decide who would be the best target.

Remy's hand tightened around Bijou's and he stepped close to her—so close the heat from his body washed over her. She could feel strength flowing through him. His fingers bit into her hand. She glanced at him. His eyes had gone that strange green, nearly glowing. He shook his head, an almost imperceptible movement as he brought his mouth close to her ear. "Just breathe."

"I'm glad you called ahead, Remy," Eulalie continued, clearly unaware of the tension in the room. "I was about to leave for a couple weeks. I put off traveling until tomorrow so I could look at this for you. Is it the same man that was killing a few years ago when you brought me the photographs to look at?"

Bijou was aware of everything in the room. The position of each item. Scents. The windows. She knew someone else lurked in the back room behind the veil of beads—a man, and he was somehow connected to Eulalie. Her scent was all over him. Sounds were acute, so much so that she could hear conversations outside the shop and knew that several fans as well as a couple of paparazzi were outside waiting.

Remy's pressure on her hand kept her grounded and she forced her lungs to work. In and out. That strange, elusive wildness unfurled, stretched and retreated, leaving her feeling limp and wrung out. What in the hell was wrong with her? She'd always been accused of being moody, but now she really was. Moody. Edgy. In desperate need of sex. Her skin itched, felt too tight on her body, and she could feel the beginnings of a bad headache.

Remy dropped his arm around her shoulders, tucking her close to him. As much as one minute ago she had wanted to claw his eyes out; now she just felt grateful that he was there, holding her up. She was going to have to go back to her therapist. Her emotions were all over the place.

"I believe he's the same man, Eulalie," Remy answered the voodoo priestess, keeping her attention centered on him. "Did you take a look at the photographs?"

Eulalie frowned. "If this is the same man, he's evolved as far as his altar from several years ago, but he is not a true practitioner."

"Clearly he's practicing black magic, summoning demons to aid him, right?"

Eulalie smiled at him. Bijou couldn't help noticing how the rows of long braids emphasized her beautiful cheekbones and the way her smile lit up her dark eyes. "You've been reading. I suspect he's reading as well, but he's never gone to a practitioner before. He's mixing things up. His altar is far better than a few years ago, I'll give him that."

"But he isn't really a follower of voodoo?" Remy prompted. "A *bokor* perhaps? One who focuses on dark magic rather than light?"

Eulalie shook her head. "Certainly not in the traditional sense. In traditional voodoo, a human sacrifice would be considered extremely objectionable. I can't say it doesn't ever go on. In any religion you have people with sadistic natures who covet power above all else, but certainly he would be the exception, and, Remy, I would hear of him."

Remy frowned and brought up their joined hands, rubbing Bijou's knuckles back and forth over his jaw. The gesture was not only unnerving, but she found it intimate. He was so used to being flirtatious he didn't even seem to notice, but she couldn't summon the will to pull away from him.

"Why don' you believe he's a real practitioner, Eulalie?"

It was her turn to frown. "Nothing is right about any of his rituals. He changes them to suit him and you just can't do that. I would have to say he's never had a teacher, at least that's my best guess. Where I might use water, he had blood. He has a sacrifice. I'd use an apple, he has an actual heart."

"He's bastardizin' actual rituals," Remy asked, trying to understand.

"Yes. Exactly. But he's also mixing them up, which makes me think he's just getting everything out of a book. The hanging man's hand must be cut off while the victim is still hanging, but then it's dried over a fire. If he truly knew what he was doing, he could eventually create a handyman as it were to carry out his orders. He did tie candles to the fingers, which, if you didn't dip the hand in oil ahead of time to use as candles, then you'd do it that way."

"I'm particularly interested in the string with the knots."

Something in Remy's voice, although he sounded very casual, maybe too casual, centered Bijou's attention on the answer. Whatever that string meant, Remy considered important.

Eulalie nodded. "Ah, yes, that is a definite misfit of a ritual in the middle of all this. The seven knots in the string can be used to bind a woman or man to you, to ask for them to love you, but the string should be put under your pillow, not into a bowl of blood. He turned the string red using the blood, but it isn't the same thing. The candle is thrown into running water. And there were no symbols on the ground anywhere. No protections. No god or deity or even a demon he's distinctly calling on. Nothing at all to say what he's doing. Remy, these rituals are sacred. We don't abuse them and we don't dare make mistakes. You don't play around with this."

"Thanks, Eulalie," Remy said. "Can I call you on your cell if I need to discuss more with you?"

"Of course. I'll help in any way I can," she assured. "Why was the string so important?"

"Because he's never done it before," Remy said.

5

IN the dark of Saria's kitchen, Remy paced restlessly back and forth. He was silent, not making a sound as he moved across the tiled floor. His leopard was riding him hard and he knew he had to let the animal out for a run, but there was danger if what he suspected was true.

Blue was leopard. Well . . . *maybe* she was leopard. Remy considered the ramifications for her. Bijou had no idea who her mother was, and in any case, her mother, had she lived, would not have been able to tell her daughter about her heritage, just in case Bijou couldn't shift. Bodrie was no leopard, and he certainly hadn't known what he had in Bijou.

Female leopards didn't emerge unless the human counterpart and the leopard both came into cycle at the same time. Only at that time could a woman's leopard emerge for the first time. It was an extremely dangerous time for all male leopards. Blue would be extremely alluring and yet, if not ready, moody and edgy.

A few days ago, there in the store, Bijou's eyes had

changed from that amazing blue to a lethal glacier blue when Eulalie had kissed him on the cheek. Maybe Remy had wanted Bijou to be the one. He had all but given up looking for a mate, and now Bijou was back in his territory and in spite of the age difference, he couldn't get his mind off of her. She was beautiful and intriguing. He knew she was intelligent. She was talented and had a good sense of humor. He liked being in her company.

He was man enough to admit to himself that he was a strong dominant and needed a woman who could stand up to him when he became too overbearing, as Saria often accused him of being. His career was important to him. He believed what he did made a difference and often he was gone long hours. He needed a woman with her own life, career and independence, yet one who would need him the way he would her.

Earlier in the week in Bijou's company, without warning, his leopard had gone from a jealous, snarling lethal cat to . . . *oh baby . . . there you are.* The moment was gone, the scent of a female close to her time was gone, but for whatever reason—his cat accepted Bijou Breaux.

He scented his sister just before she stepped into the kitchen. Like him, she was silent when she walked, and she didn't bother with the lights. She froze and turned very slowly toward the corner where the darker shadows hid him completely.

"Remy?"

"Why aren't you sleepin', Saria?" he asked.

"Drake's not here. He left yesterday for Texas to see Jake and Emma. We were hopin' to persuade them to come for a visit, but Emma just found out she's pregnant and Drake says Jake is freakin' out. The doctors weren't certain she could ever have another baby. She nearly died in childbirth. Jake was adamant that they not have another child, but apparently birth control doesn't always work on leopards."

"Jake Bannaconni? Freakin' out?" Remy shook his head. "That man is stone."

"True, unless he's around his kids or Emma," Saria said. "Drake said Jake is scary crazy over Emma. He was pretty upset that she was pregnant again. Drake went to calm him down."

"Drake's pretty good at that."

"I miss him. I thought if I drank some hot chocolate I'd feel better." She sent him a small smile. "Chocolate will keep me out of the swamp. I hate sleepin' without Drake, and nights when he's gone I usually make my trips to do my night photography so it isn't so bad without him." She sounded distracted, as if she was leaving an important piece of information out.

"Thanks for not goin'," Remy said, choosing his words carefully. "I know it's difficult for you to change your routine, especially when you've got a paying client. I really appreciate that I don' have to worry about you."

"You sound tired, Remy."

He toed a chair around and sank down into it, studying his sister's face. She looked strained, something rare for Saria. She was self-possessed, sure of herself and uncaring of other people's opinions of her. It was unlike her to be so restless with Drake gone.

"I am tired," he admitted. Handling Saria took care. One didn't leap in with her. You gave a little to get something back. He was a skilled interrogator and once in a while he could coax his independent sister to tell him what was troubling her—and something definitely was. He rubbed the back of his neck knowing her cat's eyes would be able to see the gesture there in the dark. "Talk to me."

Saria crossed to the counter, putting her hand on the coffeemaker to test the heat. "You aren't drinkin' coffee are you?"

"No. I figured I'm already jacked up, I don' need coffee to keep the buzz goin'."

"You always get this way when you're worried, Remy. Is it Pete's murder?"

Remy shrugged. "If the killer stays with the pattern he

had four years ago, he'll be hittin' tonight or tomorrow night and I'm no closer to catchin' him then I was when he struck back then. For all the evidence he leaves at the crime scene, so far, nothin' links anyone. I don' even have a single suspect, and he's goin' to kill another innocent person. Someone with a family. Pete was a damned good man."

Saria put a hand on her brother's shoulder. "Yes he was. You'll get him this time, Remy, I know you will." She pulled up the chair beside his and sat down, leaning toward him. "I know you always think you're responsible for everyone around you, but you aren't. You can only do so much."

"I suppose that's the truth," he agreed. "But it doesn't make me feel any better. Gage and I have worked night and day on this case, and we're no closer to findin' the killer. I'm just really grateful you're stayin' out of the swamps no matter the reason."

Saria pressed her lips together and pushed back into her chair. There it was. She was on the verge of telling him, but obviously hesitating. Remy made a show of massaging his neck, wincing a little.

"I do have some news," Saria said reluctantly, not looking at him directly. "Part of the reason I'm not going into the swamp is because I'm going to have a baby and I don' want to risk a problem."

"Saria!" He hadn't been expecting that. He leaned toward her, covered her hand with his. "Aren't you happy about it? What's wrong? Have you told Drake?" He'd kick his brother-in-law in the ass for leaving her when she was obviously upset.

Saria shook her head. "I haven't said anythin' to him. I wasn't certain before he left and after he was gone, I took a test. I wasn't really sure I wanted to know, but the thingie came up positive, which I have to tell you was a little shockin'."

"So you were using birth control," Remy guessed. "And it didn't work for you?"

"It certainly did not. Male leopards ought to come with

a warnin' label." She gave a small sniff and kept her head turned away from him.

Remy didn't know if she was sniffing in disdain at male leopards, or if she was on the verge of tears—and Saria rarely cried. He was treading a minefield if Saria was crying. "Do you want a baby, Saria?" He asked the question straight out. Skirting around the issue wouldn't do any good and would only make her clam up. She hadn't told Drake and she could have called him, but she hadn't. "Is everythin' all right between you and Drake?"

Saria pressed her hand to her forehead, leaning her elbow on the table in a gesture of weariness. "Drake and I are fine. It's not that." She sighed without lifting her head. "It's me, Remy. I never had a mother, or father for that matter." She did look at him then and there was stark fear in her eyes. "How would I possibly know how to be a decent parent? It's not like babies come with manuals. You're supposed to know all that before you ever have one. I was being so careful so this wouldn't happen."

Remy didn't make the mistake of reacting. He turned over what she'd revealed in his mind, studying her statement from every angle. She feared becoming a parent, and truthfully he didn't blame her. She wasn't old enough to remember their father as a happy man. He'd gotten drunk when his wife got sick and stayed that way permanently after she died. Saria had practically raised herself.

"I can see what you're thinking," Remy conceded in a thoughtful tone. "You didn't have the best example in the world of parenting, did you? I certainly wasn't any help."

"I didn't mean that," Saria said hastily, her dark eyes meeting his. "Maybe I was angry at all of you for a few minutes there, but mostly it was because I felt left out, not because I was alone with *mon pere*."

"Still, I should have protected you more. He was never really present in your life."

"I never was very good at accepting protection, Remy,"

Saria confessed. "And you were gone. In the service, travelin'. All of you had lives."

"That's no excuse, Saria. But, the point is, you took care of *mon pere*. By yourself. When you were just a little girl. You kept the house and you cooked for him. You even ran the bar when he was too drunk to do it. You fished, shrimped, and you hunted alligators. You can do anythin'. Having a baby will be nothing for you."

"That's nice of you to say, Remy," Saria said. "I wish I could believe you. I'm absolutely terrified."

He frowned at her, trying not to be upset. "Are you thinkin' of getting rid of the baby and not tellin' Drake?" He couldn't conceive of Saria doing such a thing. She was honest almost to a fault.

She looked so horrified he had his answer.

"Of course not. I'm goin' to tell him. I just need to get my head right is all. And lately, it hasn't been so right." She rubbed at her temples as if she had a headache. "It was just as well Jake called and needed Drake to make the trip to Texas. I haven't been so nice lately."

"To Drake?" Remy prompted.

"It's just that I'm horribly moody. Or edgy. I don' know the right word for it." She made a face, her eyes filled with self-loathing. "I found myself getting' jealous of Bijou, and she's one of my oldest friends." She made the confession in a little ashamed rush. "I'm not a jealous person. I'm really not, Remy. Bijou's—broken. She needs friends. She needs me and I'm actin' like an idiot. Oh, not to her face, but inside, especially when Drake's in the house, I find myself wantin' to claw her eyes out."

Remy let his breath out and sat up straighter. There it was. The confirmation he was looking for. "It's all right, Saria . . ."

"No, it's not," Saria was adamant. "I don' want to be that kind of person, especially toward a friend of mine. I've never cared about anyone being attractive—which she is. She *needs* me right now. She's afraid of somethin' and she's come home. I can't turn into a jealous, spitting, nasty cat because I'm pregnant."

"I doubt that's it," Remy soothed.

She glared at him. "What else could it be? I'm *never* like this. I don' cling to my husband. I don' distrust him around other women. I've never been just plain mean, especially to him. He doesn't say anythin', but I know he's going to soon and I'll deserve anythin' he says."

"He'll understand," Remy assured. Drake was a patient man, quick to explode into violence only when needed. As a rule he was quite calm and thoughtful. Remy couldn't imagine him getting impatient with Saria.

"I wish it was just Drake," Saria said. "I'm so jealous of poor Bijou I could spit. Sometimes, with no warnin' I just want to leap on her and scratch her eyes out, and that's a polite way of saying what I really want to do."

She blinked rapidly, and his heart jumped. Saria was definitely fighting tears and it wasn't fair to her to let her think she had suddenly become a jealous woman because she was pregnant and felt terrified at the thought of being a mother because she had no parenting.

"I think Bijou's leopard and she's on the verge of the Han Vol Dan," Remy stated quietly.

In the ensuing silence, Remy heard the clock tick and the rapid beat of his sister's heart. Her eyes went wide with shock. Her mouth opened, but no sound emerged. She shook her head. He nodded.

Saira frowned, jumping up to pace restlessly. She shook her head again. "Remy. No. That's impossible. Her father . . ."

"I know her father was no leopard, but we know nothin' of her mother or her mother's family. It's entirely possible and I'm almost certain I'm right. Your leopard would react to the close proximity of a female leopard on the verge of the Han Vol Dan. Basically, she's comin' into heat around your male and you're pregnant."

"That's just crazy." She kept shaking her head. "Bijou is . . ."

Remy felt his leopard leap in protest, or maybe it was the man. "Don' say she isn't strong. You don' know the half of what she's been through. Anyone can reach a breakin' point, Saria. Bijou found her way when she was just a child and she's still going strong."

Saria didn't reply. She simply looked at him, and there was accusation in her eyes. He knew he'd made a mistake jumping to Bijou's defense when Saria hadn't actually said anything disparaging. He didn't make mistakes like that—and Saria knew it. He cursed silently in his native Cajun French, keeping his expression blank.

"Remy . . . *no*. You are not goin' to chase after her. I mean it. You've already made her cry." She regarded with him with her dark brown eyes, her steady stare a mix of leopard and human, eyes already taking on the glow of her leopard. "I hear her at night. She won't talk to me about it so I know she's cryin' over you."

"I hear her too," Remy admitted, stretching, trying to ease sore muscles. Saria's couch was very comfortable and he wished he'd been sleeping on it. He was getting too old to be sleeping in a little chair on a cold balcony, which he'd done for three nights running. "What makes you think I have anything at all to do with her cryin'?"

"Because I know you, Remy. You make people confess to anythin' and you no doubt made that poor girl cry." Saria put both hands on her hips and stared him down. "You've been grillin' that girl about something and she's upset." She leveled her glare at him. "You haven't touched her, have you?"

"That's none of your business, *ma soeur*. She's got a stalker after her. She's not takin' it very seriously, but, Saria, I'm tellin' you this man is dangerous and he's not going to stop. He's *extremely* dangerous, the kind that ends up killin' the woman if he can't have her."

Saria was silent for a moment, but those cat's eyes never

left his face. She shook her head again. "What are you up to, Remy?"

"He's not going to like her havin' a man in her life. He'll get mad and make a mistake, and I'll be there to take him down."

"No." Saria stated the word quite fiercely.

For a woman so much younger than he was, Remy had to admire her courage. He wasn't a man most people—man or woman—ever chose to go up against. His little sister had no such qualms. He raised his eyebrow and remained silent.

"I mean it, Remy. She's . . . susceptible. You can't pretend to be her boyfriend just to bring some stalker out into the open. I know you. You'll decide she can't know because she won't act natural. You can't pretend to care for her . . ."

They both scented lavender and leopard at the exact same moment. Remy was already gliding toward the door, more leopard than man in that moment. His leopard went wild—crazy. Snarling and raking, desperate to emerge. He couldn't imagine what Saria's cat was like, scenting a female close to her time.

"I'll go." He managed to bite out the two words. "You get out of here. Go to my house in the bayou."

Saria was definitely struggling to control her female. "She heard me, Remy." Her voice had gone husky, gravelly, fur running under her skin as her leopard fought for supremacy.

His breath hissed out of his lungs. There was no more doubt, Bijou was definitely leopard and she was close to the emerging. Every single male in the lair would be driven insane, and Drake, the only voice of reason, was gone. Remy cursed as he padded down the hall on silent feet. Bijou had heard every word Saria had said and she would believe it was true. It smacked of being true. There was no doubt he was a man who might do that very thing to bring a danger-ous adversary into the light. There was every reason for Bijou to believe what Saria said. Hell. Saria believed it and she was his sister.

He moved swiftly through the halls, following the scent

of the elusive female leopard. Bijou would have no idea why her emotions were all over the place. She had no idea what was happening to her—or what could happen. His lair was fucked up. There was no other word for it. They'd been isolated for so long and had no idea of the way leopard society worked—until Drake had shown up.

Some had intermarried and produced—monsters. Others had married outside of the leopard society and weakened the lair as generations failed to produce offspring. It was a complicated situation even as Drake tried to provide guidance for them. He sent the younger men to the rain forests in the hopes of finding mates, and that was difficult. Once any of the males got a whiff of a female coming into the Han Vol Dan they would be all over her.

Remy's lips drew back in a snarl. No one would be safe. Bijou had to be claimed immediately and thoroughly so there was no doubt she was taken. Without that, chaos would reign and the males could easily turn on one another. Drake was working magic on the lair, but it was difficult to overcome generations of problems.

Remy knew the exact moment Bijou was aware he was pursuing her. Her soft footfalls sped up and almost immediately a draft rushed through the house as she went through the front door and raced toward her car. He used his animal, the cat already sensing the desirable female running from him. He leapt after her, covering twenty feet in a single jump. His leopard could easily reach thirty-five miles an hour when running. She was fumbling with the car keys, her hands trembling, hurting, as her cat rose close to the surface. She tried to unlock the car door when he landed behind her, reached around and took the keys from her hand.

Bijou spun around fast, striking out. His leopard saved him from a swift rake of nails. Her female had leapt to Bijou's defense, claws springing out for one moment to keep her human safe from attack. The claws barely missed him, and he glided back a few more steps just to be certain he was out of the danger zone.

Bijou clearly had no idea what just happened, or that her eyes were glowing an almost aquamarine blue. Her skin was nearly translucent, her hair wild. He'd never seen a woman so passionate or so alluring. His leopard had already gone insane, reacting to hers and the pheromones she was throwing out, demanding his human claim her immediately, whether she was ready or not.

Remy lifted his face to test the wind, worried that it was blowing in the direction of the bayou where so many other males might catch that elusive and potent scent. The need for sex was riding her hard, and if he read the situation correctly, she was on her way into town just for that specific purpose. Bijou, who clearly wasn't a one-night stand kind of woman, had to be scared and confused.

"Give me my car keys," she hissed at him.

His blood sang hotly in his veins. His body was on fire, aching. In need. He tasted lavender in his mouth, breathed it into his lungs. He watched her closely, unblinking, focused. The eyes of the leopard, not the man. Slowly he shook his head. "I don' think so, Blue. You're goin' into town lookin' for somethin' you're going to regret tomorrow."

Swift color surged up her neck into her face. "That's none of your business." She held out her hand for the keys.

Remy knew he had already passed the point of no return. He had never experienced such an urgent, all-consuming need. He recognized her in some strange way. He knew they would burn hot and out of control, almost as if he knew every curve, as if they'd done this all before. He caught her wrist and yanked her to him, his other fist tangling in her hair to jerk her head back as he brought his mouth down hard on hers. The world around him exploded, turned red, the ground shifting as her body melted into his.

Leopards were rough at sex, even brutal at times, and Remy's leopard was always close to the surface, his savage nature riding him hard in any situation, but far worse when it came to sex. Even at work he had to keep his temper in check, keep the intense emotions from surfacing, so he was always, always in control. Until now. Something in him snapped when his mouth found hers. All his icy control was gone, leaving nothing but hot flames burning like a wildfire out of control.

He devoured her mouth. Gave her no chance to breathe—or protest. His tongue demanded entrance, sliding along the seam of her lips, and she opened for him. He poured himself inside, nearly frantic to be skin to skin. Her hands slid under his shirt and he knew he was lost. She made small noises in her throat, an urgent kind of mewing, desperate to get as close to him as he needed to be close to her.

With his last vestige of sanity, he caught her up and took her around the house, to the back where the lake lapped at the shore and prying eyes of stalkers and paparazzi cameras couldn't possibly find them. He didn't lift his head, kissing her over and over, long, drugging kisses that kept her unaware as he leapt to her balcony, and managed to open the sliding glass door to her bedroom.

The moment he was inside, he shoved her up against the wall hard and ripped her blouse away, desperate to get at her soft skin. There was an ominous sound and he saw a crack spreading up the wall behind her back. He hadn't realized just how urgently he'd needed to touch her. To claim her. It had been in his mind since the moment he'd set eyes on her. The wall didn't matter or any damage to it, only removing every bit of material that stood between him and her soft skin.

The last three nights he'd sat in a chair on her balcony while she slept, her silent sentinel. The scent of her filled his lungs and left him hard and hurting all night, unable to sleep even in the chair. He'd known she was his instinctively, but touching her confirmed it.

She wore a lacy midnight blue bra, sexy as hell, her soft curves spilling over the tops, her nipples hard and erect, pushing through the lace to tempt him. Her breath came in ragged gasps, lifting her breasts toward his hungry mouth. Her rib cage was narrow, her waist small. The loose drawstring pants she wore rode low on her hips. She was so beautiful, so sensual, her body moving against his, her lips swollen with his kisses and her eyes slightly glazed.

He pinned her against the wall with his body, lifting his hands to her breasts, feeling the supple weight, the exquisite softness of woman, before bending his head to taste. She gasped and caught his head to her, cradling him close, while her heart pounded in his ears and the scent and taste of her engulfed him.

His mouth moved over soft flesh, tongue laving her nipples through the lace. He couldn't wait another moment, yanking the bra down and away from treasure, so that the lace pushed her full breasts upward toward him all the more. He covered her right side with his palm, his mouth drawing her left breast deep into his mouth. She moaned and writhed against him, tightening her hold on his head and pushing herself tightly into him. Her leg slipped higher, so that the soft cushion of the vee between her thighs rode his hip, inflaming him further. She was so damned sexy he was losing his mind.

He fed on her breasts, first one, then the other, tugging and rolling her nipples, his teeth nipping, tongue sliding over the ache to ease it. She was sensitive to his every touch, to his mouth and hands and he felt her reaction, the shudder of her body, her hips bucking against him, the grinding of her body tighter along his thigh. He needed her to burn just as hot as he was. She had to want him as much.

Bijou was on fire, burning from the inside out. Her body didn't feel as if it was her own, yet was more of a fit than she'd ever felt before, which made no sense to her. She'd been fine, sitting in her room, going through the plans for the renovation of her apartment above the club, when she suddenly couldn't sit still. A tidal wave of urgent demand swept over her.

Her breasts ached and tingled. Felt swollen and needy. Her skin was too tight and far too sensitive. Even her clothes hurt. Wave after wave of heat surged through her body, rushed through her veins and pooled low and mean. She couldn't stop moving, her body rippling with sensual sensations she couldn't hope to control. She'd fled her room, trying to run away from herself and the way her skin itched and her groin throbbed with need.

It wasn't as if she hadn't known Remy had gone all protective on her. He was that kind of man. She knew that going into it. She knew he felt responsible for her and admitting to him she was afraid of one of her stalkers had set him off. His kiss had ignited a fire and she couldn't put it out, no matter how many times she reminded herself his kiss had been for the cameras and the tabloids to draw out her stalker. So why had it hurt so much to hear Saria confirm what she already knew? Why had it felt as if she'd been stabbed through the heart?

She ran, her mind in chaos, her body in such urgent need she could barely catch her breath. She had never run from anything. She was a fighter, or she made a decision with her brain, not impulsively. Yet, this time, she couldn't think. She couldn't stop the blood coursing so hotly through her body. Running was the only thing to do. She had no idea what she would do when she got into town. Certainly she couldn't have been looking for a one-night stand . . . And then Remy was there, so calm and cool, so totally in charge, like nothing ever got to him.

He'd taken control, like he always did, in that charming, you're-so-young and I'm-so-grown-up-and-in-command infuriating way of his. She both detested and loved his confidence, and that just showed her how truly screwed up she really was. When he'd taken her car keys right out of her hand, smirking at her, she'd experienced a truly frightening fury.

She didn't have a temper. Certainly not one with such intensity that it would cause an all-consuming reckless, rash, *idiotic* compulsion to slash Remy in his face. She wanted to rip his face right off his skull—to wipe that smug, self-confident smirk right off his face forever. For a moment, she even thought of leaping on him and biting him. So very un-Bijou-like. There had been a roaring in her ears. Her hands ached, knuckles swollen until her fingers curled like claws and she could barely stand it.

And then he yanked her to him.

Her stomach bottomed out and the throbbing between her legs turned into a terrible drumbeat of savage need. His hand fisted in her hair and dragged her head back. The bite of pain should have had her kicking and screaming and running for her life, but instead, her body had flooded with a hot, welcoming liquid. Every cell in her body reached for him. Something wild and uninhibited rose like a tidal wave from somewhere deep inside her.

She was lost in the flames. In the intensity of his lust and her own. She didn't even know she could feel so much. There was no turning back. No brakes. No thought. Only feeling. He'd ignited a firestorm, and there was no putting it out for either of them. She wanted to be closer to him, skin to skin. Anything else hurt. She could hear herself making frantic, mewling noises, desperation showing, but she couldn't stop herself. His mouth was like a fountain of fire, a haven of molten gold she could never get enough of.

It was the most frightening, scary, exhilarating feeling she'd ever had. Her body felt more feminine than it had ever been. She was acutely aware of every curve and the effect she had on Remy's body. She reveled in her ability to inflame him, to drive him over the edge into madness, and yet, at the same time, she was terrified—because she couldn't stop. There was no stopping. No way to take a breath and just step back and think.

Her body drove her, not her brain. Not her heart. She needed his hands on her body. His mouth at her breast, his fingers inside of her. She needed him to fill her, to take the emptiness away, that terrible burning that refused to let up, consuming her with desperate lust for this one man.

He shifted her until he had cradled her in his arms, close to his chest, his mouth still feeding on hers, devouring her.

She couldn't get enough of his kisses, consumed by the taste of him, the wild exotic spice she was fast becoming addicted to. She felt herself floating, levitating, moving through the air as if in the clouds. The cool breeze from the lake rushing through the trees added to the intensity of sensation.

Remy's roped muscles bunched and rippled. She felt each defined muscle imprinted on her heated skin. She needed her clothes gone, the material literally hurt she was so sensitive. She was burning from the inside out, afraid she wouldn't live through it. She was barely aware of being inside her room, with no idea and no real caring of how she got there. Remy shoved her hard against the wall and ripped at her clothing, every bit as desperate to get the material off of her as she was, his mouth on hers, demanding her compliance.

She'd always wanted to see Remy out of control, to have him be on that edge of reason, to feel as if she could drive him that far, but she'd never once thought it would be like this—a fire raging out of control in both of them. It was as if one of them lit a match and both had accelerant poured over them, going up in raging flames the moment their lips met.

Her heart pounded with fear. She could even taste it in her mouth. She had no idea what to do, how to act, even how to have sex. Obviously, Remy knew exactly what he was doing. How in the world was she going to keep up? Her body might be driving her, but when it came down to it, what was she going to do? Even those questions didn't seem to stop her, or pour water on the fire. She couldn't stop kissing him, or touching him, or even grinding her body up against his like some hussy desperate for sex.

Remy suddenly lifted his head. His eyes glowed a strange, deep emerald green, wholly focused on her, like a predator. A great jungle cat focused on prey. The unblinking stare sent a shiver down her spine. He didn't let up on his unbreakable hold on her.

"You know there's no going back for either of us."

Bijou tried to think clearly. There was a strange roaring in her head. Her body moved constantly, rubbing against him like a cat. Her breasts ached for his mouth. She felt empty between her legs and needed him desperately to fill her. His words meant something, but he was making a statement, not asking a question. There was a wealth of possession in the glittering of his strange eyes that sent both panic and a thrill ricocheting through her body.

"I mean it, Bijou, it's too late to ever go back."

Remy read fear and confusion in her eyes. He could barely stand the clothes on his back and knew her skin was burning just as bad. There would be no going back. At the best of times his leopard was difficult, but hers had risen and accepted his. He wanted her with every cell in his body, every breath he drew. The intensity of need threw him. It was unexpected and a little crazy when he'd always been so in control.

His leopard would mark her for certain. Hell. *He* wanted to put his mark on her, his warning to all other males to stay away from her. It was a dark, primitive need he couldn't possibly ignore. He couldn't wholly blame his leopard for not keeping his hands to himself. If he was being strictly honest, the moment he'd kissed her—and he'd lied to himself—told himself he was kissing her to get in a tabloid and flush out her stalker—but he'd *wanted* to kiss her from the moment he laid eyes on her again. No, he'd *needed* to kiss her. Once he had, for him, there was no going back.

She was addictive. He couldn't stop kissing her. He never wanted to stop. The taste of her lingered in his mouth—in his mind. She'd somehow crawled down his throat to spread like a virus through his entire body, so that he was an addict. He needed to feed on that wild, elusive taste. That lavender scent mixed with her pheromones stayed with him every moment of the day and night. He'd waited, knowing her leopard was close to the surface and that it would drive her into a sexual frenzy of need. He had been ruthless enough to wait, to watch, to be close at hand so that no other had a chance to interfere or come between them.

He couldn't resist her mouth, that full lower, almost pouty lip that drove him insane. He kissed her again, drowning in her those long, addictive kisses he couldn't get enough of. He'd never be satisfied with anyone else. He knew it. She was branded in his very bones, wrapped tight inside of him. He kissed her again and again, keeping her pinned to the wall, one leg wrapped tight around his thigh. He lifted his head, once more coming up for air. There were things that had to be said. Explanations. Truths that needed to be revealed, but he couldn't think straight enough, not with her leopard so close. The emerging was soon. Another day. Maybe two. Maybe tonight.

The idea of her coming to him like this, so in need, hardened his body into a painful ache of urgency. He knew in the morning there would be tears and regret, if her leopard didn't emerge. Confusion. Perhaps even anger toward him, but he couldn't stop himself to give her the explanations of being a shifter. She probably wouldn't believe him and she was in no condition—and neither was he—to wait. Hopefully her leopard would rise and everything would turn out the way it should.

His thumb moved back and forth across the curve of the sweet temptation of her lower lip. "You'll be afraid, Blue. I know you will, but look to me. Not anyone else. I'll get you through this. Just keep looking to me."

She stood in her lacy blue bra, her nipples hard and red from his teeth and mouth. Her breasts lifted with every ragged breath she drew in, a temptation impossible to resist. Before she could reply, he was kissing her again. There was too much confusion in her eyes. Trepidation. Fear of his roughness, and he couldn't be gentle, as hard as he tried. His leopard drove him, and now, more than ever, with her female rising, his male was too close to the surface for tenderness to show.

Kissing Bijou was better than any fine wine he'd ever tasted. He tried to stop, tried to find enough semblance of control to at least reassure her he wouldn't hurt her. He managed to lift his head inches from hers, resting his forehead against hers, looking into those amazing blue leopard eyes. He brushed back her hair, looking into her eyes, trying to reassure her when he was already ripping away her innocence with his roughness.

He was far too experienced not to recognize that she was innocent, but his leopard didn't care, and neither did hers. His hands moved over her of their own accord, shaping all that soft exposed skin. His. She was his, now and for all time. Her skin was so soft, like satin, and he blazed a trail of fire from her mouth down her chin to her throat and back up to her mouth again because there was nothing else he could do. He had to kiss her. Had to touch her. Their choices were long gone.

6

BIJOU made a sound, a soft little cry that tore at Remy, inflamed him, made him all the more desperate for her. He had to get skin to skin. Blood surged hotly, pooled low and wicked, until he was one giant ache. He bent his mouth to her breast, his hand going to the other nipple as his teeth tugged and teased. He wanted her more than aroused, more than ready. He wasn't going to give her one moment to back out or change her mind. He was too far gone.

She writhed against him, pressing her back into the wall, a soft little cry somewhere between pain and pleasure escaping. He caught at her with hard hands, whirled her around and pushed her hard against the wall, his hands dropping to the waistband of her jeans. He stripped her clothes and shoes from her, holding her still with one hard hand against her back, unrelenting, not allowing her to move while he removed every bit of cloth that might come between them.

His own clothes followed, while he breathed deep, trying to keep his animal instincts at bay. He kissed his way up the

back of her legs, nuzzled her firm bottom and made her yelp
when he bit her twice, the second time deliberately leaving
his mark.

"Remy, it's too much," she whispered. Her body trembled, her arms flat against the wall, her head turned to one
side as she tried to look at him through her long fall of silky
hair.

His hand slipped between the wall and her flat belly,
continued that slide lower as he stood, until he was cupping
her hot mound while pressing himself against her back,
pinning her there to the wall. She was hotter and slicker than
anything he'd ever felt. His finger slid inside of her. She
moaned and her body clamped down tight. Her hips bucked
involuntarily. He bent his head to her shoulder, kissing her
neck, nuzzling her as his finger moved in and out in a slow
replica of what he wanted most.

Her buttocks rubbed against him as she gasped and
moved, unable to be still. He sank his teeth into soft skin
and she cried out, hot liquid pouring over his finger, lubri-
cating her enough that he could sink two fingers deep.

"What are you doing?" Her voice was muffled. Husky.
Desperate.

His tongue lapped at the marks on her shoulder and neck.
"Getting you ready for me."

"I don' know what I'm doin'," she confided. "I've never
been with a man." She took a breath. "Teach me, Remy. I
want to please you."

He'd known that. Deep down inside, he'd known she'd
waited for him. He slowly removed his fingers and brought
them close to his face. She smelled like lavender all over.
Even there. He licked at his fingers. "You even taste like
lavender. Your scent drives me wild."

Before she could respond, he whirled her around, hands
hard on her skin, taking her down to the bed, sprawling her
out for him like a banquet. Bijou gasped, her long lashes
fluttering, but he gave her no chance to protest, his mouth
coming down hard on hers, robbing her of breath. He kissed

her until her body melted into his, soft and pliant, once more moving restlessly beneath him.

With one hand he caught both of hers, and stretched her arms above her head, pinning her wrists to the mattress. Slipping one leg between her thighs, he opened her to him. Her scent was as wild and as elusive as she was. For so long, he'd always felt empty. He'd tried filling his nights with women, and when that didn't work, he turned to his career. Nothing seemed to help, until this night. This woman. He hadn't had her yet, but the taste and scent of her filled his every empty space until he burned for her. Knew her. Would never be complete again without her.

Maybe he'd never been complete and that was why his leopard was always prowling and hungry, so close to the surface. He recognized her in some strange, primitive way. She belonged with him. They belonged. His fingers curled around her throat, tipping her head back to expose her throat to him. He bent his head and kissed that long, slender line. She smelled so good, and her skin was unbelievably soft.

Her body kept moving, undulating, her hips bucking, her leopard pressing close to the surface helping to drive her need to mate. Her breath came in ragged gasps, each lifting her breasts and pushing them temptingly toward him. He kissed his way down to one taut peak and blew warm air over her nipple.

He stared down into those wild, glowing eyes. So beautiful. Her leopard was close, driving her so that her body couldn't stop moving beneath his, rubbing along his, until the roaring in his ears became a demand.

He stroked his palm down her throat, along her collarbone to the swell of her breasts. The rise and fall as her ragged breath left her lungs only added to the terrible temptation. He lowered his head and drew one dark nipple into his mouth. She cried out, and thrashed beneath him. He suckled, using the edge of his teeth to tug and pull, the weight of his body keeping her pinned and open to his exploration.

The little sounds escaping her throat drove him wild. His mouth pulled strongly at her breast while his fingers tugged and rolled her other nipple. She gasped and arched her body. He knew she was too innocent for such rough play but he couldn't stop himself. Each time he tugged and pulled, each time he bit, her hips bucked and she thrashed deliciously.

"Remy!" She tried to reach for him, but he stopped her, pushing her hands back against the mattress.

"Shh, Blue, just let me have my way right now," he cautioned. There was no turning back at this point, the scent of lavender and honey drifted up to him, calling, and he was lost.

Bijou couldn't take her eyes off the man she'd fantasized over nearly her entire life. No one else had ever measured up. No one else had ever made her body grow tight and needy or made her breasts ache or caused a flood of hot, welcoming liquid.

Physically, Remy was beautiful. There was no other word for it. He was the most sensual, sexy man she'd ever encountered. She dreamt of him, erotic, hot dreams she didn't dare remember when she was awake. He was tall and broad-shouldered with hard, defined muscles that rippled every time he moved. And when he moved, it was with such grace even that affected her, robbing her of her ability to think reasonably at times.

His hands moved over her with such expertise, rough against her sensitive breasts and soft, inner thighs. He had the most seductive mouth and he used it, his strong white teeth nipping and tugging, occasionally biting gently or with enough pressure to make her yelp, even as his tongue eased the sting.

She couldn't catch her breath, her head tossing on the pillow, but she couldn't take her eyes from him. He wrapped one arm around her hips, pinning her down, the other hand pushing her legs apart so he could wedge his broad shoulders between her thighs.

"Stay still, Blue. I've been waiting a long time for this."

His voice growled with hunger, and his eyes glowed a fierce nearly golden color. He looked as if he might devour her. Her heart went crazy, pounding in her chest and if she had one single iota of self-preservation, she would have run for her life, but she was desperate for him, for anything he would give her.

Her body was impatient for his, undulating without inhibition on the bed, trying to entice him, to tempt him. She wanted him as out of control as she was, her fists gripping the sheets, twisting and holding to stay still as he'd commanded.

He kissed his way down her breasts, across her flat belly. Her breath exploded from her lungs when his tongue dipped in her navel and licked and flicked there. She heard herself pant and her hips jerked, but he held her pinned with his casual strength. Again she felt the edge of his teeth as a warning, but that only inflamed her more.

His hand stroked up and down her thigh, and her entire body shuddered in response. She swore her temperature had soared out of control and each time his hand slipped over her thigh, hot liquid seeped from her body and deep inside her muscles contracted and pulsed in need.

He looked down at her with his strange cat's eyes, at the moisture seeping from her body and her writhing hips. A smile of pure male satisfaction, of total possession, as if what he was looking at belonged solely to him, softened the curve of his mouth. And she supposed she did belong to him. A small sob escaped.

"Remy, please. I'm not goin' to live through this. You have to do something."

She couldn't believe that was her, pleading. Begging. She would be utterly humiliated under any other circumstances, but her body was on fire and she couldn't stop herself. Pulsing. Throbbing. Desperate for him to do something. Anything. Just give her some relief. Her blood roared in her ears, a thunder like no other she'd ever heard.

He spread her thighs even wider, until his impossibly

broad shoulders held her legs apart, digging into her inner thighs. Her breath caught and held in her lungs as his head slowly descended. She felt his breath first. He blew warm air over her quivering mound. Every muscle tensed. Contracted. Waited. The room was utterly silent except for the pounding of her heart.

He looked at her again, this time without raising his head, and for a moment fear swept through her. He made a hot, snarly sound, much like the growl of an animal about to pounce on prey and devour it. She jerked, her fingers curling harder around the sheets.

The first swipe of his tongue through the hot, slick folds of her core had her crying out. Her entire body shuddered and if he hadn't been holding her down, she would have come up off the bed.

He lifted his head, glaring in reprimand, his eyes piercing and furious. "Don't." It was a single command.

Bijou realized Remy wasn't in control any more than she was. Of her, yes, but not necessarily of himself. He had said there would be no stopping, no going back, and she realized why. He had gone over that cliff with her and they both were in the throes of some passionate frenzy neither could stop.

He licked at her, his tongue much rougher than she expected. Her breath slammed out of her lungs. Her stomach muscles bunched painfully. Her breasts strained and ached. He held her down with one arm, licking at her like a large, hungry cat, devouring an endless supply of hot cream. Her head thrashed from side to side as she felt the tight muscles of her empty sheath spasm, sending more cream to be lapped up greedily.

Pleasure washed over her in strong, rippling waves. The sheet shredded beneath her fingernails, long rips she barely noticed. She couldn't stand much more. Her body was on fire, burning from the inside out. She could barely catch her breath, but he wouldn't stop. He refused to stop even when she tried pushing at his shoulders to warn him it was too much.

Her hips bucked again and again as his wicked tongue stabbed and explored. She felt his teeth on her most sensitive spot and she exploded, came apart, her body thrusting against his fingers and mouth while she mewled at the tormenting pleasure. He gave one last lick to her shuddering, swollen body and knelt up, dragging her closer to him.

His face could have been carved in stone. Sensuality was etched deep in every line. His eyes were hooded, piercing and watchful, but filled with such dark lust there was no resisting him. "You're mine," he whispered.

He may as well have shouted the words. His voice was low, a mere thread of sound, but the words blazed through her mind and burned into her soul.

"You belong to me." The head of his cock pressed hard against her slick entrance. "Do you understand? You're mine."

Giving up her soul seemed a small price to pay just to get him inside of her. The roaring in her head was rolling thunder now, an endless, shocking scream her own bloodstream demanded. She couldn't help herself. She nodded. Panted. Begged him. There was no stopping that desperate female voice, pleading with him to enter her. She'd give him anything he wanted. Just tell her.

He leaned forward, pressing the burning thick head of his cock inside of her, stretching her in spite of the slick cream she welcomed him with.

"All of you. Everything you are belongs to me."

She was depraved and shameless and wanton, but it didn't matter. A sob escaped. He had to be inside of her. Nothing else could stop the terrible burning. The need. Nothing else could fill her up and sate the wild, relentless demands of her body.

"Yes. Everything I am," she hissed. "Please, Remy. Please."

He slammed into her hard, ripping through her innocence, driving through tight, never-used muscles like a battering ram, invading her body with his thick, hard, hot shaft.

Lightning zigzagged through her body, forks of burning fire. His hands were rough on her hips, holding her pinned down so he could thrust deep and hard over and over, setting a ferocious pace.

There was no time to catch her breath. No time to register pain before pleasure swamped her. Her body gripped his fiercely, pulsing and gushing, holding on tightly. Her sheath felt far too small. He was too large, stretching her mercilessly, but that only added to the tortuous pleasure. Her body grew tighter. More tense. The fire kept building higher and higher. There was no release. No way to stop.

He slammed into her over and over, rocking her with every brutal thrust. His fingers dug into flesh and he began jerking her into him each time he surged forward, sending whips of lightning dancing through her body, flicking her, flogging her with heat and fire. She opened her mouth to scream, to beg, but he just kept going, his eyes twin points of intensity, his face a mask of carved sensuality.

The bed rocked beneath them, shook and seemed alive. An ominous crack signaled a board beneath them snapping but he didn't stop. He drove between her thighs like a madman possessed, pummeling her with such force and so deep she was afraid he would drive through her. Still, she didn't want him to stop. Fear snaked through her that she wouldn't survive the intensity of their sexual heat, but that didn't matter either. The only thing that mattered to her was that living jackhammer pounding into her with such erotic fury.

She heard her own voice begging, but the roaring in her ears didn't allow interpretation. She just needed. She simply burned. She wanted to burn up with him. She felt him swelling, the friction impossibly increasing until she was afraid actual flames would burst from her. Still, that didn't matter to her, only that he find a way to make the terrible pressure, the never-ending need stop for just a moment.

Tension wound tighter as the frenzy of lust grew between them. His face was a mask of absolute resolve. He slammed into her again and again, a driving rhythm of furious, relentless passion. She heard her voice building in time with the rising pressure in her body. A raging inferno began slow, moving through her deceptively, and then picking up speed to spread fast, to engulf every part of her body.

She screamed. Went rigid. Felt his cock pulsing, swelling. All the while her body gripped his in a terrible stranglehold, the friction burning hotter than ever. She felt him stiffen. Gather himself. He thrust hard, driving deep and the heated spray of seed soaked her tender walls.

She fought to find her breath while her body rippled with life, squeezing and milking him, insisting she get every last drop. Moistening dry lips, she forced her lashes to stay up so she could look at his face. Beads of sweat clung to his hair and she felt a few of her own trickling down the side of her face and more between her breasts.

She couldn't move. Her body felt limp, a rag doll, no more. She could barely look at him. She'd been insane. In the thralls of some madness. She had never acted that way in her life and her behavior terrified her. Was she like Bodrie after all?

Remy leaned over her and brushed kisses to the corner of her eyes, his lips sipping as if tasting tears. She wasn't crying. She wouldn't allow herself to be such a baby, not when her body still pulsed around Remy's and blood, seed and cream from her own body were trickling down her thighs.

He kissed the corner of her mouth, the tip of her breast and with a soft groan, slipped from her body and rolled over. The action caused her body to ripple and heat more, like a terrible itch that just refused to go away. She pressed her lips together tightly and put her arm over her eyes. She was horrible. Insatiable. What the hell was wrong with her?

She'd had wild, crazy very rough sex. Her body was sore. Every muscle hurt, but deep inside, she could already feel the hunger growing. Maybe she had a sex addiction, but knowing it and stopping it were two different things. The fire between her legs grew. The tension gathered until it was no small itch, but a craving she wasn't going to be able to resist. She had to get away from Remy.

Bijou rolled off the bed and landed on her hands and knees, desperate to escape herself.

"Where the hell do you think you're going?" Remy demanded, a snarl in his voice.

She looked over her shoulder at him. Bijou knew she shouldn't have been afraid. He was rough, but every time he touched her, he made certain she felt pleasure. She was too sensitive, her body on fire. It didn't make any sense to her that she hadn't felt sated. In a way she found it terrifying. She was as afraid of herself as she was of him.

Remy's eyes went totally feral. He reminded her of a great jungle cat about to devour his prey. A single sound escaped, a small note of confusion, or worse, excitement, and she turned away from, him, scrambling across the floor on all fours.

She tried to crawl away, her body still shuddering with pleasure, hungry for more, but afraid and confused by her own desperate needs. Near tears, Bijou couldn't imagine how she'd gone from being frigid with no physical interest in a man to such an insatiable, sensual creature who kept enticing and inciting Remy to more.

He growled a warning and was on her with the speed of a cat, catching her from behind and dragging her hips back into him. His heavy erection pressed against her slick body from behind. Remy wrapped one arm around her waist, holding her still while he thrust into her, filling her. She was so slick with the mixture of their sex, and she should have been easy to enter, but she wasn't, her body fighting the invasion and giving way reluctantly. That stretching sensation had a bite to it, but she didn't care. The small edge of pain only heightened the pleasure for her, humiliating her more. What was wrong with her?

He licked along her back, lapping at the tiny beads of sweat. His breath was hot as he alternated between teeth and tongue, making his way up her spine to the back of her neck. He ceased moving, holding her still, his body locked with hers. She pushed and bucked, but he refused to move, holding her there. Waiting.

Her heart began to pound again. Her breasts swayed. Her hair hung in damp tangles around her face, sweeping the floor. His shaft swelled, pushed deep and spread her tight sheath muscles even more when it didn't seem possible.

Hot breath blasted her. For a moment she swore she felt the slide of fur along her shoulder and then teeth drove deep, long, razor-sharp canines, in a holding bite. She cried out and thrashed beneath him, but he refused to let go. Deep inside, that wild, feral other rose until she felt an itch running like waves under her skin and fire burned between her thighs. She dropped her head, panting away the pain, accepting of Remy and his crazy, rough sex. Whatever was inside of her embraced him. Needed him. Wanted him. And was every bit as savage as he was.

Slowly the teeth slipped from her skin and his tongue lapped at the wounds. He began to move, sending streaks of fire racing over her body, burning through her veins and settling into her battered sheath. She never wanted him to stop. The sensations were stronger than ever, pleasure rushing over her while he slammed into her with furious intent. She couldn't stop the all-encompassing orgasm, the way it took her belly and breasts and rode down to her thighs.

Remy caught her by the hair and jerked her head back, adding a myriad of sensations burning through her body, increasing the strength of her muscles contracting around his shaft. Still he didn't stop and neither did her orgasm. Her body shuddered and pulsed in frenzied insanity. She heard herself scream as another orgasm ripped through her. Remy emptied himself into her as she pulsed around him.

Too weak to hold herself up, Bijou would have collapsed on the floor if Remy hadn't held on to her.

"What in the world did you do to me?" she whispered. "What's wrong with me?"

"Nothin' is wrong with you," Remy assured, kissing her spine.

She made a derisive sound in her throat. There was something very much wrong with her, but she didn't have the energy to argue. "I can't move. I really can't. I'm so exhausted I think I'll sleep here. Just leave me."

Remy slipped out of her. She didn't turn around, but let herself collapse right there on the floor. She closed her eyes and heard him move. The bed creaked and groaned as if a heavy weight had landed on it. She heard ripping as if something tore apart the heavy drapes or the walls, but honestly, she wasn't about to lift her head, even if she could. It felt good to just lie there and listen to her heart beating semi-normally.

The terrible thunder was gone, and for the moment, she felt sated, the burning gone between her legs. Terrified the sensation would start again, she kept her eyes closed tight so she couldn't see Remy, afraid he was the trigger. She hoped she'd just go to sleep and wake up to find the entire episode was only one of her erotic dreams about him. True, she'd never quite dreamt so vividly or imagined in any way that sex with Remy would be so perfect or brutal, but in her own right she was an artist and entitled to a vivid imagination.

She heard the water go on in the bathtub and smelled lavender. She couldn't move. Remy had to leave. It was nice of him to run a bath for her, which she was certain he was doing, but she wasn't about to face him even if she could. Which she couldn't because she couldn't get off the floor. Satisfied that she made perfect sense, she kept her eyes closed.

"Come on, Blue. We have to get you into hot water."

She managed to wiggle her fingers, trying to shoo him. "Go away. Really, Remy. I'm not movin'. I'm sleepin' right here and I'll think about all this tomorrow."

He laughed softly. "If you don' get into that bath, *chere*, you won' be walkin' tomorrow. Come on."

Ignoring her murmur of protest and the hand that tried to bat him away, Remy lifted her into his arms and cradled her against his chest. It wasn't fair that he still had strength and she was virtually spaghetti. Every muscle felt deliciously bruised and battered. Her body felt used and decadent.

In a horrible, secret part of her mind, she was elated—shocked, of course—but so intensely happy that she had it in her to keep up just a bit with Remy Boudreaux. Or even that he wanted her for a single night, let alone made her state that she was his alone.

She realized her thighs were sticky and she was an absolute mess. How did a woman gracefully retreat after crazy sex? She had no idea, but she had to open her eyes soon and she could tell he was staring down at her. She could feel those piercing, intelligent eyes focused on her face.

Bijou took a deep breath and opened her eyes, looking, not at him, but at the room she rented from Saria. One wall had a caved-in spot with several cracks racing up it. Another wall, over by the bed, had furrows dug deep as if a large tiger or a bear had raked it with two claws. The bed sagged from the broken board. The sheets were in bloodstained strips and a lamp was knocked over and broken on the floor.

"Oh, my God." She covered her red face with her hands. "What am I goin' to tell Saria? We've ruined her beautiful room."

Not only was she going to have to face Remy in the daylight, but there was no way to keep Saria from finding out what had taken place in this room. Or just how crazy she'd acted with Remy.

"I'm puttin' you in the water, *chere*. Don' be thinking about the room. We can fix the room up. This is going to sting a little. I put some salts in there as well."

He didn't lower her feet as she expected, but stepped into the tub with her and just sank down. Frankly, she was too exhausted to care how she got in the water, but the moment the extreme heat hit her sex she tried to scramble out of his arms. Remy tightened his hold on her and forced her down into the water.

"Your body needs this whether you think so or not."

She blew out her breath, but already, the hot water was beginning to soothe her sore, raw body. "I guess I'll let you live a little longer," she said grudgingly. "But you really do have to stop bossin' me around."

He laughed softly, shifting her off his lap and over to one side of the large claw-foot tub. "That's not likely to ever happen, woman, so don' hold your breath."

She leaned her head against the high back and allowed her lashes to drift down again. "My arms feel like noodles. I don' think I'll ever be able to walk again either."

"Give yourself a few minutes, Blue. The water will revive you in no time." Remy cleared his throat. Waited until she looked at him from under her long lashes. Guilt rode him hard. "Listen, honey, I knew you were a virgin and I should have taken more care with you. I didn't hold back or take that into consideration at all and I apologize."

Her lashes fluttered and she closed her eyes again. A small smile curved her lower lip. That fantasy lower lip he wanted to lean forward and bite.

"Seriously? Remy, I think it's a little too late for either of us to think about that now. I know you want your apology to be sincere, but how could it be after the way we were together?" She frowned. "Or is that the way it always is when one has sex, because if so, I've been missing out."

She had a point. Still, he wished he could have been just a little gentler initially. He winced a little at that, "when one has sex." She didn't say "make love" like every other woman he knew would have. He had definitely had savage, brutal leopard sex with her, but still . . .

He didn't understand why her female hadn't emerged and it worried him just a little bit. He was certain he was right about Bijou and her cat, he'd even felt his male reacting to what he thought was her female, yet Bijou hadn't been forced to shift.

He pushed both hands through his hair and studied her face. There were shadows there and around her neck little smudges and love bites. The back of her neck had been marked by his cat, claiming her. She was sore, bruised and feeling guilty as sin. How did he explain her leopard to her?

"Sex will never be like that with anyone else," Remy said honestly, "so you're better off sticking with me."

That faint smile appeared again. "Or I could be dead in a week after spending time with you." A blush crept up her chest and neck. She still wouldn't look at him.

He couldn't imagine how she felt. She'd shed every inhibition and had absolutely no idea why. If he blurted out, "Hon, you're a leopard, just like me,"' she'd run for the hills and he couldn't blame her. He should have tried to explain before they'd ever gotten started, but he was too far gone, too far into the frenzied thrall of mating.

"It would be a hell of a way to go," Remy said, injecting humor into his voice. He could still lose her. She was out of her depth and fighting not to be ashamed of herself when there was nothing to be ashamed of.

"Wouldn't it?" She tilted her chin. "Why haven't you ever married?"

That was a loaded question if he ever heard one. He turned her around and picked up the spray nozzle so he could wash her hair. "I never found the right person. For me it was far better to be alone than to be with the wrong woman. I'll never be an easy man to live with and my woman will have to put up with a lot, so there was no doubt in my mind I'd better find the right one if I was going to be with someone."

He massaged her scalp, trying to ease some of the tension from her. The bite mark on the back of her neck was deeper than he had intended. He couldn't help but lean forward and brush a kiss over the wound. She seemed to drift a little while he rinsed, towel dried and then braided her hair into a long, thick rope.

Bijou suddenly jerked away, turning her head toward him, her eyes wide with fear and shock. "Remy." She said his name like a talisman, her white knight, the only man she could trust in a frightening situation.

He stood up quickly, pulling the drain on the water and drawing her with him. Taking her out of the water, he wrapped a towel around her. Her body shuddered, sensitive to the slightest touch. She moistened her lips and looked up at him, her jeweled eyes meeting his. "It's happening again. I can feel it—a hunger spreading like fire through me. Is it you? Have you given me something like a drug? A chemical to make this happen? Have I turned into a nymphomaniac? Is it in my blood?"

He shook his head. "Don' be silly. It's none of those things. Just know that when it happens to you, it also happens to me. We're in this together, Blue, and I'll get you through it. Look at me, I had you not even an hour ago and I'm all jacked up again."

Bijou looked at him with rapt attention, at the size of his cock, and he felt himself jerk in response. They'd had violent sex, and yet that didn't matter. He knew she was sore. He knew her body needed rest. Hell. So did his. That didn't matter either, it seemed. His wayward cock had a mind of its own, just as her poor abused body did.

He reached out and caught the nape of her neck, leaning a little toward her. "I sat on that damned balcony three nights in a row, so hard I thought I'd break into pieces if I dared to even move. I made up stories in my mind, all those erotic images of you kneeling at my feet, your beautiful lips wrapped around my cock givin' me relief."

She bit down on her lower lip, her blue eyes rising to meet his. The impact hit him hard, like a punch to the gut. The tip of her tongue came out and she licked at her lips as if the thought was intriguing. "I want to, Remy. I dreamt of pleasin' you that way, maybe a million times, but I honestly don't know how. I'm a fast learner," she added. "I read books just in case you wanted me. I didn't want to disappoint you."

"You could never disappoint me, Bijou. The key to being good at this is to enjoy it. If you do, and I know you want me like that and that you enjoy having me in your mouth, lovin' me that way, anything you do will be perfect."

"Would you help me learn? If you talk me through it and have patience . . ." She trailed off.

The hopeful note in her voice tugged at his heart. She was squirming again. The Han Vol Dan was so close and her leopard was definitely a very sexual passionate animal, just as his was. She wouldn't give Bijou any relief, her heat driving her to mate.

He put a little pressure on her shoulders, silently commanding her to kneel. "I'm a very good teacher," he told her hoarsely.

He was not going to last long, his passion rising to meet hers. He would have to be inside of her soon. The thrall was on both of them, not just Bijou, and he couldn't stop himself from taking her again and again, no matter the cost to either of them.

Who could resist the sight of Bijou, her long hair falling around her soft skin, on her knees looking up at him with dark desire in her incredible eyes? He needed her mouth wrapped around his cock. He was already dripping in anticipation.

Her breasts rose and fell, her nipples harder than ever. She wanted this every bit as much as he did, and that had him nearly falling to his own knees. He nudged her knees a little farther apart with his foot, enjoying the reality of her rather than an image. Her body was open to his, needy like his, and she licked her lips again as if she couldn't wait to taste him.

Already he could scent her call, that wild lavender honey wafting up from between her thighs to tease his senses and drive him insane with need all over again. She was leopard, she would take to every passionate, erotic lesson he gave her. He let her look her fill and then he caught her hair in his fist and urged her chin up. "Explore with your tongue. Get to know me. Every part of me. I belong to you, so take your time and enjoy yourself."

He wasn't altogether certain he could give her that time, but he found he needed this from her. Her hands touched him tentatively at first, stroking little caresses that made him want to growl. Then she touched with more confidence, testing his weight, his girth, holding his balls and rolling them gently. He threw back his head at the first stroke of her tongue. Featherlight. Velvet soft. He wasn't going to survive this night.

He used the back of his hand to gently caress the sides of her face, encouraging her as she built up her courage. It was all he could do not to force himself to thrust his cock into her mouth. Fire burned over him when her tongue stroked and licked and then she sucked at his heavy sac. This wasn't going to work, not when she was so sensuous and obviously into pleasing his every whim. He would never last.

"Blue, I need your mouth around me. Suck on me hard." Now his voice was nearly gone, just a hard command that was more growl than voice.

Bijou licked up the shaft, swirled her tongue around the ridge and down under the head of his cock. His breath hissed out of him as she licked over the head and then pushed down, taking it into the heat of her mouth. The suction was tight and her tongue teased over his hard flesh. He forgot all about teaching her anything. There was no way he could allow her to explore much longer, not if he planned on being inside of her.

Her scent beckoned him, a wild call he couldn't ignore, not even for the ecstasy of her mouth moving over him with such care. She was squirming, her hips undulating in desperation, yet she still did her best to please him.

He tugged at her hair, waiting until she looked up at him. Her eyes were nearly pure cat, glowing at him like two glittering jewels in the night.

"I need to be inside you, *chere*. Right now. There's all the time in the world for you to pleasure me like this, but right now, I need something else." He drew her up and pointed to the bed. "Kneel down there."

Bijou did as he commanded without question. He knew exhaustion didn't matter. Inhibitions didn't count. She had no more choice than he did. All he could do was make their joining the most pleasurable and passionate he could.

In the end, as dawn crept in, and she finally fell into a fitful sleep, he had no real idea of how many times he had taken her, only that each time she had screamed in pleasure, her body riding his as he took them both to paradise again and again.

Remy looked down at Bijou sprawled across the bed, her skin marred with his fingermarks, and the teeth of his leopard. He'd marked her—claimed her in the manner of his people, a primitive ritual, but it served its purpose of warning off other males, and making certain the emerging female leopard accepted the male. Bijou Breaux was formally now and forever . . . his.

7

"YOU really pissed off someone," Gage said, hands on his hips, as he surveyed the damage to his brother's apartment.

Remy noted with an inner smile that his younger brother had positioned himself protectively just a little in front of Remy. He knew without a doubt, if there was trouble, he could shove his brother out of the way, but it would slow him down by a second or two. On the other hand, it was a good feeling to know his brother had those protective instincts—for him.

"I guess I did," Remy admitted with some satisfaction. He looked around the small apartment he rented in New Orleans. His home would always be the bayou, but it wasn't always convenient to make his way that distance every night, so he kept a place closer to the police station.

"He really tore up your apartment," Gage said. "I don' think there's anythin' left."

"I don' keep anythin' of value here," Remy replied and took a long, slow look around the sitting room of his apartment.

Everything was smashed. His end tables, his lamps. The

television set that had been on the wall was shattered, leaving a huge hole in the Sheetrock. The couch and recliner cushions were slashed and the stuffing torn out.

"I'd say he was in a rage," Gage said. He glanced at his brother. "What did you do?"

Remy shrugged. "I kissed a girl."

"I hope she was worth it," Gage said, and stepped back, closer to his brother in order to peer into the bedroom.

Remy knew the exact moment Gage inhaled and caught his scent. His head swung around, eyes wide with shock.

"What the hell have you done, Remy?" he asked, swinging around to fully face his brother. "You have Bijou's scent all over you. There's no mistakin' . . ." He trailed off, suddenly catching that other much more elusive scent shadowing Bijou's. He inhaled sharply. "She's . . ."

Remy nodded. "Leopard. *Mine*." He made that very clear. "This bastard has been stalkin' her. He's not going to get away with it."

Gage held up his hand, shaking his head. "Wait a minute. I need a moment here. You *claimed* Bijou Breaux? The multimillionaire, born with a silver spoon in her mouth, daughter of a *legend*? Are you out of your mind?"

"I've been asked that more than once, and watch your mouth." Remy shrugged lightly, but his hands closed into fists, the ache in his knuckles telling him his leopard was close.

"Get real, Remy. She's slummin', comin' back to New Orleans. You think she's a hometown girl? She's never been one of us. She's elegant and stylish and she's restless as hell. She's used to livin' a lifestyle on red carpets with jet-setters and private jets. We don' belong there and never have. She's come here on a whim, putting her club together and her cutesy little apartment." Gage laid a hand on his brother's arm. "She's goin' to rip your heart apart. She'll never stay."

"Watch what you say, Gage. She's my mate. No one's goin' to take her away from me. And I'm not goin' to let anyone, including my brother, make her life miserable. She'll stay. She belongs with me whether she knows it or not." His voice was resolute. Implacable. Bijou might try to run, but she wouldn't get far.

He feared his rising anger at his brother was because Gage was voicing his own concerns. Bijou didn't belong in the homes on the bayou—and he did. She didn't belong in a fucked-up leopard's lair—she was made for far greater things. Money meant little to him, it was nothing more than another tool to get through life, and the amount she had was nearly unimaginable. It wasn't her money, it was Bijou herself. She was elegant, a lady, just as Gage had said. Her passion came from her leopard driving her. What happened if her leopard didn't emerge?

"A week ago you didn't even know she was in town, Remy. Now you're actin' like an idiot, drawin' some crazed fan out so you can be a hero."

Remy smiled, but his eyes had gone cat. He knew because he was seeing distorted heat images. "You don' have to like her, Gage, but you do have to be respectful. I'll defend her with everything I am. She's my choice. And just for your information, I would have been an idiot and drawn out any stalker if a woman had come to me for help. Bijou didn't ask. I insisted."

Gage opened his mouth and closed it abruptly, shaking his head. "You may have bitten off more than you can chew with this one, brother. But I'll back your play. You want Bijou Breaux, then I'm all for it."

Remy inhaled sharply. The stalker had left his scent everywhere throughout Remy's apartment. He had cleaned up the scenes forensically, but he couldn't fail to leave behind his scent. Unlike the crime scene the serial killer had left behind, there was no blood and fear to contaminate the nose of a leopard.

"Have you come across this scent before?" he asked Gage.

Gage took another sniff. "No. But I'll know him if I run into him."

"Have all the boys come in and smell him. I want them

all lookin'. The moment someone scents him, have them call me." Remy sounded like he was giving orders—and he was. He was head of his household and his brothers would do as he said. When Drake wasn't in residence, the rest of the lair relied on him as well. He wanted all of them out searching for Bijou's stalker.

The man's anger toward Bijou was escalating, but his rage toward Remy was all consuming. Remy stepped closer to the long wall in his sitting room—the wall the stalker had nearly destroyed. There was a picture ripped from the tabloid of Remy kissing Bijou and another frame where he'd lifted his head and looked directly at the camera. His body was slightly in front of Bijou's blocking her face from the shot, but there was no denying it was her.

His face had been scribbled over with a black marker—permanent, he was certain. A knife had stabbed at the region of Bijou's stomach and then jabbed at his body repeatedly, over and over, each tear in the photograph larger and deeper into the wall then the last. Forensics had already told him there were no prints on the knife and the knife itself was most likely untraceable, but it mattered little. The stalker had fallen into Remy's trap, and it was only a matter of time before one of the shifters got his scent.

"I'll get them on it," Gage said, "but watch your back."

Remy moved through the small apartment toward the back where the bedroom was. "He was very methodical here." He glanced at Gage over his shoulder. "He was searching for something."

Gage crowded closer, his eyebrow raised. There wasn't a single thing in the bedroom untouched—or unbroken. "Searching for what?"

"Evidence that Bijou has been here."

Gage opened and closed his mouth again. "Damn, bro. This isn't a good situation."

"He didn't find anythin'," Remy stated. "I'm not about to set her up as a target of that kind of anger. I took enough of a chance kissing her publicly. I was fairly certain he'd come after me, and I knew if he came here, he would be satisfied that Bijou has never been here."

"You took a big risk, Remy," Gage pointed out. "Look at the rage this stalker exhibits. He almost acts as if he owns her. She's in real danger and kissin' her probably added to that."

"It was a calculated risk," Remy admitted. "And necessary to draw him out." He gestured toward the bed. "I think he was makin' a statement."

There was nothing left of the bed. Even the frame was in splinters. The mattress was slashed, ripped and stabbed repeatedly, the guts all over the room. Remy was thankful his good mattress was in his home in the bayou. On the wall, like the wall of the sitting room, a giant eye was painted in dripping red paint, the meaning clear. He was being watched. Bijou was being watched.

"Yeah, I get it," he murmured under his breath. "Tell everyone to be careful, Gage. If they scent this man, I don' want anyone approachin' him. Just have them ID him to me."

Gage nodded. "I'll get everyone in here."

"I have to get back to the Inn. Saria had to leave because her leopard was goin' crazy with Bijou there."

"Did Bijou's leopard actually emerge?" Gage asked, his tone cautious.

"No." Remy's abrupt answer didn't invite discussion.

Gage ignored him. "Her mother? Bodrie?"

"Not Bodrie," Remy said firmly. "He didn't have any leopard in him."

"You certain about that?" Gage replied. "His sexual excesses were legendary. That's a by-product of a leopard without a mate."

Remy shook his head. "I would have known. My leopard would have known. I was around him a few times." There was distaste in his voice. He couldn't help it. Taking an eight-year-old child into a room filled with naked men and women and endless drugs sickened him, and every time he thought of how he'd chosen the easy way out—palming her off on Pauline and taking off—he wanted to kick himself all over again. "Bodrie was no leopard," he repeated.

"You can't know that for certain. It isn't as if we haven't had our own mess here in the lair with half leopards and crazed leopards doin' things they shouldn't. Look at Bannaconni's family. And right here, Tregre's family. Not all leopards are worth anything," Gage reminded.

Remy swung around. "What kind of crack is that?"

Gage didn't back up even a step, although Remy was once again seeing in heat images. "It's no crack. I know you didn't like Bodrie. You never talked about why, but you had to have a reason. I liked his music, but I didn't know the man. I wasn't referrin' to Bijou."

Remy took a breath. The stench of the stalker felt like an infection in his lungs. "Sorry, Gage. I'm a little jumpy. Her leopard didn't emerge last night and when she wakes up . . ." He shook his head. "She isn't a one-night stand kind of woman. I was pretty brutal last night with her and she was innocent. I need to get to her and explain what's goin' on before she takes it into her head to bolt."

"*Imbecile.* Remy, are you insane? She wasn't even experienced and you just *left* her? What if her leopard decides she's ready and you're not around? She goes runnin' in the swamp or bayous and half the lair will be chasin' her whether you've marked her as yours or not. You know what happens to males when a female is in her time."

"She's exhausted." Remy glanced at his watch. Like everything he'd done, there were risks. He calculated them against the benefits. He didn't have much more time, which was why he was directing his brother to get the members of the lair to his apartment now that the forensic team was finished.

"She'd better be." Gage shook his head in disgust. "You're a damn good detective and a smart son of a bitch, but you don' know jack about women, bro."

Remy was beginning to be more than uneasy about leaving Bijou. Gage was right, although he wasn't going to admit it.

"Have you talked to Saria? Is she back at the Inn?" There was worry in Gage's voice.

Remy realized he relied heavily on his own reputation. The males in the lair had grown up around him. They knew him and his leopard. Few could hope to best him in a challenge, even if they tried double-teaming him as they had Drake. If you crossed one Boudreux, you crossed all of them. Remy had the reputation of swift and terrifying punishment, and the males had always backed off if he stepped into a fight. But an unmated female was rare in their lair. More, Bijou was a celebrity with millions of dollars. On top of that she was beautiful and intelligent. Perhaps Gage had a point and he'd overestimated his lair's fear of him.

His gut churned. Turned over. Yeah. He'd been an idiot to leave her. He needed to get back to the Inn as soon as possible.

BIJOU pried her lashes open, groaning, afraid to face the light—or herself. Even the slightest movement sent pain crashing through her body. Every muscle hurt. She hurt in places she hadn't known existed. Bijou groaned and threw her hand over her eyes. Last night had been the most intense, exhilarating and absolute best night of her life. So why couldn't she just admit she loved every second of it and move on?

Why lie in bed and feel like she could never face Remy again? She was grown up, for God's sake. She could have a night of crazy sex and face him the next day, couldn't she? She let her breath out slowly and forced herself to sit up, drawing her knees up and rocking herself gently back and forth. She was traumatized, that's why. Totally, absolutely traumatized. She'd never done anything like this in her life. What had gotten into her?

She'd been utterly shameless. She groaned and wiped her hand over her face. Did it have to be Remy? *Her* Remy? Her white knight? Her fictionalized, fantasy Remy who was her dream man. She'd had a one-night stand with him. Given up her virginity to him in a wild night of crazed sex. She'd done things she hadn't ever imagined—or even knew she could do—and she loved it. She was some kind of pervert when it came to sex.

She always thought she had inhibitions, scarred from seeing her father on the floor having sex with multiple women. How many times had she walked into the kitchen, or their enormous living room or gone out to the pool and found him actually having sex. He didn't even stop when she walked in, just looked up and asked her what she wanted.

She'd been around three when she began to realize what he was doing with those women. Her nannies. The housekeeper. The maids. They came and went as he tired of them. When she was seven her teacher came to the house to talk to Bodrie about absences. He'd had sex with her right there, nearly on the front steps, right in front of Bijou. When Bodrie refused to see her after that, she'd tried using Bijou to get to him. When that plan failed, she'd hated Bijou and had made her life miserable.

How could she possibly have turned out like Bodrie? But she would have had sex with Remy on the front lawn. On the hood of her own car. Anywhere. She wouldn't have even recognized she was in a public place. She was a nymphomaniac. There could be no other explanation.

A sound escaped. A low, keening moan. She rocked herself back and forth for comfort. There was no blaming Remy. She would have gone into town and seduced someone, maybe—God help her—a total stranger. Remy at least had saved her from that humiliation.

How could she have gone from someone who refused to have sex with a man even when she was semi-interested, to such a total crazed, nymphomaniac? The last couple of days she and Saria had been out of step. Had she inadvertently flirted with Drake? Could she possibly be the kind of woman who would sleep with her best—her *only*—friend's husband?

She groaned again and once more covered her face with her hands. Her first inclination was to pack up everything and just get the hell out of New Orleans, but she knew from experience, she couldn't outrun who she was. No one could. The only good thing that would be accomplished would be not having to face Remy and not acting like her father in front of him ever again.

She didn't want to lose Saria as a friend. All she could do was apologize and move out. She could easily stay at a hotel until the renovations on her apartment were done. Avoiding Remy wouldn't be easy if he didn't want to be avoided, but she didn't trust herself around him. And maybe, hopefully, the physical attraction she felt toward him had been simply confused with her fantasies of him, and now that they'd had sex, she wouldn't think about him anymore.

Yeah. Right. She drew in a sharp, harsh breath. There was no other explanation. She really was just like her father. She had always said she would be nothing like him. She'd be responsible. She'd vowed to be the complete opposite of Bodrie, and yet here she was, a wild animal in bed. She hadn't been able to control herself, she hadn't even tried, not once Remy had kissed her. His mouth still burned on hers, his taste still potent and addictive.

She had to force her aching body to move. Every step into the bathroom just served as a reminder that she'd screwed up big-time. Sheets stuffed in the clothes hamper were stained with blood. Remy had put them there, but they were ripped up, useless, and she didn't want Saria to see or have to deal with them.

She moaned again and looked into the mirror. Her eyes had dark circles under them. Her lips seemed swollen. There were strawberry bites all over her neck and throat. A clear path of love bites went from her throat to both her breasts and even lower still. She blushed, thinking about what her inner thighs might look like.

To wake herself up, and give herself more time to think, she stepped into the shower. She couldn't help thinking about how Remy had run a hot bath while she dozed on the floor. He'd carried her into the bath and carefully washed and then braided her hair. It was still wet and would be if she didn't pull out the braid and dry it. She'd felt . . . cared for. His hands had been gentle, at odds with his near savage sex. She couldn't remember a time in her life when anyone had ever made her feel as if she mattered to them, other than when Remy had dragged her from a hotel room the night she'd made up her mind to end her life.

She slid down the wall of the shower stall, sinking onto the tile in a crouch while the hot water poured over her. It took several minutes to realize she was crying. She'd been alone for so long in the midst of a crowd. She'd been surrounded, her entire life, by managers and handlers, and she'd been so lonely, yearning for so long for a family. For a real friend. For one person to care whether she was alive or dead.

Remy had cared all those years ago and so had Saria. She'd come back to them, looking for something that had always been out of her reach. She had all the money in the world, and no one to share her life. She knew she had issues. She'd worked hard to overcome them, but trust just didn't come easily to her.

She let out her breath slowly and forced herself to stand up. She'd made a mistake, but she didn't have it in her to take the easy way out and run. She'd picked New Orleans to make a stand. She loved everything about her home city. The people and the music. The bayous and swamps called to her. She loved the food and the fishing boats. The laughter and hard work. She loved the sunsets and the birds. She even enjoyed the alligators. New Orleans was the only place that felt like home. Her own stupidity wasn't going to run her out of town.

She dressed slowly, taking her time with her makeup and hair. If she had to face Saria and confess her sins, whatever they might be, she needed a little armor. She was feeling extremely vulnerable and she had the feeling if she lost Saria, it would be a blow she might not readily recover from.

She could hear the cell phone she'd left on the nightstand playing the song her manager loved the most. It was a good five years old, one of the first that had been truly a big hit, rising to number one on the charts almost immediately. She hesitated answering. Lately they'd argued. Well, he argued. She'd made up her mind. No more touring. No more huge venues.

She hadn't talked to Remy about her manager being so angry with her. When she'd made the decision to stop the circus, a lot of people were very upset, and she couldn't blame them—she'd made them a lot of money. She let the phone pick up another message from him—as she'd been doing for the last few days. She was ashamed of herself for ducking his calls, but she couldn't face him yelling at her again over the same thing, not after waking up a total, absolute wreck.

She shoved the cell in her pocket, sighing, trying to ignore the way her skin itched in waves, as if something alive ran beneath the surface, settled and then repeated the movement. She had the sudden urge to grab the handrail and leap over the railing to the floor below. Her fingers curled, her knuckles throbbing, her fingertips feeling as though they might burst any moment. Every muscle ached and her skin felt too tight as if it was stretched over a larger frame and didn't quite fit.

She found, once she went downstairs to make herself coffee, that the Inn was empty. Saria was gone as well as Drake and she was the only guest, which allowed her a little extra time to think things through. It was very weird, but she swore her sense of smell was heightened. She could almost track Remy's every move throughout the house after he'd left her bedroom.

The moment his scent filled her lungs, her body went into some sort of heat flash. Blood surged hotly. Pooled. She closed her eyes and switched directions; she needed to be outside. Remy was everywhere, surrounding her, making it impossible to breathe properly.

The phone vibrated and she pulled it out impatiently and nearly dropped it, her heart pounding and her breath catching in her throat. *Remy Boudreaux*. Immediately her hand shook. What a freaking coward she was becoming. She shoved the phone back into her pocket with a trembling hand, and rubbed both palms down her thighs as if she could wipe the effect he had on her away.

Her jaw hurt, a deep pain in the bones she couldn't escape. Her teeth seemed to have grown overnight and felt too big to fit into her mouth. The terrible itch beneath her skin persisted and she scratched her arm, hoping to make it stop. Instead, she tore a strip of skin from her arm, a terrible rake mark that bled like crazy. She cursed softly in Cajun French, something she'd done since she was a child, but well under her breath so her teachers couldn't add that sin to the long list she'd had back then. Could the day get any worse?

She examined the horrendous scrape down her arm. It looked as if she'd been clawed by a jungle cat and felt like it as well. The cut was deep and long. She frowned at her fingernails. They were long, but not that long. Shaking her head, she wrapped her arm in a towel she found in the car.

She needed a distraction, and that meant getting away from the Inn and Remy's overwhelming scent. Sliding into her car, she turned up her music and took off driving. She was performing at her club in the evening, but she could do a little exploring and maybe give her body a little reprieve. For some reason even Remy's masculine smell sent her into a sexual meltdown.

The farther from the Inn she got, the more her body seemed to settle down and become her own. After a few miles the air didn't feel as if it was being squeezed out of her lungs, and she could breathe properly again. She heaved a sigh of relief. Even the terrible itch between her legs subsided, giving her a reprieve—hopefully for a very long time.

She found herself relaxing as she drove along the bayous. At night the roads could be spooky. She had grown up with reports of strange sightings and whispers of ghosts and legendary creatures prowling the swamps and bayous.

She almost missed the SUV pulled into the shadow of

the cypress grove leading out to the water's edge. She saw it at the last moment and braked quickly, her reaction far faster than she anticipated. She was out on one of the back roads, and if the SUV had gone off the road, whoever it was wouldn't have cell service and might be in trouble. Backing up, she cautiously maneuvered her much smaller car into the grove, but well away from the water.

Again she was cautious as she stepped out of her car, suddenly aware of the absolutely remote area she was in. Edging carefully around the SUV, she immediately saw a man's suit jacket tossed carelessly on the hood. He was bent over, tying a rope to the hitch of his vehicle, using two locking carabiners for one master point to slip the rope through.

"Are you all right?" she greeted, trying not to startle him.

He straightened, swinging around to face her and relief flooded her system instantly. She hadn't realized how tense she'd been. She recognized him instantly. Arnaud Lefevre, the famous sculptor whose work was even shown in the Louvre in France. His work sold for hundreds of thousands and he was grinning at her from the shade of the cypress grove on the edge of the swamp. He was dressed in his immaculate thousand-dollar suit, white shirt and hiking boots. That was Arnaud, an eccentric, but extremely talented and versatile.

"What in the world are you doin'?" Bijou demanded. "Arnaud, you can't just come out here alone. This is a dangerous area."

"I do it all the time." He stepped forward and hugged her in welcome, kissing both cheeks before releasing her. "It's a treasure trove here for me. I discovered it years ago."

She laughed, suddenly feeling carefree. "That's so you, Arnaud. Why are you wearing a suit? This is swamp right here just in case you hadn't noticed."

He raised a black eyebrow. "Woman, I always wear a suit. You should know that. You never know who you'll meet out in the middle of nowhere and you have to look your best to impress." He took ahold of her arm. "You want to tell me what happened here?"

Bijou frowned down at her arm, carefully unwrapping the material she'd tied over the rake marks. "I don' honestly know, Arnaud."

He very gently turned her arm over. "It looks like a very large and angry cat scratched it. Did you get into a fight with another woman?"

She pulled her arm away. "That sounds so like me."

He laughed and went around her to open the passenger door. "I brought food and coffee. You up for something?"

"Sure. But what were you doin' with that rope and your hitch?" Deliberately she looked around and up, as if looking for a cliff. "We don' do a lot of climbin' in Louisiana."

"Every time I see you, I'm surprised again by your ac cent." He glanced back at her over his shoulder, his gray eyes sparkling with laughter. "And you climb. I'd forgotten that as well. Come with me." He pointed down to the edge of the embankment, a thirty-foot drop, with eroding rock, dirt and root structures. One tree was actually tilted, its weight over time slowly pulling it down.

She moved cautiously to the edge of the trees lining the bank and peered over the side. "Down there? Are you searching for alligators?"

Knobby cypress trees rose out of the water like giant stick figures, branches reaching like arms, moss hanging from them in drapes. The water pooled, dark and forbidding around the barren, misshapen trunks and lapped at the thin strip of a ledge only inches above the surface.

"Rocks," he said, coming up behind her, and handing her a coffee mug over her shoulder. "You take it black, right?"

She took the coffee cup, frowning at him. "Rocks?"

"For my work. I pulverize them and get a variety of subtle color as well as texture. I get them from all over. Contrary to popular belief, Louisiana has some beautiful rocks and crystals, you just have to know where to look. Just below us, along the bank, there's a vein of beautiful agate. That might not sound like much to you, but for me, the colors are perfect for my work. I don't manage to get here that often, so every time I come, I make certain to get a few rocks."

"You aren't kiddin', are you?" Bijou asked. She could hear the ring of truth in his voice, and more, he sounded boyishly enthusiastic.

"No, the rocks are beautiful in color and just the right texture for my sculptures. I don't mine much of it, just a bit each visit, so hopefully I'm not contributing to the bank eroding."

Arnaud pulled out a folding chair one-handed and opened it expertly, putting it under the shade of the cypress trees. "Sit down, drink your coffee." He pulled out a second chair and sat down beside her.

"You do know there's a killer hangin' around, don' you?" Bijou said as gently as possible. She hated to put a damper on his enthusiasm, but he had to take the warning seriously. It had never occurred to her that Arnaud Lefevre haunted the swamps looking for rocks for his sculptures. He was handsome and sophisticated with his thousand-dollar suit and hiking shoes he'd paid a fortune for. She knew he was a bit of an adventurer, but she hadn't ever considered that he might go into the swamp—especially alone.

"I read something about it," he admitted. "But what are the chances? I'm only here a few times a year and come to these places no one else knows about. There's a lot of land out here, Bijou, and I doubt that our paths would ever cross."

She scowled at him over the coffee cup. "Still, you shouldn't come here alone."

"I don't have to worry now that you're here," he pointed out.

She rolled her eyes and laughed in spite of herself. He was good company. He always had been. He was intense when he was working, his mind wholly into his art. He didn't notice anyone or anything when he was creating something new.

He leaned over and pulled at the chain, lifting the pendant—his jewelry. "This is a beautiful piece," he said, impartially, as if he hadn't been the one to create it. "I used chambersite, a rare crystal found here in this state, and ground petrified palm. I made the piece for you and I knew the one place you always called home was Louisiana, so I made certain nearly everything was from your state."

"Sometimes, Arnaud, you're so sweet you make me want to cry," Bijou said honestly. Why couldn't she be attracted to him? He was handsome. He had money in his own right—he certainly wasn't after hers. When they were together, they laughed and talked about everything. Conversations were always interesting and lively. She even relaxed in his company. He loved some of the same things she did—such as climbing. She bet he had a climbing bag with his gear in his SUV just as she had hers locked in the trunk of her car. He traveled far more than she ever would want to, but still . . . Yet there was just no chemistry between them—not on either side.

Bijou sighed. It was Remy who made her wild and crazy. It was Remy she had always trusted, even though she hadn't really known it. After her behavior last night, who knew what he thought of her.

"Tell me," he urged, leaning close. "I can see you're worried about something. I told you about my secret stash of agate and if you insist, I'll trade your worries for the location of chambersite," he teased gently.

She flashed him a smile. No way was she going to tell anyone about her wanton uncharacteristic behavior with Remy. She shrugged. "My manager is really, really angry with me. I can't really blame him." That was strictly the truth, so she didn't feel too bad misleading him. She pushed back the stray strands of hair that had pulled free of her braid and were annoying her by falling into her face. She really should have dried it before she left the Inn. It would be a mess for the show. "I made up my mind not to tour anymore. I want to settle here and just sing in my club and record in the studio. I'll be makin' considerably less money."

"So will he, I take it," Arnaud summed up the problem

quickly. He sat back in his chair, his gaze on her face. "Have I met him? Rob something, right?"

She nodded. "Rob Butterfield. You met him briefly in New York when I went to one of your shows. I feel bad about not touring, but I just don' want that life anymore. He says I'm selfish and only thinkin' of myself." She sighed. "It's probably true too, but I honestly couldn't live that life anymore. I'm not cut out for the spotlight. I don' like it. Don' get me wrong, I love music and I have to sing, that part makes me happy, but all the rest . . ." She broke off, looking at the artist a little helplessly.

Outsiders looking at her life always thought she had it made. She had a famous father. All the money in the world. She could do anything she wanted. She had a voice that was a blend of smoke and fire according to all the critics, and she could draw thousands to a concert and easily sell over a million albums almost within the first week she put her recordings out. Outsiders would say, what the hell was wrong with her. That was her manager. Keep working. Keep going, no matter how unhappy the lifestyle made her.

Arnaud leaned close and laid his hand on her wrist, smiling at her. "In the end, Bijou, you must do what is right for you. This is a place I come to visit because it inspires me, but I couldn't live here all year-round. The mosquitoes alone would drive me to drink."

He laughed at himself, making her smile.

"I enjoy New York. The nightlife, the way the city makes its own music. I feel inspired there. I enjoy Paris, and believe it or not, Istanbul. I like to travel and see the world, but in the end, my studio is where I need to be."

"Do you have secret places you get rocks everywhere you go?" she teased.

"Of course." He finished off his coffee. "How about you come rock hunting with me?"

"I have a show to do tonight at the club, but it isn't for hours. As long as this doesn't take too long," she said.

There was safety in numbers. Whoever was murdering

people caught them alone—at least so far that seemed to be the way. In any case, she didn't want to go back to the Inn, see her manager or Remy. Playing hooky in the swamp with Arnaud might be the cure.

"I'll tell you what, *chere*, do some climbing with me and I'll go to your show tonight and buy you dinner."

What else did she have to do, but feel sorry for herself? She could spend the day in Arnaud's company, have a good time and then do her show. Singing always made her feel better.

"Sounds good to me," she said and finished off her coffee as well. "But I'm not usin' that hitch to tie off my rope. I'm using that very strong tree trunk."

"You're such a chicken," Arnaud protested. "I use the hitch all the time."

"I'm not fallin' into the disgustin' water," Bijou said with a small shudder. "Laugh it up, Arnaud, I'm not smellin' for a month to prove a point. That water has enough germs in it to kill half of Louisiana."

"You really are a girl," he teased. He slapped at his arm. "Damn mosquitoes. How come they aren't eating you alive?"

" 'Cuz I'm a girl, not a mean Frenchman," Bijou said and folded up her chair. She had no idea why mosquitoes didn't ever bite her, but even as a child, when everyone else was getting attacked, the insects veered away from her and went after someone else.

She sent him a smug look. "Louisiana mosquitos know the natives and just go after the tourists, especially hot French tourists."

"At least you think I'm hot." He made a face at her as he put her folding chair in the back of his rented SUV. "Let's hope your climbing skills haven't been affected by your sense of humor."

She peered over the ledge. "I don' have any intention of endin' up in that water. I've got my own equipment in the trunk of my car."

"A girl after my own heart. If you have a helmet, you might want to use it. The bank is unstable and juts out in places overhead," he cautioned. "I get debris falling at times."

The wind shifted, blowing a slight breeze through the trees. She felt the now familiar itch rising like a wave under her skin and took a deep breath trying to control the need to scratch. For a brief moment, a scent drifted to her and just that quickly was gone. Elusive. She knew it, and yet she hadn't gotten enough time before the capricious wind changed direction again to identify it. A chill crept down her spine and the hairs on the back of her neck stood up.

Bijou swung around, looking slowly. "Arnaud, do you feel as if someone is watchin' us?"

Arnaud didn't snicker or act as if she was crazy. He took her seriously, stepping out from behind the vehicle to inspect the road running along the bayou with a slow, careful perusal. Bijou rubbed at the itch racing up and down her arm. Just that fast the sensation faded, along with the odd feeling they were being watched, leaving her feeling foolish. Whatever strange thing was taking place in her body, was making her moody, edgy and jumpy.

"I don't see anything, Bijou," Arnaud said. "But if you're worried, we can skip getting the rocks and I can come back another day."

"No, that would be silly. We're already here," Bijou replied. "I was looking forward to seeing your cache." She took one more careful look around and drew in a lungful of air. Nothing. She had no idea what had set her off, making her so uncomfortable, but there was nothing to indicate they weren't alone.

8

"YOU don't want a lot of stretch in your line," Arnaud cautioned. "Use a static line, maybe ten to twenty meters. I use a Grigri. It's simple, and I don't like a fuss when I'm working. I rappel down, work out the rocks I want, put them in my bag and use an ascender coming up. I've found my hiking boots are better for this than climbing boots."

Arnaud was a serious climber and he'd gone into his serious mode the moment they brought out the gear. He helped her wrap nylon webbing around a live tree that was about ten inches thick. Near the base of the tree, he created friction between the webbing and the tree. Leaving two equal length ends, he tied overhand knots on a bite.

Bijou handed him two locking carabiners for each end. After finding the middle of the rope, he created two overhands on a bite ten inches apart and attached each to one of the lockers on the webbing.

"One for each of us," he said as he tossed the ropes off

the edge, leaving them two secure lines to rappel down. "Happy?"

"Much happier," Bijou said.

He took her helmet out of her hand and plunked it on her head. "That's so you don't have half the embankment falling on you."

Bijou stepped into her harness, laughing as he had to pull the trouser legs of his suit through. "Great climbing pants," she teased.

He grinned at her, his eyes laughing. "Keep making fun of me, woman, and you may be alligator fodder after all."

Bijou attached the Grigri to her line, near the point where they attached to the webbing on the tree and waited for Arnaud to do the same. Both attached their Grigri to the belay loop on their harness using a locking carabiner, double-checking that they each locked theirs.

"Let's do this," Arnaud said, a hint of excitement in his voice for the first time.

Bijou realized Arnaud rarely showed emotion. He did laugh occasionally, but she'd never seen him do so with anyone but her and even with her, it had taken a great deal of time before he'd let her in enough to relax around her. He seemed disconnected from people, his passion completely kept for his work, which probably explained why there was no real physical attraction between them. Every sport he chose was dangerous and solitary.

She nodded, and after going over a safety check, they started to rappel down the slope. Clearly Arnaud had been over the embankment numerous times and was confident. Bijou went far more slowly, taking her time and watching the outcropping above her. The dirt was definitely loose and occasionally rained down in a little burst. Arnaud ignored it as he found a purchase on the slim ledge.

"There isn't much room on this ledge," Bijou pointed out, peering out across the water, half expecting an alligator to be swimming toward her.

"I'm never here long and so far I've never seen evidence

of a gator trying to come up on the ledge. It's too narrow for even a medium-sized one." Arnaud wrapped the tail of his rope around his leg five times.

Bijou made a face as she cautiously settled her feet onto the muddy surface. Very carefully she wrapped the tail of her rope around her leg as well, creating a friction backup.

Now that his hands were free, Arnaud selected a small brush from his tool belt and showed it to her. "I use this to brush aside some of the dirt to check the color of the stone before I remove any. Do you want to try? You have to be very careful not to disturb too much of the embankment."

He was offering her the brush, but he sounded reluctant. She realized this was something of great importance to him, not just a lark. She smiled at him, shaking her head. "I'd rather watch you, if you don' mind. I love watchin' you create art and this seems similar."

She said the right thing, because Arnaud flashed her a genuine smile and crouched down beside her.

Bijou studied the embankment above them. Small rocks and the root structures of trees seemed to be the only thing holding the crumbling dirt together. Some roots jutted out like gangly, boney arms, moss hanging from them. A few larger rocks were scattered along the wall, but for the most part, the bank seemed nothing but loose dirt.

She found it impossible not to be a little nervous. Behind were the gator-infested waters and in front of her a tall wall of soil, some of which was already falling like dust on top of her head and shoulders.

She cleared her throat. "Arnaud, I have to hand it to you. You're very dedicated to your art. Couldn't you have someone else do this for you?"

He examined the wall approximately three feet from the bottom. Intrigued, she squatted low and peered at the dirt, trying to see what he was looking for.

"No one else can find exactly what I need for each project. I actually scheduled a visit to the gallery here because I need some of the colors I can get from this little cache. I can get the banded agate, but here . . ." He broke off, using the brush like an archeology tool, exposing the rock beneath. "Here I can find various hues you don't find very many other places."

"I had no idea," Bijou admitted, finding the entire idea of elegant, sophisticated Arnaud Lefevre, in his thousand-dollar suit, mining for stone in a dangerous, mosquito-infested swamp fascinating. He was totally focused on the task of gently brushing away the dirt to find his hidden treasure. She'd seen him in the studio and he clearly hadn't even noticed anyone around him, time passing or anything else. He was the same way now, taking the same care with his hunt for the perfect color agate for his sculpture.

His patient brushing revealed a small vein of pale blue, almost purple and blue-green rocks. He continued brushing away the loose dirt so more colors were exposed.

Bijou gasped. "Those colors are beautiful."

"Even more so when I work with them," he said almost absently. He took the fork and meticulously began prying the pastel purple rock free. He was careful not to scrape it, digging around the edges to free the small stone.

"Do you already know what you're goin' to use it for?" Bijou asked. "Do you actually have a sculpture in mind?"

He nodded. "I draw what's in my head and then figure out which mediums I'm going to use and how best to get what's in my head to come to life."

"Arnaud." She waited until he turned his head to look at her over his shoulder. "You know you're a genius, don' you? No one in the world can do what you do."

He studied her face for a long time. "No one ever says the things to me that you do, Bijou, not and really mean them. I can see honesty in your eyes and hear it in your voice. You always have inspired me with your generosity of spirit. Sometimes when I read the tabloids, I find myself getting angry at the way they portray you, and it surprises me. I don't get angry, or feel much emotion unless I'm cre-ating."

Bijou couldn't help but hear the sincerity in his voice. He wasn't making a declaration of love—he never did. She could tell he felt great affection for her, as she did him, but something just didn't quite gel between them, not in a romantic way.

"That's the nicest thing anyone's ever said to me, Arnaud. Thank you," she said. "And yes, the tabloids seem to really enjoy making up an entirely different life for me. There's one photographer who is the biggest pain in the neck. He loves to follow me around, take pictures when I'm unaware and then make up some ridiculous story behind the photograph." She sighed. "He's here in New Orleans and already dogging my every footstep."

Arnaud turned back to brushing away dirt from the stones. "Can't you file a harassment suit? There must be some way to get rid of him."

She shrugged. "Someone else would just take his place, and I guess it's a case of the devil you know. Bob Carson used to live with my father. He was about fourteen or fifteen when I was born. When he moved out of our home, he'd still come over every day to see Bodrie."

"So he was your friend and now he hounds you to make money off of you?" Arnaud asked, as he carefully began to pry the small stone free.

"I wouldn't say we were ever friends. By the time I was old enough to know who he was, he was takin' advantage of the women around Bodrie, usin' drugs and drinkin'. He traveled with Bodrie as his personal photographer and made a huge name for himself in the business. Of course he always made Bodrie look good."

Bob Carson had taken her to the hotel the night Remy found her, bringing his friends and drugs and alcohol. She was still embarrassed to be around him. Remy hadn't recognized that young man he'd beat to a bloody pulp that night—or if he had he hadn't said anything to her when Bob had photographed him kissing her.

Arnaud glanced at her over his shoulder as if reading her

mind. "He makes you uneasy." He dropped a purplish stone into his bag.

She hadn't meant to reveal so much. "All paparazzi make me uneasy," she hedged.

He laughed softly. "The thing is, Bijou, you can't lie worth a damn. It's one of the many reasons why you can't stand the business you're in. You tell the truth, and when you don't, you're embarrassed. I'm your friend. You can tell me he makes you uneasy and it isn't going to end up in the tabloids. I keep your confidences and your secrets. I always have."

"I know. I'm sorry, Arnaud. I think I'm so used to being careful about what I say, that it's habit." She did feel ashamed. She didn't see Arnaud often, but when she did, he was always the same. Steady. Calm. Definitely someone who valued his friendship with her and asked for nothing in return. He didn't seem to care who her father was, or how much money she had. He never changed. "I'm grateful for our friendship."

"Me too."

Already the moment was over and he was looking at his precious stones, sinking another one inside his bag with almost loving care and turning his attention to his next choice.

Bijou shook her head. Arnaud was trying, but clearly she wasn't really there. He was totally absorbed in what he was doing. She watched quietly for a few minutes, admiring his dedication and somewhat fascinated by his complete concentration. He was wholly focused on what he was doing, prying two more rocks free and dropping them carefully in the bag hanging from his tool belt. She had the feeling if an alligator did get curious and rushed at them from the water he wouldn't notice.

Without warning a shiver went down her spine. That strange wave beneath her skin rose like an itch that couldn't be scratched. More, something wild and feral deep inside unfurled, leapt and pushed against her in alarm. She turned toward the water, half expecting a huge alligator to be attacking. Only then was she aware of the silence. The bayous and swamps were never really silent. As a rule, insects droned incessantly and they had suddenly ceased making any noise above their heads.

Glancing down at her vibrating rope attached to her harness, she touched it lightly, feeling the sudden tension. Instinctively she stepped around Arnaud, her body shielding his, her head down, hands gripping a root overhead. Both ropes slithered down, dropping over the top of them along with a landslide of debris and rock. Small rocks hit her shoulders and back. She dropped one hand onto Arnaud's shoulder. The ropes slid off the narrow ledge and dropped into the muddy waters, the weight jerking at both of them. She kept herself braced, trying to stay as small as possible while protecting Arnaud.

The mini landslide subsided and silence reigned once more. Bijou remained still, a little worried that whoever had cut their lines and thrown them over the edge was still above them, prepared to knock more dirt on them. Or worse, had a gun and was going to shoot them. Arnaud stirred and tilted his head to look up at her a bit quizzically. Trust Arnaud to remain calm.

She pointed above them and laid a finger over her lips, counting in her head while she listened for movement. A few minutes later a trickle of dirt rained down as if someone stood on the edge looking over. Her mouth went dry, her heart pounding. Was the killer above them? He couldn't get down to them if he was.

Arnaud wrapped his hand around her ankle and that small gesture of camaraderie steadied her. They were safe. They might be trapped on the small ledge, but whoever was above them couldn't get to them, even if they couldn't get back up. Eventually someone would come along and see the cars and think they might be in trouble.

Another avalanche of rocks and stones came down. She heard muttering, but couldn't identify whether it was a man or a woman above them. A branch snapped. Silence. The

SUV started up. Her heart jerked hard. It was definitely Arnaud's vehicle. Her fingers dug deep into his shoulder. She knew what was coming. Hurriedly she bent down and placed her mouth close against his ear.

"Stand up and flatten yourself against the bank. He's goin' to push the car over the edge down onto us."

Arnaud didn't hesitate. As she stepped back to give him room to stand, he was up instantly with that same unemotional, calm expression. Both pressed themselves tightly against the bank as the motor roared, bursting the silence like a bomb. Arnaud reached out and put his hand over Bijou's as they both made themselves as small and as thin as possible.

The earth above them shook. Rocks and debris rained down. A tree crashed into the water, the root structure tearing a hole in the bank. The SUV leapt from the cliff above them to drop front end first straight down into the bayou. The back tires missed them by a breath, seeming to skim down their backs, although neither was actually touched.

Bijou closed her eyes and tried not to shake. Arnaud didn't so much as tremble, his nerves like steel. She hadn't expected that of him. He was so creative, and she associated creativity with emotion—maybe because she was so emotional. Most of her problems over the years in the business she was in had been due to being too emotional. She couldn't handle the fame. She never liked being in the spotlight, and yet she'd been born into the glare of one and had pursued a career that kept her there.

Footsteps overhead kept them still. Bijou pressed her lips together tightly and waited, sending up a prayer that whoever was above them didn't have a gun. There was still her car, and she'd left the keys in the ignition, just as Arnaud had. Whoever the madman was, he swore again and spit into the water as the SUV tilted and slowly began to sink beneath the murky water. He kicked more dirt down onto them, although clearly he couldn't see them.

Silence descended. A few minutes later the insects began to buzz, filling the silence with normalcy. Bijou stirred, but Arnaud tightened his fingers around her hand warning her to wait a few more moments. The insects grew louder. He relaxed and allowed himself to push away from the wall, casually dusting off his suit. The gesture made Bijou smile, stealing some of the tension from her. No matter what, Arnaud was aware of his appearance.

"Do you think he's gone?" she whispered.

"I don't hear him starting up your car, but stay as close to the bank as you can," Arnaud cautioned.

She found it took a minute to make her body move away from the protection of the embankment. She looked up. "It's a long climb back up there and it looks unstable."

"We'll be fine," Arnaud assured. He looked at her for a long time, a puzzled look on his face. "Why did you do that?" Arnaud asked, his voice expressionless.

Bijou frowned at him. "Do what?"

"Protect me. When you first knew he was there, you covered my body with yours."

She shrugged. "You're my friend."

He shook his head. "That's not the reason, Bijou. Do you remember how we met?"

"Of course." She flashed a smile in spite of the situation. "It was very dramatic."

"I had been at your concert. I sat in the front row and just watched you. I *watched* you more than heard you. When you came out, surrounded by bodyguards, you were still signing autographs. They didn't want you to do it, but there were people outside who hadn't been able to get to you and they mattered to you. You were a few feet away . . ."

"And you were starin' at me."

He nodded solemnly. No smile. Just remembering something that was obviously important to him. "I couldn't help myself. You had the most perfect bone structure I'd ever seen. I kept thinking if I could sculpt you—somehow get that perfection in one of my creations. I didn't realize until much later that I was making you uncomfortable. I was so focused on memorizing every detail of your face."

"You weren't paying any attention at all to traffic and you stepped backward."

He nodded. "I was trying to see your face in a different light. No one moved but you. Not a single one of your bodyguards. Just you. I remember you rushing toward me, catching at me, and we both went tumbling. I felt the air as the car went by. It was so close. You saved my life, Bijou, and risked your own to do it. Not a single other person moved to help. Just you. You didn't know me then, but you still did it."

Bijou shrugged, a little embarrassed. She hadn't thought before she moved, seeing the car bearing down on him. "I'm glad I did, Arnaud, whatever the reason. I've got three people in the world I count as friends and you're one of them."

He stared at her for a long time. "I've got one friend, Bijou, and you're it."

She blinked. Found herself smiling. "We're a pathetic little lot, aren't we? Our darin' enemy up there probably despises my singin' or your sculptures and he's just expressin' himself."

"He's throwing a tantrum is what he's doing," Arnaud corrected.

Again, Bijou was caught by Arnaud's lack of emotion. He wasn't angry, even with his SUV sinking in the bayou.

"I'm sorry about your car. Did you have anything important in it, aside from your climbing gear?" she asked with regret. She was angry for him. For both of them.

He shrugged and once more looked up the embankment. "Nothing I can't replace. You're alive. I am. We're good. The real question is, how are we going to climb up this thing without bringing the entire bank down on top of us?"

Bijou remained silent, studying the overhang above them and the very unstable bank. She didn't have the answer to that very good question.

Arnaud sighed. "We've got rope." He began to haul the

end that had fallen from above into the water back out, looping it as he went.

"You can't climb using a slimy rope," she protested.

"I'll try to climb without one and just use if for safety.
You can belay from below," he said. "If I can find a stable
place to put in a few anchors, or even use a good solid root,
I might make it to the top and then I can bring you up."

"I'm lighter, Arnaud," Bijou said a little reluctantly. She
was smaller and wouldn't have the reach he had. Wingspan
could be everything when climbing, and Arnaud would have
an advantage of height, but with less weight pulling on the
rocks and roots, she might have a better chance to make the
climb.

Arnaud paused for a moment and looked at her, cocking
his head to one side and then slowly shaking it. "I'm a better climber, Bijou. You're not going up that wall. It's very
unstable. I wouldn't be trying it if I thought someone would
come along and rescue us. And I don't want to chance that
madman coming back for another try at us."

A sudden thought occurred to her. "Arnaud. What if that
was the killer and we interrupted him? Or he wanted to
make certain there were no witnesses. If you go up there
and he's in the middle of murderin' someone, he'll *have* to
kill you."

A hint of a smile teased Arnaud's mouth. "You're a funny
girl, Bijou. I've never met anyone else like you. I suppose
we could spend the night here, fighting off alligators."

Bijou grinned at him. "I'm from the bayou, my friend.
We'll be eatin' one of those gators if they come around."
The smile faded. "Let's just wait another hour before you
try it."

He glanced at the sky. "Okay. But only an hour. I'm not
going to be on this ledge after dark."

REMY glanced at his watch and once more called Bijou on
his cell phone, swearing under his breath repeatedly. He'd

looked for her at the Inn. Talked to Saria, and just about everyone else, and no one had seen her. Her car was gone, but she hadn't packed up her things.

"Blue," he whispered aloud between his teeth. "Where the hell are you?"

She had a show to do. She was too much of a professional to miss it. She just wouldn't do that, but she hadn't come to the rehearsal and no band member had heard from her all day, which, according to them, was unlike her.

He stood still there in the street, staring at the club across from him. He'd harassed the band members, the bartender and three waitresses. Who was left? Saria hadn't seen or talked to her. He'd made Saria call her twice, just in case she wasn't answering him, but Bijou hadn't picked up. Okay, he'd even called Gage and asked him to have the sheriffs patrolling to keep a look out for her car.

His leopard was as uneasy as he was, close to the surface, raking a bit for freedom—and maybe that wasn't a bad idea. Maybe his leopard could find her when he—with all his resources—couldn't.

"Remy, get the hell out of the street," Gage called.

Remy swung around abruptly, hope surging. "Did you locate her?" He crossed the street to his brother in several long strides. More and more the feeling of urgency was on him. He couldn't shake that she was in trouble.

At first, when he'd gotten to the Inn with the intention of talking to her—explaining about her heritage as best he could without seeing the actual proof of her leopard—he'd been angry that she was gone. He feared she'd run from him, but she wouldn't have left her clothes and jewelry behind. There were too many personal items in the room. She'd had time to pack her most important things if she was leaving permanently and she hadn't done that.

As he stepped onto the sidewalk beside his brother, Gage shook his head. "Everyone's been out lookin' but no one has spotted her car. Do you want me to put out an official request?"

Remy took a breath. He could feel something was wrong, but he had another solution to try. "Not yet. I'm goin' back to the Inn and let my leopard try to track her. I'll take a radio and call in if I find her or need backup."

"It's daylight."

Swift impatience crossed Remy's face. His fists clenched and he took an automatic step back, away from his brother. His temper was as out of control as his leopard felt. He was terrified she'd left him and he'd bungled everything because he couldn't stop himself last night. He was angry as hell at himself. Even Gage had been shocked that he'd left his mate in a state of emergence. The Han Vol Dan was brutal on a woman, especially when she had no idea of what was happening.

"I don' give a damn if it's daylight. My leopard can keep to the groves and grasses. He'll track her."

He'd put work first. It had been so important to him to find Bijou's stalker. He'd deliberately set himself up and then, when he knew her stalker had been drawn out, he'd been so impatient to get there, he'd left her behind without so much as talking to her about what had transpired between them. He knew her. He knew her better than anyone, whether she thought so or not. Maybe better than she knew herself. He had known she'd wake up and be horrified at her behavior. And she'd attribute it to her father's genetics, not her mother's.

"Don' go off all crazy, Remy," Gage cautioned. "You can't have a leopard runnin' free in daylight hours, not confined to the swamp. Everyone is packin'. You get some good ole boys spottin' a leopard and they'll go huntin' and then we'll really have a problem on our hands."

He'd let her down when she needed him most and he sure as hell wasn't going to let her down again. He *knew* she was in trouble. He felt it. His leopard felt it. Gage could think he was going off crazy, but it wasn't that. His leopard was—extraordinary. Difficult but extraordinary. He'd find her.

"I'm goin' to find her, Gage. I'll start at the Inn and track her from there. If you're worried, follow at a distance and keep everyone off of me."

"Has anyone ever told you not only are you a mean son of a bitch, but you're stubborn too?" Gage snapped.

Remy sent him a cool, calm look that said everything. "I believe our father told me that long before you ever did."

"And what the hell really happened to put that bruise on your face? Did she beat you up?"

Remy was distracted for a moment, memories washing over him so strong, with such intensity, that for a moment he froze. After he'd marked Bijou, his leopard had emerged to rake the walls and in the process, as he'd shifted back, he'd run into a lamp. Hard with the side of his face. He'd been in the throes of passion, not caring about furniture.

Abruptly he turned on his heel and headed for his car. He heard Gage swear again and then the brush of material as Gage raced to his own car, but the urgency in him was growing—a feeling of dread and fear. Leopards were said to find the same mate, each time they were reborn. Sometimes those connections grew strong enough that they could even speak to one another without saying a word, using a form of telepathy. Remy had no idea if that were true, but he did know he felt connected to Bijou in some way—and that connection was very strong.

He drove fast. His leopard's vision and quick reflexes gave him an advantage on the road, and everywhere else for that matter. He used every bit of his leopard's abilities, pushing the car to the maximum on the narrow roads, outdistancing his brother. The moment he pulled up to the Inn, he caught sight of Saria in the front yard.

He threw his keys on the seat and reached back for the leopard pack every self-respecting leopard kept close. Saria ran over to him.

"I searched her room. I swear she didn't take anything at all with her, Remy. She didn't leave, but she isn't answering her cell." There was worry in Saria's voice. "What happened last night? Was she upset?" Her gaze slid from his. "I found the sheets. And the room is . . . wrecked."

Remy glanced at her. "I'll do the repairs. Don' worry."

"I'm not worried about a room, Remy, just Bijou. Did somethin' happen last night? Did you two fight? She wouldn't . . ." She trailed off, looking more upset than ever.

He shook his head adamantly. "She wouldn't do anything dumb. I'm goin' after her. Using my leopard. He'll track her."

Saria's eyes went wide with shock. "Those photographers have been by lookin' for Bijou, Remy. You can't take that chance. They know she's here and for all we know they're lurkin' in the bushes, or have set up shop down the road with a zoom lens."

He moved around the house to the back, away from the street. The property stretched down to the lake and edged the bayou on one side. Saria followed him. Remy ignored her, jerking off his shoes and tossing them aside.

"Are you serious?" Saria objected, trying again to reason with him. "Remy, it's too dangerous. She wouldn't want you doin' this."

"I'm strippin', little sister, so if you don' want an eyeful, you might want to leave."

"You're so stubborn!" Exasperated, she threw her hands into the air and turned her back on him. "If you get yourself killed, that's not goin' to help Bijou."

He didn't reply. Already his leopard raked and clawed for freedom, eager to find her. Fur ran beneath his skin, a wave that itched beyond reason. His knuckles ached and the tips of his fingers burned and throbbed. Joints popped, painful to the point that he squatted, unable to stand while he tried to grasp his jeans to get the material off his burning skin. His vision had already begun to blur, to change color, and his sense of smell heightened.

"At least let me make certain no one's around before you go out onto the street," Saria said, desperation edging her voice. "I wish Drake was here to talk sense into you."

Drake couldn't have stopped him. No one could. The need to find Bijou had grown so strong it was beyond a compulsion. He shed the rest of his clothes and willed the change, embracing his leopard, calling him out. He'd always been fast at shifting, but his leopard had been so eager to emerge that it had taken longer to remove his clothing, but now he had barely time enough to circle his neck with his pack and boots. His was nearly all leopard by the time he stashed his weapons in his pack and zipped it closed, just making it before his hands curved and claws burst through skin.

Black fur, darker rosettes set deep, covered roped muscles and powerful legs. He forced his leopard to wait for Saria's call. He counted heartbeats, his breath huffing out in deep chest breaths as he tried for restraint, concentrating on the actual math in his head. Waiting. Snarling. His nose already scenting, whiskers acting like radar.

"Clear, Remy," Saria called.

He rushed around the corner, swerved to avoid his sister and raced to where Bijou had parked her car the night before. He went still, absorbing the scent until her car was a distinct marker in his lungs—until the unique blend of lavender with oil and gas and her particular vehicle penetrated deep into his bones. He paced up and down, making certain he could follow her particular car anywhere.

Remy whirled around and raced down the street, moving fast. His presence set dogs barking two residences away from the Inn, but by the time the dogs knew there was a big cat in the neighborhood, he had found a semblance of cover in the trees lining the street leading to the maze of trees. He cut into the grove and followed the road until it branched, moving fast. She could only go one way, and he could stay out of sight until he came to the fork.

At the fork, he slowed to a stop, hidden in the brush while a car went by. Taking a careful sweep in each direction, scenting the air, Remy determined he had a few moments necessary to catch which way Bijou's car went. He stepped out into the road and made for the fork, padding silently on large paws, all the while taking in every smell along the pavement.

Bijou's car had gone to the right, toward the bayou and away from town. He huffed out his breath and started down the road, moving fast, angling toward the cover of trees. The tree line stopped a good fifty yards and heavy grasses replaced the grove, but the grass wasn't particularly tall. He took the chance anyway, streaking across the open field to the grass, listening for cars while he raced toward the strip of road separating the bayous. The sound of a car had him sinking down, nearly in plain sight, holding himself still, not a muscle moving. The car went by, and his brother's patrol car swept up beside him. Gage reached back and opened the door and Remy leapt in.

"You're totally insane," Gage snapped. "I'll drive you to the next fork. There's no way you'll be able to find enough shelter to keep from being seen."

Remy lay down on the seat, keeping low to avoid anyone looking into the back of the car, but if they met a truck, he could be in trouble—and so would Gage—maybe the entire lair. What he was doing was endangering everyone. Drake would definitely have a few words to say to him when he returned from his trip and found out.

Gage let him out at the next fork where there was far more cover for the leopard. He tracked Bijou's car for several miles when he heard voices just ahead of him. Remy crouched low in the brush, the leopard's heart beating fast, a silent snarl rising. The three men in the pickup truck stank of booze and pot. He recognized all three.

Ryan Cooper and his friends had come into the café to get an autograph from Bijou and made trouble. Brent Underwood and Tom Berlander nearly always accompanied Cooper. To Remy's disappointment, sometimes Robert Lanoux, one of the leopards, did as well. Fortunately not this time. Cooper had a bad reputation. The cat struggled against his control, wanting to creep up behind them. A bottle came crashing into the brush, hitting a foot from where the cat crouched. Remy held him still when the cat's instinct was to bolt—or attack. He could make short work of all three men fast.

Ryan Cooper pulled out a pistol and shot the bottle, shattering it. The leopard whirled and ran toward deeper grass, just as another vehicle came along the road. The Land Cruiser swerved, did a U-turn and stopped almost in the center of the road. Bob Carson, the photographer, got out of the driver's side, a camera slung around his neck. He peered into the brush where the leopard had just been. Remy dropped to earth and began a slow, almost freeze-frame crawl away from danger just as Gage drove up in the patrol car.

Cooper and his friends began swearing. Carson continued to block the road, looking no doubt for Remy. Remy kept moving away from the group, but so slowly and stealthily that he could hear Gage's drawling sarcasm.

"What the hell are you doin', Cooper? You and the boys drink yourselves sick and then get behind the wheel of your truck and drive that way?"

"You don' see us drivin'," Cooper objected, his voice slurred, but belligerent. "We're just out here mindin' our own business and you can just do the same."

Gage turned his head slowly to look at Bob Carson. "What are you doin' blockin' traffic? Have you been drinkin' with them?"

"I just saw a . . . leopard. I think it was a leopard."

The three men standing by the truck suddenly looked sober, casting wary glances around them. "You saw the Rougarou," Cooper said in a low, frightened tone. "Here?"

Carson frowned. "What's a Rougarou?"

"He'll tear you apart and leave no blood left in your body," Cooper said.

"Local legend," Gage said, walking around the truck to the hood. He lifted it and stuck his head inside, rooting around. "Most of the time when we get calls it's nothing but a normal break-in, but once in a while, we find bodies torn apart and not a drop of blood left in them." Satisfaction colored his tone. He held up his hand, wires bunched and hanging. "You can collect these at the office, Coop. You're not drivin' drunk."

"You can't just leave us for the Rougarou to kill," Cooper protested.

"Maybe you can talk this guy"—Gage sent his thumb in Carson's direction—"into givin' you a ride. Offer him money, or I'll call you a cab. A cab comin' all the way out here to collect your sorry asses won't be much money for you at all."

The slight breeze shifted just a little, a playful gust swirled leaves and grasses into the air and just as quickly subsided. The leopard whirled around, almost forgetting it needed to stay low and out of sight. A stench filled his lungs. He knew that scent. Recognized it. But which man? He wasn't close enough. Hopefully Gage was and could separate the individual scents of the four men. The leopard snarled and continued his journey to find his mate.

9

"ARNAUD, you're goin' to kill yourself. You have to stop," Bijou pleaded. "That root system isn't goin' to hold. You've climbed to it three times and every time the bank crumbles. You nearly ended up in the bayou twice. Please come down."

Not to mention the dirt and rocks pouring down on top of her. She didn't want to think about what would happen if he fell. She'd managed to keep him on the narrow ledge the last time he'd come plummeting down, but she'd wrenched her shoulder and nearly hadn't held him safe. It was a nightmare. The sun was thinking about sinking, and no one had come along to investigate. Maybe her car had been stolen and there was no evidence they were even there.

"No worries." As usual, Arnaud's voice was mild, no panic. "We can't just sit out here all night. We've waited for someone to come along, but no one has. This has to be done." There was absolute conviction—and resolution—in his voice.

The man wasn't human. She was panicking—trying not

to—but she couldn't figure out what to do next. Clearly climbing to the top was not feasible, even with the rope and equipment and Arnaud's excellent climbing abilities. Every foot- and toehold he found disintegrated beneath him. Mini avalanches trickled dirt continually and if he moved, more fell along with rocks. The root he had clipped his carabiner to slowly inched outward, as if that too would fall, and with it the small tree leaning over the embankment. The SUV must have grazed the tree as it tumbled over, and now that too was precarious.

Even as she thought it, with a horrible roaring sound, the tree tipped over in what looked like slow motion. Dirt and debris pounded down on her. She covered her head, grateful for the helmet, trying to stay as close to the bank as possible and make herself small. The sounds above her were horrible, grating and cracking, the tree groaning and then a terrible, ominous whoosh as the tree began to fall over the side. For a moment it teetered, and then the weight pulled the roots from the bank.

Bijou instinctively grabbed her flashlight and turned it on, sticking it in her mouth to leave her hands free as she turned from facing the bank, still crouching low and covering her head as more stones and dirt poured down. There was no time for Arnaud to get himself free of the root system. The tree dragged him over the edge and into the murky waters of the bayou. She held firmly to the rope, hoping to feel him come up.

When he didn't and there was tension on the rope, she knew he was trapped and she didn't have much time. She jumped in after him. The water was cold, the odor disgusting, but when her feet didn't hit bottom, she took her flashlight out of her mouth, drew a deep breath and followed the tree down. She strained to see more than a few inches in front of her. Debris floated all around her, sometimes brushing up against her. Using the rope, she rapidly dragged it toward her, looping it over her arm as she followed it down toward the tree, the tangle of branches and Arnaud.

Her heart pounded so hard in her chest, she feared it might explode. Going underwater with such poor vision was terrifying. Alligators lurked, and only God knew what else was in that awful cesspool of bacteria. Something solid touched her foot and she whirled around, afraid she might faint from sheer terror. The knobby broken trunk of a cypress tree rose from the floor, one of the branches reaching out with greedy fingers for her.

Bijou forced herself to keep swimming, looking right and left, trying to find Arnaud in the underworld grove of broken trees. The rope jerked and she kicked harder, following that trail. She swam deeper until she spotted the rope tangled in tree limbs. She struggled through the branches, wondering how Arnaud had ended up *under* the tree instead of on top of it. Her lungs began to burn and she worried she'd have to go back up for air and Arnaud would drown.

She spotted him thrashing, fighting to get himself free. His hands were at the harness, trying to get it off when the tangle of rope and the branch pinning him to the soft muddy floor prevented him from unlinking the carabiner. She swam fast, now that she had a location, using the rope to help pull her along. The moment she got to him, she pulled the knife from her tool belt and cut him free. Arnaud continued to thrash. His foot was pinned beneath the tree trunk.

She could see that the rope had wrapped around the tree as it rolled, which had pulled Arnaud beneath it as it sank. She signaled to him and he went still, his gaze wide, clinging to hers. A calm descended over her as she swam to the bottom and examined the problem. She only had seconds now and she would be forced to surface for air. She would not abandon him. If she went to the top, so would Arnaud.

His hiking boot was trapped in the crook of one of the largest branches. She immediately took hold of the boot and tried to pry it loose. Instantly she knew it was impossible. Arnaud had been trying to do so all along. He wasn't a man to panic and he would have thought of that. She sliced through the laces, jerking them free, opening the boot as best she could. Arnaud wiggled his foot out and kicked strongly for the surface.

Her lungs were burning and she couldn't imagine what his felt like. Along the edges of her vision, a strange red had begun to shade out images. She kicked as hard as she could, desperate for air, afraid she wouldn't hold out. The idea of drowning in the bayou with alligators feeding on her body spurred her last desperate kick. She exploded to the surface gasping for air. She'd never held her breath for so long in her life. Frantically she looked around. Everything seemed a little hazy. She felt weak, her pulse pounding in her temples.

A hand brushed her shoulder, and Bijou suppressed a scream. Arnaud wrapped one arm around her, putting his mouth close to her ear. "Can you swim?"

She nodded, ashamed of the weak moment. Arnaud had it so much worse and yet he was already calm, treading water even as he drew a great lungful of air deep. Bijou struck out for the ledge, looking around and peering below her, afraid all the thrashing around might have drawn an alligator to them.

The water was so slow moving it appeared stagnant and it was definitely brackish. She had the feeling that when the tide came in their tiny ledge would disappear. Crawfish and shrimp thrived, but there was no telling what kind of litter, chemicals or other things had found their way to the channel.

She concentrated on putting one arm in front of the other and pulled weakly, conscious that Arnaud had dropped behind her to make certain she made it back to the ledge. She dragged herself up, clawing at the muddy surface. Arnaud shoved her up by her butt and followed her onto the narrow strip. Both lay motionless, legs still in the water while they fought to breathe.

Bijou moved first, turning over, uncaring that she was lying in mud, pulling up her knees so unless an alligator exploded out of the water, she was relatively safe for a moment. She was freezing. Shaking. And she stank. Badly.

Very, very badly. Beside her, Arnaud did the same, rolling over and pulling up his legs.

"Thanks again, Bijou." He turned his head to look at her, confusion in his eyes. "You're making a habit of saving my life."

"I'm gettin' really good at it." She tried to make light of the moment. She huffed out her breath. "I don' want to sound like a girl here, but I swear bugs and germs are totally crawlin' all over my skin. They have to be in my hair too." She squeezed her eyes closed tight. "I'm not lookin' until I can take a long hot shower. Maybe for several hours."

"Um, Bijou . . ." Arnaud paused. "You do sound like a girl."

She couldn't help herself. She laughed. They were alive. No alligator got them. "I stink like sewage, but then so do you—the latest in cool perfume. Thank God no one else can smell us."

"Although we might smell like rotten meat to an alligator," Arnaud said.

"That's *so* not funny," she said, trying not to laugh. She was afraid she might be on the edge of hysteria. "I'm freezin'."

"So am I." He glanced at the sky. "It's going to be night soon."

"Don' you *dare* talk about climbin' up that bank. I'll push you back in myself."

There was no sound above them other than the drone of insects. No trickle of dirt to alert them. Nothing at all, but she suddenly knew with absolute certainty they weren't alone. She wrapped her fingers around his wrist to get his attention and put her finger to her lips signaling above them.

They both lay in silence, Arnaud, frowning, trying to hear whatever had spooked her. He put his mouth against her ear. "I can hear the insects."

"Someone's there," she whispered back. She knew she was right. Her entire body had gone on alert. Deep inside something shifted and moved. That strange itch raced like a tidal wave just under her skin, rushing through her body in alarm.

"Bijou!"

Her heart dropped. She'd recognize that arrogant commanding voice anywhere. Remy Boudreax was up above them. Of *course* it had to be him that would come along when she was at her absolute worst. She moaned and covered her face with her hands, smearing mud all over her cheeks and chin.

"Bijou, answer me." The imperious command left her in no doubt that Remy was searching above the bank for her.

Arnaud started to roll over in an effort to get to his feet.

"Shh," Bijou cautioned, panic-stricken. She put her hand over his mouth "Don' say a word. Seriously. I'd rather an alligator eat me than have him see me like this."

The voice above them rose in volume. "Damn it, Blue. You'd better be alive. Answer me. Where the hell are you?"

"That's a friend of yours I take it," Arnaud drawled around her hand.

"He is not goin' to get the satisfaction of seein' and smellin' me like this," she hissed.

Something moved along the edge above them, clearly following the path of the SUV. There was a lot of cursing in Cajun French.

"We have to be rescued before dark," Arnaud pointed out in his usual pragmatic way.

She was silent a moment, then she snapped her fingers, already moving, trying to curl herself into a little ball. "You get rescued, and then come back for me."

"You really like this man, don't you?" There was a trace of amusement in his voice.

"Don' laugh at a desperate woman, Arnaud," she warned. "You'll be goin' back in that really smelly, disgustin' water."

"Blue? Where the hell are you? You damn well better not be in that sunken SUV."

Arnaud raised his voice. "We're here, trapped below you. A little worse for wear but we're alive."

"Traitor," Bijou hissed between her teeth. She covered her face again, smearing more mud. "I'll never live this down."

"Bijou?" Remy's voice was directly overhead. A small amount of dirt rained down.

"The ledge is crumbling," Arnaud cautioned. "You'll have to stay back from it."

"*Well* back," Bijou whispered. "Like the other side of the bayou. Why do these things always happen to me?"

"Bijou." There was a short pause. "I need to hear your voice. Are you all right?" This time the tone wasn't so commanding and for some insane reason tugged at her heartstrings.

She sighed, resigned, and sat up slowly, shoving dripping hair from around her face. "If you can call smelling like sewer and being covered in germs all right, then I'm perfectly fine."

"Damn it, woman." Relief poured into Remy's voice. "You took a few years off my life."

"Poor you," she called back. "You should have been here for the last few hours."

"You really are fine," Remy said. "If you can come back with your sassy sarcasm."

"Well, for heaven's sake, Remy, I was the one someone was tryin' to kill. *And*, I'm the one who ended up in the bayou, not you."

"I was wonderin' what that smell was," Remy called back.

She hissed out a swear word between her teeth.

Arnaud grinned at her, his eyes briefly warming. "You really *do* like this man."

"No, I don'. At least not right at this very moment." She raised her voice. "Is my car still there, Remy?"

"Sort of. It's been vandalized. Your fan was here and must have been in a really bad mood."

That now-familiar uncomfortable heat whenever she was in Remy's presence was beginning to drift through her body,

warming her in spite of the wet clothes. She closed her eyes
and shook her head. She stank. She was in an impossible
situation, looked like a drowned rat and she was getting all
hot and bothered just at the sound of his voice.

Remy stretched out carefully in the dirt and peered over
the side. He needed to see for himself that she was alive and
in one piece.

"Look at me, Blue."

He could see she was reluctant. He wasn't going to tell
her that she looked beautiful, with mud smeared all over her
and her thick braid looking like a drowned tail, but she did.
He was thankful she was alive, although her shirt was nearly
transparent and she was lying very close to another man—
too close. He waited until her long lashes lifted and she
looked him straight in the eye. The impact on his body felt
like a wicked punch.

His eyes met hers, assessing the damage. "You look like
a drowned rat." She was close to tears, and if he said anything nice at all she would cry and then she wouldn't forgive
him. His gaze shifted speculatively to Arnaud and then back
to her. "What happened to your arm?"

She huffed at him. He desperately needed to gather her
up and hold her. She was hanging on by a thread—by her
pride. She was cold, miserable and exhausted as well as
embarrassed for him to see her looking and smelling as if
she'd just gone for a swim in the bayou.

The relief Remy felt at seeing Bijou alive made him feel
weak. He was grateful he was lying on his belly, stretching
his weight along the bank to keep it from crumbling. That
gave him an excuse not to stand, because at that precise
moment he wasn't altogether certain he could. He didn't like
the close proximity of the other male. His leopard liked it
even less, raging and snarling as wild and hard to control
as Remy had ever known him to be.

Bijou had to be close to the emerging for his leopard to
be so difficult. That, and the scare she'd given them. When
he'd seen the tracks of the SUV going over the bank, the cut

ropes and saw the mess the stalker had made of her car, he'd felt physically ill.

"I have more rope in the trunk of my car, Remy," Bijou said. "If you thread it through the master anchor we have on the tree and knot it, using the same knots, we can climb out of here."

"No problem," Remy said, and slithered backward until he was certain he wouldn't bring the cliff down on top of them when he stood up.

Gage came striding through the cypress grove. "What the hell happened here, Remy?" He demanded. "Is your woman alive? Okay?"

"If he has a woman, she isn't here," Bijou called. "Should I expect *la famille* to show up, all one hundred of you, because I can assure you, I'm not adequately dressed for company."

"I have a woman," Remy snapped between his teeth, "and she's extremely difficult. You should have stayed put, Blue." He walked quickly away before he erupted in temper. The leopard was pushing so hard he wanted to leap down and shake her. She'd scared him past anything he'd ever known before. Or his leopard. However it worked, they were connected, and she didn't have the right to run off because she was a little uncomfortable with how her first time had gone.

"Of course you can expect *la famille* to show up. We get in each other's business. It's what we do best," Gage called down to her, unapologetic. "Glad you're alive there, Bijou. Who's your friend?"

Remy halted in midstride. Yeah. Just who was her friend? What the hell were they doing together? And why would her leopard even allow him in such close proximity? He was going to have trouble with Bijou Breaux.

"Stop snarlin'," Gage advised softly. "She's obviously gone through hell, Remy. That leopard of yours is gettin' out of control."

"Arnaud Lefevre is with me," Bijou called out. "His SUV

was driven over the side with all of his things by that crazy person."

"Were the two of you inside?" Remy asked, lifting the trunk of her car and rummaging for her climbing bag. The thought of the suave, wealthy, sophisticated famous sculptor and Bijou together in his backseat was enough to have claws bursting through aching fingers. He breathed away the pain and forced his leopard under control.

"No, we weren't inside." Impatience edged Bijou's voice. Her teeth were chattering.

"We were really worried about you, Bijou," Gage intervened, shooting a glare at his brother. "You obviously ended up in the bayou. We'd like to know what happened."

Bijou blinked back tears. "*No* one can be nice to me right now, Gage," she cautioned. She hated the quiver in her voice. She would *not* turn into a baby in front of Remy. She pressed a hand to her mouth. She needed to be alone, just for a few minutes to compose herself. It would help if she'd stop shaking.

Remy mouthed the word *see* to his brother, frowning in caution. The last thing he wanted was for Bijou to cry in front of everyone and then blame him. He wouldn't be able to be cool with her tears and that would only embarrass her more. Gage might not like the way he handled things, but he knew Bijou better than she knew herself.

Arnaud touched Bijou's arm awkwardly. "We'll get you out of here in time for your performance tonight."

Bijou hadn't even thought of singing at the club. How could she have forgotten? She worked so hard to pull the club together, but all she wanted to do right now was crawl in bed and pull the covers over her head—after a long hot shower of course.

"You'll be awesome tonight, Bijou," Arnaud assured her as if guessing her thoughts. "You're the consummate professional. You'll handle it just fine."

Now she really had no choice but to buck up and be the

professional, which was probably why Arnaud had said it. He knew she was an emotional wreck and was bolstering her up. He was right too. Both had survived when things could have gone very bad at any time. She took a deep breath and let it out.

"I've got the rope," Remy called down to them, studying the webbing around the tree. The original carabiners were in place. The ropes had been cut off past those carabiners. He made short work of tying new knots, grateful for his time in the service and all the special training he'd had.

Arnaud sent Bijou up first and he followed right behind her. Once they were safe, Remy stood absolutely still, almost without breathing, drinking in the sight of Bijou. She did smell like the bayou, but it didn't matter. The only thing that mattered to him was that she was alive. He didn't give a damn what she said or thought. He yanked her into his arms, holding her tightly against his body, his hands moving over her, reassuring himself she was uninjured. She didn't melt into him, but rather held herself very stiff and aloof. Yeah, he was in trouble.

Bijou pulled away from him almost immediately. "I'm getting you all wet and you'll have to throw away those clothes."

"Do you think I give a damn about clothes? You could have died. What were you thinkin'? You should have stayed put and waited for me."

She shook her head, a slow crimson creeping up her neck at the memory of waking to the ruined room and having to possibly face Saria, not knowing where Remy went or even if he intended to return. "No, Remy, *you* should have stayed put."

She turned on her heel and walked away from him. Head up. Shoulders square. She looked regal in spite of the mud and wet clothes. She looked . . . magnificent.

"You got it bad, bro," Gage whispered as he walked past Remy, a wide grin on his face. "You might want to close your mouth before somethin' flies into or out of it."

Bijou went straight to her car and stood, unmoving, looking at the damage. Arnaud came up beside her, setting Remy's teeth on edge. She didn't look at Arnaud as if she wanted nothing to do with him.

"What a mess," Arnaud said. "Why would someone do this?"

Remy watched Bijou carefully. She inhaled sharply and stiffened. She knew. She'd caught the scent. The leopard in her was merging with her, becoming part of her, and with her acute sense of smell, she recognized the scent of the man who been stalking her.

"Who is it, Blue?" Remy asked.

She shook her head.

"You know. He trashed my apartment this morning and left behind the picture of me kissing you. It wasn't pretty, Bijou. He's escalating his behavior."

"It doesn't make sense. Bob Carson grew up in Bodrie's house. I've known him my entire life. He wouldn't do this."

Remy's eyes met Gage's. Gage nodded. The moment he'd caught Carson's scent out on the road, he was certain it was the photographer who was stalking Bijou.

"Don' kid yourself, honey," Remy said. "Tell me why he would take an eight-year-old child to a hotel room with a bunch of men and try to pump her full of drugs. He was probably figuring he'd get rid of you and Bodrie would leave everything to him."

"You *did* remember him then. You didn't say a word."

"I had a very primitive reaction to seeing him—I wanted to pound him into the ground." Remy paused, his gaze holding hers. "And you didn't say anything."

"He has no reason to want to hurt me."

"Of course he does. His mother lived with Bodrie until your mother came along. He probably fantasized he was Bodrie's son. If he could prove he was, he would have come forward already, so that means his fantasy became a reality in his head. You took it all away from him, the house, the women, the drugs, the lifestyle. He became a photographer

and inserted himself back into Bodrie's life, and once again
he was somebody. But he couldn't have it all because there
you are, standin' in his way."

Bijou shook her head.

"On one hand, he probably fantasizes you're his sister,
and on the other, he wants you gone so he can inherit."

She scowled at Remy. "I'm not stupid, I have a will."

"Which is probably the only reason you aren't dead. He
hasn't figured out a way to inherit everythin' from you."

"I don' know if it's him," Bijou insisted. "You can't do
anything without proof anyway, so don' go after him, Remy.
Please. I have to think about this."

"You know it's him," Remy said quietly. "Bijou, you don'
have a mean bone in your body. This man is escalatin' in
his behavior and we both know it. That's why you even
considered allowin' me to see the letters, otherwise you
would never have said a word about them. You knew you
were in trouble with him."

"He's got to be ill," Bijou said. "To do this, he has to be ill."

She touched the hood of her car. The tires were slashed
and punctured repeatedly, obviously with a knife. The seats
had been slashed and punctured, the insides ripped out and
thrown all over the ground. On the outside of both sides of
the car, a giant eye had been carved into the doors. "I see
you" had been keyed in with crude sticklike letters. She'd
seen the letters so many times with the same phrase on the
walls of her home as well as in Bodrie's homes.

Bijou shivered. Remy strode over to the sheriff's car and
pulled out a jacket. Arnaud simply stood observing everyone.

Gage cleared his throat. "We'll have a tow truck bring
up your vehicle, but most likely it's a total loss. You might
be able to recover some of your things though."

Arnaud shrugged. "I didn't have anything I couldn't replace with me. Mostly my climbing gear and things I use
for my sculptures. Rocks, petrified wood, different mediums
I mix together. Those can be replaced. It will just take a
little time to find the ones I need again." He patted the bag

at his waist. "At least I didn't lose these rocks. It's what I came here for."

"I'm so sorry about your truck and your things, Arnaud," Bijou said. "I feel like it's my fault this happened. I'll replace . . ."

Arnaud held up his hand. "Don't be silly, Bijou. I'm just sorry this man is targeting you." He glanced at his watch. "You don't have much time to clean up before your show. Maybe the sheriff wouldn't mind giving us both a lift into town."

Remy wrapped the coat around Bijou's shivering body. "You don' have to do that show tonight, Blue. We can tell the band to cover for you."

It was tempting. She was exhausted, confused, afraid, and she wanted to crawl into a hole and lick her wounds. They were all waiting. Arnaud with his expressionless face, just watching her. Remy and Gage clearly wanting her to go back to the Inn and forget about singing in the club, especially with Carson running loose. She knew he'd be there too. He always showed up to her performances.

She lifted her chin. If she didn't sing tonight, Carson won. His ugly behavior had already taken its toll on her, but she couldn't allow him to win, especially after what he'd done to Arnaud. She could smell Bob Carson all over her vehicle. She didn't know why her sense of smell was so acute, but she definitely knew he'd been the one to destroy Arnaud's SUV and her car.

"I'll be singin' tonight at the club, and if I don' get cleaned up fast, they'll have to fumigate the place after I leave."

Gage gestured toward his car. "Your chariot. I've got a couple of officers on the way. They'll take care of the tow truck and photograph your car and all the evidence here, so Arnaud, if you'd like a ride as well, I'll be happy to take you back to your hotel."

"I'd appreciate that," Arnaud said.

"You'll both have to ride in the back so I can hose off the seats after," Gage added with a small grin.

"I can't say as I blame you," Bijou said. "I'm holdin' my breath as best I can so I don' have to smell me."

"Let's hope Saria doesn't make you hose off outside," Gage teased.

Remy kept glancing back at Bijou huddled in the backseat. She didn't say another word, but stared out the window, her face set. Sad. Thoughtful. He was certain he was right about Bob Carson—that the night he'd interrupted them in the hotel so many years ago, the man had intended she die there. It made sense. If Carson believed Bijou and her mother had pushed Carson and his mother from Bodrie's life, he would certainly want her out of the way.

He made a mental note to check on what happened to Carson's mother and where they'd lived during the years they'd been away from Bodrie's mansion. He glanced again into the rearview mirror. He should have been gentler with Bijou. She'd been through hell. She looked as if she had smudges under her eyes. and he winced a little when he saw the faint bruising along her neck. The rake marks on her arm could only have been put there by a leopard. He suspected she'd done that to herself without realizing what happened.

Saria was outside waiting when the sheriff's car pulled up. She rushed to the door, yanking it open. "What happened to you?" Saria demanded, her voice filled with concern.

Bijou blinked back unexpected tears she hadn't known were so close. Clearly her emotions were far rawer than she'd realized. She attempted a small smile. "Remy pushed me into the bayou."

Saria glared at her brother. Remy backed up a step and held up both hands in surrender.

"She went swimmin' on her own. She must have gotten all hot and bothered thinkin' about me," Remy said hastily.

Bijou rolled her eyes. "Yeah, that was it. I'm sorry about the room, Saria."

"My brother can be sorry about the room, not you," Saria said, shooting another glare at Remy.

"What happened to the room?" Gage asked with a deliberate drawl.

Bijou felt color creeping up her neck and throat. "I have to get ready for my performance tonight, Saria. I'll scrub the shower when I get back. Do you have a trash bag so I can throw away these clothes?"

"Go away, Gage," Remy ordered. "And I mean right now."

"Thanks for taking Arnaud to his hotel," Bijou said as she turned to enter the Inn.

"No problem, although I think he stank more than you do," Gage replied with a wink.

"He was underwater a lot longer. He was trapped, and I had to cut him loose," Bijou admitted. "We were lucky neither of us drowned."

Remy frowned at her. "What do you mean you nearly drowned? What the hell happened? I thought you bailed when the SUV went over the bank."

Saria looked horrified. "Bijou, how awful. I'll make some tea. You take a shower and I'll have it ready for you."

"Answer me," Remy insisted, catching Bijou's arm before she could step inside.

No one had moved. Bijou took a deep breath. Reliving it only made the entire episode worse. "Our ropes were cut first, leaving us trapped on that very tiny ledge. Then the SUV was pushed over the bank, nearly on top of us. We waited a long time, hours really, before Arnaud insisted he climb out and then get me up. He tried three times, and the bank kept crumblin'. He waited between each climb because I was pretty freaked out, afraid he'd be killed, but night was fallin' and he felt we had no choice."

Bijou lifted her gaze to Remy's face. He was absolutely still. His face could have been one of Arnaud's sculptures, so utterly without expression, frozen. Her heart did a funny little flip and a million butterflies took flight in her stomach. She looked away.

"He finally used a tree root to tie off just in case he fell again and it would save him from going into the bayou.

Unfortunately, what neither of us knew was that the tree above us had been hit by the SUV when it went over and was already unstable. To make a long story short, the tree went, takin' Arnaud with it. I followed him in just in case and it was a good thing I did."

"Did it occur to you at any time," Remy asked, "that an alligator most likely was in that water?"

"Of course. I was scared, if that's what you want to hear." She couldn't help the belligerence creeping into her tone. "Don' tell me you wouldn't have gone in after him, because I know you would have."

"That's not the same," Remy snapped.

Deliberately, Saria stepped between them. "What happened, Bijou?"

Grateful for Saria's presence, Bijou focused on her. "The tree rolled, and he couldn't get out of the rope and harness so it took him with it. I cut him free but he was still trapped. His hikin' boot was wedged in the crook of the branch. I had to cut him out of that as well. I didn't think either of us was goin' to make it out of there alive."

"Thank God you were there," Saria said, casting a warning glance at her brothers when both moved as if to protest. "Arnaud would be dead if you hadn't gone in after him. I'll get the tea made, you take a shower and we'll disinfect those scratches on your arm before you have to go to work."

"Thanks, Saria," Bijou said. She hurried into the house before either of the Boudreaux brothers could say another word to her.

Bijou stripped the moment she was safe in her bathroom, tossing her ruined clothes onto a plastic bag she found inside the trash can. It was small, but it worked. The hot water felt wonderful and she let it pour over her head as she worked the long, thick braid loose so she could wash her hair.

"You know you could have been killed."

She screamed and threw the bottle of shower gel at the intruder, nearly jumping out of her skin. So much for her early warning system. "I locked the door. How did you get in here?"

Remy shrugged. "You didn't lock your balcony door, and in any case I'm very good at pickin' locks."

"Get *out* of here."

"We need to talk," Remy said, resting one hip on the sink.

"We should have talked this morning, you cretin. Not now. Get out of my room right this minute. I'm naked."

"It's a little late to suddenly become modest, don't you think?"

"It really isn't a good idea for you to be remindin' me about last night," Bijou snapped. "Get out of my bathroom right now. I'm hangin' on by a thread, Remy, and I've got a show to do tonight."

"We're goin' to talk."

"Fine. But not now. Go away, and don' be thinkin' you have the right to come into my personal space anytime you like. I mean it, Remy. Just because we . . . We . . . Whatever you call what happened last night, doesn't mean it's goin' to happen again. Go away."

"It's goin' to happen again."

She wasn't going to argue that point. If he kept sitting there, all arrogant and hot-looking it might happen again and she needed him gone. Now. This instant. Her body was already coming alive, that terrible craving starting. He had to go.

"Please go, Remy. Please."

He sighed and straightened up. "But we're talkin' after your show tonight. I know you're goin' to be tired, *chere*, but it's important."

She didn't answer, but turned away from him, mostly out of self-preservation. She was truly in trouble around Remy. Her body seemed to rule her head, not the other way around, and she had to find a way to conquer her need of him.

10

REMY stood in the back of the packed club, leaning against the wall, his arms crossed over his chest, his gaze moving over the crowd restlessly. His leopard had never liked being indoors, let alone in the midst of a throng as big as this one. He was surprised the fire marshal, who was sitting in the crowd, hadn't complained.

He spotted Arnaud at a table up front, clearly a welcome guest. Just the sight of the man set his teeth on edge and if Bijou smiled at him one more time, he just might have to go drag the sculptor right out of the club and throw him in the bayou again. What the hell was she thinking? Leopards weren't nice about sharing mates. They were jealous and bad tempered, and his leopard was one of the worst. Remy disliked Arnaud on principle, but his leopard despised him.

Basically, he despised any man who came near Bijou, but especially the ones she smiled at—or sang to. Remy's gaze went back to Bijou. She always astonished him when she sang. Her voice was such a blend of smoke and sex.

There was a husky, sinful quality to her vocals, rich and beautiful, the tone unique. She had some of the gravel her father was famous for, and the wide, wide range, but the soft, sensual quality was all her own.

She looked beautiful. There was no other word for it. She was in a long gown that hugged her phenomenal figure, emphasizing her small waist and drawing attention to her full breasts and rounded hips. She was breathtaking as far as Remy was concerned and he had the feeling that a good number of the men in the audience felt the same.

Each set seemed better than the last. He knew she'd suffered trauma, and yet she was totally relaxed, genuinely smiling and very friendly to her audience—completely different while performing than when she was simply Bijou. Bijou was shy and withdrawn, but as a singer, she was confident and smooth, and very sexy.

Her voice burned through his skin to sink into his bones. It sounded like a cliché to him but she took his breath away standing up there, belting out her soulful, bluesy song so effortlessly, the notes so clean and pure, yet blending one into the other until she took them all on a journey with her of heartache and need.

He was a man who was extremely cynical. Even more than that, he didn't trust anyone, not with his job, yet when he looked at her, his heart pounded, his mouth went dry and his body went as hard as a rock. He was a man always in control, and yet with Bijou, he was on the edge, or lost it completely. His mind was always logical, everything in his world had to make sense, because the killing never did. It wasn't logical to fall for Bijou Breaux.

She had too many interested men gawking at her. He was the jealous type—well—not him—his leopard. She had too much money. He couldn't even conceive of the kind of money she had. She was in need of rescuing and refused to even consider that possibility. Worse, she stood up to him, which was exactly what he wanted and needed in a woman, but not when it didn't suit him.

He swore under his breath for about the tenth time. And that was another thing wrong with her—she made him swear and he wasn't the swearing kind.

Gage nudged him. "You're doin' it again, bro. You're actin' like a fish out of water gaspin' for breath." He grinned at Remy's dark scowl. "I've never seen anyone have it so bad. Not even Drake, and he was just a fool for our sister. You can't stop starin' at her, and you're lookin' at her like any moment you're going to be carryin' her off to a cave somewhere."

"It's not a bad idea," Remy snapped, unrepentant. "The cavemen had something going for them after all. She doesn't have to do that thing with her hips when she's walkin' through the crowd. What's up with that?"

"You're supposed to be lookin' out for her, not gettin' all hot and bothered," Gage pointed out. "You're losin' your edge, Remy."

"That's a little difficult," Remy admitted, and forced himself to look around the room. Ryan Cooper, Brent Underwood and Tom Berlander were at a table close to the front with Robert Lanoux and two men who looked vaguely familiar. All of them were drinking heavily, even Robert, and shifters just didn't do that to their leopards. Remy didn't like the way any of them was looking at Bijou. Every now and then the two men he should have been able to identify, but couldn't, leaned close to whisper something to Ryan and Ryan would scowl up at Bijou and mutter something.

Remy nudged Gage. "Those two men with Ryan Cooper, do you know them?"

"Jean and Juste Rousseau, a couple of punks who always seem just on the outside of the play, but I've suspected for a very long time they're the ringleaders. I see them around some of the criminal elements, but they're always quiet and we've never caught them at anything."

"I recognize the names, now that you say them. Their names came up in the investigation of the bone harvester four years ago. They were friends with one of the victims and I remember bringin' them in and askin' questions . . . but they don' look the same."

Gage nodded. "Yeah, they changed their hair color from dark to that sandy blond. I think they're tryin' to be surfers. They went out to California for a while to visit their mama and I guess the idea of bein' surfin' bums was too much to pass up." He snickered. "They've been gone a few years. Maybe their mama got tired of supportin' their lifestyle and sent them back to their daddy."

"How do you know so much about them?" Remy asked. "I only interviewed them once, they didn't seem a good fit, and had nothin' to add to the investigation, so I put them out of my mind."

"You haven't driven the streets like I've been doin'. A few years ago, around the time of the killin's, there was petty vandalism goin' on, mostly homes of the elderly and the poor, but someone was beatin' the hell out of the occupants. None of the incidents occurred in New Orleans, but more in the outlying parish. No one died, but it was pretty ugly."

"And they were suspects?" Remy's gaze flickered once more to the table where Cooper and his friends were getting louder.

He'd always wondered at the possibility of two men committing the murders. The murders were messy and all over the place, yet the altar was exact, meticulous even. He could never find evidence of two killers, but the bone harvester could easily be a team.

"I had a hunch, but there was never any hard evidence at any of the break-ins." Gage shrugged. "Now that they're back, the break-ins have started again."

Remy observed the two men for a few minutes. "They whisper to Ryan, and they're the ones buying the drinks. I think they're eggin' him on."

"I noticed that as well," Gage said.

Remy had always respected Gage. He held all of his brothers in high esteem, but since Gage had become the sheriff, he'd grown very serious about his work and he was damn good at it. "Is it possible they're a killin' team?"

Gage frowned, studying the two men. "Are they capable of it? I would say yes. I think sooner or later they will kill someone. These break-ins are definitely not about the money. Whoever is beatin' the elderly is doin' it for fun."

"You don' get a scent?"

Remy's pulse jumped. There was never a scent left behind at the bone harvester's kills. Not one that Remy could catch, and his leopard was always close to the surface. The victim was always so fearful, sweat pouring off of them, the blood and intestines and bowels obliterating any scent the leopard might pick up, which was highly unusual. Leopards had a tremendous sense of smell, and Remy's had always been a huge asset to his career, yet his cat had never been able to pick up the scent of the bone harvester. How could Gage's leopard not pick up the scent of the violent home invaders?

"I definitely have caught their scents at the homes, but the problem is, they work odd jobs and they've done work at all the homes. They aren't the only ones either. It's a perfect way to get an in with those livin' in the houses, and every single one of the victims describes the masked intruders differently."

"I don' like that Robert is runnin' with them," Remy commented, frowning.

"Yeah, I've been particularly worried about the relationship for some time, and I know his brother Dion has tried to get him away from them," Gage responded.

"Could the Rousseau brothers be runnin' a crew to do the break-ins?"

Gage shrugged. "I'd believe anything is possible at this point. But they'd have to be very smart to pull it off and never get caught. Why would they think if their crew got popped, they wouldn't be named?"

"Because they are smart. Maybe they're certain nothin' can be traced back to them."

"Still," Gage said, "it's possible you might want to look

a little closer at them for the bone harvester's murders. They left around the time the murders stopped and they've been back long enough to establish themselves and begin again."

"You should have told me about them," Remy pointed out. His leopard was snarling and raking at him, wanting freedom with the two brothers in such close proximity to Bijou.

Gage shrugged. "I had no idea you were considerin' them for the murders."

Remy had to be fair, although he didn't feel fair; he felt like raging and raking his claws up and down the walls to claim his territory and warn all others away. He'd spotted several leopard males in the room, all with their attention focused, even fixated on Bijou as she performed. She looked alluring, sexy, her body moving subtly beneath that figure-hugging gown. She'd caught his attention again and he couldn't pull his gaze away from her.

"That's true," he murmured.

There she went again, moving through the crowd instead of staying on the small stage close to the band where her bodyguards could stop any trouble before it started. He winced visibly when she stepped backward so gracefully, her hips swaying as she poured herself into her music. That small step took her a little too close to Arnaud, and his leopard pushed close to the surface, causing a wave of itching as fur threatened to burst through his skin. His joints hurt. His jaw ached.

Remy breathed deep and called on years of discipline to subdue his leopard. He breathed away the pain and worked his jaw to keep teeth from bursting through.

Gage nudged him, clearly attempting to distract him. Both knew just how dangerous a male leopard could be with his mate emerging for the first time. "See that man, third table to the right, fourth row. He was the one starin' through the window of the café when Bijou was there. You asked everyone to keep their eyes out for him. His name is Jason Durang and he works for Bijou's manager. Rob Butterfield, her manager, has been in town awhile now. They both arrived within a few days of Bijou. Durang has been doggin' her, followin' her everywhere and reportin' back to her manager."

Remy frowned. "He's not her stalker. Bob Carson is definitely the man stalking her. I smelled his scent all over her car and even on the ropes he cut. He makes more sense. He has to blame her for his life. I called Angelina at the office and asked her to look up Carson and what happened to him during the years with his mother after they left Bodrie's mansion. She was a major drug user and became a prostitute to feed her habit. Her son was dragged around from city to city, following Bodrie wherever he was, but they weren't allowed to live in the mansion until after Bijou's mother died."

"How did Bijou's mother die?" Gage asked.

"She died under suspicious circumstances, which only gained Bodrie more sympathy. She'd just had Bijou, and Bodrie went on a tour. Bijou's mother left the baby at the mansion and supposedly went for a drive. Her car and body were found over in the next parish, the car wrapped around a tree. It didn't make sense for her to leave the baby behind. And some of the officers put in their reports that they didn't believe she was the driver."

"You don' believe it now, either, do you?"

"If Carson's mother decided to kill Bodrie's wife, and she had her son help her at such an impressionable age, he would be one mixed-up kid," Remy said.

"But if she was leopard . . ." Gage protested.

"She had head injuries and the medical examiner couldn't tell if she had some prior to the accident. The case remained open because he wouldn't rule either way."

"Damn it, Remy, Bijou is in real trouble, isn't she?"

Remy nodded slowly. "I don' believe her manager has her best interests at heart either. I don' know what he has in mind, but clearly he's here for a reason and it can't be good. They're comin' at her from every direction."

Gage's jaw tightened. "Are you certain she's your mate?"

"You keep askin' me that, Gage, what do you think?"

Gage swore under his breath. "Then it's war, Remy. She's one of ours, and if they come at one of us, they're goin' to have to take us all on. I'll call the boys."

"Have one of them stay on her manager and that jackass who keeps starin' at her. I don' like his expression. It isn't admiration," Remy pointed out.

Gage turned to observe Durang and Butterfield. They kept putting their heads together whispering, all the while watching Bijou perform. The crowd had gone wild with her last song and now was eerily silent, as she sang a weeping, bluesy ballad that was heartrending. There was something about her voice that crawled under the skin, sank deep into bones and stayed there, making anyone hearing her feel every emotion as she poured her heart out.

Clearly her manager and Durang had heard her many times and weren't quite as enamored with her as the rest of the crowd. Butterfield stared at her with an ugly expression on his face, one that had Remy's leopard snarling and raking at him all over again.

"I'm goin' to have Angelina dig around a little into both of their backgrounds and see what she can uncover," Remy said. "Butterfield doesn't want Bijoux doing this, but he can't exactly kill the golden goose."

"Do managers take out insurance policies on their big-name clients?" Gage asked.

Remy turned his head slowly to look at his brother. Their eyes met. Remy swore and stepped out of the club to use his cell phone. He wanted the information fast. He needed it. Bijou's life could very well depend on it. Angelina was very good at her job, and he had no doubt he'd know a lot more about Bijou's manager and his shadowy friend within the hour.

Remy stepped back into the club just as the band swang into a sultry, steamy number. Bijou's voice seduced the crowd until they appeared almost mesmerized. He'd seen her do the same thing at a concert, a few years back when he couldn't stop himself from going to see her perform. Curiosity, nothing more, he'd assured himself.

She stood on the stage and looked ethereal, beautiful and so not of the world, Remy hadn't believed it was actually Bijou. Her hair fell to her waist, thick and glossy, the kind of hair a man got lost in. She'd been far too seductive to equate her with the gawky teen he'd caught glimpses of when she hung out with his sister. She was even more beautiful now.

Remy found he didn't dare look at her, not if he was going to protect her. There was an undercurrent in the room his leopard sensed that kept the cat prowling close to the surface. It was an expectation, an awareness of danger. His belly was in knots, his muscles coiled and ready. He didn't know for certain where the threat would come from, but it was safe to say, it would come.

Remy frowned as two of Drake's men shifted positions. They were acting as bodyguards for Bijou, and he wasn't entirely happy about it. Joshua Tregre had shaggy sun-bleached hair and piercing green-blue eyes. He was a man with a strong build, carrying the heavy muscles of their kind—a leopard—and he was fast. Very fast. Remy appreciated that trait, but he knew how dangerous the emerging of a female leopard could be, and just how difficult it could be on any male in the vicinity.

Elijah Lospostos was a steely-eyed, far too handsome man, with a wealth of gleaming black hair spilling into eyes the color of mercury one moment and as dark as night the next. He was tough and extremely dangerous, a good man to have on Bijou's side—but he also was an unmated leopard. Drake had chosen both men to work at Bijou's club on her nights to perform because they were dangerous and fast and could protect. The leader of the lair hadn't known Bijou was leopard as well and that she was entering the Han Vol Dan.

Remy gritted his teeth and took a long, slow look around the room. What had the two leopards up front, close to Bijou, seen that he hadn't from his position in the back of the room? He shifted, his gaze scanning the large overcrowded club. He spotted several male leopards in the room, not surprising because their lair was small, but most of the males were unmated and that added to the undercurrent of danger.

The song ended and the crowd went wild, clapping and stomping feet. Bijou smiled and gracefully made her way to Arnaud's table as the band went into an upbeat, dance melody. A few couples bravely took to the dance floor while others sipped at their drinks and tried to work up the courage to ask for Bijou's autograph.

Remy frowned as Arnaud rose to hold her chair for her. She shouldn't be sitting with him, she should be with Remy—under Remy's protection.

"You're rumbling," Gage cautioned. "Remy, this is turning into a bad situation. Have you thought about asking her to leave with you?"

He'd thought about throwing her over his shoulder and just taking her out whether she liked it or not, but it wouldn't earn him any points with her. No way was she going to be reasonable if he said he needed to talk to her. The time to talk had been when she woke up.

"She's only got one more set and she's done," Remy said. "If we're lucky we can get through that, and I'll get her out of here and have the talk with her."

Gage snorted. "Yeah, I'm sure you'll be talkin' to her."

"I have to tell her about her leopard."

"And if for some reason her female never emerges?"

Remy took a deep breath. "Then she'll think I'm crazy, and I'll have to prove to her I'm not. Either way, she's mine and I'm goin' to tell her the truth about what I am and what she is."

Gage's gaze shifted to Bijou. Her profile was to him and she was laughing. Lights shifted over her face as she leaned toward Arnaud and said something. "Are you certain she's your mate? This isn't about sex? Because she's beautiful, Remy, and it would be easy enough to get things mixed up."

"Damn it, Gage." Remy's frustration nearly exploded at his brother. "Quit askin' the same damn thing every few minutes. Nothin' has changed and nothin' can change. I've marked her as mine. She is mine. There's just a little matter of persuadin' her, and it's done. I don' care if her leopard emerges or not, she belongs to me and no one and nothin' is goin' to stand in my way. Is that clear enough?"

Gage shrugged, hiding his grin and deliberately goading his brother further. "Lust has a funny way of colorin' a man's perspective, brother, but since you're so certain and all, I've got a text from the boys sayin' they're on the way, so we should have reinforcements soon."

"Good. The feelin' of impendin' doom is not goin' away." And if his brother kept asking him the same question over and over, doomsday was going to start with Gage.

Remy spotted the older couple, Mr. and Mrs. Chambridge, from the café in the crowd seated at one of the tables in the middle of the room. Emile and Thereze were there as well, Emile looking mesmerized.

Cooper's table was growing louder and more obnoxious by the moment. He knew if Bijou was singing, the bouncers would likely throw the men out, but she was on a break and they were getting away with their noise. He ground his teeth together and held on to his foul temper with every bit of discipline he had, commanding his leopard to back off and let him handle things.

His jaw ached permanently now. He could feel the roped muscles coiled and ready. Fur itched beneath his skin and the tips of his fingers and toes burned. He tried breathing away the fire, but the more he tried not to look at Bijou, the more his gaze was pulled in her direction and his body hardened beyond his comprehension. He didn't have that kind of gut-wrenching reaction to a woman, ever, not until now.

He was the kind of man who could walk away any time he needed to—fully intact. Until Bijou. That was how he knew the leopard mating ritual was real. He had become fixated on her, his body reacting almost before he scented her or saw her. Having other men around her was torture, but knowing other male leopards were close to her was worse. Yeah, Gage had it right when he said Remy had it bad.

His phone vibrated and he pulled it out to check it. There was nothing like an ongoing investigation running through the night, but his sense of urgency kept increasing and he always trusted his gut instincts. Angelina had sent him information on both Rob Butterfield and Jason Durang. She hadn't found out yet if there was an insurance policy on Bijou taken out by her manager or his company, but even in that short period of time, she'd uncovered quite a bit on both men.

Ron Butterfield had a gambling habit that over the years had caused him grief. Twice his home had been broken into and everything destroyed because he'd failed to pay back a loan he'd taken out from the wrong person. Once he'd been beaten senseless, and several times over the years he'd been accused of embezzling from his own company.

Butterfield's friend Jason Durang had a long record of assault. He'd come in contact with Butterfield when Butterfield briefly served time in prison for embezzlement. Butterfield hired Durang the moment Durang was out of prison, but no one seemed to know what the man actually did for him. He had a reputation for being an enforcer, and he'd been hanging around Butterfield for the past four years.

Remy handed his phone to his brother and let him read the data Angelina had provided. "She's still diggin', but I don' think there's much doubt that Butterfield has an insurance policy on Bijou."

Remy took a deep breath. He didn't want to say it aloud and breathe life into the idea, but it was a perfect time for a copycat killer to dispose of someone who was in their way. If Bijou was considering firing Butterfield, and if he continued to push her to do something she didn't want to do, she had to be considering it, then his money train was over and she was of no more use to him alive.

Gage's eyes met his. Remy read the same thought. He shook his head. Things were getting worse by the minute. Bijou's life hadn't improved much even after her father had died. He tried not to snarl as he turned his head to look at her. She lifted her head. The impact of her amazing eyes on him was frightening. He could fall into her eyes and stay there forever. She smiled at him and nodded, and just like that his breath slammed out of his lungs and his blood surged hot and wild through his veins. She stood up with her fluid grace, looking more sensual than ever and began her rounds through the club before she took the stage again. She spoke briefly to the people at each table, smiling and listening to the various comments and greetings. She was gracious, royal even, occasionally signing autographs before moving on.

"I have to hand it to you, brother," Gage said, "the woman is gorgeous. A handful, but gorgeous. I can see why none of the girls in school liked her. Saria said that to me once, but I put it down to her daddy's money and how privileged she was."

"Yeah, she was privileged all right," Remy said, anger welling up out of nowhere, remembering that little eight-year-old girl with the solemn eyes telling him she didn't expect to make it through the night. Bringing her home and finding naked men and women scattered throughout her house, so causally doing drugs and in alcohol stupors. "No doubt about it, Gage, Bijou had a very privileged childhood."

"I can do without the sarcasm, bro," Gage said, handing back Remy's phone. "I'm not as dense as you think I am. Clearly her childhood wasn't great, and she isn't the stuck-up bitch I always thought she was." He turned and looked at the woman who, if Remy had his way, would be his sister-in-law. "She does look . . . unreachable. A dream or fantasy, but definitely untouchable. And a little haughty. She has an attitude, Remy, distant and beautiful and so very far above us."

"She damn well better be unreachable or untouchable," Remy snapped.

Gage laughed at him. "I've never seen you so messed up in my life. Wait until the boys get here and see you like this."

"I've got a gun, Gage, and I'm not afraid to use it," Remy warned his brother.

The smile faded from Gage's face. "You already stuck me with a knife. And I've got about a million scars from your leopard beatin' the crap out of me for some silly indiscretion when our leopards were just playin' around. There's no shootin' me. I'd be damned mad if you did."

"Quit bein' such a baby. It was just a little slice and you should have been payin' more attention. I told you a million times you weren't judgin' the distance correctly and don' be gettin' into a knife fight until you practice a whole hell of a lot more. You didn't believe me so I made my point." Remy deliberately sounded self-righteous. He was the older brother just helping his younger brother out and making certain he stayed alive. "That leopard of yours doesn't take anythin' seriously, not even trainin'. I'm savin' your life whether you like it or not."

"I don' have to like your methods. Your leopard is a tyrant and must be obeyed in all things." Gage made a face. "Oh, wait. That would be his human counterpart."

Bijou had reached the tables at the rear of the club and moved around them laughing softly at something someone said before approaching the two of them. "Are you all right, Remy? You look . . . upset."

It was her voice, that sensual, sexy, voice of hers, there was no blaming his leopard—or even himself. Later he would swear it had to have been her voice that turned him into a complete idiot. Remy circled the nape of her neck with his palm, his fingers nearly wrapping around her throat. He pulled her to him, savoring the feel of her body so close to his—savoring the fire burning hot in his veins. The moment he touched her, the moment her breasts brushed his chest and the scent of lavender surrounded him, sinking into his lungs, the world faded until there was only Bijou.

His eyes met hers. He felt her body melt into his as her

breasts rose and fell, her breathing ragged. Those amazing eyes, that deep cornflower blue, began to take on a glow. He bent his head to hers, holding her gaze as his head slowly descended toward hers. Her long lashes fluttered.

"Remy," she whispered his name.

A protest? Consent? She didn't pull away. Her eyes closed and his mouth found hers. Flames raced over his skin, through his body and lodged like a roaring fire in his groin. His cock lengthened and hardened until he was so thick he was afraid he might burst the material of his jeans. His leopard roared and raked his belly in an effort to call to his mate.

Bijou gasped and pushed at him, her eyes glittering, her face flushed. She made a small sound of distress and stepped back, shaking her head. He could see her leopard had risen and was close to the surface. She didn't understand what was happening and she was afraid, probably equating the unfamiliar feelings and body pains with their intense and rather brutal sexual encounter.

"Come with me," he whispered, trying to entice her. Seduce her. Hell, whatever it took. He just needed her to stop looking at him with fear. "*Chere*, let me explain what's happenin'."

She took another step back, shaking her head, one hand going defensively to her throat. "I'm workin', Remy. This isn't the time."

"It might be too late in another half hour or so," he pleaded. Her eyes definitely had turned cat.

She was afraid of him—or herself. Either way, she was retreating, and he couldn't blame her. She had every reason to be frightened. Her body no longer belonged to her. She ached. She hurt. She had no one to turn to. Remy knew he threatened her on an elemental level. He should have stayed, not taken the chance, and explained everything to her.

He swore under his breath as she retreated farther from him. Every male leopard in the room would scent the rise of the female. They would know she was close to the emerging and their leopards would be ready to fight for her. She had no way of knowing the havoc she would cause, or the danger she was in—because he hadn't told her. He hadn't explained.

"It's too late," Gage whispered as Bijou turned and made her way through the crowded club back toward the stage. "We'll just have to trust that if any of the others get near her, they'll catch your scent and it will be sufficient to warn them off."

"At least every leopard in here will protect her if anyone tries to harm her," Remy consoled himself.

Remy didn't take his eyes off of Bijou as she moved closer to the front of the room. He knew the exact moment both bodyguards realized she was a female leopard. Joshua swung around abruptly, shock on his face. Elijah was expressionless, only a small tick in his jaw giving his surprise away. The two men exchanged a long look.

Remy's vision went cat. He was aware of every rustle, murmur and clink of ice in the room. The smells were difficult to sort out, but he breathed in lavender, fear and the intoxicating scent of a female close to her time.

"What's up?" Lojos Boudreaux, the youngest of his brothers entered, followed closely by Mahieu and Dash.

The three brothers inhaled and swung around, shocked, staring at Bijou. She had reached Ryan Cooper's table and was moving past it when Cooper reached out and caught her wrist, stopping her.

"If you're giving out kisses, you little whore, I'll be happy to oblige." He jerked her down, trying to put her across his lap.

Bob Carson leapt up, camera in hand.

Jean and Juste Rousseau both laughed uproariously, snapping pictures with their cell phones. Robert Lanoux and Brent Underwood moved back in their chairs as if distancing themselves, while Tom Berlander grinned like an ape.

"Plant one on her, Ryan," Juste yelled. "We'll have the proof."

"We can sell it to a magazine," Jean encouraged. "Make thousands."

Both laughed again as Bijou fought Ryan's hold on her wrist.

Remy leapt over a table and sprinted toward the front of the club. Joshua and Elijah got there first. Elijah caught Ryan's head and slammed it down on the tabletop as Joshua pulled Bijou to safety, thrusting her to the other side of him to keep his body between her and trouble.

The male leopards in the room came to their feet, rushing to the front of the club to form a loose, protective circle around one of their females. Lojos and Dash hit Bob Carson from the back, driving him to the ground, Lojos holding him still with one knee planted in his back. Remy made it to the circle and snarled. Instantly the two male leopards facing him opened a path for him. Remy noted the only leopard from his lair not to stand for Bijou was Robert.

Remy caught Bijou's wrists. "You're comin' with me, now. No arguin'. You can see it isn't safe."

Bijou pressed her lips together. He could feel her trembling, her eyes searching his. She nodded slowly, and relief poured through him. At least she wasn't going to fight him on this issue. The club was a powder keg ready to blow at any moment and the human counterparts of the male leopards were holding on to their human forms by a thread. He couldn't imagine what it would be like if even one leopard succeeded in shifting.

He knew to those in the club it would simply look like her protection stepped in and removed her. "We're goin' out the back way, behind the stage. I'm not takin' you through the club. The boys will hold everyone while we make our escape."

Her teeth chewed on her lower lip. "I think Joshua and Elijah took care of the real threat."

He wasn't convinced that Ryan Cooper was the real threat to Bijou but he wasn't going to argue the point. He swung her around, drawing her beneath the protection of his shoulder, his arm circling her waist, the other hand on his gun. He moved fast, relying on his leopard's radar to tell him what was ahead, behind or to either side of them.

Bijou hurried to keep up with his fast pace. "Remy, no one's after us, there was a wall between us and anyone else. No one would ever be so stupid as to challenge all those men. What's goin' on? This isn't about those drunken idiots is it? Somethin' else is goin' on."

"Yes, but I need somewhere far away from here to tell you. Somewhere safe where we can be alone."

Bijou shook her head. "Nowhere is safe if we're alone." She looked up at him, her eyes meeting his. "Is it?"

If she was seeking reassurance, he couldn't give it to her. His body was already on fire, his leopard almost mad with the need for hers. He knew her body was reacting to his, and her leopard was so close he doubted if they would make it too far before she began to insist on emerging. He didn't have a lot of time to get Bijou back to the privacy of the swamp.

"My car's straight ahead. Keep movin'."

"I feel sick, Remy," she admitted, pressing a hand to her stomach. "And hot." She pushed at her hair, her hand coming away damp. "I'm so hot. I feel like I'm runnin' a high fever."

"I know. Just get in the car." He yanked open the passenger door for her.

She slipped inside and he rushed around to the driver's side. He jumped inside and kicked off his shoes. She didn't notice. She was too uncomfortable, squirming, her female leopard in a frenzy after the close proximity of all the male leopards.

Bijou continually rubbed her hands and knuckles. He knew how bad it hurt that first time, the terrible, brutal, yet wonderful gift of shifting. Every joint, her jaw and mouth would be painful, while the tips of her fingers and toes burned as if she was touching flames. Worse than all of it was the ferocious drive to have sex.

"Remy." Bijou cleared her throat repeatedly in an effort to talk. "Why does this happen to me every time I'm with you?"

"I'll explain everythin' to you, *chere*, but you have to trust me. It's all goin' to sound like somethin' out of a movie. Right now, the only thing that matters is to strip. And do it fast."

She frowned at him. "I'm not havin' sex with you in the car, Remy." She breathed deep, put her head down as if to keep from fainting and then sat back up, glaring at him as she touched her breasts through the material of her dress as if they were hurting. "I'm not." But she didn't sound as certain as she wanted.

Remy put his foot on the gas pedal and floored it, racing for the swamp. "Take off your clothes. Right now, Bijou." He used his most commanding voice. "Hurry. Kick off your shoes and get out of that gown. Now."

11

BIJOU kicked her heels off and looked through the window out into the night. No other cars were on the narrow road leading to the Inn.

"Do it now," Remy snapped. "Get undressed."

Bijou winced at the gravely sound of his voice, but she slipped her gown from one shoulder and then the other, holding it over her breasts with her hands.

"Bijou," Remy said between his teeth. His hands shook and he felt the claws so close to bursting through his fingertips. "We don' have much time. Listen to me while you're undressing. I'm goin' to sound crazy, but just listen, don' interrupt. And damn it," he added, "get out of those clothes now. Even your underwear. Keep breathin' deep."

Bijou allowed the gown to slip down over her bare breasts down to her waist. Remy tried not to look. He was in as much trouble as she was. It didn't help that her breasts were perfect, just exactly what he liked. She was flushed, breathing hard, her nipples taut, drawing his attention when he needed to be in total control. She wiggled the formfitting gown down to her waist so that her narrow rib cage was exposed.

She was beautiful. Her skin gleamed at him even in the darkness of the car. The scent of lavender intoxicated him. He gritted his teeth, trying to hold on to his control. His jaw ached, and already it was becoming difficult to grip the steering wheel properly.

"Do you know what a shape-shifter is?"

Her eyebrow shot up and she stopped wiggling the gown down past her waist to look at him. "The Rougarou?" She rolled her eyes. "Of course I've heard of it. Every child growin' up near the swamp and bayous has heard of the Rougarou." She had to clear her voice several times as if her throat was swollen.

Bijou lifted her buttocks and shimmied the tight-fitting gown down her hips and thighs.

"Leopards, Blue, not the Rougarou. There's an entire lair of leopards here in the swamp. Bodrie wasn't leopard, but he met your mother on tour. I believe your mother was leopard, and she passed her gift on to you."

Bijou chuffed out a breath. "You've lost your mind, Remy."

But she was still slipping the gown down her thighs and legs. She began to peel her sheer stockings from her legs.

"Maybe, but if I'm right, and I'm certain I am, your leopard is close to emergin'. Your joints hurt. Your jaw. Your body feels like it's on fire, burning from the inside out. And you have to have sex. Right now. Even in the car with me on the edge of the road. Would you ever really do somethin' like that if you weren't under extraordinary circumstances?"

He wasn't explaining things very well and she didn't have much time.

"I want sex every time I'm anywhere near you, Remy," she admitted, tossing the stockings into the backseat. The only thing she had left on was a lace panty that didn't cover much but enhanced and intrigued. "That doesn't make me a leopard, it makes me like my father, with no self-control and clearly some kind of sex addiction."

Remy winced at the distaste and self-loathing in her voice. He glanced at her. "Ouch. You could at least pretend you think I'm so overwhelmin'ly sexy that you can't possibly resist me." He let out his breath trying to concentrate on the narrow road to get them to safety. "Take off your panties, Blue."

Bijou could barely use her hands. Her knuckles felt inflamed. Her mouth hurt. Even her scalp hurt. There wasn't a joint in her body that wasn't sore. Most of all, her body was on fire. She felt desperate for sex.

She hooked her thumbs in the lace and drew them down, balling them in her fist and holding them almost protectively against her. She had no idea how that tiny scrap of sheer lace was going to protect her against the man she craved like a drug, but if he didn't pull over soon and let her out of the car, she wasn't going to be responsible for what happened.

"Now, what?" Her breasts ached, felt swollen and needy. She took a deep breath, utterly aware of her naked body and the way she was affecting Remy. She could feel the heat pouring off him.

She didn't like the spotlight unless she was performing. Maybe she turned into someone else when she sang, but she liked feeling as if she could fade into the background, quiet and observant rather than being the center of attention— until tonight in the club when all those men had surrounded her so protectively. She'd been aware of every one of them— just as she was aware of her bare skin, the heat and Remy right now. She detested herself for that.

Her attraction had at least been reserved to Remy exclusively. It had been humiliating enough to be so crazy for him that she'd done things she hadn't even known possible. Now, to think that even for a moment she'd been so insane, feeling sensual and alluring surrounded by the men. She'd smelled them, the various scents so acute, in some way affecting her, and that shamed her. Now what was she doing? She was riding in a car totally naked, doing exactly what Remy wanted of her so she could have wild uninhibited, *ferocious* sex with him. It was all she could think about.

"Take off my jacket." He'd worn the dress jacket as a concession to her elegant club. Jacket, white shirt and his jeans. It was the best he could do when he had known clothes would be coming off fast.

She didn't argue with him but pulled at his sleeve as he lifted one hand off the steering wheel. She jerked his sleeve off and as he leaned forward, took off his jacket for him. It went sailing into the backseat to land over the top of her gown.

When she started to settle back down, he shook his head. "Now my shirt," Remy ordered. "Hurry, Blue. It's goin' to be too late in another few minutes."

She didn't know what he meant by too late, but she leaned into him to unbutton the immaculate white dress shirt. He'd looked so handsome when he'd walked into the club. Her heart had nearly stopped, and then began pounding hard. She loved the way he walked with such confidence. The moment she saw him again, she knew she was lost. Remy was her hero, and he always would be. She had no idea she would have such a physical reaction to him, especially when as a teenager and during her college years she had never once been tempted to give herself to a man.

Her hands were clumsy on the buttons, her knuckles aching, the tips of her fingers on fire. She could barely breathe as she slipped the buttons free of the openings. Her hands kept brushing his bare skin, sending little electrical shocks racing over her own. She swallowed hard, trying to clear what felt like an obstruction in her throat. Her skin itched in waves, over and over, and her skull felt too tight as if it didn't quite fit. She tugged on the shirt and managed to get it off of him, sending it flying into the backseat along with everything else.

"Now my jeans."

His voice was husky, a velvet brush of sensuality that sent more electrical charges streaking through her bloodstream. She gasped, licked her lips and reached for the band of his low-riding jeans. He wore button-up denim rather than a zipper and again she found she had even more of a difficult time releasing his straining cock. Her breath came in ragged, desperate puffs, her lungs burning for air as she slowly managed to get the buttons undone.

Remy lifted his buttocks so she could wiggle the material down his hips to the strong column of his thighs. Her hands felt clumsy. Burning. Too big. Her fingers didn't want to work. Her body felt as if it had burst into flames, so hot she could barely stand it. She turned to roll down the window.

"Get my jeans all the way off. Hurry."

His voice had gone raspy, but the urgency in his tone caught at her. The car turned onto the drive leading to the Inn. She could smell the lake, the swamp, individual grasses and plants.

"I'm burnin' up," she admitted. "I can barely breathe." With wanting him. The moment she could see his heavy erection, long and thick and so very hard for her, the burning between her legs became a firestorm, slick and hot until craving turned to desperate need.

"I know, *chere*, I am too." He gritted his teeth. "Just get my jeans down."

To do that, she had to shift in her seat, lean down, her bare breasts brushing his strong muscular thighs with all those intriguing roped muscles. She nearly sobbed with wanting him. His masculine scent enveloped her, went deep into her lungs so she didn't know where his sexual need started and hers left off. Heat radiated off his body, and his eyes were dark green, almost glowing with his hunger for her.

To her utter horror, he had become an obsession. Her only consolation was that judging from his heavy erection, the heat pouring off his skin and the dark hunger in his eyes, he was just as obsessed with her. One hand fisted in her hair, as if he was going to push her face toward his jerking cock. She could see his stomach muscles rippling, his hips bucking a little as she shoved his jeans farther down his legs.

She felt the bump as he steered the car onto the grass, blowing past the Inn, around to the back. The Inn was dark and she was glad Saria wasn't there. She was stark-naked, nearly sobbing and so close to losing every shred of common sense and dignity she'd ever had. She'd do anything to have him, and that was just insanity. She'd have to wake up some time and face herself and her foolish actions. Right at that moment, nothing else mattered but to feel him, all that silky heat, in her mouth.

She leaned closer, her nipples so hard they scraped along his thigh. His fist tightened in her hair, guiding her to his pulsing erection. Her fingers stroked while she inhaled his wild, almost feral scent. She glanced up at his face, so intent, so dark with desire.

He slammed the brakes on before the car rolled into the lake, turning off the ignition. She wanted to sob in frustration as he shoved open the door and yanked her out through the driver's side door, one hand still in her hair, using that too to get her out of the car. He jerked her into his arms, the hand in her hair, pulling her head back, his mouth coming down on hers hard.

Even the pain in her scalp sent more flames pulsing through her body. His kiss made her weak, knees shaking, his taste making her feel almost intoxicated. His free hand swept down her back to her buttocks, pressing her close to him.

"Remy." She broke the kiss, panting, near tears. "I need you in me. Please. Right now. I'm burnin' up and I need you now." She felt empty. Incomplete. And so hot she was afraid she might just go up like a stick of dynamite.

Remy pushed her against the car, half lifting her. "Legs around my waist." His voice was nothing but gravel now, a growl really. A command.

He was feeling a little desperate himself. He knew the

emerging could be any moment, but he had to be inside of her. He had no choice. He had to feel that impossibly tight silken sheath surrounding him, that sweet friction taking him to paradise.

Her tongue frantically tasted his skin, driving him nearly insane with his need to have her, to claim her as his own. He felt as if he'd waited a lifetime for this woman—maybe more. She moaned softly, her teeth sinking into his shoulder as she complied, her legs wrapping him in a soft, firm tangle. She hooked her ankles and lowered herself over him, all that slick fire engulfing his cock.

He threw his head back, feeling as if he were burning alive, catching flame from her, leaning her back against the car for better leverage before he began to move. She rode him, setting the pace at first, a little frantic, but such a hot tight glove gripping him that her body sent waves of pleasure coursing through him.

Her panting little cries only added to the need building in him so rapidly. He took over, his hands on her hips, guiding her into a stronger, steadier rhythm, one that robbed him of breath and sanity and took him into a world of feeling. They rocketed toward the precipice, coming apart at the same time, the world around him going red, thunder rolling in his ears.

Still, she didn't stop moving, gasping, panting, her cries even more frantic.

"Don' stop, Remy. I'm burnin' up. You can't stop." She nearly sobbed her plea.

Remy brought himself up short. He wanted to stay locked inside of her more than anything, but he knew he was being a selfish ass, letting go of all control when she needed him most. He took a few deep calming breaths and went motionless, still buried deep. She squirmed, her muscles clamping down hard on him, hot as fiery hell, so tight she was practically strangling him. He could hear the roaring in his head and felt his leopard pushing and raking, snarling to be let free.

"You have to listen to me, Blue. This is important. I can't keep gettin' distracted when you need this information. My leopard is rakin' at me, desperate to get at yours. She'll be emergin' any moment and we have to allow them to be with one another. In fact, there's not goin' to be any real way to stop them. Mine chose you, chose your leopard. He's so crazy for her, and I'm just as driven for you."

Bijou went still. Very still. Her breath caught in her throat as she repeated his words in her mind. He really believed what he said about the leopard.

"I should have explained more to you. The shiftin'. How it's done. It's just that every time I get near you I can't resist havin' you."

She moistened suddenly dry lips, slowly lifting her head from Remy's shoulder to look into his eyes. They glowed a piercing green, much like a cat's in the dark. Her vision was strange, banded with color, as if she was seeing through heat binoculars. "What do you mean, your leopard is crazy for mine? You're with me because you think your leopard wants mine?"

Her heart pounded hard in her chest. Of course it was all too good to be true. Remy didn't love her. He barely knew her. What had she been thinking? The fairy tale? Happily ever after? He was talking about pure sex, not love. She was an adult and she knew better.

"Of course," Remy said. He frowned as she slowly dropped her legs so that her feet touched the ground. He grinned at her, holding her to him by her buttocks. "The added bonus is the crazy sex."

She couldn't even blame the whole thing on him. She'd been a willing participant. More, she'd practically torn her clothes off and then his. She would have done anything at all for him and to have him. She stepped away from him, allowing him to slip out of her. He was still hard, leaving her feeling empty and lost.

Before she could say anything more, her belly cramped and she doubled over, clutching her stomach. Sweat poured out of her skin. She scented something wild and feral. Deep inside something came alive, moving under her skin like a parasite. She gasped and dropped to her knees, her body nearly convulsing.

"Don' fight, Blue. Let her take you over. You'll still be there, just let go."

Dimly she heard Remy talking to her, but what he was saying made no sense, unless he really was telling the truth. An impossibility, but her face contorted. Her teeth felt sharp and too full for her mouth. She wanted to scream. What kind of monster was she?

"Breathe, *chere*. Breathe deep and try to relax. This is an amazing moment. Not all females emerge." Remy sounded hoarse, but eager. "Your cycle has to coincide with hers, and some females wait a lifetime for that."

What was he saying? That she could get pregnant? Carry a leopard? Every horror movie she'd ever watched played through her mind. She tried to wipe the beads of sweat dripping down her face off, only to find that her hands were no longer human. She stared at the misshapen, fur-covered claws, the long curved nails springing from them. It couldn't be happening, not for real. What kind of monster had her mother been? She knew her father was one, but all this time she'd clung to the idea that she could be like her mother. Terrified, she twisted away from Remy when he reached to touch her, in an attempt to reassure her.

Those other men in her club, had they been leopards? All waiting for her to emerge, and then what? What was expected of her? Was she supposed to accept all of them? Did leopards have more than one mate? She didn't even know the answer. A sob escaped, but it came out a strange mewing sound. None of this was about her at all. Remy wasn't attracted to her and neither were those men. It was about whatever was inside her struggling to come out.

Her body contorted again, joints popping and cracking. Pain burst through her. Out of self-preservation she tried to listen to Remy's distant voice. Her lungs burned, and her body felt as if it was turning inside out. The itching was horrendous, as fur began to burst through her skin. Her jaw lengthened.

She tried to crawl away, a silly, desperate move, trying to flee, to get away from her own body. Most of all, she wanted away from Remy. She didn't want him witnessing what was happening to her, and worse, she didn't want her leopard, if that was what she was, to mate with his. She felt like she was living a nightmare, a horror movie and there was no way out.

"Blue." Remy's voice penetrated the roaring in her ears and the sheer terror of her body becoming something else. "Look at me. See me. I can get you through this. You're afraid and it's my fault. Instead of havin' sex with you every time I saw you, I should have been preparin' you for this. Please, *chere*, just let me do this for you."

Her body twisted, rolled, so that she came up on her hands and knees, only they weren't her hands or her knees any longer. She turned her head slowly, anger burning through her belly and raging in her heart. She swiped at him.

Remy leapt back. It was only his leopard's reflexes that saved him from a nasty rake across his face. His lady was really, really angry with him. There was something in her eyes that alarmed him. She was definitely distancing herself from him, and that was terribly dangerous, especially now.

One more roll and a silent scream and Blue was fully leopard. She came to her feet gingerly, regarding him warily, wild and feral and all female. Before he could move, she whirled around and sprinted toward the swamp. He changed on the run, using more speed than he ever had. He wasn't going to lose her, not now, not when he was so close to making her his.

His leopard charged after Bijou, leaping over a fallen log and easily following her scent. The swamp closed around him, giving him the sense of freedom and wild he craved. This was his real world, one he understood and needed. That was part of the danger of being leopard, especially in shift-

ing for the first time. There was no real way to explain to
someone else the absolute freedom of being cat, and the
temptation to stay in that form was always present.

Bijou was frightened and he'd clearly handled things
wrong with her, so the lure of staying in the large cat's form
would be doubly so. He tried to stay rational, to use logic as
he followed her trail, reasoning when his brain wanted to
go feral on him. Usually, the first hour or so, when he ran
free, he didn't allow his human side to feel anything at all.
He stayed fully animal, but he couldn't afford to make any
mistakes.

Bijou's leopard was small, very sleek with luxurious light
buff, almost white fur with darker rosettes scattered everywhere. He was large for a leopard, even a male leopard, his
coat a rare black with darker rosettes set into the fur so that
they were barely discernible. He was powerful and enormously strong, thanks to the roped muscles covering his
body. He had plenty of scars from numerous fights, and he'd
always come away the victor. None of the males wanted to
tangle with him—but over a female in heat—that could
change. He didn't want to kill a friend because he'd handled
things with Bijou badly.

He was aware he was extremely dangerous in leopard
form. His leopard was aggressive and cunning, a predator
high up in the food chain, often surly and bad-tempered.
With his female running from him, he was even more difficult and Remy sent up a silent prayer that no fisherman or
local would be hunting in the swamp.

He spotted the female running along the embankment,
splashing at the puddles with a delicate paw and jumping
over small downed branches of cypress trees. Bijou had
allowed the leopard to take over and was obviously enjoying
her freedom, dropping low to slink under some branches
and leaping effortlessly over others. She displayed agility
and grace, easily making jumps to low branches and climbing the trunks of trees.

Every movement was sinuous and filled with grace. She

twisted and turned, this way and that, showing off her flexible spine, clearly getting used to her new form, arching her back in a half circle and then leaping straight up to change direction in midair through a quick rotation of her hips. She looked beautiful as she moved with effortless elegance. She seemed to be playing, even as she exhibited the behavior of a female in heat.

She called out occasionally, and her voice would carry on the night, luring any males within hearing to her. She rubbed along the tree trunks, leaving a tantalizing scent behind. Seductively she rolled and stretched along the ground, among leaves and vegetation, just as quickly coming to her feet and moving deeper into the interior of the swamp.

He came up behind her as stealthily as possible, getting close enough to protect her and warn any other males off, without putting himself in danger. A female rebuffing a male could be very dangerous. He chuffed at her, calling out a soft hello, letting her know she wasn't alone and he was answering her call.

The female whirled around, ears flat on her head, snarling, warning him off. He kept a respectful distance. Bijou was totally angry with him, and her cat protected her, even to warning off her mate. Remy swore at himself. He'd always bulldozed his way when he wanted something. He'd never really needed finesse. He was intelligent and like his leopard, cunning, strong and bad-tempered. He had control and discipline to offset the more negative traits of his leopard.

He chuffed at her again, letting her know he found her beautiful and alluring. She snarled again and took a swipe at the leaves in front of her, sending them into the air. She whirled and ran, heading deeper into the swamp.

The large male leopard followed her, keeping an exact safe distance, waiting for her to give him a sign she was more receptive to his advances. They traveled several miles in a light rain. The leaves overhead protected them from the water, but neither really noticed or cared. She was making her way in a steady line away from the Inn, and the male leopard circled to get in front of her and change her direction.

The small female lifted her lip at him, growling and spitting, but she was tiring, and the demanding hormones were slowly edging out the rage. She allowed him to change her direction, and he moved closer to her, tentatively approaching. She rubbed along several more tree trunks, a small boulder and rolled in the grass. When she crouched, he moved closer. Instantly she was up, extending her claws and hissing her displeasure of him.

She was up again and moving away from him. Patience was required of a male leopard, and with the little female already disoriented and frightened, just finding herself in her animal form, he had plenty of patience. Once again, he fell in behind her and followed her as she moved through the swamp.

A small trickle of water became a larger ribbon, cutting through the wet land, and she padded through the inches of shallow water, splashing playfully and leaping back onto firmer ground. Just as she did, the black leopard slammed into her, driving her sideways, away from the thicker tree line. A golden male burst through the brush and circled her, coming to an abrupt halt when he caught sight of Remy's black leopard, roaring a challenge as he attempted to stare down the black leopard.

Remy recognized Robert Lanoux instantly. He was a member of the lair, single, and he'd given them trouble more than once. He had a reputation for not fighting fair, and usually, he traveled with his brother, Dion. Remy didn't wait for the intruder to make his move, but rushed him, hitting him hard in the side and driving him off of his feet.

The golden leopard rolled fast as the larger leopard drove after him, Remy relentless, wanting to end the fight fast without killing a member of his lair. Remy followed up his advantage with a punishing slap of his paw, claws slashing the side and neck of his adversary. Streaks of blood instantly matted fur. Robert kept rolling until he slipped into a tight opening in the brush.

Remy's leopard slammed into the shrubs, ripping through branches and leaves, using his superior weight and heavy muscles. He landed on the back of the golden leopard, driving him to the ground. Instantly, he flipped the smaller leopard and settled his teeth around Robert's throat. Silence instantly descended in the swamp until there was only the sound of ragged, hot breathing coming in gasping puffs.

The two leopards stared at one another, Remy not giving an inch. It wouldn't be difficult to bite down and suffocate the smaller male if he made one wrong move. His leopard raged at the control he was imposing, furious that the intruder had challenged him for his mate. His mark was on her, his scent. There was a code of honor within the lair, and Robert had ignored it. He was within his rights under their laws to kill the challenger.

Movement to his left had him biting down a little harder in a threat. He hadn't smelled Robert's brother Dion, but they were rarely separated, although he'd noticed that more and more Dion had seemed upset by his brother's bullying ways. His gaze shifted for just one moment. The little female watched intently, curled up to make herself smaller. Bijou had risen closer to the surface, and he could scent fear along with the female's excitement of the courtship rituals. The female trembled, her coat damp.

There was no way to reassure her in his present form. Killing Robert in front of her wouldn't give her cause to trust him either. Beneath him, Robert's leopard suddenly relaxed and submitted. Remy held him that little bit longer to warn him not to be stupid. It took everything he had to hold his leopard back from the kill.

Disgusted, his leopard dropped the golden leopard's throat and backed off, snarling as he did so. Twice he charged the smaller male, roaring as he did, swiping his enormous paw in the grass and leaves, sending vegetation into the air. It took a few minutes for the leopard to settle enough that Robert could get up cautiously and slink off into the heavier brush and sprint away.

The moment he was gone, the female leopard took off in the opposite direction as if running for her life—and maybe she felt as if she were. He couldn't imagine what it was like for Bijou to discover at such a late date that she had an animal form living inside of her. She didn't know how she could move between forms, how she would come to control her leopard and keep the animal's emotions from affecting her too much. Her leopard was probably just as confused and scared as she was.

Once again Bijou had headed away from the Inn and he circled to get in front of her, needing to drive her back. She halted abruptly when he appeared in front of her, baring her teeth, ears flat against her head, signaling her displeasure with him. He approached her carefully, and she slapped leaves and twigs at him. He rushed her, hitting her with his shoulder, turning her back toward the Inn and springing away before she could retaliate.

The female leopard hissed at him, whirling around in a circle, trying to get past him, but he blocked her every way until she took the only out left to her and headed in the direction the male wanted her to go. This time she didn't run from him, clearly already tired from trying the impossible—fighting the demands of her hormones and the urgent need to mate.

Again, he was careful, keeping a safe distance, but this time he paced alongside of her, testing the air to ensure they were once again alone. Every now and then, the female would rub along the trees. Eventually the action became more frequent and she would roll in the vegetation almost playfully, submissively, but when she crouched for the first time and he approached her, she spat at him and leapt away.

Remy retreated farther to allow the female leopard more freedom. No other leopards—or humans—appeared to be in the area, and clearly Bijou had withdrawn once again to allow her female her time. Her buff-colored coat with the dark rosettes allowed her to nearly disappear at times as she padded on her silent paws through the vegetation and trees. Every few feet she would stop and crouch, but if the male got to close, she would rebuff him.

The rebuffs became less and less threatening and her actions more and more enticing. She lured the male closer still, with tantalizing chemical messages, vocal calls, seductive rolls and sensuous stretches, all directed toward the large male. The male became more aggressive and possessive as she crouched again, this time blanketing her, driving his teeth into the back of her neck to hold her in place.

Hours later, exhausted, both cats broke apart, the little female retreating to the shade of the trees as the dawn began to break. The male lay close to her, watching over her and resting for a few minutes before getting to his feet and nudging her up. Reluctantly she obeyed, too tired to fight him as he pushed her onward.

The male leopard retreated enough to allow Remy to think logically. He was exhausted, and Bijou had to be as well. The two leopards had had sex for hours, over and over as their species did. They still had to make it back to the Inn before they could be seen.

It took only a few minutes to make it to the edge of the swamp and circle around to the lake where the back of Saria's property stretched out in front of them. Remy kept them inside the grove of trees as long as possible, testing the wind and air for signs of human activity before they sprinted across the open grass for the Inn itself.

He leapt up to the branches of the tree closest to her second-story balcony, showing her the way back to her room. The next leap took him onto the railing and then to the floor of the balcony. The smaller leopard followed him, head down, sides heaving, barely making it over the rail to flop down onto her side.

Remy shifted to his human form, opened the French door and stepped back to allow the small leopard into her bedroom. "Shift back, Blue," he encouraged. "Just let her go, take your form back."

The cat looked at him. There was something in her eyes that made him uncomfortable. He could shift fast enough to protect himself if she launched an attack. Her leopard was exhausted—hell—they both were exhausted. Bijou would barely be able to move once she returned to her human form. That first shifting was exhilarating, but it was definitely draining. Instead of launching herself at him, the small female leopard walked past him, nose in the air. He'd never seen an animal look so haughty and regal and dignified.

She went straight into the bathroom and the door slammed behind her. Remy let out his breath, unaware he'd even been holding it. He caught up a towel and wrapped it around his hips, sinking down into the comfortable chair facing the French doors. He felt every muscle in his body, sore and bruised from the fight with the other male and long sessions of rough sex. His leopard might not be sore, but it was different for him as a human.

He glanced toward the bathroom door. The silence went on for so long he stirred, determined to go to her, but then the water in the shower went on. He leaned back and pressed his fingers to his eyes. He needed sleep—a very long sleep, but there was no way it was going to happen until he talked to Bijou and found out why she was so angry with him.

The water seemed to go on forever. He sighed. He needed a shower as well. His muscles were going to get stiff sitting there; he had to make himself move. He stood up, stretched and went to the French doors to pull the drapes. Hand on the pull cord, he paused, movement catching his eye. Down by the edge of the swamp, something moved in the brush, just enough to stir the leaves the wrong direction.

Not wanting to draw the eye to him, he inched freeze-frame, much like his leopard counterpart, until he was back in the shadows, but able to see out the French doors. He

waited patiently, all fatigue forgotten, holding still and sending up a silent prayer that Bijou wouldn't choose that moment to walk into the room.

As he watched, a golden leopard thrust his head through
the brush to look up at the Inn. It stood there for a long while,
just staring, and scenting the air. Very carefully the leopard
emerged, until it was fully in the open, something none of
them did unless absolutely necessary—as Remy had done
in order to track Bijou. Robert Lanoux was up to something,
and it couldn't be good.

Remy had considered that the killer might be leopard.
He knew it was possible to disguise any odor, even from a
leopard. It had been done by one of his kind before and
everyone in the lair was aware of those gruesome killings.
Any shifter could hunt as a leopard and kill as a man or vice
versa. As he watched, the golden leopard reached high and
raked one of the trees near the Inn. He scent-marked several
others before whirling around and rushing back into the
safety of the swamp.

Remy frowned. Had Drake been home, he would have
taken Robert's actions as a challenge for leadership. To come
onto Drake's property and scent mark and leave rake signs
on trees would garner swift retaliation by the lair's leader—
and Robert had fought and lost to Drake before. In fact, it
was apparent that Drake could have killed him easily. So
why would Robert take such a chance? Nothing about Robert's actions made any sense. He knew Remy could kill him.
He knew Remy's leopard could as well.

The water went off abruptly, and Remy pulled the drapes,
darkening the room, certain that Robert had retreated to the
safety of his own property, but taking no chances. He swung
around to face Bijou as she emerged. Her hair was wrapped
in a towel and she wore a robe. There were shadows under
her eyes, bruises and love bites on her neck. He didn't think
it would have mattered if she'd come out wrapped in a gar-
bage bag, his body immediately reacted with urgent

demands—and he was damned tired. There was no getting around it and there was no hiding it.

He saw the flare of desire in her eyes, quickly veiled by her long lashes. She shook her head. "Don' you have a place to sleep?"

He glanced at the bed.

Bijou sighed. "It's not goin' to happen, Remy. I need sleep desperately, and right now, I don' like you very much."

"Why? What the hell did I do wrong?"

She recoiled for just a moment at his tone, and then her chin went up. "Figure it out. In the meantime, I'm goin' to bed to sleep, so go away."

"That's not goin' to happen, Blue." He threw her words right back at her. "I'm stayin' right here with you."

"You can't tell me Saria won't give you a place to sleep." Bijou stalked across the room to the edge of the bed, yanked down the covers, and tossed her robe aside.

Before she could hide, he saw the dark smudges on her body. She moved a little stiffly as if, like him, her body ached. He reached out and caught the covers, holding them open for her so she could crawl in the bed.

"I'm takin' a quick shower, and then I'll be sleepin' right next to you," he warned.

Bijou slid into bed and turned on her side, clearly savoring the feel of the mattress and soft sheets. "Do whatever, Remy. I'm too tired to argue. Just please don' wake me, because I don' want to have sex with you."

"I'm waitin' for lightning to strike you, woman," he replied.

She didn't even look at him, her lashes already veiling her eyes so he couldn't read her expression. It didn't matter. He knew. She craved him every bit as much as he did her.

Remy took a long shower, allowing the hot water to run over his tired muscles, washing his hair and going over everything that had happened between them. Had she still been angry with him for leaving her earlier? Most likely, although for a short while she'd seemed to have forgiven him.

He sighed and made his way back into the bedroom. Bijou clearly had fallen asleep and the towel she'd wrapped her hair in had come loose. Her long hair was everywhere, still damp. She looked young to him, too young for the kinds of things he'd done to her.

He slipped into the bed and wrapped his arm around her waist, pulling her into the protection of his body. She was warm and soft. He buried his face in her shoulder, kissing the bite marks along her neck. He laid back, content to just be with her, so close, his body tight against hers, his cock nestled between the firm globes of her buttocks and her breast in his palm. He drifted off to sleep with the scent of lavender surrounding him.

12

REMY woke to pounding on the door. He kept his eyes closed just that little bit longer, holding Bijou close to him, enjoying the warmth and softness of her body. Beside him she stirred, moving with a low groan of protest.

"Remy! Your cell phone is off. They need you at work right away," Saria called out. "There's been another murder."

He dropped his head on Bijou's shoulder and swore softly under his breath. "Not again. This can' be happenin' again to us."

The pounding continued.

"I hear you, Saria. I'm on it, thanks," he called out reluctantly.

Bijou rolled over in his arms, her gaze meeting his. Her eyes were such a deep, perfect color of blue. He knew he'd never get enough of falling into them and just drowning.

"I'm sorry, Blue, I'm goin' to have to go again. I know we need to talk . . ."

She sat up and pushed back her heavy fall of wild hair.

"Remy, I'm perfectly fine. I'm some kind of freak, but I'm fine. We have great sex and no attachment, but guess what, I'm still fine. I'm all grown up and I'm just as responsible for what happens every time we get together. The freaky change into an animal thing, I'm just goin' to ignore until I've had my coffee. I might give it some thought then."

He rubbed his palm down the length of her spine, needing the contact with her. "Great sex with no attachment? We're havin' a long talk about that misconception. But you make me laugh. You wake up grumpy, don' you?"

"Only when I've destroyed an entire room in my only friend's beautiful Inn with some kind of depraved sex and then turn into an animal and run around the swamp like a sex-starved cat hussy. Otherwise, no, I'm perfectly fine when I wake up."

He leaned over and brushed a kiss over her temple, keeping his lips against her skin. "And you aren't sex-starved anymore. We've taken care of that," he whispered.

"Says who?" Bijou asked. "Don' be thinkin' you're all that, Remy Boudreaux. You're not *that* good."

He trailed kisses to the corner of her mouth. "I know I'm that good. Stay the hell out of the swamp."

"Don' be tellin' me what to do. We might have sex once in a while but you *never* get to tell me what to do."

She managed a haughty expression even with his mouth moving on down her neck to the swell of her breast. He heard her breath catch in her throat, and she pushed him away. "Go, Remy. You need to catch whoever is murderin' people."

"Are you goin' to stay put this time?" He narrowed his eyes and pinned her with a hard gaze. It usually worked for him, but she gave a little sniff. "I mean it, Blue. I don' want to have to put every cop in the city and every sheriff in the surroundin' parishes on alert lookin' for you. If I have to do that, believe me, *mon pitit*, you'll be hauled back in handcuffs."

"Delightful." Sarcasm dripped from her voice. "And I'm not your *mon pitit*."

"You're my anything I need or want you to be." He leaned closer and licked her already taut nipple.

She shuddered, one arm circling his head. She didn't pull him away or push him closer, she simply stayed still, looking down at him.

His mouth closed over the temptation of her breast, pulling strongly, teeth scraping. He lifted his head and pressed his forehead against hers. "Leavin' you is difficult."

"So is murder. Get goin', Remy." Even as she commanded him, her fingers fisted in his hair and she pulled his head up.

Remy held his mouth inches from hers, looking straight into her eyes, so she'd know he meant what he said. "Don' you go off anywhere alone. Stay with Saria and stay inside until I get back."

She frowned at him. "Do you think I'm in danger?"

"I know you are."

"Then stop makin' everything an order and just ask nice like a normal person."

Remy opened his mouth and then closed it again with a little bite of his teeth. "Blue, please do me a favor and stay here with my sister and be safe while I go try to catch a murderer."

"Of course," Bijou replied. "I don' mind restin'. I've got a lot of thinking to do."

Remy breathed a sigh of relief, caught the nape of her neck and kissed her hard. She tried to hold herself away from him, but he refused to back off, deepening the kiss until she relaxed into him with a little sigh of resignation. He kept kissing her. She finally kissed him back. It took discipline to stop when all he wanted to do was be a part of her, to lose himself in her fire and addictive taste.

He pressed his forehead tight against hers. "Restin' is good. As much as you can. But no thinkin' about anything. You have to wait for me to talk this out. I know it was a shock to find out about your leopard, but there are more of us than you think. We have rules that govern us and you have to abide by them. Saria is leopard, and she can answer any questions you have until I get back. Clearly, it isn't something known and we don' ever talk about it to outsiders."

"Because you'd all be locked up as insane," Bijou pointed out pulling back. She reached for the sheet and pulled it up over her breasts in sudden modesty.

"Because *we'd* be hunted and killed," Remy corrected, needing her to understand the importance of absolute secrecy. He cupped her breasts through the sheet, making his claim on her and her body. Satisfaction flooded when his thumb found her nipple a hard peak.

Bijou recoiled subtly, a slight withdrawing, not quite pulling away from him, but he felt her retreat as a stab around his heart. He actually put his palm over his heart to ease the ache. He and Bijou had a long way to go, and he realized she had trusted him before, so easily, but now there was a space between them and he couldn't quite breach it. She definitely was his physically, but she'd moved away from him emotionally and he wanted her back.

He sighed as he slid out of bed. "I know you're confused about us and the leopard . . ."

She held up her hand and shook her head. "I'm not thinkin' about that yet. I'm just pretending you bit me and infected me with some rare blood disease and it will all go away."

She made him smile. No matter what, her sense of humor crept in at times when she was afraid or even angry. She had every right to be confused.

"Talk to Saria, *chere*, if you need questions answered before I can get back. This will take some time."

"I'm fine with it takin' time. Take all the time you need."

That wasn't her sense of humor. She was quite serious. She wanted him gone, just as she hadn't wanted him in her bed when they'd returned from the swamp. He went into the bathroom and pulled himself together as fast as possible, brushing his teeth and inspecting the rake marks across his side and chest. Robert had gotten in a few licks of his own and Remy hadn't even noticed. There were a few bad bruises, the consequences of a strong leopard hitting another one. Robert would wake up with far worse.

He returned to the bedroom fully dressed to find Bijou wrapped in her robe, sitting by the open drapes. "I didn't infect you with some rare blood thing, Blue. You do know that, don' you? Your *mere* had to be leopard."

Bijou deliberately pointed to the door. "Go." The word didn't come out as commanding as she would have liked.

Her treacherous heart melted every time she looked at him. She had to get over her adolescent hero worship. She'd been so silly, proving just how young and inexperienced she was by thinking he had real feelings for her. It was just sex between them, he'd admitted as much to her. She couldn't even claim he had his own physical attraction to her— -it was his leopard's fascination with her leopard, which somehow made the entire affair even seedier.

She looked around her at the cracks and long rake marks down the walls. Now it all made sense. She knew exactly what made those claw marks. She groaned and covered her face with her hands.

Remy was an amazing man. Pure and simple. He was intelligent, had a good sense of humor, loved and protected family and he made her feel beautiful and safe. He knew what her life had really been like, not the fairy tale everyone else wanted to believe. She'd been so happy when he'd acted interested in her and when he'd kissed her . . . There was no going back.

There was a hesitant knock on her door, then Saria's voice. "Are you hungry? I have a brunch made. Come get food."

Bijou wanted to crawl back in bed and pull the covers over her head, but she refused to be a coward. She couldn't blame Remy for her actions, and she couldn't pretend she hadn't had mad, crazy sex with him. Saria knew everything. She probably even knew about her wild romp in the swamp.

"I'll be down in five minutes," she called back.

She took a deep breath and held the sheet against her face for a moment, cooling the color, before tossing it aside in resignation and going to the dresser where her clothes were neatly folded. At least the dresser hadn't sustained too much damage, but she found herself blushing at the memory of Remy sitting her atop it, his mouth and hands driving her insane.

"Maybe it's the room," she muttered aloud, glaring as she looked around. "Some kind of strange Cajun curse on anyone stayin' here and they turn into the Rougarou. What other real explanation is there?"

She looked down at her body. She was bruised, but there was no fur. When she looked in the mirror her teeth looked like perfectly normal teeth. Bijou sighed and ran a brush through her thick, wild hair. That's what she got for going to bed with wet hair. There was no taming it, but on the other hand, she had hair, not fur. It was black, not covered in rosettes.

She walked down the stairs a little reluctantly. There were so many questions she had, but more importantly, she had to apologize to her friend and offer to leave if she'd been flirtatious inadvertently with Saria's husband. Whatever had put Saria on edge had to be her fault and she wanted to make certain they were okay. She didn't have a lot of real friends, and she definitely didn't want to lose Saria.

The moment she pushed open the door to the kitchen, the aroma of coffee hit her. She went straight to the coffee-pot and poured herself a mug, aware of Saria putting plates on the small table in the kitchen. It was far more intimate than the guest dining room and ordinarily, Bijou much preferred it, but knowing she had to apologize made her even more self-conscious than normal.

She turned slowly, leaning against the counter as she faced Saria.

Saria flashed an encouraging smile. "I'll get the food out of the warmer."

"Before you do, I just want to say how sorry I am. I know you've been upset with me and I honestly—I *swear* to you, Saria—I didn't realize how flirty and awful I've been. I'm not usually like that, I had no idea I was doin' anything that might disturb you or Drake."

Saria's eyebrow shot up. "What are you talkin' about?"

"You've been upset with me. Don' deny it. And you're not like that, so I had to have been doin' something to get you riled." Bijou ducked her head. "My father was some sort of sex addict and it colored my life. I didn't want to be like him so I stayed away from men. Bodrie always made sex seem so cheap. And then I came here and . . ." She shook her head as her eyes stung and burned and the lump in her throat grew so big she couldn't talk around it.

"Bijou, don' be silly. You're not at all like Bodrie. Not for one moment."

Bijou took a deep breath to try to stop herself from crying. "You didn't see me with Remy, Saria. I was a crazy person. Worse than Bodrie ever was. And I figured out that you must have noticed me flirtin' with Drake, but if I was, I didn't know it, I didn't mean to do it."

"Bijou, seriously, you didn' do anything at all. I'm pregnant. I told Drake this mornin' and he's on his way home." Her voice changed, the laughter fading. "I was jealous. You look so beautiful, and I had no idea I was pregnant. But your leopard was comin' into heat and my leopard was crazy, which made me that way." Her words came out in a little rush. "I didn't have any idea you were leopard or maybe I would have put the two together, but instead I had my jealous pants on. *I'm* the one who's sorry, Bijou. I hope you can forgive me. When you needed me most, I was actin' silly."

Bijou allowed herself to breathe again. "You're pregnant? That's so awesome, Saria."

Saria smiled. "It kinda is, isn't it? I'm still gettin' used to the idea."

Bijou carried her mug to the table and put it down so she could finish setting the table while Saria got the food. The relief she felt that everything between her and Saria had gotten back to normal was tremendous. She placed flatware carefully and added napkins before sitting down to finish her coffee.

"I turned into sex pants and that's far worse than jealous

pants," she admitted. "It was horrible. And we destroyed your room. I'll pay to have it fixed, Saria."

Saria burst out laughing. "My brother has already taken care of it. He and Drake can put it all back together. His leopard was the crazy one, rakin' the walls."

"Not exactly." Bijou felt compelled to be strictly honest. "I definitely helped, and there was no leopard involved."

"*You* are the leopard, Bijou," Saria pointed out. "I know it's difficult to take in . . ."

Bijou scowled at her. "Difficult?" She interrupted. "Insane. Impossible to believe. The memory is tryin' to fade. I'm tryin' to convince myself that there's some kind of Cajun curse on that room, or your brother bit me and instead of the werewolf, I became a leopard."

"When I was little, I followed my brothers into the swamp and saw them shift into leopards. I watched them. It was horrible because at first they stripped and who *ever* would want to see their brothers naked? I knew I'd be traumatized for life!"

Bijou scooped up fluffy scrambled eggs mixed with crabmeat and rice. "You're talkin' to the queen of trauma, remember? My father and his band and their groupies thought group sex in the livin' room was appropriate behavior."

"I suppose I can't top that," Saria agreed with a slight grin, "*but* I was still *horribly* traumatized."

Bijou gave a little smirk. "I'm certain I would have been too."

Saria laughed. "You little hussy. You'd only be lookin' at Remy."

Bijou's smile faded. "I know. He's all I've ever looked at, and a fat lot of good that did me. Maybe if I'd seen him shift into a leopard I would have run for the hills and never come back. How did you feel about the entire leopard business?"

"I was jealous. I wanted to be like them. The brotherhood, you know. They were so close and I always felt like an outsider," Saria admitted. "We used to talk about that, remember?"

Bijou shook her head. "You were crazy about your brothers. You thought they walked on water. You never complained about them."

"I didn't?" Saria added, as she added panfried trout to her plate.

Bijou took a hot beignet. "The first thing I did when I came back home was go to the Café Du Monde and order coffee and beignets. I missed them so much." She took a bite. "These are wonderful, Saria. You always were such a good cook. I guess all that cooking for your *pere* really helped. I'm not so good. We had a chef—well, several. Mostly women, and believe me, they didn't want me in their kitchen."

"It should have been *your* kitchen." Saria was indignant on her behalf.

Bijou shrugged. "That satisfaction was in knowin' they wouldn't last very long. Bodrie would get tired of havin' sex with them and the way they would cling to him. He'd fire them and hire the next pretty face." She added the trout to her plate as well. "I took a cookin' class once. It was a disaster. I'll have to try some of your recipes when I get in my own place."

Saria pressed her lips together for a moment, clearly contemplating how to word her next sentence, putting Bijou on alert. "You know my brother isn't goin' to let you out of his sight. He'll be expecting to share your place or have you move in with him."

Bijou forced a casual shrug. "Clearly we're not on the same page about that. Wild sex might be fun, Saria, but it will never be enough for me. I want a man to look at me and love me the way Drake does you. I've waited a long time for that. I can't help it if his leopard is crazy about mine and that's why he's so physically attracted to me."

Saria frowned, stopping with a forkful of eggs halfway to her mouth. "That's not why he's attracted to you. Where would you get an insane notion like that?"

"Straight out of his mouth," Bijou said, forcing herself to admit the truth and trying not to choke on the words. She picked up her coffee cup and took a sip just to give herself time to control the tears burning behind her eyelids. Damn Remy anyway for turning her into a weepy female.

"No way did he say that!"

Bijou nodded slowly. "He definitely told me last night, that it was all about the leopards and our uninhibited and wild and crazy sex was just an added bonus." She blinked rapidly and looked down into the coffee cup. Luckily, Saria made it strong. She preferred tea in the afternoons, but when she first woke up, nothing tasted better than Cajun coffee.

"My brother is an idiot. I love him, and in most things, he's right, but when it comes to women, I'm afraid he needs a good smack in the head."

Bijou forced another shrug. "He can' help the way he feels. And I can' help the way I do. The leopards are just goin' to have to get over it."

"Mmm, sweetie, they won't get over it. They bond life-time after lifetime. They seek each other out. If you think Remy is goin' to let you go easily, you've got another think comin'."

"I don' care," Bijou said, lifting her chin stubbornly. "I'm not goin' to be his sex toy. I'm not."

"Are you sayin' you don' have feelings for him?" Saria asked, curiosity in her voice.

"He's my biggest fantasy. He always has been. Maybe I even came back here to see if he was the man I always thought he was. No one else ever lived up to him, but it doesn't matter how I feel. Not now. I'm not goin' to play second fiddle to a leopard."

"It isn't like that," Saria denied.

"Not for you, because Drake actually loves you. I was foolin' myself that a man like Remy would fall in love with me."

"And why wouldn't he?" Saria demanded.

"He knows exactly who he is and what he wants," Bijou said. "The truth is, I'm just findin' that out about myself. It's taken me this long just to realize I don' want to tour or play huge venues. I don' want the kind of life where I have no home or family. I didn't even know until I came here that this was where home is to me."

"You said yourself that Remy is someone you admire and respect—that he's everythin' you want in a man and no one compares to him."

Bijou wasn't going to deny it. She didn't think she would find another man to compare with Remy. She found him the most beautiful man she'd ever come across. He had the heart to go with his looks.

"I'm so much younger than he is and he can't help but look at me like I'm still a kid. I don' blame him. I haven't exactly acted mature. I fell into his bed immediately. Probably every woman he wants does that. I'm nothin' special to him." She managed a smile. "He didn't fall in love with me, how dare him."

"Okay, that's not true. You're leopard, Bijou . . ." Saria trailed off realizing she'd just said the wrong thing.

Bijou nodded. "Sadly, I'm well aware of that. Do you really think my mother was leopard? How would she ever have met Bodrie?"

"Bodrie had a lot of fans from all over the world and he traveled extensively. We aren't the only lair, Bijou," Saria pointed out. "Most of them are in the rain forests. Drake came from one in Borneo, but there are other places. Everyone likes music, and Bodrie, no matter what anyone says about him, was a music man. She probably went to his concert and he somehow spotted her."

"I wouldn't doubt that, Bodrie could spot a beautiful woman miles out. And she was beautiful," Bijou conceded. "I saw a picture of her once. He had it in his room, by his bed, and I went in to get some money for lunch and it was there. He never took women into his bedroom, and he was really mad when he found me there."

"You never went back to his bedroom?"

"Of course I did. The picture wasn't there anymore. But I know there are things in the main mansion. I just haven't gone there. I was hopin' you'd go with me when I finally got up the nerve."

"Of course I'll go. Anythin' you need me to do," Saria said sincerely.

Bijou took a deep breath. She'd been skirting around the subject, but she was going to have to face the truth. "Tell me about being a leopard."

"Drake and Remy can answer questions better than I can, but actually, Bijou, it's really great. I've noticed we all prefer to stay near the swamp and bayous rather than the city, which is probably one of the reasons why you were driven to give up touring." She turned her head toward the door leading to the dining room. Her hand went up indicating the need for silence. "Someone else is here."

Bijou inhaled in an effort to catch the scent that may have alerted Saria to another's presence. Her leopard appeared to be fast asleep and was no help whatsoever, at least until the door to the kitchen was shoved inward. Bijou leapt from her chair and instinctively placed herself between the door and Saria.

The man didn't look familiar; she knew most of the locals—yet everyone had changed so much in the years she'd been gone—but he *smelled* familiar. He smelled like the golden leopard from the night before—but not quite.

"Dion." Saria stood up, her voice wary. "You didn't call, what's wrong?" She wasn't looking at the man in front of her, but staring past her toward the door. "Where's your brother? Where's Robert?"

The tension in the room went up until Bijou felt as if she was choking on it. Saria was very still, but her hands were curled, almost like claws and her dark brown eyes were now flecked with glittering gold.

Bijou realized Dion wasn't the threat, it was the one unseen. The golden leopard was there in the house, close. She moved away from Dion, circling the table to reach the block of knives Saria kept on the counter.

"Robert's here, Saria. We've come for help. We need Drake."

"You didn't call first," Saria pointed out. "There's just bein' polite. You can't just walk into my house and expect to be welcome."

"We didn't have time for that," Dion said brusquely. "Where's Drake?"

Bijou's hand closed over the handle of the knife, but didn't pull it loose. She stood with her body blocking her actions, just waiting, listening for sounds of the other male.

"Get out of my house, Dion, before I call my brothers."

The tension in the room was definitely escalating. Saria was pregnant and she had to be feeling vulnerable. Bijou hadn't thought of calling for help. She didn't have brothers or a family. She should have reached for her cell phone, not the knife. Silently cursing her own stupidity, she let out her breath and let go of the knife.

"I'm Bijou Breaux," she introduced herself. "I don' believe we met, unless it was back when we were still in school."

Dion turned cool eyes on her. "Oh, we met, but you were too cool to notice my brother or me."

"That's it," Saria snarled. "Get the hell out of my house, Dion. Right now. You're not goin' to break in to my home uninvited and then be rude to my friends. Get. Out."

"Saria, we've been friends a long time," Dion said, "I'm tellin' you, we need help."

"Then act like it instead of bein' a jackass, Dion," Saria replied, not backing down an inch. "I expect this behavior from Robert, but not you. One of you has to be reasonable, and you know it isn't goin' to be your brother. So tell him to either come in here and sit down at my table and explain to me what's goin' on, or both of you get out and wait for my husband."

There was such hard authority in Saria's voice that Bijou could have hugged her. She had that same air of command

and confidence that Remy and the rest of the Boudreaux exuded. Clearly she wasn't intimidated by Dion or his brother.

"His brother came after me last night in the swamp, Saria," Bijou advised her. "And he fought with Remy."

Dion's eyes took on a slow glow. "Robert's pretty beat-up," he agreed. "He was drunk last night and he did things he shouldn't have. We need to talk to Drake, or Robert's goin' to be in real trouble, Saria. He's a screwup sometimes, but he has a good heart. I'm askin' you, as our friend, to help us out."

Saria glanced at Bijou. "Remy beat him up? Was it a terrible battle? You must have been horribly frightened."

"I was terrified," Bijou admitted frankly. "I'd never seen anythin' like that in my life. Or even imagined it."

"Bijou was already marked," Saria said. "No other had a claim on her but Remy. You know the rules as well as Robert. Remy was within his rights to kill Robert last night, but he didn't. If you're comin' here to complain . . ."

Dion shook his head. "Can I get a cup of coffee?"

"If you make that fool of a brother come in like a normal person," Saria said. "Bijou won't bite him, if that's what he's afraid of."

Dion raised his voice. "Robert come in here, right now. If we're goin' to keep your sorry ass out of jail, you'd better try to get Saria on your side." He dragged a chair from the table and dropped into it, pressing the heel of his hand against his head.

"Remy isn't goin' to throw Robert in jail because he dared to challenge him for Bijou last night. The fight was between leopards, not humans," Saria pointed out, going to the cupboard and pulling out two more mugs. She handed them to Bijou, who was closest to the coffeepot.

The kitchen door pushed inward slowly and Robert slunk in, walking carefully, hunched over, his face swollen and black and blue. He kept his arms in close to his sides as if protecting broken ribs. He didn't look at either woman, but gratefully took the chair his brother toed around for him.

"Milk? Sugar?" Bijou asked, feeling a little more solicitous now that she could see Robert wasn't a real threat. Remy's leopard had really done injury to him.

Both men shook their heads. Even when she set the coffee in front of him, Robert still didn't look up, but appeared more miserable than ever.

"We really need Drake, Saria. He's the only one who can prevent Remy from arrestin' Robert," Dion said. "We can ask for him to be the judge."

"He's on his way back home," Saria said, "but it's goin' to take some time. So if you want help, you've got me and that's it. Have some brunch and stop being so melodramatic. Tell me what happened and let's see what we can do. I can call Drake and let him know there's a problem, and he can figure it out on his way home."

Robert stirred, winced and tried to drink from swollen lips. He cleared his throat several times, glancing warily at his brother.

Dion scowled at him. "Spit it out, Robert, if you've got somethin' to say."

"There was one other thin' I didn't mention, but you'd better know before Drake gets home." His guilty gaze flicked to Saria's face and then moved quickly away.

Dion stiffened. "What the hell else have you done?" he demanded.

Robert hunched more. "I was drunk, Dion."

He sounded whiny, and Bijou took the chair closest the counter where the knives were. She'd calculated the distance and in her mind practiced drawing the chosen blade over and over until she was certain she could do so smoothly. It was evident that Saria had confidence in herself and that she knew both men very well—she spoke to them in a tone reserved for close friends one could get angry with—but Bijou didn't trust anyone. Saria was pregnant, and as far as she was concerned, the two men hadn't left when Saria told them to. She would sit and listen, but she'd be on alert every single moment.

"I came here last night," Robert blurted out. "Remy had pissed me off. I was hurt, but not feelin' it so much because of the drinkin' . . ."

"You know we can't drink," Dion interrupted, fury gathering in his eyes. "*Drake* lives here with his wife. He's the leader of our lair. What were you thinkin'? If Drake had been here, were you plannin' on challenging him? He'd wipe up the floor with you. You'd already gotten your ass handed to you by Remy, and you were damned lucky you weren't killed, but challenging Drake is just plain stupidity, especially after the beatin' you took."

Saria stirred as if she might say something, but Dion slammed his coffee cup down on the table and leaned toward his brother. His eyes were all glowing now, cat's eyes, his temper rising to the surface.

"You're not getting' me killed, Robert. Drake is savin' this lair. Savin' all of us, and I've had enough of your drinking and your lousy friends and the trouble you're always in. If you think I'm goin' to be turning on Drake or defendin' you to him, you're dead wrong."

Robert kept his head down, portraying an absolutely miserable man, but Bijou wasn't buying it. He was obviously good at manipulating his brother. Dion felt responsible for him, and Robert was taking his outburst as another lecture, not an absolute vow.

Saria pushed the warmer containing beignets toward Robert. "What did you do here, last night, Robert? Perhaps if you just tell us what happened, we can figure this all out."

"I went to *her* club last night," Robert said, making it an accusation—a whiny one at that. He jerked his thumb toward Bijou but still didn't look at her. "She's still as hoity-toity as she always was. She passed right by me without sayin' a word."

Bijou gave a little sniff. "I'm so like that."

Saria coughed, holding her hand over her mouth. Dion glanced at Bijou and then away. Faint color crept up his neck. Bijou wasn't certain what that was all about. He'd insulted her the moment he'd seen her and yet he refused to look at her for more than a second or two. Each time he did, he looked red and uncomfortable.

Robert glared at her. "I told my friends I knew you, that you grew up here, but they didn't believe me. They took bets."

"What friends?" Saria asked. "We all grew up in the same lair . . ."

"*Not* leopard," Robert snarled. "I don' hang out with just leopards like the rest of you. I have a life and lots of other friends."

Dion snorted. "They aren't friends when they're gettin' you in trouble all the time, Robert. You get stinkin' drunk with them and they put you up to all sorts of things."

"You're just jealous because I have friends," Robert countered. "You think you're so high and mighty, Dion, but you slave away in that stupid office of yours and you're jealous because I don' have to."

"You might not work, but you always have money, don' you, Robert," Dion accused. "Wherever you're gettin' it, you certainly don' want to admit where it comes from, which means you're ashamed. You know damn well you shouldn't be doin' whatever it is you are."

"It's none of your business," Robert whined. "I don' have to tell you how I make my money."

Saria heaved a very loud sigh. "Robert, focus. I need to know what you did when you came here last night."

Robert ducked his head again, his defiant gaze sliding away quickly. "It was Remy's fault." He lifted his head and glared at Bijou. "And *hers*. They got my leopard riled up and I couldn't control him last night. First he went after her, and when Remy went so crazy, hitting me from behind when I wasn't even doin' anything, my leopard just lost it."

"I see. None of this is your responsibility at all," Saria said.

Robert didn't seem to notice the sarcasm in her voice. "No, it isn't. Look, I did a few drugs with the guys. Nothin' big, not like heroin, but my brain was a little scrambled. So after the snotty woman lost me the bet and I owed big-time, I drank a little on top of it and that made it difficult to control my leopard. All she had to do was acknowledge me," he said. "That's not askin' so much, is it?"

"I'm hearin' a lot of excuses, Robert, but nothin' I need to hear," Saria persisted.

"My leopard wouldn't calm down and he came here last night and raked a tree and marked the yard up, that's all." The confession came out in a hurried rush.

There was a long silence. Clearly Saria was horrified. Bijou didn't quite understand why Robert's deed was so horrible so she remained very quiet, just waiting.

"You challenged Drake for leadership?" Saria asked, incredulous. "Are you crazy?"

Robert hastily shook his head. "No. No way. I'm tellin' you, my leopard was insane with the smell of a female hussy, and she was flirtin' with me. It wasn't my fault. You have to tell Drake that. You have to explain about Remy jumpin' me."

"Remy did *not* jump you," Bijou snapped, unable to stop herself. "You charged him. I was there, and you can't exactly pretend you're innocent when there was an eyewitness."

Robert refused to look at her, instead looking to his brother. "She'd lie for Remy. She'd do anythin' for him. She's his whore . . ."

Saria slapped him hard. "Get out of my house now. Dion, get him out of here before I call Drake and tell him the whole sorry story."

Robert howled, grabbing his already bruised face. "You can't throw me out. You can't. Remy already hates me and he's goin' to come in here and accuse me of murder. Last night. I was there. He'll know I was there and he'll arrest me just to get me out of his way." He glared at his brother. "I told Dion everything and he betrayed me. He called it in anonymously, but now everyone will know I was there."

13

Remy stared at the body hanging from the tree there in the swamp. They were very close to Saria's property, at the very point where he and Bijou had been last night. The murder had to have taken place no more than an hour after they'd passed through the area, if that. He tried to remember if he'd heard or scented anything unusual as he moved closer to the crime scene. His leopard had been concentrating on only one thing—his mate in heat. He hadn't been the least bit interested in anything else.

He took two more steps and immediately recognized the man. Ryan Cooper had died hard. He'd been alive when he'd been cut open, the noose tight around his throat, restricting his breathing but not doing its job before the bone harvester had begun carving him up. Remy hadn't liked Cooper, but no one deserved to die this way.

It seemed a little surreal that just hours earlier he'd been angry with the man for taunting Bijou and then daring to lay his hands on her and now, not only was he dead, but he'd died so close to where the leopards had been running. Was it really a coincidence?

"This is ugly," Gage said. "Really ugly. Cooper was alive for a while."

"The altar is, as usual, immaculate, but the blood spatter and pools go everywhere else." Blood ran in ribbons and streams, all over the ground, soaking into the vegetation and coloring all the grasses a dark red. The ground looked macabre, a hellish nightmare of a stained leaves and dark, twisted branches.

Remy crouched down and studied the ground. Something was off. He'd been at four similar crime scenes years earlier and Pete Morgan's murder in the swamp just days earlier. They'd all been identical other than the strange seven-knot string found in the bowl of Pete's blood. Each crime scene had been immaculate, not a single footprint, no hair or fiber to be found. There were no prints on anything, not the rocks making up the frame of the altar or anywhere else. But . . .

Remy stiffened. "Gage." He glanced up at his brother, waited until Gage made his way over and very subtly, covering the gesture, pointed to the smudged, partial print hidden among the leaves.

Gage closed his eyes briefly. "Leopard," he mouthed.

Remy nodded and indicated with his chin the few hairs stuck in the blood on a cypress trunk. "One of ours, and I think I know who," he whispered softly. "Damn him for this. It's goin' to cause a huge mess. Every hunter from here to hell and back is goin' to be in the swamp with guns."

"And every missin' animal and strange death will be blamed on the Rougarou. We'll be getting' calls every night from nervous drunks and people alone to go check out their homes for them," Gage added. "Who?"

"Last night, Robert Lanoux challenged me for Bijou. My leopard drove his off and I made certain he'd feel his lesson for the next week or two, but it didn't deter him at all. Later, he showed up at the Inn and left a challenge for Drake for leadership of the lair."

"Is he out of his mind?" Gage asked, disbelief in his voice. "Robert can't take Drake. He's never been great in battle. In fact, I thought Drake had discussed Robert goin' to Borneo to learn a few skills."

"He refused to go," Remy said. "Drake didn't push it, because there was no proof he was doin' anything that could put the lair in harm's way."

"Could he be our killer?" Gage asked. "He was pretty tight with Cooper. They drank a lot together, and Dion suspected they might be runnin' drugs or doing something else illegal because Robert has a *lot* of money, but wasn't workin'. He questioned Robert about the money and Robert refused to talk to him about it. Dion was pretty worried about what he might have gotten himself into."

"No way is Robert capable of doin' this," Remy disagreed. "He'd puke his guts out. He's still a kid, a stupid one, wantin' to take the easy way out, but he's no murderer. Not like this. Whoever is doin' this is as cold as ice. Robert is a hothead. He would no more plan ahead and have his equipment ready and a way to keep from leavin' evidence behind, like this killer. I don' believe for one minute that Robert did this, but I wouldn't mind arresting his sorry butt and throwin' him in jail for a good long time."

"Leopards don' do well caged," Gage said uneasily.

"Just what that little bastard could use, a good lesson in what could happen if he continues his ways." Remy sighed and looked once more to the ground and the proof that said a leopard had been on the scene. "It does worry me that we can't catch the scent. The killer should be sweatin'."

"The odor of fear is coverin' everything else," Gage pointed out.

"That's part of it," Remy admitted reluctantly, "but it shouldn't completely mask the killer's scent from a leopard. If he isn't leopard, and I see no sign that he is . . ."

"Until now. We can't be certain this wasn't Robert," Gage said. "If you're wrong, then we've got another killer in our lair. Our leopards are definitely dangerous, and when one goes wrong, it can be very bad."

"Iris Mercier was able to mask her scent when she made kills," Remy said. "Every leopard in the lair became aware of it after she was killed. None of these kills feel like leopard, not even this one, but Charisse was still workin' on the product that consumed all scents. She did tell me she was far more careful since her mother had used her work to get away with killin', but it's possible someone managed to get ahold of her experiments."

Gage studied Remy's face. "Your gut is sayin' this isn't leopard."

"I don' believe it is, but Robert's managed to muddy the water. I've got to call Drake and tell him to get back here now. We'll need him when forensics identifies this as leopard fur."

"Obviously planted by the killer," Gage suggested. "Who would ever find a leopard runnin' around here?"

"Drake will have to order everyone not to shift for a while. We can't take any chances with the locals thinkin' the Rougarou is haunting the swamp. The last time two people shot their neighbors, convinced they were shifters," Remy said.

Remy stood up slowly, looking around. "There was obviously a party of some sort right over there." He skirted the crime scene and made his way to the flat spot where beer cans were strewn everywhere. There was an empty tequila bottle as well as a Jack Daniels bottle.

"He must have come here with his friends."

Remy and Gage exchanged a long look.

"Jean and Juste Rousseau," Gage said.

"And also Robert Lanoux," Remy said. "He was here partyin' with the Rousseau brothers and their other friends. At least three others, probably the same ones who sat together at the club."

"Funny how the Rousseau brothers keep turnin' up," Gage said. "I'm likin' this group for the break-ins."

"And they definitely were partyin' with Alan Potier. He was the third victim four years ago. The brothers were with him when they were partyin' behind the school. Potier was a local boy found in the tree just past the football field there, that giant oak tree. He and the Rousseau brothers had been drinkin' under the bleachers that night. They claimed they passed out and when they woke up, Potier was gone. They walked home from the school and never saw Potier alive again."

"You didn't smell a lie?"

Remy shook his head. "They were nervous, but in a murder investigation, most people are. I looked at them for a while, so clearly I wasn't completely convinced—it seemed a little strange to me that they wouldn't notice the body in the tree. The tree was a good distance away from them, but it still seemed unlikely to me that they wouldn't have seen the body. Wouldn't you look around for a friend if you passed out when he was there and then when you woke up, he was gone? At least take a little look around?"

Gage shrugged. "We would, Remy, but we're talkin' about the Rousseau brothers. I don' think they've ever been responsible in their lives. They like stirrin' the pot. And don' ever underestimate them, they have high IQs. I absolutely believe they have a little ring of thieves they control and they case the places and send their crew in to do the actual robberies."

"And the beatin's?" Remy asked.

"It's them. Just like you know this murderer isn't leopard, I know the Rousseau brothers are masterminding the break-ins." Gage studied the body, his face expressionless. Clearly he had to fight to separate himself from the victim. Gage had talked with Ryan Cooper yesterday afternoon. Cooper had been drinking then. The Rousseau brothers hadn't been with him, but his two companions had been sitting in the club with the brothers and Robert.

"Robert's goin' to be worried sick that either Drake or I

will kill him. He'll tell Drake whatever Drake wants to know, includin' everything he knows about the robberies if he's involved, and I'm bettin' he is," Remy said in an effort to help distract his brother. "If you can get the Rousseau brothers on that charge, and they have anythin' to do with this, it will buy us time to find evidence against them for the murders."

"Robert's many things, but he's no snitch. And he's got a sense of loyalty when it comes to his friends."

"Too bad he doesn't have the same loyalty to our lair," Remy said. "In any case, if he won't give them up to Drake, I'll get involved, and then he'll be headin' out to Borneo. The lair there will teach him a few needed lessons."

"You're a bloodthirsty man, Remy," Gage said, and then looked down at the ground. "I shouldn't have said that. Not here."

Remy forced himself to look at Ryan Cooper's body hanging from the tree limb. The body looked very much like the others he'd seen. He switched his attention to the altar. The rocks were set precisely with the same meticulous care he recognized. Leaves, and other ornamental rocks and shells were set in a pattern. The strange string of seven knots was set in the bowl of Cooper's blood. The heart was in place. The altar was exact and meticulously perfect. Yet . . .

Something was off. Not the partial leopard print. Not the fur. Something about the crime scene was just wrong. But what? Remy frowned as he paced first one way and then the other, studying it from all angles. He held up his hand for silence. All motion and whispered chatter from the others stopped. Even the medical examiner stepped back. They'd worked with Remy and trusted him implicitly. That was a good feeling, but at times like now, an added pressure.

He just knew something didn't quite fit. He inhaled, trying not to choke on the terrible scent of sheer terror and the overwhelming stench of blood and death. His gaze continually strayed back to the body. It was there. He was missing something important, and it was there on Ryan Cooper's torn body.

He took several steps back, circled and came back. Each time he attempted to examine the altar, his attention was pulled back to the body. It was there. It had to be, but . . . Remy stepped even closer, peering at the wounds.

"Look at his neck and throat, Gage, tell me what you see? The way the bones were taken so carefully. Try not to see Cooper, just the way he was killed."

Gage shook his head, but he stepped up close. The medical examiner, Dr. Louis LeBrun, moved closer as well.

"He's finally made his first mistake," Remy said. "He got a little careless."

LeBrun and Gage looked at each other, both looking blank.

"Remy," LeBrun said, "there's nothin' careless about this man's work. He's absolutely meticulous. He could be a surgeon the way he removes those bones."

"Yes, but he carves the victims up without a single thought, like they aren't human. He doesn't care what kills them. He doesn't even notice. He's never noticed. The victim is his donor and nothing more to him. I never got the feeling he knew the person or even that he recognized his victim had a family or a life. The murder itself was messy and unorganized. Only the harvesting of the bones matters to him, so he's meticulous about that. I doubt that ordinarily he notices when or even if his victim dies."

The medical examiner swung around and stared at the body. "The killer was much more careful at first not to hit a major artery. He didn't slash him up or rip him open like he always has in the past. Look here on his neck and throat. The rope burns are numerous, as if our killer tightened just enough to hold him still and then released him when he was too close to death."

Remy nodded. "He made it personal. He knew Ryan Cooper."

"I'll have the boys pick up the Rousseau brothers and have them taken to your headquarters, Remy, so you can interrogate them."

"Make certain to keep them comfortable," Remy said. "We don' want them to think we suspect them of the murders. We want them thinkin' we just want to question them because they were one of the last to see him alive."

"And Robert?"

Remy shook his head. "We'll wait for Drake and then question him. Bring in Tom Berlander and Brent Underwood as well, but put them all in separate rooms. I don' want them comin' up with the same story. I'm bettin' they partied last night in the swamp with Cooper and the Rousseau brothers."

"Are you goin' to find Robert?" Gage asked.

Remy nodded. "I'll keep him under wraps until Drake gets back. I don' want him tryin' to take off, not after finding he was here at the crime scene and he didn't even call it in."

"We're tryin' to find out who did," Gage said.

"Probably Dion. Robert would have gone runnin' for his brother to fix his mess. That's what he's always done."

"He's gotten so much worse since Saria married Drake," Gage pointed out. "I'm bettin' he thought he'd someday wind up with her."

Remy's hand closed over his gun, almost a reflex action. He didn't even realize he'd done it until he felt the familiar butt of his gun in his palm. "Over my dead body. That boy has a lot of growin' to do before he can be with one of our women."

Gage hesitated, and then he spoke in a rush. "You've got to make certain that these killin's aren't in any way connected to Bijou."

Remy scowled at his brother. "What the hell are you talkin' about? Bijou was with me last night. There is no possible way . . ."

Gage held up his hand to cut off his brother's rising temper. "Damn, Remy, sometimes you're as mean as a damned snake. I don' think Bijou killed anyone, but she was there at the first scene with Saria and now this one. You just have to make certain there's no connection."

"There was no connection to the first four murders four years ago," Remy snapped.

"Don' bite my head off, Remy. She was in New Orleans four years ago. She came back for her father's funeral. I'm just sayin' you're too close to this with her and aren't considerin' even the remote possibility. Just to be safe. Maybe she knew the other victims."

Remy sighed. He detested that Gage was right. He couldn't ignore any possibility, no matter how crazy it sounded. "Maybe, but she would have said."

"Four years ago, she wasn't thinkin' about murder, Remy. And she hightailed it out of here the moment she buried her father. She might not have even known there was a murderer carvin' people up."

Remy nodded. He didn't want to question Bijou about the murders or any of the victims. He'd already blown it with her so many times he was afraid if he kept making mistakes with her, she'd get it in her head to take off. She had enough money to go anywhere in the world and if she wanted to disappear, he had no doubt that she could make it happen.

"It's a long shot, but I'll ask. Right now, let's concentrate on the Rousseau brothers and their friends. I'd also like to know the whereabouts of Rob Butterfield, her manager, and his little enforcer friend Jason Durang last night. If they don' have a good alibi, I'll be wantin' to talk to them as well. And, Gage . . ." Remy waited until his brother turned back to face him. "If they alibi each other, and no one else can corroborate, that doesn't count as a decent alibi."

Gage sighed. "I was hopin' this would never happen again. Especially on our turf."

"I'm with you there, Gage," Remy admitted. "This is one sick man. I thought it was bad enough when his victims were nothin' but meat to him, but he stayed cold as ice, even through the butcherin' of Cooper alive. Nothin' else changed. His hands weren't shakin'. He didn't leave prints or any other evidence behind. But he knew Cooper. And he had some kind of grudge against him."

"Or maybe Cooper decided he didn't like bein' told to break into old folks' homes and beat them up. Maybe he'd had enough and was goin' to start talkin' to us," Gage suggested.

"Or he was drunk and was talkin' smack," Remy said. "That's more likely. If you're right about the Rousseau brothers, they'd take action."

"Or kill him for kicks," Gage suggested.

LeBrun shook his head. "This wasn't for kicks. Whoever carves those bones wasn't doin' it for the fun of it."

"Is there a possibility that there are two of them?" Remy asked LeBrun. He respected the man. Louis LeBrun wasn't leopard, but he was very good at his job and he didn't miss much.

"Of course," LeBrun said, "but whoever harvested the bones is an expert. It has to be the same man every time. One could be doin' the hangin' while the other does the carvin', but believe me, Remy, the carver is the same every single time. There's no mistakin' his work."

"The murder itself is messy and careless," Remy said, "but the harvester is meticulous. If you look at that altar, I'd have to say the same man put that together, payin' special attention to every detail. There's never one single drop of blood on his altar other than the bowl of blood provided by his victim, and if you look at the bowl, that's not even messy."

LeBrun nodded. "I don' know how you're goin' to solve this one, Remy." He swept his hand toward the body. "With all this every time he kills, you'd think he'd leave some forensic evidence behind, but the crime scene, in spite of the blood everywhere, is pristine, isn't it?"

Remy steadfastly refused to look down at the partial leopard print. Forensics would find it, that and the fur, but he preferred not to help them. He and Drake needed time to warn the leopard community and get damage control underway before the news broke. He would suggest the fur and print were easy enough to fake, and clearly no animal had committed such a crime, not even the legendary Rougarou.

"Call me the minute you have anythin' at all for me," Remy instructed LeBrun. "I'm headin' back to the station."

LeBrun nodded, and Remy abruptly turned away. Gage fell into step beside him as he made his way to the sheriff's boat. The moment he was in range to use his cell phone, Remy called Drake and told him everything that had transpired.

"Drake's already on his way back. Robert and Dion are at the Inn with Saria and Bijou," Remy told Gage. "I don' like that one little bit. I can't get back there to protect Bijou, and neither can you."

Gage grinned at him. "I get your meanin'. The Lanoux boys are about to meet up with Lojos, Dash and Mahieu. They'll be enjoyin' their time with our brothers while we take care of business."

"You know Saria won' like it," Remy said.

"Which is why you're makin' me make the call," Gage guessed. "But that's all right. I figure a man should be in trouble with only one woman at a time. From the way you're tiptoein' around I'd say your lady was truly aggravated with you. And probably for good reason."

"Why would you say that?" Remy demanded.

"Because you're smooth with all the ladies you don' care about and a bit of a jackass with the ones you do care about."

Remy glared at him, although he had a suspicion Gage's observation might have some truth to it. "I'm smooth."

Gage snorted. "You're an idiot, and I say that with love in my heart." Dramatically he placed his hand over his heart, his eyes laughing at his brother.

"I've got a gun," Remy reminded. "You're pushin' the borders of my leopard's ability to rein in his temper."

"You blame that poor leopard for everythin'. You're the one with the foul temper. Is that what happened? Did you manage to lose your temper and yell at that poor woman?"

"No, I didn't yell at her. Although I thought about it. She could make Mother Teresa angry."

Gage snorted again. "You're so clueless, bro. Seriously. You've got the catch of the century and leave it up to you to blow it."

"You're the one who said she'd leave." Just the thought of Bijou leaving him, let alone saying the words aloud, sent a stabbing pain through the region of his heart. He knew his brother was teasing him, probably crowing because Remy had always attracted women easily and Bijou wasn't quite the easy conquest he'd expected. More, he hadn't expected to be consumed by her. He couldn't stop thinking about her. She was there with every breath he drew and the moment he scented lavender, his body reacted with urgent, hot demand.

"Her leopard won' let her run too far and you know it. She might try, and if she's smart, she'll definitely give you a run for your money . . ."

"That's it. You're about to go the hospital and have a bullet dug out of your ass."

Gage burst out laughing. "You're plannin' on shooting me in the butt?"

"Well, it's the only safe place, and it might be a bit embarrassin' if you get a cute nurse, which, for the record, would be an added bonus."

"I did say you were about the meanest man alive," Gage pointed out.

Remy tried a blacker scowl to intimidate his younger brother. Ever since Bijou had come back home, Gage had been having way too much fun tweaking him.

"Just get the boys to the Inn fast," Remy said. Otherwise, there would be no keeping his mind on interrogating the Rousseau brothers or Bijou's manager and his assistant. He had to put her out of his mind and tell himself she was perfectly safe with Saria and his brothers.

She seemed so fragile to him. Saria was small, but she could take care of herself in any situation. Bijou needed . . . care. He just had to convince her that she did.

He drove back to the station house, refusing to give in to the temptation to call Bijou just to hear her voice and know she was all right. And he absolutely refused to believe he *needed* to hear her voice. It was just that with Robert going to the Inn, she might be scared and needing to hear *his* voice.

He should probably call her to reassure her that his brothers were on the way. She'd feel much safer and calmer knowing he was thinking of her and making certain his brothers would protect her while he had to be away from her.

Satisfied that it was Bijou who needed to hear from him, and not the other way around, Remy parked in front of the station and whipped out his cell phone. She was under *Blue* and he found himself smiling for no reason at all. His thumb traced over her name before he could stop the automatic reaction. He looked around to make certain no one had seen that involuntary, silly reaction, more of a caress than anything else. If Gage or one of his other brothers had witnessed that incredibly ridiculous moment, he'd never live it down.

There was no response on Bijou's cell. He left three voice mails and texted her three times, still to no avail. Swearing under his breath, he strode into the station house, straight to his office. Apparently everyone saw his face and quickly looked away, not greeting him. He picked up the phone and called the Inn.

Saria answered.

"Where the hell is Bijou? And why isn't she takin' my calls?" He demanded, furious, worried, and more than a little inclined to drive straight out to the Inn and the hell with interrogating anyone but his stubborn woman. "What the hell is wrong with women, anyway? How difficult is it to pick up the damn phone?" His voice went low, mean and gravelly, a sign his leopard's temper was turning into a rage.

"She's sittin' right here, Remy." Saria's voice became soothing. "Her phone must be upstairs. What's wrong?"

Okay, now he really looked like an idiot. He hadn't considered she didn't have her phone on her. And why didn't she? "What the hell use is a cell phone if you don' have it on you? That woman is so damned difficult."

"Is she?" There was laughter in Saria's voice that only served to make him angrier.

"I was worried about her, Saria. I knew Robert went there, and last night he challenged me for her. Then he challenged

Drake. He's a complete idiot and can't be trusted. She's such a fragile little thing and I knew she'd be really frightened." He forced himself to sound reasonable when he still wanted to drive out to the Inn and see for himself Bijou was alive and well.

"Fragile?" Saria snorted. "You should have seen her reachin' for the butcher knife when Dion refused to leave and we knew Robert was in the house but he refused to come out where we could see him. She even jumped up and put herself between Dion and me to protect me."

His belly knotted up. "Is she crazy?" His voice dropped low. His scary voice. He even scared himself a little when he used that tone. He never knew exactly what he'd do. Robert and Dion Lanoux were going to get a visit from him in the dead of night and both would learn manners. No one threatened his mate or his sister. And certainly not in the home of the leader of the lair, or on Boudreaux property. They'd be lucky if they lived through the next night.

"I'd just told her I was pregnant, Remy. You would have been proud of her. I know you're probably really upset with Dion and Robert but . . ."

"*Don'* defend them," he snapped, cutting her off. Saria had always had a soft spot for the two brothers. "They have to live by lair rules just like the rest of us. They don' get to go into your home scarin' you or threaten' you and not leavin' when you tell them to."

"I know," Saria said, all reasonable, which only pissed him off more, "But there were extenuating circumstances."

"They're men, Saria. I know Robert was at the crime scene. He stupidly left a partial paw print and even some fur. Forensics will find it, and what do you think is goin' to happen to all of us? We'll be hunted. No one will be safe lettin' their leopards run and if we can' shift and they're caged up, you know what will happen. Robert's a man. He needs to take responsibility instead of whinin' to his brother and then whinin' to you."

He truly wanted to beat Robert Lanoux within an inch

of his life. There would be chaos in the lair and Drake had worked hard to get everyone under control. Everyone who lived or worked in or around the swamp and bayou would be under scrutiny by their neighbor.

"They're waitin' here for Drake. Robert knows he screwed up and to be honest, I think Dion's had it with him. I put them in the sittin' room."

"Are the boys there?"

"They arrived just a few minutes ago."

He could tell by her voice that she was somewhere between annoyance and laughter. "I do believe Robert is properly intimidated, which I hope, for your sake, was your motivation. I can take care of myself and so can Bijou."

He wasn't touching that one. Anything he said could get him in trouble with his independent and touchy sister. Of course his brothers were there to protect both women. Saria was pregnant, wasn't she? He admitted silently to himself that he would have sent the boys pregnancy or not. "Put Bijou on, please." At least he remembered his manners. Saria could turn stubborn fast and he wasn't taking any chances.

There was a moment of silence and then Bijou answered. "Hello."

His heart did some strange nonsensical bullshit that alarmed him. Maybe it was time for a checkup. Worse, that sultry, bluesy tone got under his skin and sent an electrical charge snaking through his bloodstream.

"Are you all right?"

"I was until your brothers showed up. They're all starin' at me and grinnin' like idiots."

The laughter in her voice sent a shaft of relief spiraling through him. "Don' feel alone, they've taken to doin' the very same thing to me," he admitted. "Robert didn't hurt you, did he?"

"No, of course not."

"I'm sorry I can't be there to get him the hell out of there."

"I think what you're doin' is far more important than

bein' here at the moment. I'm sure your brothers will insist
he go if he makes any threats." There was a small silence
and then she made a small sound. "Um, Remy . . ." She
broke off, hesitant, and her voice had dropped nearly to a
whisper.

He liked that she was connecting them intimately
whether she knew it or not. "What is it, Blue?" he prompted.

"When Robert came in, I felt her. You know. *Her*. It was
a little disconcertin'."

He stopped himself from grinding his teeth. "Did your
leopard act happy to see him? Did you get that feelin'?" He
was killing Robert Lanoux if her leopard dared to even en-
tertain the notion of accepting the idiot. He couldn't imagine it. She'd mated with his leopard, but Bijou was so
confused, maybe her leopard was as well.

"No, she was definitely not happy. And I found myself
fightin' to maintain. Is that normal? Quite frankly, I felt a
little scared that I might not be able to control her. I don'
think anyone noticed."

"That's good, *chere*, and very normal." He tried to keep
the relief out of his voice and stay neutral and informative,
as matter-of-fact as possible. Deep inside he was rejoicing.
"Your leopard is mated to mine and she won' tolerate any
other male interested in her. I know I've got a lot more to
explain to you, but just so this makes sense, we find our
mates over and over from one life to the next. At least, that's
the way it's supposed to work. Our leopards recognize one
another, even if it's the first cycle of life. I promise we'll
discuss more when I get there."

He glanced at his watch. "Unfortunately, I don' know
how long this will take, but when Drake gets close, he'll
give me a call. I'll have to come there to talk with Robert
and Dion."

"Remy," she whispered. "You wouldn't really kill him,
would you? He keeps actin' like you want to kill him."

He sighed. He'd told himself he wouldn't lie to her. Not
ever. Not about anything. But why the hell did she have to

ask the complicated questions? "My leopard would definitely kill his if he persisted in tryin' to get to you. So, yes, he'd be dead." He had skirted the issue, blaming his cat, but he'd told the truth. His leopard would kill Robert's in a heartbeat if it found the golden leopard anywhere near Bijou's female.

"That's just a little scary."

"I know, Blue. I know this all must not only be shockin' but very frightenin' as well. I've got to go after this murderer, but I swore to you I'd get you through this and I will. Just please stay put for me. Don' go off anywhere alone. I need to ask you a few questions though, about some things pertainin' to the murders, just because the victim was at your club and harassin' you."

"Would it help if I come there?" Bijou asked. "I wouldn't mind gettin' away from here. If you don' want me to come alone, I can ask one of your brothers to drive me there. My car's a wreck anyway."

"That might be a good idea," Remy said. He knew it wasn't, not with all the suspects there, and all the work he had to do, but he wanted to see her. It was definitely want, not need. He'd never admit to needing to see her. His leopard was all growly because he was worried, that was all. "Have Mahieu drive you. He's got a brain and isn't crazy in a car."

"I'll be there as soon as I can," Bijou said.

There was relief in her voice. Was she glad to get away from Robert and Dion, or did she want to see him?

"Just wait for me in my office. I'll come out when I'm able."

"Sounds good to me. I've gotten a couple of text messages from my manager. He wants to meet with me and discuss some business. I've been puttin' him off for a couple of weeks now and I've got to do it."

"Not yet, no way." He nearly snapped it. As it was it came out as an order.

There was a small silence. "Remy, if you know somethin'

about my manager, and you must to have a reaction like that, please tell me."

He cursed again under his breath. This time, blistering, hot Cajun French, directed at himself. "Listen, *chere*, I'm still investigatin' him, but I've discovered a few things that worry me. I was waitin' until I had all the information before I said anythin' to you one way or the other." He paused. "The thing is, Bijou, I know you care about Rob Butterfield. I didn't want you hurt again."

"I sort of grew up around him. He's the nephew of Bodrie's manager. I've known him most of my life."

For some reason, that piece of information just irritated him more—that and the dejected note in her voice. Everyone who had anything at all to do with her father was out for themselves and using Bijou as a means to pad their bank accounts. Were they all so used to easy money that they'd put out a hit on her to get insurance money? Or arrange an accident? With a serial killer in town, what better way to get rid of her?

Maybe he was paranoid—his chosen job certainly made him think everyone was a potential killer—but he didn't trust a single friend she had. With a killer on the loose, he didn't want to let her out of his sight.

"I'm glad you're comin' down, Blue. I'll get the information on your manager as fast as I can. I know you must feel like everyone you've ever known has betrayed you."

There was a silence. "I have trust issues for a reason, Remy."

He heard her. Heard what she was trying to tell him. The thing was, he'd known it all along, he just thought he'd be exempt.

"I know you do, *chere*. We'll work around them."

14

BIJOU had no idea what to do about her strange relationship with Remy. She didn't like the fact that she felt excited and happy at the prospect of seeing him. She wanted to remain aloof. Who wanted a man who only wanted her because his leopard did? She felt a little like she was in a fantasy film or a sci-fi movie. Leopard woman? She stared down at her hands. They looked so perfectly normal.

"Are you all right?" Mahieu asked. "You're awfully quiet." He glanced over at her as they made their way toward town.

Bijou nodded. "Yes, I'm just thinkin' about things. I thought I'd come back home and find peace here."

"The swamps and bayous are peaceful," Mahieu assured. "Especially for our kind. You're not alone, Bijou. You have us now. And the lair. Drake will introduce you to everyone in a formal ceremony and you'll find you're part of a much larger and tight-knit community."

She raised an eyebrow. "I met Robert and Dion Lanoux today."

"I won't say our lair doesn't have big problems. Until Drake came along, we were cut off from other lairs and had no idea of their existence. We didn't even know much about our history or the rules of our society and Drake taught us. We're comin' together, though.

"Remy will catch this killer. He's very good at his job. I know things are a bit difficult right now, but hang in there. The public will get used to your singing in your club and eventually you won't get so hounded. Everyone will protect you."

She gave him a faint smile. "I'm Bodrie Breaux's daughter. I made a career singin' rock and roll, just like him. Now I've turned my back on that and I sing what I've always wanted. I don' do tours and I've let the world down, not followin' my daddy's legacy. You should see the hate mail. Most people come into that club because they want to see a piece of Bodrie."

Mahieu whistled softly. "You really don' know how good you are, do you?"

Bijou shrugged and sent him a small smile. "That's the nicest thing anyone's said to me in a long time." She twisted her fingers together in her lap. "I spent so much time tryin' to be what I thought everyone wanted me to be instead of bein' myself. I was a rocker, like Bodrie, and everyone accepted me that way. I made a lot of money, but the life wasn't anythin' like what I wanted—or even needed."

"It takes courage to turn your back on success," Mahieu observed.

A small grin escaped. "I was terrified. Everyone was angry with me and told me it was a terrible mistake. I knew I couldn't live that life. I just couldn't do it. The drugs and drinkin' reminded me too much of the way I grew up."

She stared out the window as they drove along the bayou. She loved being close to the bayou, the bay, the swamp, all of it. She loved the French Quarter and New Orleans. She felt as if finally, she could carve out a place for herself, not Bodrie's daughter, but Bijou Breaux. She wanted to live a quiet life, own her club and sing when she wanted.

She glanced at Mahieu. "I'm actually quite good at find-ing young, up-and-coming jazz and blues singers and bands. I know some great chefs and bartenders. I think I can make a success of the club. I love the idea of livin' in the apartment above the club. It has great views and really nice balconies."

Mahieu smiled. "Your leopard won' like it much. She'll need to run in the swamp. Remy keeps a house there, so no worries."

"Does everyone expect me to live with Remy? Because I don' see that happenin'."

Mahieu's brief smile turned into a grin. "You don'? Well now. That's downright interestin'. Have you mentioned that to Remy yet?"

"I didn't think I had to."

There was laughter in Mahieu's eyes. "Please tell him when I'm around. Even if you do it when I'm across the room. The fireworks will be a thing of beauty."

"You and your brothers seem to be misguided about Remy's feelin's toward me," Bijou informed him, using her haughtiest voice and sticking out her chin.

Mahieu didn't seem to be the least bit affected by her tone. His grin didn't diminish in the least. She was begin-ning to believe the Boudreaux brothers lived to tease one another. She couldn't help herself, she wanted to laugh. Mahieu was enjoying himself far too much at her expense.

"I don' think you have a clue what you're talkin' about, Miss Breaux, but that's perfectly all right. We do love the way you've got our big brother dancin' like a marionette on a string. Please keep it up."

She gave a little sniff. His laughter was infectious and she wasn't going to give him the satisfaction. "I have no idea what you're talkin' about. Remy doesn't dance to anyone's beat but his own. You know that."

"We all *thought* that," Mahieu said. "But times have changed. And her name is Bijou Breaux."

Bijou tried not to feel elated. Mahieu was giving her hope where Remy hadn't given her any. She was not going to be wanted for her leopard. She'd come home to New Orleans to live her life her way. She wanted to be loved for herself. Not for being Bodrie's daughter. Not for her money. Certainly not for her leopard. Maybe what she was asking was impossible, but she'd rather not be with anyone at all than to be with someone for the wrong reasons. Remy wanted her for all the wrong reasons, but his family didn't seem to understand that.

She shook her head. Drake appeared to be madly in love with Saria, and she knew without a shadow of a doubt that Saria loved Drake. They weren't together because of their leopards.

She stayed silent until they pulled up to the curb and Mahieu parked. She sat for a moment, trying to calm her suddenly rapidly beating heart. She detested that she was so excited at the prospect of seeing Remy. She could admit to herself that he was the man she dreamt of, the one she considered a hero, the man no other man could measure up to, but she absolutely refused to believe she might be falling in love with him. Not now. Not when she knew there was nothing between them but leopards and sex. Everyone had choices. Her choice was not to be in love with a man who didn't love her.

Mahieu came around and opened the door for her. "I texted Remy to let him know you're here. He's in interrogation, but he'll come out as soon as he's done." He walked with her up to the door of the station house and reached to open that door for her.

"I'll be fine. You don' have to wait with me," Bijou assured.

Mahieu gave her his cocky grin. "Not a chance, Bijou. Remy doesn't want you goin' anywhere without an escort right now. He's gotten all paranoid between the murders, you getttin' harassed last night at the club and Robert actin' like an idiot. You're goin' to have to be a little patient with Remy until he figures things out. He's got a protective streak a mile wide when it comes to you."

"I'd love to feel very special, Mahieu, but the truth is, Remy feels protective over everyone. That's why he's a cop."

She went inside and stepped back to allow him to lead the way. The truth was, everyone was going to stare at her, and she didn't mind Mahieu running interference. He was a big man, much like his brother, all muscle with that smooth, fluid way of walking. He exuded confidence, just like all the Boudreaux brothers and Saria. She wanted to be like that and was determined that she would be, given a few months. For too long she'd tried to be someone she wasn't and in the end she just couldn't sustain it.

Following Mahieu through the bull pen, she rounded a corner to find the homicide division. Remy's office was in the corner, with several desks out on the floor. Mahieu waved her to a chair, but there were several policemen looking at her, staring, some sporting grins. She didn't feel like sitting there on display for them all. Mahieu went over to talk with someone he knew, and she wandered around the room, trying to get a feel for Remy's work.

Set up in the middle of the largest wall was a huge whiteboard with pictures of Pete Morgan and the altar. Alongside that were pictures of Ryan Cooper and the altar. The pictures were in horrible, gruesome detail, and although it was one of those situations where one could almost not stop looking at the train wreck, she managed to shift her gaze.

In a line down either side of the grisly murder pictures were photographs of men. Her manager, Rob Butterfield, and his friend Jason Durang were among them. Bob Carson was up on the wall as well. She recognized a few other faces from the men who had been in her club and had harassed her. She couldn't imagine why any of them had been singled out and would be considered suspects.

Above the pictures, a map caught her eye. It was of both the United States and Europe. There were red pins in various cities. She moved closer and studied the map. It took a moment or two for the significance to sink in. She stood there, staring, biting her lip, suddenly very much afraid.

"Come away from there," Remy said.

She whirled around to face him, one hand going defensively

to her throat. She felt the color drain out of her face. "What is this, Remy?"

"Don' be lookin' at that, Blue," he cautioned. "Come into my office. You shouldn't see that. There's no reason." He took her hand and tugged.

"No, I need to know. What is this?"

He sighed, his fingers stroking the back of her hand in a caress. "It's a murder board. It helps me keep all the facts straight. Putting everything up, I can work the pieces like a puzzle until eventually it all comes together."

"You have Rob Butterfield up there. You even have Bob."

"I'm not calling them suspects, but they are persons of interest. All of them were here four years ago when the first series of murders happened here in New Orleans. All of these men were. I have to rule people out and so far, I haven't quite gotten there with them, but I'm certain I will. Among others, I'm talkin' with them now. Of course not together. I like to keep my persons of interest separated so they can't come up with the same story."

"Why would they even be suspects?" She wasn't buying his "persons of interest" story for a moment.

"They were in the wrong place at the wrong time with no real alibi." He gave a careful, casual shrug. "Come away from here now."

Bijou resisted the tug on her hand. "Why are all those cities flagged with red pins?"

Remy went very still, her actions suddenly really catching his attention. "Do you really want to know?"

"I wouldn't ask if I didn't," she replied. Her heart pounded hard. Her mouth went dry. She felt the rise of her leopard coming close to the surface as if offering to take her place.

"These are his kills over the last four years. The first that we found with the same pattern was in New York City."

Bijou closed her eyes briefly. "And the days, months and year written above each pin are *when* he killed?"

Remy nodded grimly. "Four kills in each city. Even in Europe, but we know of only three sites there."

She *had* to tell him. She felt sick to her stomach. "I need to sit down, Remy. Maybe a glass of water?"

Remy regarded her carefully, his piercing eyes sharp with intelligence. She knew she'd gone pale and that her skin had suddenly become clammy. There was no way to hide it from him since he was holding her hand. His thumb slid innocently over her pulse. He was well aware something was radically wrong. She wasn't a wilting flower. Her distress had nothing to do with the detailed pictures of the two men she knew who had been brutally murdered.

He didn't question her further, simply led her into his office, put her into a chair and went to get her a glass of water. She leaned her head into her hand. Nothing made sense anymore.

Remy returned and carefully closed the door. "Drink this, *chere*, and then tell me what's wrong."

Bijou took a long, cool sip, hoping it would help. Her mind raced with possibilities. "Remy, those cities on your murder map, I played shows in every single one of them. Includin' the places in Europe."

He went very still, his hip on the desk, his eyes locked on hers. She couldn't have looked away if she wanted to.

"The same days, the same months. Every time I was in a city playin' a concert, the killer was there too. That can't be a coincidence."

She twisted her fingers together to keep her hands from trembling. "And the first set of murders, I was here in New Orleans for Bodrie's funeral." She looked up at him. "What do you think that means?"

"It means your manager, his mysterious friend and your stalker just moved to the head of the list." Remy toed a chair around and straddled it, sitting close, facing her so he could watch her every expression. "Were you at any time aware of the murders before Pete was killed?"

"After I left town, which I did fast after Bodrie's funeral, I read about a serial killer in the Garden District. It was in the news on the television as well. But I didn't know about any of the other killings. When I'm on tour, it's exhaustin'. I spend most of my time goin' from city to city, so when I have the chance, I spend my time relaxin'."

Bijou looked down at her hands, her fingers twisted together. She hated confessing to him, making herself look like a loser. Those years had taken their toll on her. She didn't believe in herself, or people anymore. She'd lost who she was. "I don' trust easily, Remy. I saw the people who surrounded Bodrie. They weren't his friends. They were usin' him."

Remy leaned toward her, reaching out to cover her hands with one of his. "*Chere*, they weren't real. You know the difference."

"I spent most of the time alone in hotel rooms, readin' books. I love to read. I guess that's my form of escape. Not drugs or alcohol, but books. I disappear into them, and durin' that time of my life, I needed them. I wasn't watchin' television or readin' magazines because I was afraid I'd see or hear something about me. I know that sounds vain, but I just don' have the personality to be in the spotlight. I realized I'd chosen the wrong profession, but I didn't know how to get off the merry-go-round."

"Being a public figure doesn't necessarily mean you have to give up your privacy."

"That's naïve, Remy, and I think you know it. Anyone chosin' to be in the public eye is free game. Being Bodrie's daughter I was already there from the time I was born. Like an idiot, tryin' to prove something to myself and to others . . ."

"What, Bijou? What did you ever need to prove to anyone, let alone yourself?" Remy asked, his thumb sliding gently back and forth across the backs of her hands.

She ducked her head. "That I was good enough. Everyone wanted me to be him and when I first started singin', people were saying things like, 'What does she think she's doin'. She has no talent.' They always compared me to him, and of course I came off second best."

"Are you crazy? You're a total success in your own right. Half the planet is in love with you and your voice."

She shrugged. "It didn't start out that way, but by the time I'd made a name for myself I realized that wasn't my world—that I didn't even want it. Can you imagine how that made me feel? I was a success and people loved my music. I felt like the ungrateful brat the tabloids and all of Bodrie's fans thought me. Here I had everything I'd wanted and dreamt of and I still wasn't happy." She looked him in the eye, wanting him to understand. "I was so miserable I could barely drag myself out of my room, but I performed nearly every night. I found myself exhausted and so unhappy I couldn't look at myself in the mirror."

She took a deep breath. "I guess I'm just tryin' to explain to you why I wasn't up on the news. I hid from everyone while I was on tour and then when I made the decision to quit, I hid from my manager because he was so angry with me. I needed time to figure out what I really wanted to do."

Quite frankly she was ashamed of having to tell him she didn't have her life together, not even when she was young. She wanted him to see only her good side, not all the floundering and angst she'd gone through before she realized what she needed—and wanted in her life. For all the crazy things going on around her now, she knew she was right to have come home. She loved her club. She loved the intimacy of it and the fact that she could control when she performed and how often. She was certain she would fit into the community given time, and the paparazzi would lose interest and eventually leave her alone.

She didn't want him to think she was a loser sitting in her hotel room, feeling sorry for herself and not even watching the news when other people were suffering, being murdered and he was trying hard to put a stop to it.

"I'm glad you've come home. Butterfield's upset because he's losing his money ticket."

"He says I'm letting my fans down," she said. "And I suppose he's right."

"If they're fans, Blue, they'll love what you love. Just

because you aren't singin' rock and roll like your father, that doesn't take away your voice."

She smiled at him. She couldn't help it. He talked in that velvety smooth tone and looked at her with those piercing, *amazing* eyes of his and her stomach did flip-flops. Her heart beat far too fast and her mouth went dry. He just had so much charisma, a magnetic pull she couldn't seem to ever resist. She knew better than to fall for his charm—he'd made it very clear his attraction had little to do with her—but still, she found it hard not to react to him.

"Thanks, Remy. I hope you're right, but if not, I know the club is what I want."

"Good girl. I think the club suits you, but more than that, you need to do what makes you happy."

"I didn't have anything at all to do with those murders, Remy," she said, making certain to look him in the eye. She was in the same city where every one of the murders occurred.

"I know that. I can't imagine you hoisting a grown man up a tree, let alone carvin' him up. I didn't think for one moment you had anything to do with the murders, Bijou," Remy said. "But it's very possible you know the killer."

She wanted to protest, but her gaze strayed through the glass toward the map on the murder board. There was no denying the fact that where every single murder took place, she had been present. "I do have a few extremely devoted fans," she admitted. "They follow me from one concert to the next. Some even followed me out of the country on my world tour. There's a special group that run a fan club and the members are the first ones to be able to buy tickets and backstage passes."

"Can we get a list of their names? Do you know them all by sight?"

"I'd recognize the ones who come backstage on a regular basis, but if they don', and not all of them do, there's no way I'd be able to recognize them. In any case, Remy, I can't remember who was at what concert."

Remy tightened his hands around Bijou's. She was extremely distressed, but holding herself together. He could feel the tension in her. Her hands trembled beneath his. The idea of knowing a serial killer, that he might be traveling to her concerts and killing at every event, sickened her.

"Could I have done somethin' to make this happen? A song? Ignorin' someone? There're so many people and I really try hard to autograph for as many as possible and talk a little with anyone I meet, but I'm exhausted after every concert and maybe I didn't take the time I should have." Bijou delivered the confession in a little rush.

Remy shook his head. "I don' know what the trigger was for this man to begin killin', Blue, or even if he has anythin' to do with goin' to your concerts, but it has nothin' to do with *you*. I've run into killers before, many times, but no one has ever been this cold. Believe me, *chere*, this man was born a psychopath."

Bijou shivered. "Why would he be followin' me around?"

"If you were a target, he'd have killed you already," Remy stated bluntly. "He doesn't seem to have any trouble gettin' to his victims. But you've really helped me by givin' me this information, Blue. I'll be able to ask the right questions now."

He sat back in his chair and regarded her steadily. "Does your manager have an insurance policy on you?"

"Yes. He took one out ages ago, when I first signed with him."

"Were you aware he served time in prison and that's where he met Jason Durang?"

"I knew about Rob, of course, he disclosed that he'd gotten in trouble with the IRS and had served time. He hadn't paid the employees' taxes, but he knew Bodrie and he had a good reputation in the industry."

"He's a gambler."

She nodded. "But he doesn't gamble. He goes to regular meetings."

"Is that what he tells you?"

She swallowed hard. "Remy, if you have somethin' to tell me, just get to it."

He shook his head. He had no proof. He couldn't see her prissy manager as a cold-blooded killer. He'd thrown up when Remy had shown him the crime scene photographs, but Jason Durang was an altogether different proposition. He hadn't looked away or even showed any reaction whatsoever. Neither had the Rousseau brothers. Regardless, he believed Rob Butterfield and Jason Durang presented a danger to her.

"What about Durang?"

"I've seen him with Butterfield a few times, but I've never talked to him. He always avoided me. I don' know what he does."

"I'll drive you back home. I got a call from Drake and he wants me to meet him at the Inn to talk to Robert and Dion."

"You don' have to do that. I should check on the apartment and see how that's comin'. I was hopin' I could move in soon."

She sounded innocent. Her gaze didn't waver and there wasn't a single hint of being coy. He was tempted to reach out and shake some sense into her. Whatever sin he'd committed she hadn't forgiven him. She'd come to his office to get out of the Inn and away from Robert and his brother. She'd been glad to see him, she hadn't even attempted to hide that fact from him, but she wasn't planning a wedding anytime soon.

He didn't know whether to be hurt or angry, or just plain both. "You know you're probably pregnant with my child," he said bluntly. "Birth control doesn't work so well on leopards." He sounded smug even to his own ears.

Her lashes fluttered, veiling her expression. Her lips made a little moue. He saw the "tell" in her fingers rather than her face. Her hands curled into fists, but she immediately straightened them and clasped them primly together in her lap.

"Well, we'll have to see, won't we, Remy? The idea was very scary when you first mentioned it, but I've had time to think about it and I have no doubts I'll be able to handle havin' a child."

She sounded downright haughty, as if he wasn't in the picture at all. He leaned toward her, his eyes locking with hers. *"We'll* be able to handle it, Blue. There's no more 'I' here. If you think you're walkin' out on me, you can just think again. In fact, set a damn weddin' date and let's just get it over with. Talk to your idiot lawyers, I'll sign whatever prenup they want signed, but we're gettin' it done soon. And when I say soon, I mean no more than a couple of weeks."

She scowled at him, her eyebrows emphasizing her complete disgust. Both hands went to her hips. She stalked to the door, yanked it open and turned back. "Remy Boudreaux, you don' have a *single* romantic bone in your body and I'm ignorin' everything you just said and might say from now on. In fact, it would be better if you just didn't speak."

The entire bull pen turned around, including Mahieu. His brother was the only one who dared to grin.

"Blue . . ." Remy started.

She cut him off. *"Don't* say another word to me right now." She actually held up her hand to stop him. "For your information, lookin' hot and relyin' on your charm only carries you so far. Bein' good-lookin' doesn't give you a free pass to be a . . . a . . ."

"Jackass," Mahieu supplied helpfully.

Bijou nodded her head. "Thank you, Mahieu. That fits perfectly."

Several of the detectives coughed hard, turning their backs on their boss. Mahieu bowed. Bijou marched toward his brother, turning her back completely to him. She had a really nice sway to her hips that caught his eye.

"Mahieu would you mind givin' me a lift back to the Inn?"

That was enough. "If you value your life and don' want me spendin' the rest of mine behind bars, Mahieu, you'll politely decline," Remy warned. He'd already grabbed his jacket and shrugged into it, as he trailed behind Bijou.

Mahieu held up both hands in surrender. "When he's like this, it's best to just give him whatever he wants, Bijou."

She gave a little delicate sniff, but didn't turn around and didn't protest. Deliberately, Remy put his hand possessively on her back, down low, close to the curve of her buttocks. She glanced at him over her shoulder, but she kept walking. He heard the wave of laughter rippling behind him as they walked out.

"You did that on purpose, didn't you?" he demanded, moving up beside her, sliding her beneath his shoulder, one arm wrapping around her waist.

"A little bit, yes," she admitted, a hint of laughter in her voice. "But you deserved it." The amusement faded from her voice. "Never talk to me like that again. I don' like to be ordered around. Even if I'm pregnant, doesn't mean I want to run off and marry a man who just likes havin' me around for great sex."

"At least you admit it is great sex," he muttered.

Clearly she found him attractive and even amusing, that was true, but she wasn't conceding an inch. Bijou Breaux was not as easily charmed as he'd first thought she would be. He was older. More experienced. She definitely looked up to him and yet, she was elusive, just out of reach. Every time he thought he had her wrapped up, she found a way to elude him. Quite frankly, it was maddening.

Bijou didn't respond but went with him to his car. He opened the door and she slid inside. For a moment his heart pounded hard just looking at her sitting there. Composed. Beautiful. *His*. He had never really considered that he'd find *the* woman. She stared straight ahead, her little nose in the air. Damned if he didn't even find that cute. He'd never admit it to Gage, but maybe he really did have "it" bad. He just wasn't going to define what "it" was, not now. Not yet. He needed time to figure a few things out.

Like what the hell he was going to do with her when they weren't having sex. Maybe lock her up somewhere where he knew she'd be safe, because as it was, it seemed like every person he met was bent on causing her harm in some way.

He stalked around to the driver's side door, noting Bob Carson was down the street with a camera, clearly using a lens that would bring Bijou close. He considered how many years he might get in prison for "accidentally" running the fool over with his car. He slammed his door with unnecessary violence, earning him a look from Bijou.

He started the engine and indicated Carson with his chin. "You know, you do need rescuin' whether you want to believe it or not."

She made a face at him. "I'm not a wimp, Remy, no matter what you believe."

"I believe half of New Orleans is tryin' to kill you and the other half wants to go to bed with you."

Her mouth twitched and she covered her lips with her palm, coughing delicately and then clearing her throat several times.

Remy glared at her. "Woman, you'd better not be laughin' at me."

"Just a little. I think you take your job far too seriously. Bein' a homicide detective has made you a little bit paranoid, Remy. Yes, this situation with these murders is bizarre, but you said yourself if he wanted me dead, he would have already gone after me."

A growl rumbled through his chest. Usually that was more than sufficient to stop any arguing from his siblings or fellow detectives. She simply raised an eyebrow, not looking very intimidated.

"The serial killer is probably the only one *not* out to get you," he groused.

"Don' sound so happy about it," Bijou said.

He reached out and took her hand, threading his fingers through hers. It seemed a small victory when she didn't pull away from the contact. He took the gesture a step further and locked her hand against his heart. "Is that what you think, Blue? I'm in it just for the sex?"

She turned her head then and looked at him, hunching a little, as if he'd struck a body blow. Her amazing blue eyes always sent an electrical charge sizzling through his body. She blinked, drawing his attention to her impossibly long lashes. Before he drove straight into the bayou, he forced his gaze back onto the road.

"You jump around in the conversation, Remy. I'm havin' trouble keepin' up."

"No, you aren't. Now you're just stallin'. I told you a long time ago, *chere*, you're no coward, and it's time you just told me what was upsetting you. I'm gettin' the feelin' you think our relationship is about sex and nothing else."

He glanced at her again and just before her long lashes veiled her expression, he caught a flash of pain in her eyes. Instantly he felt as if a giant hand squeezed his heart hard. Upsetting her was one thing, but genuine pain was another. He didn't like ever being the cause of that. She'd had enough pain in her life and he would bet his last dollar she was facing more.

He was positive her agent and his murky friend were up to no good. And he knew Bob Carson was. The man followed her everywhere taking photographs and selling out her privacy. He couldn't yet prove that Carson was stalking her and destroying her property, even frightening her, but he would find the proof. She knew all three men, had known two of them for years, and it would hurt to find out that they really cared nothing for her . . .

The moment the thought entered his mind, he cursed himself. Of course. What an idiot. His brothers were right. Bijou had never been important to her father or her nannies. She'd never been loved by anyone. She probably had no idea what it felt like to have someone caring for her. He'd talked about the sex and little else.

"I think our relationship is about your leopard bein' crazy about mine, as well as the great sex," Bijou stated. "I think that because you said it. More than once."

Remy tightened his fingers around her hand, keeping her

palm pressed tightly against his heart. "Then I'm a moron if I made you believe that." Looking back, he realized he had said just that. He shook his head.

Bijou shrugged. Her lower lip trembled and she bit down with her small teeth. "It's all right, Remy. I'm not askin' anythin' from you. I'm a grown-up. I was there, just like you were. I wanted to have sex with you. It's not like you forced me. I'm well aware people have casual sex all the time."

"What we had was *not* casual sex. Had you ever had sex before, believe me, *chere*, you would never even consider attaching the word *casual* to what we have together."

"Remy, I'm well aware we barely know one another. I'm not one to jump into bed with just anyone . . ."

"I know that. I was there, remember? I should have been much more careful with you that first time," he admitted.

"I wasn't sayin' that. I just mean, you don' know me any better than I know you."

"You'd be surprised at how well I know you, Bijou. I didn't lose track of you over the years. And I'm a cop."

She turned cool eyes on him, although again, there was that tiny hint of amusement. "You investigated me?"

"Of course. Did you expect anythin' less?"

"No, I guess not. But that doesn't mean you know me, Remy. Nor do I know you. I didn't even know about the leopard business." She lowered her voice when she used the word *leopard*, clearly still uncomfortable with the idea of being a shifter.

He pulled her hand up to his mouth, brushing his lips over her knuckles. "I'm not good with words. I know that. Not with anyone I care about, but there's a hell of a lot more to our relationship than our leopards—or great sex— regardless of what I may have said earlier."

"See, I don' know you that well, or I'd know whether you were just sayin' that to make me feel better, and keep me around for your leopard, or if you mean it."

"I've never once told you a lie. We do have great sex. And my leopard is crazy about yours. Maybe I left out how

I feel, but only because I've never actually felt this way about a woman before. It's new to me as well, Blue. Just give us time. We're interrupted every two minutes and I have to find this killer. But you're on my mind, every moment, you're on my mind."

Bijou smiled at him a little tentatively, but her smile reached her eyes. "I'm apparently not the most lovable person in the world."

"That's bullshit."

"You said yourself half of New Orleans wants me dead."

"True, I did say that, which is why you're goin' to stick close to the Inn when I'm not around. My brothers will keep their eyes on you when I'm workin'. Do you have anything important goin' on in the next couple of days?"

"Arnaud asked me to go to the openin' of his gallery showin'. That's tomorrow night." Her smile widened. "It gives me a chance to dress up. It's a black tie affair."

"*Don'* be usin' the word *affair* in the same breath when referrin' to that Frenchman," Remy groused. "He's all over you."

"No, he isn't. We're just good friends. I'm worried about him. He doesn't pay any attention to the news or what's happenin' around him. He spends half his time drawin' and the other half workin' on his sculptures. It's rare for him to show up at a gallery and actually talk to anyone who wants to purchase his work. I don' want him to be an easy target for this killer."

"You're worried that if he's around you, he might be next."

She pressed her lips together and nodded. "I'm worried about you too, Remy."

He gave her his leopard grin. Dangerous. Predatory. "Worry about the other guy, *chere*."

15

REMY glanced out the window of the Inn and froze. "What idiot let him go out there *before* he talked to Robert?" He swung around to glare at his brothers.

"You know Drake. He just gets that look on his face and you back off and let him do whatever he wants to do."

Saria moved up beside her brother to stare out at her husband. She gasped, one hand going defensively to her throat. "Can you stop him if he tries to kill Robert?"

"What do you mean, *tries*?" Remy demanded. "Robert doesn't stand a chance against Drake. Not even if Dion was stupid enough to try to help him. Robert challenged him, and you're pregnant. What do you think his leopard is goin' to do?"

"No one said anythin' about Saria bein' pregnant," Lojos pointed out with a pious expression.

"Do you have any idea how bad this is?" Remy asked, worry edging his tone. "Two male members of Drake's lair came into his home uninvited. His pregnant wife asked them to leave repeatedly and they didn't. One laid out a challenge for leadership of the lair in Drake's own backyard. He's always in control of his leopard, but this is too much. Mine would be killin' both of them by now."

Bijou slipped her hand into Remy's back pocket. He glanced over his shoulder at her. Her face looked pale.

"The laws of civilization don' apply to leopards. We aren't exactly civilized," Remy explained, trying to gentle the words with a softer tone.

"Absolutely lethal," she whispered. "That's what you're sayin'."

"Yes. I'm sorry. That's who we are. Robert has been leopard for years and he *chose* to take such a risk." Remy's gaze went back to the large leopard tearing up the trees in a rage. Drake wasn't known for being a hothead. If anything, he was always the voice of reason. If there was one man who could always keep his leopard under control, it was definitely Drake. He didn't look under control at the moment.

"I shouldn't have been so detailed when he asked me," Saria whispered, looking up at her brother. "Maybe if I'd skipped the part about Dion and Robert just comin' in . . ."

Remy put his finger over his sister's lips. "Leopards don' lie to one another. Especially mates. You had to tell Drake, and both Robert and Dion knew the chance they were takin' goin' into this." He looked out the window again. "You'll just have to trust Drake as your husband and our leader to know the right way to handle this."

He stepped back from the window and turned to face the two men sitting straight in their armchairs. Dion appeared resigned, but Robert looked as if he might try to bolt at any moment.

"Before Drake gets in here, Saria," Dion said. "I didn't know you were pregnant and I never would have brought this to you had I known. I know that doesn't much matter now, but I wanted you to know, I am sorry we upset you."

Remy reached behind him and took Bijou's hand. He had

nothing normal to give her. There was nothing typical about their lives nor would there ever be. She had never been normal and now, for certain, she never would be. She was a gentle person, a caring soul. He knew all about the foundations she'd established and the way she took care of the people she'd employed for so long. It was no wonder Rob Butterfield didn't want to lose his meal ticket.

"You don' have to be here for this," Remy said. "You can go up to your room. You're safe either way. Drake would never harm you, not even in a leopard's rage."

The door banged open and Drake Donovan strode in. He didn't look right or left, just stared straight at Robert. He was barefoot, his jeans riding low on his hips and his shirt open, revealing roped muscles and numerous scars.

"Dion, get the hell out of my home, *now*, before I decide you've got a beating coming. Don't hesitate. Don't argue. Just go while you still can."

Drake's eyes had gone a deep gold-green, his wealth of thick blond hair falling in a wild array over his forehead. There were telltale signs of the change, the darker shadow of rosettes deep within the strands of gold.

Remy swept Bijou behind him, just as a precautionary measure, his body shielding hers. Drake's rage was under control, but it was there, smoldering beneath the surface, and with any leopard, that wasn't a good sign. Remy's own leopard reacted, snarling and raking at him, ready to leap forward to protect him as well as his mate.

The tension in the room rose as Dion slowly stood. Robert cringed and caught at his brother's shirt. "You can't leave. You know he's goin' to kill me."

Dion shook his head, his face a mask of sorrow. "I don' know what happened to you, Robert. But you did this and you have to face the consequences. I can't keep coverin' up for you. I did my best to pull you out of the things you'd gotten into, but you refused. You challenged Remy and then Drake. You're my brother and I love you, but I can't fix this one for you."

He looked straight at Saria. "Once again, I'm sorry I dumped this in your lap."

He turned and walked out without looking back at Robert, his shoulders stiff and his head up. Remy was proud of him. He didn't know if he would have the same courage to leave one of his brothers to face an enraged leader of the lair. Drake, according to their laws, could force Robert to fight him as a leopard—and he would be well within his rights to kill him.

The silence stretched out, tension building. Drake's eyes were nearly completely gold, never once leaving Robert's face, never blinking. His entire being focused on the man slumped in the chair in front of him. Robert's expression was sulky and a little defiant, even though fear permeated the room, oozing through his pores along with every breath he exhaled.

"I need to know if you're a member of this lair," Drake snapped, his voice like a whip. "Where do your loyalties lie? Answer now, Robert."

Robert blinked rapidly. Remy felt Bijou's fist twist in the back of his shirt. He laid his palm lightly against her thigh. She was trembling. He wanted to reassure her, but right now, he was Drake's second and protector—not that Drake needed one—but that was the way of the lair.

"With the lair," Robert mumbled. "I was drunk, Drake. I would never challenge for leadership. Never. My leopard was in a frenzy because there was a female . . ."

"Do *not* place blame with your leopard. It's my job to know every leopard in this lair, their strength and weaknesses and their abilities. Your leopard isn't difficult to handle. Remy's is a fighter, continually looking for supremacy, and he always keeps his leopard under control—as I do mine. If you exhibited just a little control yourself and a little bit of discipline, you would never have a problem. *You're* to blame. You're responsible for the behavior of your cat at all times."

"It was *her*." Robert pointed a finger at Bijou. "Her leopard led mine on."

A growl rumbled deep in Remy's chest. He bared his teeth at Robert, but he remained absolutely still. Drake was the leader, and he was following the plan they'd devised. Robert had to state his loyalty so there was no safely going back.

"So you're telling me you're incapable of controlling your leopard, no matter the circumstances."

Drake's voice had gone very quiet, quiet enough to send a chill down Remy's spine. If that tone had sent a message to him, he couldn't imagine what Robert was feeling. It was a question no shifter wanted to be asked. If he couldn't control his leopard, it was a virtual death sentence. No shifter could be around humans if his leopard, with its intense mood swings and violent outbursts, ruled.

Robert shook his head. "No. No. I control my leopard. The circumstances . . ."

"Don't matter," Drake interrupted. "Either you're in control at all times or you're not. Which is it?"

"*I'm* in control," Robert admitted hastily. He was trapped and he knew it. He was facing life or death and there was no getting out of it.

"You were drunk and you allowed your leopard loose when you weren't one hundred percent," Drake accused. "You're totally responsible, not Bijou, not Remy and certainly not your leopard. *You* challenged me and you went after a claimed female. Whether or not she'd mated with her chosen one, she was off limits and should have been under your protection."

Robert said nothing, holding himself stiff in his chair, clearly terrified as Drake laid out the charges against him.

"Last night at the club, a female leopard of our lair was threatened and every member present with the exception of you leapt to protect her. One of our most sacred laws is to protect our females and our children. I'm waiting for an explanation." Drake's voice was lower than ever, and that made him sound all the more lethal.

Robert opened and closed his mouth several times, looking like a fish gasping for air. Sweat beaded on his forehead. "I was with my friends—"

"To clarify," Drake interrupted, "these are the friends that were harassing one of our women."

"I didn't know she was one of ours," Robert lied.

The room shook with the force of Drake's roar. He leapt forward and struck Robert's face, openhanded, but his hand was a large claw and the razor-sharp tips ripped Robert's cheek open, leaving four distinct rake marks with blood welling up.

Robert howled and cowered back in his seat. Bijou hid her face against Remy's back. He could feel her trembling more than ever. Bijou had steeled herself to remain in the room and learn as much as she could about leopard law. He had to hand it to her, she had courage.

Saria gently put her hand on Bijou's shoulder in a gesture of camaraderie as well as to try to tell her to trust in Drake. He glanced at Saria, grateful for the way she read Bijou's feelings. Drake was scaring the crap out of Robert on purpose. Remy had no doubt that if Robert told any more lies, the retaliation would be swift and painful—that was their law.

Bijou had no brothers. She hadn't grown up in the environment Saria had. She knew about neglect and debauchery. She knew what alcohol and drugs could do to a man. But she had never experienced real violence, not like leopards were capable of. Remy couldn't take his eyes off Drake. His leopard was at the ready. If for any reason, Drake needed him, he had to respond within seconds, and that meant he couldn't be the one to reassure Bijou, no matter how much he wanted to do so.

"I lied. I lied," Robert admitted, holding the side of his face. Blood seeped through his fingers and trickled down his arms. "I did know she was leopard. It was obvious at one point. I didn't want Jean or Juste to think I'd turned on them."

There it was—exactly where Drake had been leading Robert all along. Had Robert not claimed his loyalty was to the lair, Drake would have challenged him in a battle between leopards and Robert surely would have died. As it was, he *had* to answer any questions Remy or Drake posed, whether he liked it or not. Drake had been careful to keep every subject in the context of lair business. That was what Remy admired most about Drake. His leopard might be enraged, but he always kept his cool and thought clearly through every crisis. That trait was what made him such a great leader.

"I see," Drake said. Deliberately he allowed the silence to stretch out, until Robert squirmed in his chair. "I'm going to give you one chance to come clean. We know about the break-ins, Robert. I want you to give Remy every detail. Every piece of evidence you can provide, anything at all that will help him put those men behind bars."

The color drained out of Robert's face. He opened his mouth but Drake held up his hand to stop him from speaking.

"One chance, Robert. I'll know if you lie. Remy will know if you lie. You have a death sentence hanging over your head, so whatever the Rousseau brothers have on you, it will never be as bad as what I'll do to you. Start talking."

Robert licked his suddenly dry lips. Immediately Saria left the room to get him a drink of water. He swallowed several times. "They'll kill me. They like to kill. They both call themselves *bokor*, a kind of priest for voodoo black magic. I don' know if they really know what they're doin', but they hold regular rituals out in the swamp and sacrifice animals. They love to cut the heads off of chickens and spray the blood around. They call on demons. They even have a human skull they use for their rituals."

He confessed in a rush and gratefully took the glass of water Saria handed to him, drinking it down almost in one gulp. He almost sounded relieved to be telling someone, anyone. "They're crazy, you know. But smart. Real smart. They have eyes and ears everywhere." He shivered. "Maybe they really have demons looking out for them. I swear, they're the devil on earth."

"They masterminded the gang robbing and beatings of the elderly," Remy stated.

Robert nodded. "We all had to participate. I joined not knowin' what I was getting into. It seemed like a party at first, the initiation and all. They promised huge amounts of money and great kicks. Ryan Cooper and Brent Underwood both told me I'd make tons of money. So I went with them."

"Went where?" Remy prompted.

"They have this place in the swamp where they conduct their rituals." His entire body shuddered, and he lifted the glass to his mouth, not realizing it was empty. "They took me out there blindfolded the first time. We were all drinkin' and then Jean and Juste began to undress and got naked except for loincloths. Both drew intricate symbols in the dirt. I laughed, thinkin' it was all part of the party until I noticed no one else was laughin' and the others looked scared."

Robert shook his head and drew his hand over his face as if wiping the memory away. "They cut the throat of a pig and watched it bleed out, dancin' around and invokin' some demon, and then they painted us with the blood of the pig." He looked at Remy with stricken eyes. "Once in, you can't ever get out."

"Did Ryan Cooper want out?" Remy asked.

"Coop was always talkin' like he was goin' to get out if Jean and Juste didn't give him a bigger cut, but it was all talk. He didn't want to chance crossin' them any more than the rest of us. He didn't want the money to stop, but he thought he should get more than the rest of us because he did a lot of the beatings. Brent and I kind of hung back most of the time. Juste and Jean liked hurtin' people and every single time it seemed to get worse. I was afraid they'd kill someone. It was almost as if they each tried to outdo the other."

"Your leopard could tear both of them apart," Drake pointed out.

Robert shook his head. "They're demons. The devil. No one can stop them. I've seen them do things no one can do."

"How is it we don' catch the scent of anyone but the Rousseau brothers in the break-ins?" Remy asked.

Robert ducked his head, refusing to meet Remy's eyes.

"You gave them Charisse Mercier's experiment that masks all scent, didn't you?" Remy prompted.

"I had to contribute somethin'," Robert burst out. "I *had* to. I wasn't beatin' up old people. And if I didn't do somethin' to help, they were goin' after Dion." He looked up at his leader. "That's the gospel truth, Drake. I was in way over my head."

"You should have come to me," Drake stated. "You have a responsibility to this lair as well as to your brother and the community." There was no sympathy in his voice and no back up in him. "The Rousseau brothers clearly are a threat to everyone in your community. There's no excuse for not coming forward."

Robert pushed his forehead into the heel of his hand. "You don' know them." His voice was filled with loathing and despair. "They'll kill Dion and me. They'll use their voodoo magic and kill us both."

"Is there a stash of stolen articles somewhere?" Remy asked.

"In the swamp where they conduct their rituals," Robert said. "But you'll never stop them, Remy. They really have made a pact with the demons, and they're protected. They can get away with anything."

"Have they been to Europe?"

Robert blinked several times. He frowned. "Why? What has that got to do with anything?"

"Just answer him," Drake snapped.

"They've mentioned traveling in Europe," Robert said hastily.

"Is Bijou a particular favorite of theirs? Do they listen to her music a lot?" Remy demanded.

Robert nodded. "They're kind of obsessed with her. They play her stuff all the time." He ducked his head to avoid eye contact again. "They've been tryin' to get onto the crew workin' on her new apartment so they could put in cameras and maybe a few ways to get in without anyone knowin'."

Remy turned away to keep from leaping on the man. Robert was leopard. He knew Bijou was. It had become evident to all of them in the club, and yet he hadn't immediately come forward to report a threat toward one of their women. Fingertips burned. His jaw ached. He was close, so close. His leopard was strong and territorial. Also protective. All his life he'd had to work at keeping his leopard in check. Robert was making it very difficult. Any threat to Bijou could not be tolerated.

He took several deep breaths to keep control, breathing away his leopard's rage. "Have they gotten onto the work crew?" It helped that Bijou rubbed the middle of his back in a soothing pattern. He could hear her breathing and it hadn't changed. She was used to threats, he realized. Threats were a daily occurrence for her. That was why she hadn't gone to the authorities when her stalker had escalated his behavior. She was just too used to threats.

"Not yet," Robert answered. "But they were arrangin' an accident so that the contractor would be shorthanded. Tom and Ryan were supposed to help them with that."

"Tom Berlander?" Remy guessed. Berlander hung out with Ryan Cooper and Brent Underwood as well as the Rousseau brothers, so it was easy enough to guess, but Remy wanted Robert's clear identification.

Robert nodded. "He's gotten pretty violent, along with Ryan. Brent hangs back as much as possible. He's even claimed he's been sick when we were supposed to hit a place." He sighed and shook his head, slumping a little more.

"I don' know how you're goin' to catch Jean and Juste. No one can catch them. They work at the houses and the people they work for love them. They would never suspect them. They leave their prints everywhere on purpose. The elderly couples would go to court and say how wonderful they are. Jean and Juste actually bring them groceries and pick up medications, all the while laughin', knowin' they're goin' to rob and beat them."

Remy's stomach knotted. The more he heard, the more he wanted his leopard to meet the Rousseau brothers out in the swamp.

"Do you know if they're the ones committing these murders and harvestin' bones?" Remy asked.

Robert frowned, remaining silent, clearly thinking it over. Finally he shrugged. "I don' know, but they have human bones there in the swamp. I've seen them." He looked straight at Remy, honesty on his face and in his voice and eyes. "If they did, they would never be sorry. They like hurting animals and watching the life fade out of them. They like beating the old people and knowin' they had their trust. They really travel in the company of demons, just like they claim, and once you've made a pact with them, even if you were drunk and didn't mean it, you can never be free of them."

"Is that why you began drinkin' so much, Robert? And doin' drugs? To live with the things you were doin'? You knew they were wrong," Remy said.

Robert nodded, pressing his fingers to his eyes, shaking his head. "I got in too deep, Remy. There was nowhere to go."

"That's bullshit, Robert," Drake snarled. He began to pace back and forth. "You're a member of this lair. There is no excuse not to inform me of what is happening in our territory. You say they threatened your brother. He's a member and under my protection. You knew you should come to me. If I hear another lie coming out of your mouth, I'll take your damned head off and consequences be damned."

Robert pushed back in his chair, his face nearly frozen with fear. "I could get drugs any time I wanted. Drugs, alcohol, even women. Ryan had a thing going with Juste and Jean at the strip joint where he worked and the women did whatever he said. I had money and just about anything else I wanted and I just told myself I was keeping Dion safe."

"Are you sayin' the Rousseau brothers are also runnin' a prostitution ring?" Remy demanded.

"No. No." Robert shook his head. "No one pays them. They're strippers. They do what Jean and Juste say to do."

"Out of fear? Do the brothers threaten the women?"

Robert squirmed. "I don' want to talk about this. They're just strippers. I never paid for sex. They put out whenever they're told."

Saria gasped and made a soft growl in the back of her throat. Her dark chocolate eyes had gone nearly gold, a bad sign.

Bijou's fingers dug into Remy's back. He felt her tremble, but not with fear, more with rage. Her breath felt hot on the back of his neck and just for one moment, fur brushed over his exposed skin. She breathed deeply, pulling her leopard back, getting her under control.

Remy was proud of her. He knew Saria could hold back her leopard, but Bijou was new to the world of leopards, and yet she instinctively exerted dominion over her cat. Tension ran high in the room. The male leopards moved just below the surface of their human counterparts, enraged at the sniveling male who acted as if it was perfectly all right to force a woman to do his bidding simply because she worked as an exotic dancer.

"We're goin' to talk about it," Remy snapped, his voice unusually gravelly. "Whether you like it or not. Women who work in clubs don' have to have sex with men because the men demand it. They have the right to say no. Why would you think otherwise?"

Drake prowled up and down the room, coiled and ready. He shot Robert a glare from nearly golden eyes. "Be very careful about lying, Robert. I've run out of patience with you."

Robert shrank back in his chair, his face going pale. "It's not like we have a lot of women around here, and the ones we do have are taken. Those strippers expect to have to put out. It comes with the territory."

"How did they get the girls to cooperate?" Remy persisted.

"One girl, Candy Jacobson, refused when Ryan tried to fuck her out in the alley. She even slapped his face. Juste beat the livin' daylights out of her. He wanted the other girls to see what would happen if they said no. He made certain the others saw her, he took them to her room and then she disappeared. He told everyone she left town, but . . ." He trailed off, shaking his head and looking up at Remy with fear.

"You believe she's dead," Remy prompted.

Robert nodded. "Brent and I went to the swamp early the day she disappeared. Jean and Juste kept their stash of drugs there and we both were hurtin'. There was supposed to be a job that night. Neither one of us wanted to go and we thought if we got wasted, it would be easier."

"And?" Remy insisted through gritted teeth.

"The brothers had weighted somethin' down and shoved it underwater. Both of us caught a glimpse of red material. Candy had been wearin' a red nightgown in her bed when Juste and Jean brought the other girls in to see her."

"You knew they killed this woman and you still didn't come forward?" Remy demanded.

"You really are a worthless human being and an even worse leopard," Drake snarled.

"I didn't know for certain," Robert defended his inaction. "I wasn't about to try to bring up whatever the Rousseaus had put in the water."

Remy felt Bijou press her face against his back. The anger had faded to be replaced by something altogether different. Fear had a distinct smell to it, and Bijou was afraid. His world was dark and violent. Most of the time he lived in the shadows. He tracked murderers and spent his time looking at crime scenes. Bijou lived very differently. She was alone a lot, but in some ways she was protected from the outside world. On tour she'd had a team of bodyguards to watch over her.

Being newly introduced to the world of leopards she had to be a little freaked out. Robert was no example of what they were like, she had to know that, but the rage in both Remy and Drake was tangible and that had to scare her. If nothing else, she had to consider whether or not she wanted to live in a world where the rules were kill or be killed. Make a mistake and the law of the jungle was brought down on one's head. Robert was under a death sentence, and it wasn't just talk. The more he revealed the extent of and his attitude toward the crimes he'd committed, the worse it was for him. No leopard could be jailed for long. The results would be catastrophic. To protect their lair and all of their kind, a rotten apple like Robert had to be dealt with immediately and permanently.

Remy wanted to comfort Bijou, but there was no way to do that. He glanced at his sister. There were tears in her eyes. She knew Robert had dug himself a deep hole. Robert and Dion had always been her friends. She had to be wondering how he could sink so low so fast.

Leopards didn't tolerate drugs or alcohol. Most of the time none of the shifters bothered because one had to really suppress his leopard to feel the effects, and it took a lot. Robert had clearly chosen drugs and alcohol over his own leopard—another major sin in their world.

"Robert," Remy said quietly. He kept breathing deep to keep his own leopard in check. The animal was difficult at the best of times and right now, he wanted free reign to take care of what he considered a traitor to their people. "You're goin' to take me to the site. I don' want an argument so just don' bother protesting. You know the Rousseau brothers are capable of murder. Did you think Jean and Juste might have killed Pete Morgan?" Remy asked grimly.

"I don' know. I thought about it. Brent and I even talked about it. We were supposed to meet up with them that night, but they didn't show. Juste had a run-in with Morgan a few nights earlier. He'd heard Bijou had asked around lookin' for a guide into the swamp and someone recommended Pete Morgan. Juste confronted Morgan because accordin' to Juste and Jean, he had no business actin' like a guide. Pete was a shrimper and fisherman and they didn't want him . . ."

Drake leapt past Remy, a blur of motion, claws raking the other side of Robert's face, furious that Robert knew Saria and every other guide in the swamp might be in danger from the Rousseau brothers, and he handn't come forward to tell. Robert ducked, trying to scramble backward in the chair, but Drake had been far too fast and he was seconds too late. Blood ran down the other side of his face and trickled onto his shirt in four tiny streams.

Bijou shuddered, twisting her fingers deeper into the back of Remy's shirt. She made a soft sound of pure distress in her throat. Remy wanted to fold her into his arms, hold her next to his heart to shelter her from everything else. He reached behind him to run his fingers down her arm in a small, reassuring caress. It was the best he could do under the circumstances.

"They were expandin' their business and wanted money from anyone guidin' in the swamp. Pete laughed at them and refused to pay," Robert howled. "It wasn't my idea. I told them no one livin' and workin' around the bayous or swamps would pay, but they wouldn't listen. They said all they needed was a couple of good examples and everyone would get in line."

"So you knew all this and still you kept quiet. Saria guides tourists," Remy pointed out. "My sister. The wife of your leader, and your friend."

"They didn't threaten Saria," Robert denied. "They didn't."

"You're going to write this all down and then you're going to lead us into the swamp where they conduct these rituals," Remy said. "Don' shake your head, Robert. You've broken just about every single law we have. I'm takin' these two down, and you're goin' to help me do it. I want them for the break-ins and the beatin's. Even if I can't prove they killed Pete Morgan and Ryan Cooper, I'll have them behind bars, and that should give me more time to find evidence they've been committin' these murders if they have."

"We'll go as soon as it's dark," Drake said. "The three of us will go in to uncover the evidence and see what's there. I'll want your brothers, Remy, to be on guard here. We'll have to bring Dion back and put him in protective custody— ours. I trust our leopards to guard him. He won't like it, but that's too bad."

"You know I have to bring Robert in," Remy said.

"No!" Robert nearly jumped out of his chair. "You can't lock up a leopard. You know that. And Juste and Jean will find a way to kill me," he added.

"You don' get a pass on this one," Remy said. "You joined a gang that beat up the elderly and robbed them. The DA will make a deal with you, but you have to face this. I'll do my best to keep you out of jail, and if you do have to be there, you'll be in your own cell."

"You can't let him take me in," Robert appealed to Drake. "You know the Rousseau brothers will get to me if they know I turned them in."

"You said they would get to you no matter what," Drake reminded. "That they aren't entirely human. You can't have it both ways. Robert, you did this. You had options all along and you chose the easy way out. Get on your feet. We're going to take care of this and do as much damage control as possible."

"Gage," Remy said. "Have some of your men keep an eye on Brent Underwood and Tom Berlander. Make certain they do it from a distance. We don' want them tipped off, or worse, the Rousseau brothers to get suspicious."

"No problem," Gage agreed. "Consider it done."

"We'll stay away from the brothers for now," Remy decided. "They probably are crowin' about fooling me in interrogation. Once again, they figure they outsmarted the cops. I want them feelin' all happy, warm and fuzzy. We don' want them runnin'."

"And if they head out to the swamp while you're out there?" Gage asked.

"They'll run into leopards and it won't be pretty," Remy said, his tone unforgiving.

Bijou dropped her arms to her sides and stepped away from him. He turned to face her. She looked stricken and maybe a little sick. "These men sound dangerous, Remy," she whispered.

He reached for her hand and tugged her to him, sliding her under his shoulder and walking her out of the room— away from Robert and the stench of madness. She didn't need to see the corrupt side of leopards, not when she was first learning about her heritage. Like anything, there was both good and bad.

He didn't want to talk to her in front of Robert, or anyone else for that matter. She was intensely private and she wouldn't want him comforting her in front of the others. He took her through to the kitchen and as soon as the door closed behind them, he swung her around and tipped her chin up so he could see her eyes.

"I'm sorry about all this."

For a moment she was silent, pressing her lips together. Finally she nodded. "I never really thought about the kinds of things you have to see when you go to work. Or the kinds of people you have to associate with."

He wrapped his hand around the nape of her neck, a little shocked that her distress was more for him than for herself. "I don' think it's much different from the people you had to associate with as a child, Bijou."

"They were self-indulgent and permissive, but they didn't think it was okay to hurt and rape women and no one murdered anyone," she protested. "I might have been neglected and embarrassed by the behavior, but I never had to deal with the grisly, horrific things you see."

"I'm sorry," he said again. He caressed her cheek with the pad of his thumb. "Blue, I know we have so much to talk about and I keep askin' you to wait for me, but I need you to understand. I can't have these men runnin' loose. Even if they aren't the ones who killed Pete Morgan and Ryan Cooper, they're dangerous and I need to get them off the street."

"Of course. There's no question of that," Bijou said, frowning at him.

"The point is, I'll be workin' all night and maybe most of tomorrow."

"I figured that out for myself. Remy, I'm not a baby, and I certainly am not someone who has to be with a man every moment. I know what you do. I didn't have any idea how awful it was for you, but I got together with you knowing you're a homicide detective. I'm not about to fall apart because you have to work."

She was hesitant about it, but she cupped the side of his face with her palm. "I can be afraid for you. That's somethin' outside my control, but I'm beginning to realize you're a dangerous man and maybe you can take care of yourself after all." She sent him a faint smile.

He bent his head and kissed her, needing the taste of her. Needing to know she wouldn't pull away. He had never thought he would come to need a woman the way he did Bijou. He often reminded himself she hadn't been back that long, that he barely knew her, but somehow she found her way inside and was stamped onto his bones. He had wanted to tell himself it was his leopard, but he feared his leopard had little to do with it now.

She leaned into him, her mouth moving under his, her slender arms sliding up to circle his neck. His kiss started out gentle but once her lips moved against his and her mouth opened to him, it was as if molten fire poured from him to her. There was no stopping, no thinking, only his woman's body moving against his, her warmth seeping into his pores and the taste of her sinking into his bones.

"Are you goin' to wait for me?" he asked.

"I said I would," she murmured against his lips.

He kissed her again, that whisper of a caress too much to resist. His tongue tangled and danced with hers. "I don' want you gettin' any ideas about that Frenchman," he added. He kissed her over and over.

"Frenchman?" she asked faintly.

He lifted his head, a faint grin on his face. "That's my woman. Forget about that filthy rich, suave, very talented artist. What could he possibly have that I don'?"

"I can't possibly imagine," she said, smiling back at him.

He noticed she didn't offer to stay home from the gallery showing if he couldn't make it back in time or had to work the next night.

16

BIJOU dressed carefully for the gallery showing of Arnaud
Lefevre's work. He was always very elegant in his attire, his
suits impressive and his manners impeccable. He moved in
a far different world than Remy's. She'd lived so long like
Arnaud that dressing up was second nature to her. Red carpets, cameras and the right clothing were a way of life.

She liked her blue jeans and casual clothes, but there was
something amazing about wiggling into a designer gown,
one that covered her back and arms to hide all the evidence
of her crazy sexual nights with Remy. She styled her hair in
an elegant updo and put on her makeup carefully. Strappy
heels and swinging sapphire earrings completed the look,
making her feel very feminine.

Remy. She sighed and stared at herself in the mirror.
Apparently they'd torn up the swamp looking for evidence,
and it had taken them all night and most of the day to complete their search. They found what was left of three bodies—

all women—anchored in the water. One was the dancer Robert had spoken of.

Remy sounded tired when she'd spoken to him on the phone. She couldn't imagine what it must do to him to see the horrific things he often had to contend with. His voice had been low, almost so quiet she could barely hear him, but there was sorrow for those women. Sorrow and guilt. They lived where he worked and he hadn't known—hadn't saved them.

The forensic team had gathered human bones and a human skull as well as all sorts of items taken from the homes of the elderly. Remy was certain that prints and blood would match the Rousseau brothers. He hoped the human bones would tie them to Pete Morgan and Ryan Cooper's murders, but he definitely had enough evidence to arrest them for the robberies and beatings. Remy was certain he could get Brent Underwood to testify against them. With Robert's testimony as well, Remy believed he could keep the brothers from getting bail, giving him more time to find evidence against them to connect them to the other murders.

She touched her earring, her fingers caressing the glittering stone. She wanted to see Remy, to hold him close to her and ease his mind just a little. Instead, he was going to work all night and she was going to take her mind off his work by going to Arnaud's showing. Maybe she'd find something special in the gallery for Remy.

"Are you ready, Bijou?" Saria asked, sticking her head through the open doorway.

Bijou smiled at her. "You look beautiful, Saria. I knew that gown would be perfect on you. Does Drake look incredibly handsome?"

Saria nodded. "Yes, he does. When that man decides to dress up he takes my breath away."

Bijou burst out laughing. "That man takes your breath away all the time, and I'm betting even more so when he's *not* dressed."

Color crept up Saria's cheeks. "Okay, I'll concede that's the truth, but don' tell him. Seriously, he already knows I'm crazy about him." She didn't sound in the least upset about it, in fact, she sounded very happy. "You look so amazin', Bijou," Saria added. "Every time I see you, whether you're in jeans or dressed up in your gowns, I'm always shocked at how truly beautiful you are."

"Thank you, my friend." Bijou gave her a little bow. "You always boost my confidence. Have you gone to one of Arnaud's shows? Lots of press. He's very famous and the critics and very wealthy buyers turn out in droves." She knew she sounded proud of him—she couldn't help it. "He really is a genius when it comes to his work. Some of his sculptures are on display in the Louvre. That is an amazin' achievement."

"Poor Remy," Saria said, a cheeky grin on her face. "He's goin' to take one look at you in that dress hangin' on that hot Frenchman's arm and he's goin' to go completely ballistic."

"No, he won't," Bijou denied. "I told him I was goin' and he was fine with it. He knows I'm friends with Arnaud."

"Knownin' it and likin' it are two different things," Saria pointed out. "He's very territorial where you're concerned. He always has been. No one could ever say anythin' about you even when you were a teenager or he'd get upset."

Bijou's heart jumped. "Umm, sweetheart. I love you, I really do, but Remy was gone most of the time when we were teens."

"Most of the time, but he visited once in a while and he always asked about you and how you were doin'. Gage and the boys thought you were a little stuck-up and Remy didn't like that."

"Everyone thought I was stuck-up except you," Bijou said.

It was strange how the memories of those days still hurt. She knew she was partially to blame. She hadn't wanted anyone to know just how awful her father and his bandmates and groupies really were. She was embarrassed by his behavior. She didn't dare take a friend or teacher home for fear Bodrie might seduce them—which of course he had on more than one occasion. She was always the one blamed when he'd refuse to see the person again—not Bodrie.

"Remy never thought you were haughty," Saria denied. "He always seemed to be your staunchest supporter."

Bijou tried not to react to Saria's disclosure, but it was nice to know Remy had remembered her even during her teenage years. She'd felt very much alone during that time. Only Saria had ever really been a friend to her. Saria had no desire to meet Bodrie. She understood the concept of growing up on her own. Her brothers were grown and mostly out of the house and her father had stayed drunk most of the time. It seemed natural for the girls to gravitate toward one another.

It had been the first time in her life that Bijou had experienced true friendship. She'd been leery at first, not trusting Saria's motives, but Saria had been so laid back, disappearing for days on end into the swamp. She had never pursued the friendship, never tried to push herself on Bijou. Bijou found herself drawn to the girl who seemed the exact opposite of her. Saria was a wild child, defiant and independent. Bijou always tried to fit in and not be noticed. Saria couldn't care less what others thought of her, while Bijou seemed to be easily hurt by the things her classmates, teachers and the press said.

"You two ladies ready?" Drake asked and then stopped, whistling. "I get to take out the two most beautiful women in New Orleans."

Saria beamed at him. She slipped her hand into the crook of his arm. "You clean up nice, Drake Donovan."

Bijou took his other proffered arm. "I have to agree with Saria. You look amazin', Drake."

He flashed her a smile. He looked very different than the man who yesterday had been pacing and snarling and raking claws over Robert Lanoux's face. No one would ever suspect that Drake was anything but a gentleman. When he looked at Saria, his features softened, his eyes held the light of love and there seemed to be no trace of that dangerous, lethal animal.

Bijou was caught spellbound by that look. She recognized it on Drake's face, in his eyes, his expression, so why hadn't she recognized it on Remy's face? She memorized every bone, his strong jaw, all that luxurious dark hair spilling so carelessly into his amazing green eyes. Sometimes just looking at him made her feel as if she was free-falling off a cliff, and too far gone to save herself.

But that look she was seeing on Drake's face, the intensity when he looked at Saria, was there on Remy's face when he looked at her. For a moment the breath rushed out of her lungs and she just stood there, frozen, unable to move, shocked at the miracle that had been in front of her all along.

"Bijou?" Saria's voice sounded far away. "Are you all right?"

Remy really was in new territory. He didn't have a clue any more than she did—well, that wasn't strictly true. He had a *lot* of experience, obviously, in areas she didn't, but the emotions were as new to him as they were to her.

"I'm fine," she answered. Her heart felt lighter than it had in years.

"Is Remy going to try to join us tonight?" Drake asked.

There was a hint of laughter in his voice as if he was teasing her. She did her best to look stern. "I doubt it. He's been swamped at work and he hasn't been to bed in over twenty-four hours. If he has any time he'll be sleepin'."

Drake nudged Saria. "Remy is going to be sleeping while Bijou, dressed in that very flattering formfitting gown, is hanging on the arm of another man. Just out of curiosity, do you want to place a little wager on that?"

Bijou laughed. "I'm not about to put money down on guessing what that man may or may not do. He's unpredictable."

Drake escorted the two women down the sweeping staircase and out to the car. "If there's one thing I know about Remy, it's his being predictable when it comes to you, Bijou. Don't ever kid yourself. He's not leaving you alone with another man."

"He knows Arnaud is just a friend."

Drake groaned as he opened the door for her. "Why is it women insist on saying that?"

Bijou slid into the car with great dignity. "Because women have evolved, and they can be friends with men who are not lovers."

Drake snorted his derision as he opened the door for Saria. "We're talking leopards, first of all, and we're very territorial, and secondly, men haven't evolved and they aren't going to."

Saria and Bijou laughed as Drake stalked around the car, looking more leopard than human as he moved with his usual fluid grace. They laughed harder as he slammed the door closed and started the car.

"I hope his temper isn't quite as bad as yours over the subject of men and women being friends," Bijou said.

He glanced at her through the rearview mirror. "Poor woman. You have no idea about that man, do you? You probably are suffering from the illusion that he's sweet."

"He is sweet," Bijou professed.

"Remy has the foulest-tempered leopard of any one of us. And when it comes to you, the way he looks at it is, there are no men who want to be your friends. They're all rivals."

Bijou shook her head. "I think you both blame all of your nonsense on leopards."

Saria burst out laughing again. She nudged her husband. "She has a point there. Remy loves to blame his leopard when he gets all snarly."

Drake shrugged. "Go ahead, you two, but I notice, neither one of you are putting your money against me. Remy's going to show up."

The gallery lights sparkled in the light drizzle, spilling out onto the street along with the music and laughter from inside as they drove up to Arnaud's showing. Bijou was pleased to see the gallery was packed as expected. Arnaud was world-renowned, his sculptures considered some of the greatest in the modern world.

She spotted her manager and the man that had somehow become his shadow in the crowd, as well as a few of the men she'd recognized as bodyguards at her club. She knew they were leopards. Joshua Tregre and Elijah Lospostos, two men she knew Drake or Remy had assigned to watch over her. As if that wasn't enough, she spotted two of Remy's brothers looking elegant in suits, pretending to drink as they mingled with the crowd. There was no pretense about eating, she noted with a small laugh.

Arnaud stood off to the side, a drink in hand, looking more elegant than usual in a black suit and white shirt. He turned as she walked in, lifting his drink in salute, and managing a smile as he came toward them.

He leaned in to brush a kiss against her cheek. "Thank God you've come, Bijou. You know how I despise small talk." He took her hand and tucked it into the crook of his arm. "You've saved me." Once he had her securely anchored to his side, he smiled at Drake and Saria. "Thank you for bringing her. It was becoming a nightmare. I'm not good with people, just my art, and these shows can be excruciating."

Drake nodded, frowning a little as Arnaud set down his drink and put his palm over Bijou's hand. "I can understand. I'm not the best with people either. I like to stay in the background."

Arnaud turned toward him as if for the first time, Drake had caught his interest. "You're married to Bijou's friend," he said and held out his hand.

"Drake Donovan," Drake greeted. "My wife, Saria."

"I'm sorry, Arnaud. We've been friends for so long it didn't occur to me that you wouldn't know Drake and Saria," Bijou said. "I think I've completely forgotten my manners."

"You're forgiven as long as you do all the talking tonight and make me look good," Arnaud replied, once again covering his hand with hers. "I hope you both enjoy yourselves. We have to make the rounds."

Arnaud didn't wait for a reply, forgetting all about them as was his way. He walked Bijou over to his latest sculpture, a five-foot waterfall of color and texture that was breathtaking. "What do you think of this piece? They never come out the way I expect. As I'm working they take on a life of their own."

The piece was titled "Giving Back." The critics had given the sculpture rave reviews and several had attributed the piece to "what it feels like to fall in love."

Bijou studied the waterfall from every angle as she knew Arnaud preferred before she answered him. He had actually captured individual drops as well as the feeling of water rushing over a cliff. Looking closely she could see more than the water. Images began to emerge beneath and in the flowing waves of water.

Entranced, she moved closer. The images appeared and disappeared according to the light shining on the sculpture and whichever direction she was looking from. She studied the images, taking her time, knowing Arnaud appreciated a thorough inspection before pronouncing judgment. He stayed very silent as she moved back and forth, trying to capture each aspect.

It seemed an impossible task to find everything he'd molded into the water. Each time she thought she'd found them all, when she moved, something else revealed itself. "This is amazin', Arnaud. Incredible. I don' know how you could even manage to do this. It's one of the most beautiful things I've ever seen. The weird thing is, the more I look at it, the more beautiful it becomes."

"What do you think I'm trying to say?"

This was always the most difficult moment. Arnaud made statements with his sculptures. He didn't mind the critics getting it wrong, but it mattered to him that she saw his vision, because she was one of the few people he allowed into his small circle of friends. She walked around the sculpture one more time.

"It isn't about fallin' in love," Bijou said. She looked up at him. "At least, that's not what it says to me. All the drops are individual until they hit halfway down the waterfall and then they blend together, revealin' all the faces pourin' over the cliff and flowin' to the bottom into the pool. When I look at it, I see the life in the universe—the way each form of life is on an individual journey as we take that free fall. We come together back in the universe . . ." She bit her lip. "I'm not sayin' this very well, Arnaud, but for me it's a statement on the universe and life and death. That's what I see when I look at this piece."

A slow smile lit up his face for one brief moment and then faded away. "You always 'get' me, Bijou. I believe we all free-fall through the world and then the universe absorbs us back into it one way or another and we give back to it."

"No matter what it means to others, Arnaud, and that's the true beauty of art, everyone sees what they need to see, this sculpture is truly wonderful."

"It's my favorite of all of them."

"You didn't just do faces like everyone would expect," she observed. There was the curve of hair, a perfect mouth, animals and plants, bits and pieces of various living things captured in his sculpture.

"Our life-form shares the planet with millions of other life-forms," he said. "And then all of us go back to dust to feed the Earth."

"I don' know if that's beautiful or terrifyin'," Bijou said.

"Of course it's beautiful. Our life-form is beautiful, but not always those that inhabit the form are. You happen to be very rare, Bijou." He looked around the crowded room, the people in dozens of conversations, sipping on expensive wine and champagne and eating from the hors d'oeuvres trays the waiters passed around. "I think you've found a few friends who seem to be very much like you."

He paused, forced a smile and waved at several people greeting him. Bijou immediately took over for him, making the conversation, easing him into it occasionally. She tucked her hand back into the crook of his arm, a small way of us-ing code between them. When Arnaud needed a little space from the crowd grouped around them, he pressed his palm tightly over her hand and she would find an excuse to graciously move on, giving him breathing space.

The next two hours were spent talking to couples, groups and individual fans of Arnaud's work, all eager to purchase one of his famous sculptures or a smaller item from his rare jewelry section. They worked the room together, Bijou making certain that no one felt slighted. They were all potential customers, and many were repeat buyers, millionaires and even two billionaires perusing the art. Not only did they get to talk to Arnaud, but they were more than delighted to chat with the celebrity on his arm.

The music turned dreamy and the small dance floor became crowded. Men in tuxedos and women in long, glittering gowns moved together to sway and twirl. Bijou caught sight of Saria and Drake dancing, steps perfectly matching.

"Is Drake your bodyguard?" Arnaud asked as they distanced themselves from the latest crowd of admirers.

"No, why?"

"He carries himself like a bodyguard, and he's very aware of everyone in the room and where you are. He isn't the only one either," Arnaud added.

Bijou had forgotten just how much Arnaud, as an artist, took in. He was very observant, even if he really wasn't all that social. She inclined her head, respecting him too much to lie to him. "Remy's worried that someone is tryin' to hurt me. And you know I've always had to have bodyguards. I'm tryin' to make it so that won't be necessary, but I'm not quite there yet."

"You'll get there," he assured. "Although, I like the idea that someone's looking out for you. Is this thing with Remy serious?"

"I've always been serious about him," she admitted. In some ways it seemed a relief that she could say it out loud. "He helped me when no one else would. He stood up for me and risked his job to do it. I always thought he was everythin' a man should be." She shrugged. "I guess I came home to find out if the real thing was as good or better than my fantasy."

"I hope he is," Arnaud said. "You deserve to be happy, Bijou. I hope he keeps bodyguards around you for a long time." He took her hand and brought it absently to his lips, bowing slightly, very old world.

Bijou turned her head as a series of flashes went off. Bob Carson stood only a few feet away, snapping pictures, one right after the other. Involuntarily and in a slight panic, she tightened her fingers on Arnaud's arm. She hadn't expected to see Carson after the incident in the swamp, but smelling him there wasn't the same as proving that he'd been there.

Arnaud put up a hand to shield her from the camera, turning her quickly and walking her toward the back. He glanced over his shoulder. "You definitely have bodyguards looking out for you; they're escorting him out. That's got to be the one who destroyed my car and wrote all over yours. Your stalker."

"There's no proof, but he does scare me a little bit," she admitted. "Who's escorting him out? I can't imagine him going quietly."

She stopped to watch as Gage and Remy came up on either side of Carson. Drake stood in front of him, relieving him of the camera. When he started to protest, Remy leaned in and whispered something very softly to the man. Carson went absolutely pale. He backed up, both hands going up in the air in surrender. Drake handed Carson back his camera as he and Gage walked the photographer outside. Remy turned and looked straight at her.

Her eyes met his. All that intense glittering green. Her heart gave a jump and began to pound hard. He looked extremely handsome in a black suit and tie. His shoes were a little scuffed and his tie had already been loosened, but his jacket emphasized his wide shoulders, and to her, no one could hold a candle to him.

"Have you ever noticed he has cat's eyes?" Arnaud asked. "Very unusual. Very focused. He doesn't blink. He even moves like a cat. Fluid. Graceful. I wish I could capture that particular motion."

With a sinking heart, Bijou recognized Arnaud's tone had already gone to that place she had come to recognize. He was all about the muse and was in work mode, completely forgetting where he was or what he was supposed to be doing. He studied Remy as the detective made his way across the floor, weaving in and out of the crowd easily.

There would be no distracting him, Bijou knew. He was as focused on Remy as Remy was on him. Remy's gaze had shifted to the artist and then dropped to her hand tucked so comfortably in the crook of Arnaud's arm. Faint color stole up her neck to her cheeks. Arnaud wasn't paying any attention to her at all, his artist's focus completely on Remy.

"I went to a big cat sanctuary once and sat on a bench all day just watching the various cats. Look at the way he moves. The crowd actually gets out of his way. He doesn't maneuver around them so much as they move for him, almost instinctively as if they recognized danger, someone higher on the food chain."

"That's probably the cop in him," Bijou said, a little shocked at how perceptive Arnaud was. She should have realized an artist of his caliber would notice things others didn't. "And he was in the military as well. He can handle himself." She tried to distract him.

Arnaud continued as if she hadn't spoken. "One of the most intriguing things I noticed about the large cats was their stare. They would suddenly seem to drop into a hunting zone, and once they fixed that stare on something, they never looked away."

Remy was nearly to them. She could smell him—his wild, masculine scent. He looked so good she wanted to fling herself into his arms, but he wasn't looking at her, he was staring at Arnaud. Not that Arnaud appeared to be intimidated in any way. He didn't seem to notice the danger in the stare, saw only as an artist wanting to capture the look.

The tension heightened as Remy got right up to them, his gaze locked with Arnaud's. Bijou wasn't certain how to act, how to break the near hostility emanating from Remy. Few people could understand Arnaud's obsession. Clearly he was a genius with his art, but he wasn't interested in much else.

"Look at his eyes, Bijou. They're perfection." Arnaud didn't have the least idea he might upset anyone with his comments either. He acted as though Remy couldn't hear him, that he and Bijou were having a private conversation. "Tiger eyes? What do you think? Leopard? Lion? Not lion. Amazing. And his bone structure is nearly as perfect as yours, although male, of course." The words tumbled over one another. "I don't know how I could have missed this the other day when he rescued us." He looked around almost helplessly. "I need my pad and pencils." He scowled. "There are too many people in here, Bijou. Can you get rid of them? I need to sketch him."

She caught both of Arnaud's shoulders in a tight grip. She'd seen him like this before, and it took a lot to bring him out of his nearly mesmerized state. "Arnaud. Look at me. Look at me right now."

His eyebrows came together and it took a moment for him to acknowledge her. He blinked rapidly and then looked around him as if coming out of a trance.

"We're goin' to dance now and then we'll talk to a few more people. After that, I'll get you out of here," she promised. "You can sketch Remy's face and eyes later if you still want to."

She sent Remy a quick look from under the sweep of her lashes hoping he would understand and cooperate. Arnaud could not walk out on his own show. He would not be nice to his customers if he forgot what he was supposed to be doing and disappeared back into his world of art. Arnaud was capable of simply retreating from reality, living in his art and what he was creating. These showings were important to his career, but they took a terrible toll on him.

"I'm just goin' to get a drink," Remy said. "I'll be dancin' with you before we go home, Blue. Nice to see you again, Mr. Lefevre."

Arnaud, still a little distracted, inclined his head as Bijou led him away. Arnaud was a wonderful dancer. He was good at anything he did when he decided it was something he wanted done. She slipped into his arms, smiling a little at the absolute correctness of his dancing style. He knew ballroom and his frame was always exact. He never held her too close or rubbed his body against hers. He danced beautifully, moving her with absolute confidence from one step to the next, so perfectly others stepped back to watch them. He always made her feel as if they were floating through the clouds, he was that light on his feet. He rarely talked when they danced, but he did manage to make her feel like a princess in a fairy tale as he moved her over the floor to the symphony of music.

When the dance was over, several people clapped and Arnaud dipped her with a small smile that never quite reached his eyes. When he pulled her back up, he put his mouth next to her ear. "I have to get out of here. I need to work. I have to get to New York in a few days, so I'm running out of time and everything has set me back. This is such a waste of my time."

"A few more minutes and I'll give you a clear exit," Bijou promised. She'd managed to extricate him from shows early before. "And it isn't a waste. These people love your art and they purchase it, which enables you to make more art. Think of it that way."

"Thanks." Arnaud allowed her to guide him toward two men in suits. Both had very young actresses hanging on their arms. "Tell me their names again. I always forget."

Bijou laughed and obliged. Arnaud rarely cared enough to remember someone's name, although he had amazing business sense. He was a mixture of a dreamy child, a moody, driven, obsessed genius of an artist and a man who seemed to care nothing for the social world he had to maneuver and did so with aplomb.

They spent the next fifteen minutes talking and laughing with the two customers who were two of Arnaud's biggest advocates and had purchased several of his most expensive and biggest sculptures. Bijou did most of the talking, but they were flattered to meet her and flirted outrageously with her. She made a show of glancing at her watch.

"I'm so sorry, but, Arnaud, you have to leave right now if you're going to get the right light you need for your work. If you miss this opportunity, you'll have to wait an entire month before the moon is in the right position again."

She'd used that absurd excuse on three occasions and it always worked. If someone had heard it before, well, genius took time, and if he could only work when the moon was in a specific position, they all wanted to see his next creation so they indulged his obsessive behavior.

Arnaud brushed a light kiss along her cheek and hastily waved to the crowd, disappearing through the back to make his exit fast.

Remy swept Bijou into his arms and onto the dance floor. "You are gettin' harder and harder to keep track of. It takes an army now."

She gave him her most dazzling smile as she looked up into his eyes. He looked tired, exhausted even, but more handsome than ever—and he had that look in his eyes he reserved only for her. "You didn't have to come," she whispered against his shoulder. "I know how tired you are. You need sleep."

Unlike Arnaud, Remy held her close, pressing her body into his, his hands sliding down her back, along her spine to the curve of her hips.

"I need you. You were here, so of course I would come." His lips brushed the corner of her eye and trailed kisses to the corner of her mouth. "I wouldn't want to miss seein' you like this. You look beautiful, Bijou. Absolutely stunning.

When I first saw you, across the room, you took my breath away."

She moved her body against his, melting inside and out. Warm. So much love. The intensity of her feelings for him overwhelming. She wanted to be beautiful for him. "I missed you," she admitted. "Thanks for coming tonight."

"You babysit him, don' you? There really isn't anything more than friendship between you."

"I told you."

"Tellin' me and it bein' real are two very different things."

He was surprisingly smooth on the dance floor, leading her with the same casual confidence and strength that he did everything. He moved with fluid grace and guided her unerringly across the crowded floor. Now that Arnaud wasn't there for her to concentrate on, she was more aware of people whispering and taking photographs with cell phones as she went by them. She buried her face against Remy's shoulder.

Remy bent his head down toward hers, his lips brushing her ear. "I want to take you home and make, long, slow love to you."

She reached up to circle his neck with her arms. "I can't think of anything I'd like more."

It was true. She wanted to be alone with him. She closed her eyes and allowed herself to drift with him to the music on a rising tide of lust and love. With every passing moment, her body reacted more and more to the closeness of his, but it was her heart she found was so full it hurt. She felt his erection, thick, hard and hot against her stomach, and she loved knowing he wanted her as much as she did him.

The longer she was in his arms, the more secure she felt. The world dropped away until there was only the two of them and the delicious embers slowly fanning into flames between her legs. She could feel herself growing slick and hot with need, but unlike all the other times with Remy, this was a slower and gentler build to a coiling tension.

"Come on, *chere*, before I make an ass out of myself," he whispered against her ear. "You've done your job and gotten Lefevre through it. Let the gallery owners do the rest. Come home with me."

She lifted her head and nodded, completely dazzled by him, completely bewitched by him. She would always want to be with Remy, anytime, anywhere. He wrapped his arm around her waist and walked her off the dance floor. She kept her eyes down, refusing to make eye contact with anyone, uncaring if they called her rude or haughty. She just wanted to go home.

"Is this his latest sculpture?" Remy asked.

Bijou blinked rapidly, trying to come out from under his spell and find her voice. She took a quick look around. He had halted to avoid running into a large group of people who clearly had cameras ready and wanted to ask for a picture with her.

Remy shifted his body to put himself between her and the group. Bijou deliberately stared down at the sculpture with a look of enchantment and admiration on her face. She didn't even have to work too hard to come up with the expression. She did admire and respect Arnaud's work.

"It's beautiful, isn't it? He calls it 'Giving Back,' and for him it's about life-forms returning to the Earth and once again becomin' a part of it. Sort of his take on the universe and how it all works and how we're all tied together in one form or another," she explained.

Remy moved around the sculpture just as she had. The gallery lights had been positioned in such a way that no matter where one stood, the focus was on Arnaud's piece. "I'll bet this carries a hefty price tag," he murmured as he studied the images in the fall.

"Hundreds of thousands," she admitted.

Remy shook his head. "You travel in some pretty expensive worlds, Blue."

She touched his face. "I *live* in your world. That's all that matters, isn't it?"

He caught her hand and tugged her closer. "Will you be happy with me, Bijou? Over time, as we get older and our life settles down, will that be enough?"

For the first time he didn't sound as confident as he always seemed. "Yes. I'll be happy with a quiet life, but I seriously doubt that's goin' to happen for a very long time."

His cocky grin emerged. "I plan on keepin' you pregnant, surrounded by seven boys, all as difficult as I am."

"Thanks." She risked a look under his arm at the group of hopefuls waiting by the door. "They're not going to give up, Remy. You want to go out the back? We're not supposed to, but I don' think the owner will mind. I know the way; I've been in the back with Arnaud a few times and I did happen to notice this dark closet that seemed just the right size . . ."

He groaned. "Don't tell me that."

He took her hand, turned her and they fled through the back, winding between the shelves and cupboard and tables to the back door laughing like two small guilty children. He pulled her out into the night and caught her by the nape of the neck, kissing her over and over.

"Get into my car fast or we're not going to have that long slow session of making love I promised," Remy advised.

She laughed softly, in no way intimidated. "That's not much of a threat, Remy," she told him, hiking up the hem of her gown with one hand and hurrying as fast as she could in her high heels. "I happen to know you have stamina. I can have my cake and eat it too."

He yanked open the car door for her. "What does that mean?"

His voice had dropped an octave, making her shiver with anticipation. She waited until he'd come around to the driver's side and had started the car.

"It means I'm good at removin' my clothes in your car, and I think we can make it as far as the bayou road before I start removin' *your* clothes. If you don' want to drive *into* the bayou, and I don't recommend it having been there once myself, I think you'll pull over. We can do slow and easy when we get home."

He let out his breath and drove as fast as he could without putting them in danger. She reached under her arm and un- zipped the gown slowly. He glanced sideways and caught the sight of the side of her breast. She slipped the long sleeves off her arms. The last traffic light before they left the city went red. Bijou held her gown over the tops of her breasts.

"You know Gage is goin' to stop us one of these days and find you completely naked."

The light changed and he drove faster, putting distance between them and any lights. Bijou laughed at his silly warning. Gage would know better, and she knew it. She slid the dress down her body and wiggled it down over her hips. She wore a garter belt and stockings, her heels and nothing else. "Just for you. In case you came to the showing tonight. A thank-you."

"Open your legs."

"Pay attention to the road."

"Open your legs and I will."

"You always have to have your way," Bijou pointed out. She opened her legs for him, shifting a little closer to him. The seat belt lay in between her breasts and the lap belt cinched her waist.

"I'm glad you're finally realizin' that," Remy said, unre- pentant. "I've never particularly wanted to handcuff a woman, but I think I might try that with you. Just for the fun of it."

"Who's goin' to have the fun?"

His finger dipped into her hot canal. "Both of us," he assured. "I can't believe you're still so damned tight." He pressed a second finger deep. "And so slick and hot."

"We're almost to the bayou road," Bijou warned. "I'll be out of this seat belt and goin' after what I want. You're not the only one who wants their way."

"Don' you touch me until I have the car stopped. I won't be responsible for what I do."

Butterflies took off at the growling warning in his voice. She loved teasing him. His fingers drove her insane. She couldn't sit still, no matter how hard she tried. Her hips moved with the wicked rhythm his fingers set and she could feel her body coiling tighter and tighter. She couldn't wait. He was deliberately prolonging her satisfaction. He was already on the bayou road, and yet he didn't pull over and he didn't relieve the gathering tension in her. Every time she came close to falling over the edge, he pulled back.

Her breath hissed out in a low growl of her own. He just laughed. She unlocked the seat belt in one quick flick and went after his trouser zipper. His cock sprang free and she closed her mouth around it, uncaring that her butt was up in the air. She took him deep, her tongue swirling and dancing, stroking up and down his thick shaft and finding the sensitive spot under the leaking head.

That definitely got his attention. He pulled over, finding a spot deep in the trees. She clamped her mouth tight around him, suckling hard, determined that he would be as frenzied for her as she was for him. He caught her head by two fistfuls of hair and pushed her down on him, deeper than she'd ever been. For a moment she panicked.

His hand came down hard on her buttocks. "Damn it. Do you think I'd hurt you?"

The bite of pain was more erotic than she expected. The nerve endings in her bottom spread out like waves of fire straight to her core. He guided her head, pulling her off of him enough to get air and pushing her back down to take him deep. He set the rhythm, controlling every move. Eventually, he let go with one hand and rubbed her bottom with the other.

She could feel his body begin to shudder, his erection swelling, and abruptly he pulled her head off of him.

"Nooo," she wailed. "Remy. I have to have you right now."

Swearing under his breath, Remy nearly kicked the door open, pulling her out with him, which wasn't easy. She stood there, high heels, her sexy garter and her hair tumbling wildly around her. Her beautiful mouth was swollen, her lipstick a little smeared. He placed her hands on the fender of the car and bent her over, pulling her hips back toward him.

"Hold still," he growled when she wouldn't stop moving.

"Hurry. I have to have you and you're takin' your sweet time. I'm burnin' up inside. I swear, *cher*, I'm desperate for you," Bijou pleaded.

He gave her buttocks another flat-handed smack, which only sent more heat flaring through her—he knew because her lavender honey spilled out. He entered her hard and fast, ramming deep, a brutal, savage stroke that she met with her body bucking back toward his. Her muscles clamped down hard around him, squeezing like the tightest fist. She sobbed with delight.

He kept up a harsh pace, driving into her over and over, his hand alternately soothing her bottom and smacking it. Each time he did, hot liquid poured over him. He loved the feel and intensity of it. He loved the scent of arousal and sex. He loved her sweet, hot, tight channel. He loved that no matter how rough he got, she met his every need with her own.

He held out as long as he possibly could, ignoring her cries and pleas, taking them both higher than he'd ever gone. Her muscles clamped so tight, the friction burned like hell and he was lost, exploding jet after jet of hot seed deep inside her. Her body wanted every drop, milking and draining him, while her cries disturbed the alligators in the bayou.

He fought for his breath, holding her still for a long moment, until reluctantly he slipped out of her. Remy was gentle as he helped her to straighten up. "When we get home, *chere*, I'm going to do slow and easy with you. I'll show you what making love is."

She had to lean against him, her legs unsteady. His seed trickled down her thighs, a sexy reminder that just made him want her all over again. He would never get enough of her.

"You have your clothes on," she pointed out when he lifted her to walk around the car. "I'm all sticky."

He kissed her hard. "I like you sticky, and I'm very fond of your high heels and garter. Let's go home. I want to make love to you in a bed."

17

REMY put down his phone, shaking his head, resisting the urge to punch the wall. A fat lot of good it did putting criminals in jail when a corrupt judge put them back out onto the street. He sank down on the edge of the bed and dropped his head in his hands. How was he going to stop murderers from killing again when he didn't know when and where they would strike next?

Bijou shifted her body, sitting up, pulling the sheet around her as she stroked caressing fingers through his hair. Her touch felt like heaven. He hadn't realized just how alone he often felt when he was in the middle of a murder investigation and kept coming up short, feeling as though the weight of the world was on his shoulders. He took his oath seriously, and he felt deeply the need to protect his community.

"What is it? Another murder?"

"Not yet," he said and turned toward her. She looked far too beautiful and innocent to be having a conversation about murder at six in the morning. He still couldn't believe that she belonged to him. She was a miracle, especially right at that moment when he couldn't help but feel despair.

"Judge Thomasson set bail for Jean and Juste Rousseau. He convened a special hearing and no one said a word to me. The DA was told at the last minute and didn't make it there in time, obviously on purpose, so you can bet there's goin' to be another murder. It's just a matter of when they find the body."

His gut told him in no uncertain terms that the Rousseau brothers wouldn't make a run for it, not without trying to clean up loose ends—or get revenge. They were arrogant, and they believed themselves above the law. After managing to get a judge to risk his career for them, they had to feel more powerful than ever.

"Is that even legal?" Bijou asked. "How can a judge do that?"

"No, but he did it all the same and there must be a reason for it. Maybe they threatened him, I don' know and it doesn't matter now. They're out there, and either they're runnin' or they're killin'. They can't get to Robert, Brent or Tom, so I have to try to figure out who they'd go after."

"You, Remy. They'll come after you and Gage. You're the ones who figured it out, and got the evidence against them," Bijou pointed out, her voice anxious.

He had been hoping she wouldn't think of that, but he should have known that would be her first guess. "I doubt they're that stupid. Gage and I are always armed. We're not easy targets. No, they've got someone else in mind," he said to distract her.

"The dancers at the strip joint who agreed to testify against them? You got some of them to agree but they were very scared," Bijou suggested. She massaged his back with one hand, trying to soothe him. "Are you certain Robert, Brent and Tom are all safe? Is there a way they can get to them in jail? Because if witnesses disappear . . ." She trailed off. "That's what you've been afraid of all along, isn't it?"

"There are many voodoo practitioners here in the city as well as in the outlyin' areas. If it's widely known that Jean and Juste are *bokors*, black magic priests, then there will be a great deal of fear of retaliation through voodoo spells as well as violence." Remy ran his hands through his hair again. "The worst part, Blue, is I don' think they're the bone harvesters."

"I thought you found human bones in their camp in the swamp."

He turned and swept her under his arm, needing the feel of her close to him. She was warm and soft and all his. She leaned into him without hesitation, nuzzling his neck with her lips, her breath teasing his skin.

"They killed those women, I know they did, but they didn't take their bones. Those bones were old. They robbed graves, they had to have. Look at what they do. They intimidate using voodoo. They prey on the elderly. Most of the dancers have no one looking out for them, so they make easy targets. Tom has a mean streak in him. He was always a bit of a follower and liked to hang with the bullies. Ryan was the same. Naturally they'd gravitate toward the Rousseau brothers. Robert and Brent are weak and self-indulgent."

"So you're sayin' the Rousseau brothers don't have the personalities for the kind of murders the bone harvester committed. What about tryin' to make the guides in the bayou pay protection money?"

His hands came up to fist in her hair. He loved the feel of her hair, soft and thick and as luxurious as a leopard's pelt, moving against his skin like living silk. He brought the long strands, wrapped around his fist, to his mouth, inhaling the scent of lavender that seemed so much a part of her.

"I think they're growin' bolder, trying to expand their business, like old-time gangsters, but essentially, they're cowards, preying on the weak. They're usin' a centuries-old religion to help them do it. They're intelligent and bold, and they believe they're able to outsmart everyone. With every success they've grown more confident, but they're still evol-vin'. The bone harvester has already evolved. He's been killing for years."

"I didn't consider that," Bijou said, leaning back into him. "You're right. And you know, Remy, every single time you talk about this killer, you say *he* or *him*. It's never *them*."

The sheet slipped just enough to show the tops of her breasts and her nipples barely peeking at him. As always and in spite of everything, his body reacted with an urgent jolt.

"I guess I do," Remy mused. "That doesn't mean I'm not wrong. The Rousseau brothers are definitely sociopaths and they've killed three women, which already makes them serial killers. They're certainly capable of the type of brutal crime, but if they have a ritual like harvestin' bones from their victims, why did they beat the strippers to death? Why didn't they just use their chosen ritual? Serial killers rarely deviate from a ritual. And the harvester's victims have always been men."

Bijou rubbed the back of her head against his chest, much like a cat. "Maybe they don' kill women for the bones because they aren't as dense or something. Maybe the significance is in the bones and not the victims. If the Rousseau brothers wanted the women dead, but they didn't need their bones, would they kill them in a different way?"

Remy kissed the top of her head. She had intelligent feedback and he was grateful for it. He'd considered many different reasons why the harvester only went after men. Age or race didn't seem to matter. He hadn't found a tie between any of the victims until Bijou had pointed out the murders had all occurred in places she'd held a concert. Even then, the victims hadn't necessarily attended her concerts. But maybe she was right and it was specific bones the killer wanted.

"He always takes a different set of bones from each of his four victims before he stops," Remy said, hoping she would continue to talk to him. She had a good head for puzzles and patterns. "He repeats the same pattern in every city he hits, always in the same order."

"Meaning he takes the exact bones from each victim in a certain order?" Bijou asked, sitting up.

"Yes, and he's fairly quick about it. The murders happen in a two-week span. Four dead bodies is a lot in that time period. Twice he took longer, in New York and Chicago. Less time in Paris, just over a week. Otherwise, he's on some sort of schedule only he knows. And why so long between the murders? He doesn't bother to hide them. If there were others, why haven't we heard about them?"

Bijou came up onto her knees behind him, her hands going to his shoulders, kneading the tension from his tight muscles. "You'll find him—or them, Remy." Confidence rang in her voice. "I know you will. You're gettin' closer all the time."

"I've done everything I can to protect as many people as I could think of that the Rousseau brothers might try to go after, but I can't protect random strangers."

He felt the tips of her breasts brush against his back. She was a miracle in the middle of the violent world he lived in. He had asked her if she would be bored when their lives settled down. He should have asked her how long she could stay when he lived with murder every day. Few women could do it for very long, not when he was so obsessed and driven. He had always focused on his work, and he knew that wouldn't change.

"You'll catch them," she assured him again.

She was like the calm in the middle of a storm. Her hair fell over his shoulder and he wrapped his fist in it. Love had grown when he was least expecting it. Love was strong and alive, driving out the shadows in his mind. She seemed to be able to light up his world even in his darkest hour.

Bijou kissed the top of his head, shuffled to the side of the bed and rose gracefully. Remy's breath caught in his throat. She was truly a beautiful woman. He found it astonishing that she was here, with him, discussing murder when she looked as if she belonged in a fairy-tale castle. Her hair was tousled, long, hanging to the sweet curve of her butt.

He enjoyed his hands in her hair, and every time she had it up, or in braids, he found he couldn't wait to let it fall so he could indulge himself. He'd made love to her—how many times last night—yet he wanted her again. Right then. For comfort maybe—hell—he didn't know. Maybe to make him feel like there was something worth fighting for.

He caught her hand. "Blue." He just said her name. That was all.

She turned to face him, her eyes meeting his. He didn't know if he expected rejection or a protest because of the subject matter they'd been discussing. He only knew his breath stayed caught in his lungs, and he waited silently. She had to be tired and sore. He'd ridden her hard and long over and over again, he reminded himself.

She ran one hand through his thick hair, stepping so close to him he could smell their combined scents on her. His marks were all over her body. More leopard than man at times when they made love, he could be rough. He leaned forward and kissed a dark smudge just on the inside of her thigh. She trembled. He stroked his tongue over the bruise. His hand moved higher and encountered heat.

That wild urgency settled inside of him. "You're wet for me."

"I'm always wet for you. I get wet just lookin' at you," she admitted. "It's hell on my panties."

"Don' wear the damn things," he suggested, and leaned forward to press his mouth into her center. He loved the taste of her, all that wild lavender honey. He caught her hips with both hands and dragged her to him, his tongue stabbing deep, seeking more honey, drawing it out and devouring her for his early morning pleasure.

She steadied herself by placing her hands on his shoulders, her soft little cries of pleasure escaping in spite of her desire to stay quiet. Along with all the other things he loved about her, those soft sounds were music to him. She threw her head back as he indulged himself. His tongue teased and danced and he suckled at her little clit, until her legs trembled and her soft cries grew more demanding. She actually fisted his hair to pull his head back.

He grinned at her. "Is there somethin' you wanted, *chere*?"

"You, Remy Boudreaux," she answered back, panting a little. Placing one hand on his chest, she pushed him back until he allowed himself to sprawl across the bed. "Right now. Right here."

"Has anyone ever told you, you're insatiable?"

"You started this," she pointed out, straddling his hips. "I just intend to finish it."

She settled over his heavy erection slowly, using a sliding corkscrew motion that forced the air to rush from his lungs and every nerve ending in his body to come alive. Little electric sparks leapt through his blood stream and rushed to a single point in his groin.

Bijou looked exotic and beautiful with her cat's eyes, the wealth of dark hair falling like a silken cape to caress her satin skin. Every move she made drew his attention to her full breasts, rising and falling, swaying with the rhythm as she rode him. She made those little sounds, that sexy music he couldn't wait to hear, as her muscles gripped and squeezed every time she made the descent over his rigid cock.

He reached up and cupped her breasts, his thumbs rubbing at the hard little peaks. As her body rose over his and fell, and the little small circles she made with her hips drove him mad while her muscles gripped with the strength of a fist, he used his fingers to tug and pull, to do some rolling of his own. Her gaze jumped to his, and then she threw back her head, grinding down harder, but still keeping that excruciating, slow pace. A flood of lavender honey bathed him in slick heat.

He transferred his hands to her hips. That slow, easy glide was designed to drive him insane and it was working.

"What's wrong, leopard boy?" she taunted. "Too much for you? Can't take it?"

"You're goin' to get yourself into trouble," he cautioned, his fingers digging deeper into her hips. If she did one more slow spiral, those tight muscles dragging over him with such hot friction, he might just lose his mind for real.

"I think I've proven I can take whatever you dish out," she replied, rising over him and starting another slow spin down.

"I want you to remember that the next time we have a lot of time and a location where no one can hear you when I make you beg," he warned, gritting his teeth as the muscles moved as if alive, a velvet fist so hot and tight strangling him in a fierce grip.

She rose again, a small, teasing smile on her face. He waited until she began that slow spiral down and he moved his finger into her, finding her sweet spot and making those same slow teasing circles before tugging and teasing.

Bijou cried out softly and rewarded him with a fresh flood of her hot honey, coating both his cock and fingers. He licked that lavender cream from his fingers and then when she started down again, he thrust upward hard while he dragged her down over him. Her cry was louder as he swelled more, forcing her body to accept him.

He rolled fast with her and came up on his knees, pushing her legs up and back over her shoulders so he could thrust as deep as possible. Sometimes he wanted to crawl inside of her, and share her skin and bones. He needed those soft little cries building to a crescendo. He needed her body gripping his in a stranglehold. He had to know she needed him the same way.

Bijou gave him everything he demanded of her, generously, unafraid, and made few demands of her own. She might have started out inexperienced, but she made up for it with her determination to please him—to give herself to him in any way he needed or demanded. He closed his eyes and let the rush just take him, hurtling through him like rockets going off.

Her body shuddered and rippled around his as he took her with him. She lay quiet beneath him, her breath ragged, her eyes a little glazed and her hair a wild mass of silk across the bed. Remy collapsed over her, blanketing her completely, pressing his body into hers, as if that could stamp him onto her skin.

Her arms went around his neck, hands sliding over his shoulders to his back. She held him tightly to her. He felt every heartbeat as his own, every rise and fall of her breasts as she took in air and let it out. He felt her in his mind, bathing every dark memory with light.

Remy kissed her several times before pulling back, afraid of his weight hurting her. Reluctantly, he slipped out of her. Still, he kept her pinned, one thigh over hers, looking down into her eyes. He framed her face with both hands. "Do you have any idea how I feel about you?"

"Maybe. A little. You don' talk much about it," Bijou pointed out.

"I've never told a woman I love her. Never. Not once. But you, Blue." He shook his head.

"You don' have to . . ."

He laid a finger across her lip, that amazing, fantasy lower lip he couldn't resist. "Let me say this to you. I need to. Even if it's just this once. You deserve to know."

Bijou nodded, her tongue curling around his finger and drawing it into the warmth of her mouth. His cock jerked in response.

"Everything you do is so fuckin' sensual, Blue. Everything. I tried to make this about our leopards. And then about sex. But I ran out of places to hide. I had no idea what love was. I'd never felt it before you came along. I needed time to sort it all out. I didn't honestly think it would happen for me. You came along, and you were just too damn good to be true. I had no idea the emotion would be like this. All encompassing. So intense. I feel a little like a deer caught in the headlights."

He used his finger to tease her mouth before bending his head to hers and kissing her. "What I'm tryin' to say in my own clumsy way is, I'm very much in love with you."

Bijou's long, feathery lashes swept down and up several

times. For a moment he thought tears swam in her eyes, but after she'd blinked a few times, her eyes were clear, sparkling and looking at him with everything he could have wanted.

"Say it. Tell me," he urged.

"I don' have near the confidence in myself you think I do. When I'm singing, Remy, that's someone else. When I'm me, I have no real idea of even how to be in a relationship, let alone how to love someone properly. You're taking a big risk."

He smoothed back her hair. "I told you right from the start to trust me. I'll get you through it. We'll find our own way, Blue. But you'd better tell me before I do something rash."

She laughed softly. "You're so crazy." She traced the smile on his face. "Of *course* I love you. I came back to New Orleans just for you. It's always been you."

Satisfaction went deep. He kissed her again. "Come on, honey, I can smell coffee and breakfast." He slipped off the bed and pulled her up beside him.

They took a long slow shower, Bijou washing him carefully and thoroughly, which required another, much quicker assault on her body. Remy felt relaxed and ready for work by the time they went down to breakfast. He wasn't in the least surprised to see Gage waiting for him, looking as grim and upset as Remy had been before Bijou had worked her miracle on him.

"You need a woman, Gage," he greeted and poured himself a cup of Saria's excellent coffee. "You spend too much time with murder these days." He was only half teasing. Gage did look older. He'd always been a bit of a prankster, but there was little left of the boy. He didn't care to see his brother take the same path he had, but clearly, it was too late.

"We all need the right woman," Gage said. He smiled at Bijou. "Good mornin'. How long do I have to wait to have you as my sister? It will boost my status with the voters as well as my men."

Bijou laughed. "Glad I can be of some help to you." She took the coffee he offered and sank into a chair, clearly savoring the aroma of the fresh-baked beignets. "I know this morning must be awful for you, Gage. I'm so sorry."

"Have you heard anything more?" Remy asked. "Have the Rousseau brothers been located?"

"Not so far, but Judge Thomasson was found this morning with a self-inflicted bullet hole in his head."

Remy's head came up sharply. "Are you certain it was suicide?"

Gage nodded. "He left a note, said he couldn't stop the voices whisperin' in his head, telling him to kill himself. He knew he was possessed. He had to free the Rousseau brothers, because he knew if he didn't they would send their demons to him to rob him of his soul. They wanted the charges dropped, which he couldn't do, so they sent their demons anyway."

"Voodoo," Remy said softly. "He was a believer."

"Go into the dinin' room and eat," Saria said. "Both of you. And you too, Bijou."

Remy followed Gage into the dining room and sat down at the ornate dining table. Of course Saria had made a big breakfast for them. She always made certain the men in her house had food, a leftover habit from taking care of her father, or maybe it was more likely she enjoyed cooking and feeding her family.

"Yes, he had faith, but he should have gone to Eulalie and to us. We found a recorder in his vents, motion-activated. Voices whisperin' to him to kill himself," Gage said. "The Rousseau brothers took out a little insurance to make certain their legend grew in the eyes of the voodoo community." He sat across from Remy and reached immediately for the trout.

"I would say that means they're still around. We have to figure out where they are before they get out of town and become someone else's nightmare," Remy suggested. He scooped up trout and added poached eggs and hollandaise sauce from the silver warmers set in the middle of the table.

"Fresh-squeezed orange juice," Saria announced, putting two wineglasses filled with the juice in front of her brothers. "Drink it. Neither one of you is gettin' any sleep, and if you're going to catch all the criminals lurking around the bayou, you'd better be in shape."

"Yes, ma'am," Gage said, and dutifully downed the orange juice in one long gulp. "Where's our esteemed leader?"

Saria pressed her lips together and looked away.

"Saria?" Remy dropped his voice to that one note no one ever disobeyed.

She took a deep breath and poured herself a glass of orange juice, clearly stalling. "When Gage called this mornin' and said the Rousseau brothers were gone, he went into the swamp in the hope of tracking them," she admitted, carefully not looking at either brother.

"And he didn't think it was necessary for him to have backup?" Remy demanded, his fork halting inches from his mouth.

"Of course he had backup. He said forensics hasn't come out yet with the theory of animal fur and leopard paw prints, so if they were careful, they might be able to have somethin' for you within an hour or so."

Remy lifted an eyebrow. "Lojos and Mahieu, I presume?"

Saria nodded. "He said you and Gage were workin' on a couple of hours of sleep and the lair needed to help out. He called the others and told them to be watchful, but not to actively hunt."

"And Dash. What is he doin'?" Remy asked shrewdly. "Bijou, don' just drink coffee. Eat breakfast," he added, and scooped trout and eggs onto a warm plate.

Bijou, curled up on her chair sipping at her coffee, looked startled. "I'm not hungry."

"Be hungry," he said. "Saria? What the hell does Drake have Dash doin'?"

"He's on guard duty," she said. "Bijou, you have bites all over your neck."

Remy couldn't stop his gaze from finding Bijou, even when he knew his sister was trying to throw him off track. A faint blush stole up her cheeks. She looked thoroughly loved. Taken. Claimed. Her hair tumbled down her back in a blue-black cloud, held loosely by a single clip at the nape of her neck. She wore soft blue jeans riding low on her hips and a cotton top of pale pink that wasn't quite pink but probably had some girlie name like *mauve* that complemented her skin perfectly. Both hands cupped her coffee mug, holding it in front of her like a shield.

"Blue, we need to put a ring on that finger soon." Remy made it a statement. A blue stone. Sapphire or blue diamond. He had plenty of money saved. He could spend it on a suitable ring for her.

Her blush deepened. "I thought the subject was what your brother was doin', not us."

He grinned at her and held out a fork. "Just in case you're pregnant and eatin' for two. And just so you know, you're always on my mind."

She took the proffered fork, more, he was certain, to get the attention off of her, than to eat much. Gage didn't help by grinning from ear to ear like a baboon. Even Saria smirked a little behind her hand.

"Keep it up, Gage," Bijou hissed between her teeth. "You're close enough that I could get you with this fork."

"I'm not laughin' at you, Bijou. It's just that my brother has it *so* bad. He's like a crazy man right now, and it's just really fun for me. Not to mention, when he's bossin' you, he forgets all about bossin' the rest of us."

Remy chose dignity. It was the only course of action when his brother might be stating a fact. He scooped up a couple of *couche-couche*, a Cajun-style fried cornmeal mush that Saria always made to his liking, and ignored Gage altogether.

"So where exactly is Dash at the present time?" Remy

asked his sister after downing more trout. "Is he watching over you while Drake is gone?"

"Sort of," Saria sounded a bit mischievous.

Remy sat up very straight. "Did Drake leave him behind to guard me?"

Saria nodded, the amusement fading from her dark eyes. "He's worried the Rousseau brothers will come after you and Gage, and, Remy, before you explode, it makes sense. You and Gage are relentless when you're trackin' someone. Everyone knows that. You're the ones who ruined things for them. They think they're unbelievably clever, and they believed they were invincible, that no one would dare testify against them. The two of you brought them down and they aren't the type to go quietly into the night."

Bijou made a small sound of distress and leaned toward him. "I *told* you."

Remy reached out and took her hand, bringing it under the table onto his thigh. His thumb slid back and forth in a soothing caress. He didn't need her upset or worried about him. He thought he'd dodged the bullet when he'd thrown her off with his assurances earlier.

"Did you tell Drake that?" Remy asked. His sister had always been intelligent and she thought like a lawman.

"I may have started the conversation," Saria said, unrepentant.

Bijou caught Remy's hand beneath the table to still his fingers. He could feel the slight tremble, but when he looked at her, she had her chin up.

"I told you, Blue, the chances are slim that they're that stupid. These boys are locally bred. They know our reputations, and they aren't goin' to risk their lives and freedoms by getting anywhere near us."

She was leopard. There was no hiding anything from a leopard, not once they knew you, and Bijou was beginning to know him very well.

"You think they'll come for you," she said. "You told me you'd never lie to me."

Remy shook his head. "No, *chere*, I *don'* think they're that stupid. I'm not saying the thought didn't cross my mind, and maybe I was a little wishful, but from everything I've seen of them, these are smart boys. They aren't goin' to mess with us."

She relaxed a little, letting out her breath. "Just be careful, Remy. I couldn't bear it if anything happened to you."

"What am I? Chopped liver?" Gage complained.

Saria laughed. "Not exactly, brother. You're the clever one who pegged the Rousseaus for the break-ins."

"No one beats up the elderly on my turf," Gage snapped, the smile fading from his face.

Remy looked away quickly. He was proud of Gage, more than proud of the man his brother had become. Gage carried the confidence of the people in his parish for a reason. "No, they don't, brother," he murmured and raised his coffee cup.

The sound of a leopard roaring nearly shook the house, sending chills down Remy's spine. He dove at Bijou, knocking her from her chair, taking her to the floor as Gage did the same to their sister. The bullet went straight through the dining room window, through the picture on the far wall so that glass splintered and sprayed down.

"That was Dash callin' out a warning," Remy hissed. "Move, crawl to the kitchen. Stay low. Saria, there's a safer room in your quarters. Take Bijou and go there, but both of you be ready to shift if you have to. You have guns stashed, Saria?"

Saria nodded. "I prefer my knife."

"There's the saying about don't take a knife to a gun-fight," Gage pointed out. "We'll leave Dash to watch over you. Hopefully Drake and the boys are on their way back."

Remy pushed Bijou's bottom lower as she began to crawl after Saria. "Use your elbows and toes to propel yourself forward."

Gage pushed the dining room door open to allow them to pass through. Two more bullets hit the door.

"Where are you going?" Bijou asked as they scuttled through.

"Hunting," Remy said grimly. "It's what I do best." He put his hand on her bottom and shoved. "Keep moving. Get into Saria's main livin' quarters."

"You can't go after him as a leopard," Saria protested. "He has a gun."

"A sniper rifle to be precise," Remy said. "And don' worry about me. Be worried about him. He could have shot you or Bijou. You don' mess with a man's family."

They crawled through the kitchen to Saria's side of the Inn. She had a comfortable three-bedroom home attached to the Inn. On the wall nearest the kitchen, a small hutch was in the entry way. Gage and Remy got to their feet and quickly moved the hutch, opening the entrance to the passageway behind it. Saria scrambled in with Bijou close behind.

Remy caught Bijou's shirt with his fist and pulled her to him. "Please, this one time, for me, do as Saria says. She knows the swamp like the back of her hand. She can lead you safely out of here. Don' try to help us. Gage and I will take care of the problem. Dash will have alerted the other leopards and they'll come runnin' to protect you and Saria. Just follow Saria's lead."

Bijou nodded solemnly, her eyes enormous. She leaned in to brush a kiss over his mouth. There was no crying. No hysterics. No pleading. Just her quiet acceptance—and her trust in him. Faith and trust were priceless gifts. He wasn't about to let her down.

"Be safe," she whispered against his mouth.

Remy kissed her again and then moved away from her down the passage, all business. He stripped off his shirt as he went, removed his gun and zipped it into the pack every leopard carried, adding a few extra magazines, giving him plenty of ammunition for a war should he need it. He left his shoes and jeans by the entrance to the swamp.

The passageway was covered mostly by plants and trees

and a lot of stonework, but few knew of its existence outside the family, so he was fairly certain no one was waiting. Remy shifted, allowing his large black leopard to take over. His sense of smell was acute and he would find the shooter quickly.

Gage was right behind him, and as they emerged into the damp swamp, he gave Remy room, flanking him and shifting to his left side. Almost at once, the leopard scented the intruder and the rank smell of gunpowder. Snarling, the cat went low, slinking along the ground, using its fluid, flexible spine and its large cushioned paws to move silently. He didn't disturb a single leaf or branch of a bush. There was not the slightest of warnings that the male leopard was anywhere in the swamp.

Remy glanced sideways and saw that Gage's cat had also gone to ground. Their quarry was up above them, in the crook of a cypress tree, but there was a second man, presumably spotting for the first. The stench of the Rousseau brothers filled his nostrils. The large cat snarled silently and began his approach, a freeze-frame motion, stalking his prey.

"I can't see anything," Juste reported. "We should get out of here."

"They're pinned down," Jean snapped.

"They can get out the front of the house, and no doubt they've called in reinforcements. We'll have helicopters looking for us," Juste said, the voice of reason.

"I say we go to the house and put a bullet in their heads. I want to kill the whole damn family. Wipe them out. And then I'll take my time with the women and beat them with my hands. It's been too long since I've had that pleasure," Jean said, and wiped his mouth as if the very thought made him drool in anticipation.

"You're a sick son of a bitch," Juste laughed, but his voice was strained. "Jean, we've got to go while we can. We'll come back and kill them, but not now."

The cat slipped through the brush until he was within striking distance. Smoldering intelligence shined in the focused stare. Remy's leopard had marked his target. He would take the one in the tree, and Gage's leopard, already moving into position, would go after the man already on the ground.

It was impossible to see either leopard. Gage's spots helped him to blend into the vegetation easily, and Remy's leopard had sunk so low to the ground and moved with astonishing nearly frozen, almost imperceptible increments that he blended even when he was slightly exposed. The leopards had great patience, waiting motionless, eyes and minds completely focused on their unsuspecting prey.

Inch by inch they crawled forward and then froze, belly to ground, stalking the hunters. Gage was so close to Juste he could have reached out and touched him. He waited for Remy to get into position. Jean was in the tree, lying in the crook of a branch, sniper rifle at the ready, aimed at the Inn. Remy would have to leap, using his superior weight and the force of his strike to knock Jean out of the tree and away from his rifle.

Jean glanced down at his brother, reluctance on his face. "This is such bullshit, Juste, they just got lucky." He began to pull his rifle from where he had it steadied on the tree branch.

The leopard hit him with the force of a freight train right in the chest, knocking him backward out of the tree, breaking bones, the hot breath of death in his face as the cat followed him to the ground and landed on him, teeth sinking deep in his throat.

They stared at one another. Pitiless, golden-green eyes focused solely on Jean's terrified, shocked brown ones. The leopard's suffocating bite went deep as the cat clamped down relentlessly. Jean thrashed, hitting helplessly at the creature that held him so easily with teeth and claws.

Behind him and just in the corner of his vision, the spotted leopard had hit Juste from the side with the same ferocious and calculated intensity as the black leopard had Jean. He held Juste in the same suffocating bite. Jean had his head turned toward Juste, but already the light faded from his eyes.

The two leopards held their prey in unbreakable grips, waiting for the life force to leave the bodies. The moment the brothers were dead, the humans took back control, forcing their cats away from their prey. As they did, Lojos and Drake broke through the brush in human form. Both of them carried weapons.

Remy shifted, catching the pair of jeans Drake tossed him. Gage shifted and pulled on a pair of jeans his brother Lojos provided.

"We have to get rid of the bodies quickly, before anyone comes along," Remy said. "Take them to that monster of an alligator's hole. No one ever disturbs him and he'll hide the evidence of leopard's bites better than anything else. Break the gun down and toss it in his hole as well. If we're very lucky, no one in our lifetime will find it."

"Consider it done," Lojos said. "We'll take care of it."

"We didn't find the brothers, obviously," Drake added. "But we did find another body." He paused with a small sigh. "Unfortunately, both you and Bijou know him."

18

REMY crouched down as close as he could to the bloody mess that was Bob Carson and looked him over carefully, pushing aside the fact that the body, stripped of life and dignity, so brutally tortured, had once been a man. He was nothing more than a carcass hung in the tree, like a deer carved for its meat. Only Carson had been carved for his bones.

Remy didn't like the man. Carson had stalked Bijou for years—had probably entertained the idea of getting rid of her when she was an eight-year-old child so that he had a chance of inheriting Bodrie Breaux's fortune. He'd tormented Bijou by keeping her in the tabloids, by feeding them so many misleading stories and headlines to photographs he manipulated into the worst possible lies in order to get money—and embarrass her.

Still, no one should die like this. Hard. Mean. Screaming for mercy with no one but alligators to hear. Carson had been at the gallery a few hours earlier and Remy had helped to throw him out.

"He always has his camera with him," Remy said. "Find it. And where's his car? How did he get out here? I can't see him walking out here by himself at night in those dress shoes he's still wearing. He didn't change his suit either, so he didn't go back to his hotel and change before he was killed."

Carson wasn't local. He wouldn't just be fishing or hunting nutria for his family. He had no reason to be in the swamp. Even if he'd tried to work his way around to the back of the Inn, he'd go in by the lake. This particular spot was a place not far from Bodrie's camp. Had Carson been going there when the killer ambushed him?

Drake and Remy's brothers had known better than to mess up a crime scene and they'd stayed away from the body. Mahieu had stayed behind to guard it and keep any alligators away while Drake and Lojos returned to the Inn to get Remy and Gage. Nothing had been touched, but still, something was off-kilter, just a little wrong.

He paced around the outer edges of the crime scene, looking at it from all angles. The blood spatter was worse than usual, which meant Carson was alive a very long time, but some of the other victims had also lasted longer than one would expect under the circumstances. The altar was perfect as usual, without one drop of blood other than the pint in the bowl and the heart sitting behind it. The dead man's left hand was oiled and had a candle tied to it. The rocks were arranged in the familiar rectangle with meticulous care.

He stood a distance away, frowning, surveying the scene. Gage joined him. Forensics hadn't arrived yet and the swamp seemed peaceful enough, but as always, living by its own laws. The continual drone was steady, insects buzzing around the body and feasting on what was left.

"The Rousseau brothers could have done this, Gage. They were in the swamp for certain, and not far from here."

"Yep. They could have." Gage watched his brother's face.

Every expression. Every nuance. The sharp intelligence in his eyes.

"Carson, though? That doesn't make sense. He wouldn't have been in the swamp at night alone, not dressed in his fancy gallery-showing clothes. He had to have been brought here. He's not a target of opportunity for them."

"And they have a lot of others to choose from, people they were really angry with," Gage agreed. He waited for more. Remy puzzled things out, a master at it, and learning from him would only make him better at his own job.

Remy kept looking at the body. The altar was perfect. The discarded plastic suit was in the exact position it should have been, but there was something off and he just couldn't put his finger on it.

"If the Rousseau brothers did this, and I wish they had, it makes no sense at all to choose Carson." Remy carefully moved closer to the body, wanting to examine the neck to the see if the killer had done the same thing to Carson as he had to Cooper.

"Carson could have accidentally filmed something the Rousseaus didn't want him to see," Gage ventured.

"We've got to find the camera," Remy said over his shoulder.

"Got it!" Drake triumphantly held up the very expensive camera still inside its case. "It was near the road, where the killer must have parked his car. He walked in. There are depressions in the grass. He carried Carson, so he's very strong. I couldn't find a decent print of a shoe, but he definitely walked in and it's a long way to carry a grown man."

"Two people?" Remy asked.

Drake shook his head. "I don't think so, Remy. You can take a look yourself, but it looks like one man carrying a very heavy load. If Carson had been knocked out, he'd be even heavier. If he wasn't, he would have been fighting and the steps wouldn't have been so precise and steady."

"He'd have to carry his bag of equipment as well," Remy

mused. "I doubt if he'd make two trips. His car would be on the road for any passerby to notice and if he left his victim, anything could have happened, from a poacher huntin' alligators at night to Carson coming to and getting away. He's strong. Like a leopard strong."

"Robert was in custody," Drake said, his tone neutral.

"Jason Durang was in prison," Gage said. "He worked out like most prisoners and he's an extremely strong—and dangerous—man. He could easily have overpowered Carson. Carson's not exceptionally big."

Remy kept looking at the body while Gage examined the photographs on the camera.

"We do have an excellent timeline, Remy," Gage pronounced. "Carson took a whole hell of a lot of photographs last night."

In the distance, they could hear the sheriff's boat making its way toward the spot, coming in from the water with the forensic team. Word would be spreading up and down the bayou that another murder had taken place in their backyard.

Remy continued to look at the body. Carson had taken a while to die, mostly because the killer hadn't severed any arteries when he began carving him up. But still, there were no marks on the throat indicating multiple chokings. He sighed and ran a hand down the back of his neck. It was right there in front of him, but he wasn't getting it.

"Remy, you have to take a look at these pictures Carson took," Gage said again. He walked the camera over to his brother. "Start here. There's an entire series, startin' at the gallery, inside, before we tossed him out. The first few pictures were of the sculptures in the gallery and then the more famous and wealthy jet-setters who came to fight for the right to purchase one of Lefevre's latest creations. There are many photographs of Arnaud and Bijou. He's definitely fixated on her."

"That's not news."

"He took more photos with a zoom lens from across the

street after we tossed him out, but the windows are glass and the place was lit up like a Christmas tree. Between those pictures and his scribbles for the headlines and article idea, we've at least got a timeline of his whereabouts right before his murder."

"Did we get lucky enough to get his murderer caught in the act?" Remy asked, half serious. Of course, had the murderer been on the camera, he would have ditched it in the swamp or canals. No one was that stupid.

"Take a look, Remy," Gage encouraged. "There's a hell of a lot of photographs and some are very unexpected. I'd rather not jump to conclusions or influence you in any way. See for yourself."

Remy took the camera with a gloved hand, studying the photograph Gage had brought up. Bijou, looking beautiful and far too elegant, was laughing, looking into Arnaud's eyes over his drink. The next picture was of the two of them, studying his latest creation, a look of rapt attention on her face. Arnaud seemed enthralled with Bijou, his gaze only on her. If one just looked at the series of photographs and knew nothing of Bijou and Arnaud's relationship, they would believe the two were lovers.

He moved on to the next few shots. They were taken from outside the gallery, Bijou and Arnaud dancing and then many more of Arnaud staring at Remy's face. The artist looked enraptured. Even enamored. Definitely fixated on Remy now, not Bijou.

"It's interestin' what interpretation one can put on a photograph," he murmured. "I can imagine what spin Carson was going to put on these."

There were more photographs of Remy and Bijou dancing together and they definitely looked like lovers, dancing so close their bodies were practically entwined. There was one of Bijou looking up at him and his heart clenched hard. There was love stamped on her face. She looked beautiful, so beautiful. The moment should have been private between

them, but Carson had planned on spreading it out in a tabloid, with photos of Lefevre as well and calling it "love
triangle with a twist."

Remy went still when the next set of photographs appeared. He could feel Gage watching him. Rob Butterfield
was hunched over the trunk of his car, one hand on the latch
as he talked to Jason Durang. The two looked furtive, which
had probably been the reason they drew Carson's attention.

Durang's vehicle, a four-wheel-drive Jeep, was parked very
close to Butterfield's Mercedes. The next shots showed the
Mercedes trunk open and Butterfield reaching in to extract a
large plastic tarp and more plastic sheets folded. Remy's
mouth went dry. He glanced at his brother, who looked grim.

"Keep goin'," Gage suggested.

The next shot showed Butterfield spreading a leather-type
case open on the hood of his car. Both men peered down at
it. Carson used a zoom lens to focus on the set of surgical
tools.

Remy's pulse leapt. His leopard snarled. They had
planned a murder, but whose? Bijou's? Had they planned to
kill her and make it look as if the bone harvester had done
it? He'd been worried about that for a while. Had Carson
caught them in the act and then been caught himself?

"Get a warrant, Gage. Let's search both vehicles. We
should have enough with these photographs for that."

Remy continued to examine the pictures Carson had
taken that night. After he left the parking lot, he'd gone to
the small studio Lefevre rented to work in. The room was
surrounded on three sides by mostly glass for the light.
Again there was a series of photographs, all capturing the
Frenchmen engrossed in his work, busy sketching. At times
the artist almost looked frantic, driven by his relentless need
to create. There were dozens of sketches of Remy's eyes. Of
his face. Some just of his mouth.

Remy could see how Carson could twist the photographs
into something altogether different than an artist's capti-
vated interest in facial structure and features. He could

definitely piece together photographs and make them look like a love triangle with Arnaud interested in Remy. Carson's plan was to accuse Bijou of a threesome. The headline he'd chosen was "Bijou's two lovers in love."

Arnaud clearly was totally absorbed in his work. Remy doubted, if Carson had actually been in the room with him, that the artist would have even noticed him taking photographs. Carson had zoomed in on the sketches just as he had the surgical instruments earlier in the parking lot. Remy's eyes had been drawn over and over, but Arnaud had discarded the sketches in frustration, compelled to capture the exact look he had seen in Remy's eyes and clearly failing.

The next set of photographs was of two men in the shadows who seemed to be watching Arnaud through his studio windows. They were back in the alley and Carson must have caught them by accident. The second photo showed the two men appearing to argue.

Remy realized Arnaud looked as wealthy as he was. He sat alone in a well-lit room where anyone hard up for money and willing to rob him would see. He probably appeared to be the perfect victim, a man who was so focused on his work he wouldn't notice intruders until it was too late.

"He didn't get their faces," Remy complained. "But they look as if they could be Jean and Juste Rousseau. What do you think?" He handed the camera back to his brother and turned to look at the body one more time.

The forensic team had arrived, and the photographer was busy getting shots of Carson from every angle. The sunlight came in through the cypress trees and spilled over them. Remy crouched low, angling from one side to the next to better see the body. It was right there. Right in front of him. Frustration had him rumbling low, under his breath.

"Make certain you get some good shots of the altar for comparison," he snapped.

The photographer scowled at him, but refrained from speaking. He knew his job and was irritated that Remy might not think he did.

Remy wasn't even looking at him, instead he was staring at the body. He stood up slowly, light dawning, the pieces falling into place. He knew *exactly* what was different.

"Gage." He waited until his brother turned to face him. "It's wrong. This is all wrong."

"What is?" Gage moved closer, frowning, trying to see whatever it was his brother saw.

LeBrun, the ME, stopped what he was doing. Even the photographer paused. Remy was good at his job and usually spotted discrepancies before anyone else. He had an eye for murder and an uncanny knack of solving them.

"He doesn't do this."

"This is exactly what he does," Gage argued, frowning at Remy.

Remy shook his head. "No, Gage." He indicated the torn chest with a sweep of his hand. "This is wrong. He has a pattern, and he's broken that pattern."

"I don' understand."

"The bones. He already took those bones with the first victim. He should be takin' bones from the legs, but he didn't. He follows a pattern, and he never takes the same bones," Remy said.

LeBrun nodded his head. "That held true four years ago. But maybe he doesn't always do that."

Remy shook his head. "I studied every murder he's committed that I could find over the years. He always kills four victims and he takes the bones in a specific order. He's never deviated."

"A copycat?" Gage ventured.

LeBrun huffed out his breath. "His technique can't be copied, and this is the same man who carved up the others. I would never mistake his work."

Remy nodded. "So there's definitely a reason for the change. That's twice he's deviated from his usual ritual. Cooper was personal, and now he changed his bone pattern. He's too methodical and ice-cold to have panicked and done something different. Taking the same bones from victim three as he did from victim one was as deliberate as keeping Cooper alive as long as possible."

"There's no sign of panic that I can see," LeBrun said. "This man could be a brain surgeon, operate in the middle of a war zone and never break a sweat."

Remy turned his head to look at LeBrun. "He's strong as hell, Doc. I'm beginnin' to think he's one of Jean and Juste's demons."

"Don' say that out loud," Gage advised. "Half my people believe in the Rougarou and the other half believe in voodoo. We're a superstitious lot, Remy, and this case is just adding to the growing legends around here."

Remy turned to the medical examiner. "I'd like to rule out the Rousseau brothers if possible. The tracks indicate only one man came here with Carson, but let's be certain. We'll be picking up Butterfield and Durang as soon as the warrants come through. If we're really lucky the surgical instruments will be in one of their vehicles. I'd like to see them explain that away."

He indicated the body. "Doc, if there's anything different about the bone harvestin', any reason that you can see from comparing Carson's bones to Pete's bones that might give us a reason why he took the same ones, call me right away."

"Will do," LeBrun agreed. "But, Remy, Pete was as healthy as a horse. His bones were dense and strong, and as far as I can tell, so are this man's."

Remy sighed. "Gage, I'm heading into town. I'll want those pictures developed as quickly as possible."

"We're on it," Gage said.

"I know the answer is here. I just can't grab hold of it," Remy said with a sigh.

"Durang is looking good," Gage said. "He's got a long history of particularly brutal violence. He's certainly capable."

Remy shrugged. "I wish I believed that, Gage. I want it to be Durang, I really do, but my gut is tellin' me I'm missin' something. Durang was in prison when a few of the murders took place, and we couldn't find any evidence of a passport for him. He's a two-time felon, so chances are slim he went overseas."

"Butterfield then," Gage said.

"Maybe. But I don't think he's capable of this. He'd pay someone to do it, but he'd never get his hands dirty. My guess is, he wanted Durang to kill Bijou for insurance money and Durang wanted his own insurance. He probably insisted Butterfield get the tools and other things he needed so he would be implicated if he got caught. Durang might not be terribly smart, but he's cunning. He isn't going to take the fall for Butterfield."

"I hope you're wrong too," Gage said.

Remy could tell by Gage's tone that he thought Remy was probably right in his conclusions—he usually was. Remy took a last look at the carcass that had once been Bob Carson. He didn't want to ever come across another body like Carson's. This had to be the last one. He had to figure it out. A part of him hoped Arnaud could shed some light on things—maybe he'd seen the Rousseau brothers take Carson prisoner, but somehow he knew it wasn't the brothers. Jean and Juste were violent, and they even were murderers, but they hadn't killed Morgan, Cooper or Carson—he was certain of it.

He drove through the narrow roads leading back to New Orleans, his brain trying to work out the puzzle. He had the pieces. Why didn't they fit? By now he should have figured it out and if he didn't, more people were going to die. He pulled the car over to the side of the road, and sat there for a long time.

He needed to see Bijou. Just for a moment. Maybe it was silly, but she was warm and alive and a bright light in a world of madness. He'd never realized just how dark his world was until he'd found her. He'd been driven to right the wrongs, maybe stemming from that one moment when he'd failed a child and he'd vowed it would never happen again. Funny how his world revolved around Bijou.

He pulled out his cell phone and texted her, asking where she was. Her answer surprised him. She and Saria had gone to Bodrie's estate. She was intelligent enough to mention that Dash had accompanied them, so not to worry.

His grip tightened on the steering wheel, and he sat for a moment, forcing his temper under control. Just because the Rousseau brothers were out of the picture didn't mean that she was out of danger—not until he had Rob Butterfield and Jason Durang locked up. He picked up his radio and inquired on their whereabouts. To his consternation, neither man had been at their hotel when the police had gone looking and neither car had been spotted yet.

He immediately got back on the road, driving fast, using his siren occasionally to move cars in front of him out of the way. Bodrie's estate was on the other side of the city of New Orleans. He sent Dash a message to be on the alert. He resisted the urge to send officers to the mansion to guard her. He didn't want to overreact, but he did drive faster than was probably wise.

The double ornate gates were wide open, and he swept through, going up the long winding drive to the huge house. The grounds were well kept. Bijou obviously employed a staff that took care of the estate. Just walking up to the door made him feel a little sick to his stomach. He couldn't imagine what Bijou felt. He understood why she would prefer to burn the entire building down.

He didn't bother to knock. It was Bijou's house now, and whoever she employed would just have to learn fast that he was part of her life. He entered the high-ceilinged foyer with its white gleaming marble floors. The house was quiet. Too quiet to suit him. He inhaled, testing the air for scents. He caught the faint scent of lavender, and his sister's comforting smell of spice and homemade bread. Dash smelled like cold medicine. More, he caught the scent of blood. Remy loosened his gun in his harness.

It was a large house, two stories, with numerous rooms. The house sprawled out lengthwise. He had only been in the

big room where her father seemed to do most of his enter-
taining. He went there first. Immediately he felt as if he'd
stepped back in time. The room was arranged exactly the
same as the last time he'd been there, back when Bijou had
been eight years old. It was as if someone kept the house as
a shrine to Bodrie.

His stomach lurched again. Everything Bodrie Breaux
represented went against everything Remy believed in. Had
the man never married and produced a child, Remy wouldn't
have cared how he lived. Even if he'd dumped Bijou onto
someone else to raise, Remy might have had a little more
respect for him, but Bodrie was too selfish. He liked the idea
of a single father struggling to raise his child alone. It played
well in the tabloids and always garnered him more attention.

He didn't want to search this empty mausoleum room by
room looking for Bijou and Saria. Eventually his nose would
take him to them, but in this instance, it was easier to use
his phone. He didn't want to spend one more moment in the
house than necessary. His leopard detested the place, prowling close to the surface, uneasy, and letting Remy know all
about it.

He texted Bijou. She didn't reply. He frowned. He had
full service. She'd replied earlier so he knew she had her
phone on her. He tried a second time to no avail. The unease
of his leopard began to take hold of him. He eased his gun
from his harness and let his leopard senses take over.

The scent of blood grew stronger when he rounded the
corner and entered a long hallway. The door closest to him
stood open and he glanced inside, weapon ready. Dash was
slumped on the ground, a pool stick inches from his hand.
Clearly he'd been playing pool and not paying the least bit
of attention to Remy's earlier warning.

Remy, heart beating fast, leaned down and felt for his
younger brother's pulse. It was there, strong and steady. His
skin was hot to the touch. Dash was running a fever. Dash
moved, started to groan, and his eyes snapped open when

Remy put a heavy hand over his mouth to keep any sound from escaping.

Dash looked mortified. Pale and mortified. Remy held a finger to his lips. Dash nodded and pushed himself into a sitting position. He gritted his teeth and touched the back of his head. His hand came away smeared with blood.

Remy leaned in close. "Where are the girls?" He kept his tone low, knowing Dash's leopard would hear him.

"They were goin' to the master bedroom to look for a box Bijou said her daddy kept in there. Said it was important to her and that's why she wanted to come. She told me to play a few games of pool. I thought she wanted privacy." Dash looked at the blood on his fingers. "I should have stayed with them, Remy. I'm sorry."

"Who hit you?"

"I never saw them. I never even heard them. My ears are stopped up and so is my nose. I have a hell of a cold. My leopard suddenly lunged toward the surface and stupid me, didn't realize he was tryin' to protect me." Shame and guilt came over his face. "I was too busy playin' the game. You know how much I love it and this table is awesome."

Remy let his leopard take over just enough to smell everything in the room. He'd been close enough to Jason Durang to catch his scent. "Never mind, Dash," he said grimly. "I know who it is."

Remy got one hand under his brother's arm and helped him up. He glanced around them. They were surrounded by Bodrie. His platinum and gold records were encased in glass and hung on all four walls.

Dash swayed but steadied himself. He pulled a gun from his boot and held it up. "I'm with you, Remy. The room was that way," he pointed down the hall to where one of two double doors had been left open.

The hall was wide, ceilings high. Priceless guitars hung on the walls. Remy knew each was worth a fortune, but because Bodrie had been the previous owner, each guitar could be sold for far more than he'd make in a year, and there were dozens of them.

Bijou might not realize it, but her staff was loyal to her. They weren't stealing and the temptation had to be great. He could also see why she'd left her father's estate alone for so long. Where did one even start sorting through things?

He inhaled. His woman was in the master bedroom and so was Saria. They were alone. The stench his leopard identified as Durang was too faint for him to still be there—but he had been. He didn't smell blood, but his pulse jumped at the thought that the two women had been close to Durang. Did they know it? They had to. Bijou hadn't chanced texting him back. He signaled Dash and his brother went to the left. He took the right. They entered Bodrie's master bedroom, guns drawn, sweeping the room carefully.

There was no one in sight. The room wasn't at all what Remy expected. There was no round, vibrating bed. No pictures of naked women. Nothing at all that indicated Bodrie Breaux was a rock legend—or even that he'd ever been in the room.

They continued to move silently through the room, signaling to one another as they approached the doors to the master bath. The room was enormous, with a step down to an indoor hot tub and a step up to the bathroom.

Dash leaned in, caught the doorknob and pulled open the door. Remy swept the room. The bathroom was bigger than the entire apartment he rented. They cleared the glass shower stall and the giant gold Jacuzzi tub as well as the toilet stall. There was no indication either woman had been in the dressing area or near the long makeup mirrors other than their scents.

Dash shook his head and pointed back toward the outer room's closet. Remy smelled lavender much stronger as he approached the closet. She was there and she wasn't moving. She'd been in the closet and she should have still been there.

A leopard's hearing and sense of smell were particularly acute. He knew Durang was still in the house, although his scent was much fainter. The intruder had gone up one of the winding, spiral marble staircases and was busy going from room to room. But where were Bijou and Saria?

Remy followed his cat's nose. The trail led straight into the wall of the closet. Dash raised an eyebrow. Remy ran his palm against the wall until he found the small button that served as an intercom. He leaned close.

"Bijou? Saria? Are you all right?"

There was a moment of startled silence. "Why wouldn't we be?" Bijou's voice was tearful. "Come in."

The wall creaked and a door sprang open. The safe room was quite large and furnished comfortably. The two women sat on the floor and next to them was a box of letters, some pictures and what appeared to be a diary. Bijou looked as if she'd been crying. Even Saria looked as if she quickly blinked back tears when they entered.

"What are you doing here?" Bijou asked.

"Lookin' for you as usual," Remy replied.

Both women caught the scent of blood at the same time. Saria came to her feet instantly, a slight frown on her face. "Dash? What happened?"

"There's an intruder in the house," Remy replied, never taking his eyes off of Bijou. "You don' seem to understand the word *danger.*"

She made a face at him. "I understand perfectly. The Rousseau brothers can't hurt us. And what intruder? Dash, did you get hurt?"

Dash looked more mortified than ever as his sister fussed over the back of his head and Bijou jumped up to look at the cut as well.

"He snuck up on me. I was so into my game I wasn't payin' attention to my leopard."

"He who?" Saria asked.

"Jason Durang," Remy said, his tone grim. "I'm really showin' restraint, Bijou. I'd like to shake you until you show good sense, if that's even possible."

"Jason Durang is in this house?" Saria asked. "We were

in the safe room, and unless the intercom is on, you can't hear anything. The room is sealed. Bijou guessed Bodrie kept her mother's things in here." She frowned again. "Who is Jason Durang, and what's he doin' in the house bashin' Dash over the head?"

"Shouldn't you be arrestin' him for trespassin'?" Bijou asked Remy, a mixture of challenge and defiance in her voice.

Remy caught her arm and pulled her to him, needing to touch her more than he wanted to admit. The relief at finding her safe overshadowed his anger at her for not being more careful—by just a little bit—he told himself.

"I wouldn't mind arrestin' you," he hissed at her. "You're goin' to give me gray hair if you keep this up. You knew Durang was still out there."

"Actually, I didn't think about it," Bijou said. "I'm sorry, Remy, I shouldn't have put Saria in danger, but I just got excited about findin' out about my mother."

"It was my suggestion," Saria admitted. "I thought the threat was over and it seemed a good time to find her mother's things. Who is Jason Durang and what does he want with Bijou?"

Remy detested that Bijou's soft little apology struck at his heart and that when she looked at him with her blue eyes his anger melted away. "Jason Durang does her manager's dirty work. In this instance, I believe they planned on killin' Bijou for the insurance money. They planned on makin' it look like the bone harvester killed her."

Saria gasped. "Are you certain?"

"We found Bob Carson's camera, and he caught Butterfield and Durang transferrin' plastic sheets and surgical tools into Durang's vehicle. There's an all-points out for them both, and what a shocker, Durang is right here, followin' Bijou." He knew he was being a bastard, trying to scare both women, but he never wanted to relive the last few minutes again.

"Wait a minute." Bijou went very still. "What do you

mean, you found Bob's camera? Remy, Bob is never apart from his camera."

Now he did feel like a real bastard. All the while he was listening for Durang to begin his descent down the stairs. The man was doing a room by room search, probably thinking the two women were hiding from him.

In spite of being angry with her, Remy put his arm around Bijou. "Bob Carson was last night's victim. He was murdered by the bone harvester in the swamp."

Bijou stared up at his face, shock in her eyes. "Carson is dead?"

Remy nodded. He ran a finger down the side of her face in a little caress, even though there was still a part of him that wanted to shake her for not playing it safe.

"And you think Jason Durang killed him? For Rob? Why would Rob want Carson dead? Half the time I think Rob informed Bob Carson where I'd be lately just so he could keep me in the tabloids."

"I think Durang meant to copy the harvester's murders in order to cover your murder. I intend to make Durang think I believe he did the other killings, but I'd be shocked if he did them," Remy admitted, telling her the truth.

Both women reacted with shocked gasps. They looked at each other and then at him.

"Remy, do you really believe my manager wanted to kill me?" Bijou asked in a low voice.

For the first time he wished he could lie to her and make it all better. She looked . . . broken. He couldn't blame her. She was in Bodrie's house, and it seemed that everyone she had ever known associated with the man was corrupt.

"I'm sorry, Blue. Yes. I do. I think he gambles and loses and he didn't want the money train to stop. When it did, he became desperate. The bone harvester comin' back to New Orleans at the same time you did provided him with an opportunity." He glanced at his watch. "Backup should be here. I told them to come in without sirens. This time when I say stay put, please do it, Bijou. Dash, you stay with them and don' think about anything else but protectin' them. If you forget what you're doing a second time, I'm goin' to beat the bloody hell out of you and you have my word on that."

"I won't, Remy," Dash assured.

"Get back inside that room and don't come out until I tell you we're all clear," Remy ordered. He didn't let go of Bijou even as he gave the orders. She looked stricken, pressing her lips together. He glanced down at her hands. She was holding a photograph up against her heart. He held out his hand. "Show me, Blue. Is that your mother?"

She nodded and turned the picture over. The woman looked just like her. She had to have been close to the same age as Bijou was now. He ran his finger gently over the photograph. "She's beautiful, Bijou, and you look just like her. I'll be back in a few minutes and I'll help you take all this back to the Inn." Because he couldn't help himself, he leaned into her and brushed a kiss across her mouth. "It's almost over, *chere*. Hang in there with me."

"I'm not going anywhere," she assured. When he turned away, she caught his arm. "Maybe you should take Dash with you."

He loved Dash, his younger, very sensitive brother. Dash was hell on wheels in a fight, but he was made for finer things. Remy wasn't about to risk him, not when he was injured.

Durang had a lot to lose and he knew he had the plastic sheets and surgical instruments in his car. Remy would use that against him, convince Durang he was going to be charged as the harvester in order to make him confess to the lesser crime of planning to murder Bijou. Remy wanted Rob Butterfield as well and he would do everything in his power to make certain Durang gave Bijou's manager up. Remy wasn't going to let the man get away with conspiracy to commit murder.

"I've got backup. This shouldn't take long." He winked at her and strode away.

He could hear Durang now, hurrying down the hall, back

toward the staircase. Remy chose his spot. Durang would have to go past him to get off the last stair. Bodrie's penchant for naked statues came in handy for concealment. He wasn't about to allow Durang to spot him until it was too late. There wasn't going to be a shootout. Remy couldn't risk losing Butterfield and Durang had to flip on Butterfield.

Jason Durang came down the stairs stealthily. He was certain Bijou was somewhere in the house. He just had to find her and he could take care of anyone getting in his way. Remy let him walk one step past him and he stepped out and shoved the muzzle of his gun hard behind Durang's ear.

"You're under arrest. Toss the gun aside and listen very carefully to your rights."

19

"I'M sorry, Remy," LeBrun said. "I have nothin' new for you. I can't see any discernible difference in Pete Morgan's bone and Bob Carson's. I can tell you there were traces of ketamine in Bob Carson's system. I found a small needle mark in his neck where he'd been injected."

Remy frowned. "We found ketamine in the Rousseau brother's stash of drugs for sale, and Carson had ketamine in his hotel room. This case just keeps getting murkier and murkier."

"Well, I'm sure you're aware some idiots use ketamine as a recreational drug. Carson might have bought the drug from the Rousseau brothers," LeBrun said.

"I thought of that. Robert said that Bob Carson was a longtime customer of the Rousseau brothers and he liked a variety of drugs, including ketamine. But he wouldn't have injected it into his neck."

"That would be dangerous," LeBrun agreed. "Injecting ketamine would be extremely dangerous. It's fast acting.

The person would be under before he could remove the needle from his arm."

"So someone else probably used the drug to render Carson unconscious so they could get him out to the swamp. Was there ketamine in Morgan's or Cooper's body?"

LeBrun scowled. "If there had been, even slight trace amounts, I would have included it in the report."

Remy had known that. "I'm sorry. I wasn't callin' your professionalism into question. I'm just back to square one. I'm squeezing Durang. I want him to give up Butterfield, but the surgical instruments weren't the ones used to carve bones out of our victims. Even the type of plastic sheeting doesn't match. So where does that leave us?"

"Back to the Rousseau brothers?"

"Maybe, but if I'm wrong, if I accept that because it's easy . . ."

LeBrun shook his head, hitting the top of Remy's desk with a flat palm. "Not because it's easy, because it fits. Everythin' points straight back to Jean and Juste Rousseau. The victims, the swamp, the drugs. You're too close to this, Remy. You think there must be more because it seems too wrapped up and tied in a bow for you. Sometimes, it really does happen like that."

Remy wanted the case to be solved. Everyone else thought it was solved—but it didn't feel right to him. "You said yourself, Doc, you didn't think there were two of them."

"No, I said one definitely carved the bones and, in my opinion, made the altar. In fact," LeBrun added, "you were very firm that the harvester and the man who made the altar were one and the same, yet the killin' itself didn't fit."

Remy couldn't deny he'd considered many times that there were two men doing the killings. "There was only one set of footprints goin' from the road to the swamp, carryin' Carson's body," he reminded. "Carson was tall and slender, but he weighed a significant amount. If there were two of them, why didn't they both carry him into the swamp where they were goin' to kill him?"

"I don't know, Remy, but I'm tired and I'm going to believe the Rousseau brothers did it and we'll get them eventually. They can't live in the swamp forever. As for me, I haven't seen my family forever and I'm goin' home. I suggest you do the same."

"Maybe you're right." Remy had no intentions of going home. He rubbed at the tension in the back of his neck. He knew the Rousseaus were dead, but his gut hadn't stopped churning and that was a very bad sign.

"Just give it a day or two, Remy," LeBrun encouraged. "Step back and think about other things. You've been goin' at this night and day for a couple of weeks and you've had to contend with other things as well. Go see your girl and don' think about murder."

Remy gave him a little salute and watched him leave. It was late. Most everyone had gone home already. He'd promised Bijou he'd meet her for dinner. He glanced at his watch. He still had a little time left to try to work things out. He wandered over to the murder board and studied the pictures of each suspect. Jean and Juste Rousseau were at the top of the list.

"If only it was that easy," he murmured aloud. "You two were building your own little kingdom. You liked gangster movies and thought you'd be the lords of New Orleans."

In their home, he'd found hundreds of DVDs, mostly mafia and gang movies. Jean and Juste definitely had aspired to build a large criminal network. They had murdered at least three women. They had forced women to have sex with them and their friends. They'd robbed and beaten the elderly. They sold drugs. There really wasn't much the brothers wouldn't do—so why didn't he think they were capable of carrying out the bone harvester's murders?

"He's ice," Remy said aloud. "Total ice. He doesn't ever flinch. There's no hesitation." He stared at the board. "You're one scary man. Who are you? You don' even break a sweat when you're carvin' them up."

"Remy?" Angelina came up behind him.

He could smell the cup of coffee she had in her hand for him. He turned toward her with a faint smile. She was in her late forties, married to another cop and had three children. He often considered her his secret weapon. She could find anything on anyone given time. She worked a computer with lightning speed and nothing ever stood between her and information.

"I found the insurance policy. It was taken out with Forbes and Regency. It's a big payoff if Bijou dies. Thirty million dollars, Remy." She sounded worried. "Definitely the kind of money someone kills for."

"You're an angel, Angelina," he said. "That gives me everything I need to break Durang. He'll give up Butterfield."

Angelina turned away from him, hesitated, and then turned back. "Remy, I've worked with you a long time. You have good instincts. If you aren't satisfied, don't listen to anyone else's conclusions." She looked up at the murder board, at the photographs of Juste and Jean Rousseau. "If your gut says it isn't them, then I'm putting my money on you. You'll find out who really did this one way or another."

"Thanks, Angelina. I appreciate the vote of confidence. Leave the report on my desk. I think I have just enough time to run over to the gallery and talk with Lefevre before I have to meet Bijou. She's comin' here. Would you mind stayin' and waiting for her? I'll only be a few minutes."

"Do you think he may have seen something that night?" Angelina asked. "He doesn't seem interested in anything but his art—which by the way is beautiful but so far above my pay grade I can only wish."

"He's actually quite observant. He pays close attention to details. Both Carson and the Rousseau brothers were poking around his studio the night Carson was murdered. It's a long shot that he saw something that could shed light on the murderer, but you never know. At this point, I'll take anything, long shot or not," Remy said. He pressed his fingertips to his temples, trying to clear the pounding headache.

He couldn't imagine that the famed—and very

obsessive—sculptor had seen anything of use, not after seeing the frantic sketches of Remy's facial features he'd been up all night drawing, but maybe he'd get lucky. Sometimes it was only luck solving a case.

"Sure, I don' mind waiting for Bijou Breaux," Angelina agreed. "I have every record she ever made. I know every song by heart. I never talk to her because I don't want to seem like one of her pushy, crazed fans, but every time I see her, I secretly scream."

He swung around, amused by Angelina, the consummate professional's confession. His eyebrow shot up and he found himself smiling. "Really? You? Scream? I don' believe you."

"In my head, Remy." She held up her hand when he looked smug, tossing her head like a schoolgirl. "But at her concerts I screamed with the best of them. Once I couldn't talk for two days afterward."

Remy burst out laughing. "You're priceless, Angelina. When she comes in, talk to her. She's actually quite shy. You'd never know it when she sings, but she really is. I'll just be a few minutes, I promise."

Remy caught up his jacket, shrugging into it as he hurried out. There was something driving him now, and that usually meant he was close to breaking a case. He should have considered talking to Lefevre right away. The artist *was* good with details and few people had his observation skills. He might have even noticed something earlier, when they were in the gallery itself.

He walked the short distance to the gallery where Lefevre had his showing. He wasn't surprised to see it had already closed, but the lights were on and he could see the artist inside, hunched over a large sketchbook. Several drafts of whatever he was working on were scattered at his feet. He looked as if he hadn't slept since the showing. In fact, Remy thought he might have been wearing the same suit.

He wasn't surprised to find the door unlocked. He knew the gallery owner would come by later to double-check that Lefevre had remembered to lock it. In the meantime, he had offered his place to the artist to work, knowing it would only make his gallery more prestigious with clients.

Remy stepped inside. Arnaud didn't even glance up. He worked furiously, concentration creating deep furrows between his eyebrows.

"Mr. Lefevre?" Remy said, hoping not to startle him.

The frowned deepened and impatience flickered across the Frenchman's face. He waved his hand toward the door without looking up. "Go away. I'm busy."

"I'm sorry to disturb you, but I was hoping you could help me with an ongoing investigation. I just need a few minutes of your time."

Arnaud's breath hissed out between his teeth. He looked up slowly, his expression exasperated. "What is it?" Even as he snapped the question, the aggravation disappeared.

Remy stepped closer. "Do you remember me? I'm Bijou's friend, Remy Boudreaux." He showed his badge just in case he'd spooked the artist. "I'm a homicide detective and we had a murder last night. Would you mind if I asked you a few questions?"

Arnaud's mood changed instantly. His gaze was riveted to Remy's face. He tossed his sketchpad aside and leapt up, a smile on his face. "Of course I remember you. Your eyes are extraordinary. I've been trying to capture that look, but it isn't right." He gestured to the many discarded drawings scattered around the floor. "I thought if I came here instead of the studio, I'd remember better and get the actual piercing intelligence and focused danger in your eyes." He sighed in frustration. "Maybe I could draw your face while we talk?" he said hopefully.

Lefevre *was* still wearing the same suit he'd had on the night before. Remy thought it should have been a little more rumpled since he'd worn it all night. Clearly he hadn't slept, but he still looked elegant. Even his hair seemed to fall naturally into place.

Remy sighed, grateful Bijou wasn't interested in Lefevre romantically. There was no competing with the wealthy, talented artist. Remy's leopard despised him on sight. If only he could get his leopard to understand Bijou wasn't at all interested in the man, maybe it would be easier to be around him.

"Sure." He glanced at his watch. "I don' have a lot of time, but I'll come back if you don' get whatever it is you're lookin' for."

Arnaud indicated a chair where the light spilled directly into Remy's face. "Sit there. Can you just look at me the way you did last night, when you first walked in?"

"I'll try," Remy said. "I'm not certain how I was lookin' at you."

"Like I was your prey. Very focused. What were you thinking about? Maybe that would help," Arnaud suggested as he collected his drawing pad and pencils. He sat across from Remy.

Remy had been thinking he was going to tear the artist limb from limb because Bijou was smiling up at him. He couldn't very well say that. "Last night there was a murder. A photographer by the name of Bob Carson. He's the same man who had been stalkin' Bijou."

"Yes, yes of course. He pushed my rented car into the bayou. I've got my lawyers dealing with that," Arnaud said dismissively. "Turn your head a little to the right."

Remy complied. "He was here at the gallery last night for your showing. He was taking a lot of photographs of the event as well as everyone who was here."

"Yes, I remember," Arnaud agreed, his voice almost dreamy, as if already Remy was losing him to his art. His attention seemed to be drifting away.

Remy grit his teeth. His brothers would be howling over him sitting there like an idiot while Arnaud Lefevre drew his portrait, or more specifically—his eyes.

"Did you see anything unusual in the gallery that night? Anyone who might have been watchin' Bob Carson? Did he talk to anyone?"

Arnaud scowled darkly, tore off the sheet of paper he'd been working on and flung it on the floor. He began again. "I noticed him talking to Bijou's manager. Butterfield slipped him something. But, that wasn't necessarily out of the ordinary."

Arnaud continued to draw, glancing up at Remy to look at his face and eyes, his mind on his work, rather than Remy's questions.

"Not out of the ordinary?" Remy prompted, his teeth snapping together. He detested sitting there like an idiot. His leopard snarled and raged, making it difficult to stay even-tempered. He'd known Arnaud would be difficult if he was working. He'd seen Bijou practically have to babysit him.

"Yes, they often had clandestine meetings no one was supposed to see and Butterfield always gave something to Carson. Really, it was quite childish the way they acted."

Butterfield probably had been paying Bob Carson to keep feeding the tabloids. He had no way of knowing Carson would have done it anyway.

"After you went back to the studio to work, were you aware Carson followed you?"

That got the Frenchman's attention for all of two seconds. Or maybe he just scowled and looked up because Remy wasn't giving him the focused stare he wanted to draw so badly.

"No. Why would he do that? All I did was work last night. All night. A complete waste of time." Arnaud sighed in frustration.

"He was writing an article about Bijou's love triangle."

"She doesn't have a love triangle," Arnaud said. "Turn your head a little more. Stop. Hold it right there. I think that's it." He tore off another piece of paper and began again.

"He meant you, Bijou and me," Remy said. "You didn't see him lurking around? Or anyone following him, maybe across the street?"

For the first time Arnaud lowered his pencil and really

looked at Remy. Remy was struck by the fact that he seemed to notice Remy as more than a pair of cat's eyes he was trying to draw.

"That's completely absurd."

"Of course it is, but Carson specialized in seedy headlines. He took photographs of your work with a zoom lens and was going to publish it in a tabloid, stating you were in love with me and Bijou was in love with both of us."

"He can't do a thing like that. Publishing a sketch of mine that isn't right, that I haven't finished, would be unthinkable," Arnaud protested. "I have a reputation, but more than that, I only show my best work—work I'm proud of. Those sketches last night were all wrong."

"He's dead, Arnaud," Remy said as gently as he could through gritted teeth. "He won't be publishing photographs anymore. I'm looking for the man or men who may have abducted him, took him out to the swamp and then murdered him."

"At least he's giving back to the planet and doing something constructive rather than hurting people like Bijou," Arnaud said pragmatically. "He wasn't a very good man, was he?"

Remy sighed. "I suppose not. But even men who aren't worth much need someone to stand for them."

"This isn't working. Let's try something else," Arnaud said, ignoring, or not hearing Remy's comment. "Will you allow me to put your head in the position I need you to be in?"

"I don't have very much more time," Remy said, glancing at his watch again.

"Just give me a couple more minutes," Arnaud pleaded. "I know I can do this." He jumped up, but it wasn't jumping so much as gliding. He was very graceful, a man who under any circumstances, even when he was at his most frustrated, still seemed elegant.

He hurried around Remy and caught his chin, his touch almost gentle as he turned his head. The moment Arnaud put his fingers against Remy's skin, Remy's leopard raked and snarled, forcing Remy to breathe deep to keep control. He glanced down at the floor, at Arnaud's beautifully polished immaculate dress shoes. Bits of grass and mud stuck, not to the shoes, but to one hem of his trousers. He registered the information and alarm spread. As he started to turn to face the threat, Remy felt a sting in his neck.

His leopard tried to protect him, leaping for the surface, a wave of fur moving under his skin, but the ketamine was fast acting on both of them.

BIJOU stood outside the Inn with Saria, admiring the full moon. "It sure is beautiful here, Saria. What a wonderful weddin' gift Miss Pauline gave you. The location couldn't be more perfect."

"Especially for a leopard," Saria agreed. "Miss Pauline was always in love with Amos Jeanmard. When his wife died, he married Miss Pauline, and she gave me the Inn."

"I remember him. We used to have to hide from him when we were sneakin' into the swamp at night."

"He's leopard. He was leader of the lair, but he claimed he got old and tired. Miss Pauline's leopard never emerged and he didn't marry her when they were young because he thought it would be best for the lair if only leopards mated. I think the real reason he gave up leadership was so he felt he was free to marry Miss Pauline."

Bijou leaned against Saria's car. Hers was going to need a lot of work before she could drive it—if she could make herself get into it after the things Carson had done to it. "If my leopard hadn't emerged, do you think Remy would have walked away?"

Saria frowned at her. "I always forget you lack self-confidence, which is insane when it comes to my brother. He's head over heels for you. Believe me, I've never seen him act like such a goofball."

"Remy is never a goofball," Bijou said. She looked up at

the sky again, at the stars. "I'd forgotten how to be happy until I came back here. Which is rather awful to say when all these murders are going on. I don' know how Remy does it every day."

"He's good at his job and he's passionate about it. Remy lives life to the fullest. Now that he has you, I won't worry so much about him," Saria said. "He can be so serious, and that leopard of his is so difficult."

"Are you afraid of your leopard?" Bijou asked, crossing her arms across her chest. "Because I'll admit, I find the entire idea of being a shifter very scary. What if I can't control her when she's out?"

"I felt that way at first as well," Saria admitted. "You have Remy, and he'll guide you through it. There are seven main families that live in the swamps and bayous that date back to the first settlers. They did intermarry with others who weren't leopard, but if they have one of the seven last names, you can pretty much bet, they're one of us. The thing is, Bijou, we're a small community so we're intensely loyal to one another. We have to be."

"Like Robert?"

"I don' know what happened to Robert. He was such a sweet boy when he was younger. Drake is goin' to send him to Borneo to some friends of his. It's that, or he has to follow up with his challenge for leadership and he won't survive. Drake is givin' him a chance, but if Robert refuses to take it, our world can be quite violent, but it has to be." Saria studied Bijou's face.

"I know you all grew up with Robert, but the things he did, the people who were hurt and he could have stopped it, don' you think he should at least spend time in jail?"

"A leopard can't be locked up for long, Bijou," Saria explained.

"Still, it feels like everyone else gets punished, but he's goin' to be vacationing in Borneo. How is that teaching him a lesson?"

"Drake is from Borneo," Saria said. "The men there rescue victims of kidnappers. It's dangerous and hard work. We live in civilization here. They live in the rain forest. They won't tolerate mistakes. Punishments there are brutal and fast. Robert isn't going on any picnic. He'll either grow up and become a decent man, or won't survive."

Bijou shook her head. "I don' know how you accepted all this so easily, Saria. It's a real struggle for me. Sometimes I think it's all a dream, or maybe I've gone a little insane."

"But you are a shifter, Bijou and you belong in our world. Do you understand? Because you can't run from who you are."

"Your brothers think I'm goin' to get bored or scared and leave here, don't they?" Bijou asked.

"I don't know what they think. I know better," Saria said. "We're your family. You never had one, and you always wanted one. I think you'll be more loyal and more protective than anyone else." She laughed softly. "With the exception of Remy. No one can be more protective than my big brother."

Bijou glanced at her watch. "Speaking of, if I don' leave soon, I'll be late for our dinner. He had something important he wanted to talk to me about."

"I should have known you were goin' somewhere with him. You look . . . radiant."

Bijou flashed a smile at Saria. "I do rather like that man."

"I would never have guessed. I suppose Remy's locked up just about everyone he can that he thinks might be a threat to you, so it must be safe enough."

"That's what he said. I'm meetin' him at the station house. We'll probably be home early though. He needs to get to bed." Bijou found herself blushing when Saria burst out laughing.

Saria sobered. "You know, Bijou, Remy's always going to be a cop."

"I know. But he'll be my cop."

Saria touched her teeth to her bottom lip. "A lot of women start out thinking it's cool to be with a cop, but the reality of that world gets to them after a while. Do you think you can handle it long term? Remy is very good at what he does and, although if you really were upset I think he'd stop, he wouldn't be happy."

"I'm proud of who he is, Saria, and what he does. I'm going to make a success of the club and make certain he can be just as proud of me." Her eyes met Saria's. "Your brother really is safe with me."

Saria's answering smile was serene. "I know that, I just wanted to make certain you knew it as well. Have fun tonight, although," she added mischievously, "whenever my big brother wanted to talk to me about somethin', I was usually in trouble."

Laughing, Bijou hurried to the car with a wave of her hand. Saria and her brothers definitely enjoyed teasing one another and they already had begun to include her in the warmth of their circle. She had come home looking for her white knight and she'd found him. Remy was everything she remembered and more.

She would never forget his face, the way he yanked her out of the hotel room and shook the living daylights out of her. He'd cared. He'd been alarmed. That had been the moment she realized much more would have gone on in that room than her simply overdosing. She saw it in his eyes. In the expression on his face. He'd been horrified and he'd been angry. She would never forget his eyes as long as she lived.

Everything about Remy was beautiful to her, even his famous temper. He would always be a cop, but he would be her cop and she knew she could live with that. She had a home and a family and Remy had given both to her. There was no way to describe to someone else how much she loved him. The intensity of her emotions when she was around him sometimes overwhelmed her.

She drove carefully in Saria's car. She loved fast cars and often went to racetracks and drove. She'd never mentioned that little secret to Remy, or the fact that she owned more than one high performance car. He'd never asked her much about her life and he was in for a few surprises. She did like to live simply, but that didn't mean she didn't like nice things—or really fast cars.

Laughing at the thought of his pained expression when she told him, she pulled up to the police station. At night it looked different. Somber. Even haunted. During the day people were in and out, but at night there was only a single valiant light over the door and the place appeared to be deserted.

As she walked up the stairs to the station door, she glanced around her. Night had closed in completely and fog had drifted in. Lights from street and stores appeared dull yellow halos, unable to penetrate the gathering fog. She shivered and rubbed her arms. That other inside of her was restless and she could tell the female leopard's mood was affecting her as well. She told herself she was too imaginative and the fog and deserted streets were making her edgy.

Much more sober, she walked through the station, heading back toward Remy's office. There were only a couple of people working and they looked up and waved. She lifted a hand as she went through to the homicide bull pen. Remy didn't appear to be in his office. She glanced at her watch. She was a little late. Had he left her? Forgot? That wasn't his style.

Her mouth felt dry and her heart beat too fast. The other pushed at her, wanting her freedom. Bijou was too new in the ways of leopard to know what to do to settle her down. She took several deep breaths and prayed Remy would hurry up.

A woman came around the corner, both hands wrapped around a steaming cup of coffee. She smiled at Bijou. "Remy asked me to tell you he stepped out for a couple of minutes. He'll be right back. He's just down the street at the gallery. I'm Angelina, the computer nerd."

Bijou smiled at her, relief flooding. Remy wouldn't be gone long, and he'd know what to do. "I'm Bijou Breaux."

"Remy's woman," Angelina said. "You've made him very happy."

Bijou liked Angelina immediately. "I hope so. He certainly makes me happy."

"Would you like a cup of coffee while you wait?" Angelina asked.

"That would be lovely," Bijou said.

She wandered around the room, looking at the desks and computers, marveling at how the men and women working there solved murders and various other crimes. Her path took her nearly straight to the murder board. She tried not to look, but it was impossible not to stare at the horrendous pictures of a man brutally murdered.

"You shouldn't look at that," Angelina said. "It will give you nightmares."

"It's like the train wreck you can't stop watching, isn't it?" Bijou asked as she took the coffee. Her gaze went back to the board. "It's almost mesmerizing. Who could do such things to another human being?"

"Sadly, Bijou, working here, I've learned human beings can be very cruel to one another. I stopped being shocked many years ago—until this killer came along."

Bijou studied the altar. It was so bizarre. "Is that really a bowl of blood and a human hand? His heart? This looks like something from a horror movie, not real life . . ." She trailed off, peering closer.

Her breath rushed out of her lungs. Her hands went numb. The coffee mug crashed to the floor. "Angelina," she said without turning around. "Where did you say Remy went?"

"To the gallery. Are you all right?"

"No. No, I'm not all right. Call everyone. Call them right now and send them to the gallery." She ripped her phone from her purse and took off running, hitting the only other number she had on speed dial besides Remy.

Saria answered almost immediately. Bijou burst out of the station house. "Remy's in trouble, Saria. Send Gage and everyone else to the gallery just down from his station. He's there now."

She yelled into the phone as she tried to run down the

street toward the gallery. Her high heels slowed her down so she kicked them off and ran in her stockings.

"What do you mean?"

"The stone. In the altar. It was Arnaud's. Remy went there to talk to him. I may be crazy but that stone is unmistakable." She was breathing too hard to continue talking so she just ran, her heart in her throat.

Her leopard had been trying to warn her something was wrong, but she hadn't yet gotten used to trusting her other side. There was no doubt in her mind Remy was in trouble. Everything in her screamed that he needed her. Every hair in her body stood up. Goose bumps ran up and down her arms.

"Gage says wait for help," Saria screamed into the phone.

She'd forgotten to end the call. She wasn't waiting. Was Gage crazy? Maybe he didn't believe her, but it all fell into place for her. All the clues that had been right in front of her.

Arnaud was completely disconnected from people. He didn't view them as human beings. Even his sculpture was about life-forms, not human beings. He was enormously strong from all the climbing he did over the years. He traveled all over the world and he went to most of her concerts. He had tremendous skill with cutting tools.

Remy wondered why the harvester had taken the same set of bones. Clearly he'd lost the first set. They must have been in the SUV that had gone into the bayou. Arnaud was merely replacing what he'd lost. He'd actually said to her that there was nothing in the vehicle that couldn't be replaced. He'd said he was behind on his timetable. And his sculpture . . . Oh, God, why hadn't she noticed? Why hadn't it registered? All those faces. His victims giving back.

"Please, please, please," she chanted. "Don' let me be too late."

She wrenched the door to the gallery open and ran inside without hesitation. Skidding to a halt, she could see the light coming from under the door to the back room. Heart pounding, she walked barefoot through the gallery to the door.

Her mouth was dry. Her leopard was raging. Her heart felt wild and out of control.

Bijou took a deep breath and opened the door. Arnaud was standing over Remy's body, staring down at his face with a look very close to love. Remy was lying motionless on the long table. Beside him was a spread-open leather pouch. The light shining down into Remy's face also illuminated the array of cutting tools Arnaud had spread out beside the detective.

"Arnaud?" she called out to the artist.

He looked up at her and smiled. "He's perfect, Bijou. So perfect."

"Yes, he is." She stepped closer, desperate to see if Remy was still alive. "We're supposed to go to dinner tonight. He's late."

"We're working," Arnaud told her. "I tried sketching his eyes, but I couldn't re-create that look I wanted. It was there the other night, and then it was gone."

"Yes. I remember." Bijou poured enthusiasm into her voice. She still clutched the cell phone, the line open between her and Saria. She stepped closer. She was about halfway to the table. "He was jealous of you. He looked like a hunter."

Arnaud's head jerked up. "That's it. That's it exactly, Bijou. You always get it. A large jungle cat about to leap on his prey." He frowned. "You can't stay. I have work to do."

"I know you do." She used her most soothing voice, edging closer still. "Why isn't Remy moving? He looks like he's asleep, but his eyes are open."

Arnaud shrugged. "Just a little ketamine. He can't move. He has to stay still, but I need his eyes to get that penetrating look."

"He's alive?"

"Of course." He waved her away. "I really need to work, Bijou."

"I just have to ask about the bones."

"The bones?" he echoed, already distracted. He moved

closer to the table, to the instruments spread out before him. His hand was inches away from a cutting tool.

"Yes. You took bones and some of them were lost in the SUV when Bob Carson pushed it into the bayou. What was so important about the bones? I know you needed to replace them."

Her heart beat so hard she was terrified Arnaud could hear. She was up against the table now, right next to Remy's head. His eyes shifted toward her. Those beautiful green eyes, filled with intelligence and awareness.

She reached for her leopard, bringing her close to the surface just in case. Breathing deep to keep from shifting, she laid one hand on Remy's chest, right over his heart. Protective. She was in position now and felt a little calmer.

"I use them for my work." He sounded impatient. Dismissive. She'd heard that tone many times and had dutifully taken her cue, slipping out of his studio and leaving him to get on with his creations.

"In what way?" Where were the police? She'd told Angelina to call everyone. She expected even the bomb squad to show up. How much time had passed? She knew Arnaud better than anyone. When it came to his work, he wouldn't be distracted for too long.

Bijou planned out every move in her mind. Exactly what she would do if Arnaud picked up a cutting tool. Remy tried to tell her with his eyes to get out, but she would never leave him. She smiled at Arnaud and insisted he answer. "I need to know, Arnaud."

He sighed. "I dry the bones, grind them up into a fine powder and use them as part of the sculptures for texture. The bones bring my work to life."

Bijou could see that he wanted her gone. She was losing him to his art. "What about the altar? What's important about the altar?"

"I saw one in Haiti but it wasn't perfect. It was beautiful, but not perfect. I wanted to perfect it, so I read about them and signed my work. It was my signature. How could you

not recognize my signature? Now go. I have work to do."
He waved her away and then, as always, seemed to forget
she existed.

He reached for a wicked-looking, razor-sharp implement,
and Bijou leapt over the table, using the spring action of her
leopard. She hit Arnaud full in the chest, knocking him
backward and down to the floor, landing on top of him, one
hand pinning down the hand holding the knife.

"Bijou." Arnaud looked up at her, surprised. He didn't
struggle. Didn't attempt to get away. He was enormously
strong, but he didn't even tense up. "Your eyes are like a
cat's, like his. They glow and change color. But you've got
that look. The look of the hunter."

Behind her she heard movement. "I am a hunter, Arnaud," she whispered. "So is Remy. Only you saw that in us."

"We've got him now," Gage said. "Move away from him.
The ambulance is here as well for Remy, Bijou. Just back
away."

"Give me the knife, Arnaud," she said as gently as possible. "Don' hurt him. He doesn't understand what he's
done." She glanced back at Gage in warning.

"Bijou, back off," Gage ordered.

Arnaud put the knife in her upturned palm. His fingers
stroked her wrist. "I understand, Bijou. It just doesn't matter
the way you all think it does."

Gage reached down and pulled Bijou to her feet. She
looked around her at the roomful of policemen, all with
guns drawn. Arnaud didn't even struggle. He actually smiled
at her. Calm. Serene. Forgiving.

Tears running down her face, she caught at Remy's limp
hand and brought it to her heart as they waited for the police
to give the okay to the paramedics. His green eyes locked
with hers and she felt herself tumble into him. Right where
she belonged.

"Don' look so sappy," Gage warned in a whisper. "He's
goin' to have *lots* to say to you about this when he can talk
again."

20

THE wedding was supposed to be small and simple. Bijou realized Cajuns just didn't work that way. Not the Cajuns who lived along the swamps and had big noisy families and could shift into leopards. At least there were no reporters, although picture taking was at an all-time high.

Remy swept her into his arms and they floated around the dance floor, surrounded by laughter and the sound of ice cubes tinkling in glasses. She stared up at his face. *Remy.* There never had been anyone else, and there never could be.

"You know this doesn't change anything," Remy said suddenly, bending his head to kiss her fiercely. Possessively. Something he did often since he was out of the hospital.

She kissed him back just as fiercely, uncaring they were surrounded by his brothers and she'd be teased something terrible the moment they could pounce. When he lifted his head she did a little eyelash batting and tried for innocent and puzzled. "Do you mean we're not really married? I don' understand."

"I *told* you to get out of there." His eyes went glacier blue, always a bad sign. "You could have been killed. I know you heard me. Maybe not out loud, but you knew I wanted you out of there, didn't you?"

"Yes," she admitted complacently. She snuggled closer to him.

"Gage told you to stay the hell out of there, to wait for backup, didn't he?" Remy insisted. "And you heard him."

She looked up at him. Met his beautiful cat's eyes. "Yes, I did." Totally unrepentant.

"And you ignored all of us."

She smiled at him. "Of course. Did you really think I'd leave you with him? He's a genius, an amazing creative artist, but he's totally insane. The FBI is taking over from here. They'll put him in a hospital for the criminally insane."

"Bijou, you didn't even have a weapon. Not even a gun."

"He would have cut out your eyes just to try to capture a way to reproduce them. Or maybe he would have tortured you to try to get you to look like the hunter again. Whatever he planned, Remy, I wasn't about to leave you there alone with him."

"You took a hell of a chance. He could have killed you."

Bijou wasn't going to back down or apologize, or even give him reassurances that it would never happen again. She loved Remy. He was hers. Her family. She would protect him just as fiercely as he protected everyone around them. She realized how difficult it must have been for a man like him—a man of action—an alpha leopard—to lie helpless and see his mate put herself in harm's way for him. But he had to understand and accept who she was.

"I'm probably the only person in the world who was safe from him. He saw me as a person, as real. Not one of his life-forms."

"That's not the point."

"No, it isn't. Even if I knew he'd try to kill me, I would have gone in after you and I would have done the exact same thing. Stall. Get into a position to attack him if he made a move against you, and I would have done it."

He huffed out his breath. "You're in so much trouble. The minute I get you alone."

She laughed softly, happily. "I've been in trouble every night since you got out of the hospital. Your . . . um . . . punishment is kind of sexy."

Immediately she felt his reaction. His body moved more tightly against hers, his thick hard length pressing into her through their clothing. He groaned softly. "Don' say sexy. We have to get through the celebration and be civilized for a little while here."

"You brought it up."

He bent his head to her exposed neck. Her hair was up in an intricate do that made her look more elegant and very much the lady, out of his class. He couldn't wait to start removing pins and letting all that soft silk fall all over his skin. His teeth teased at the vulnerable spot between her neck and shoulder.

"As a warnin', Bijou. I need to spank you a little bit harder to get your attention."

She laughed, winding her arms around his neck, trying to melt into his body. "You have my attention, Remy Boudreaux. You'll always have my attention. I'm madly, crazy in love with you."

"I know," he said complacently.

She dug her fingers into his ribs. He hunched a little, laughing.

"*I know*? That's your romantic response when I declare undying love for you?"

"Well, I do know." His eyes were even laughing.

"Your sexual skills are quite up to par so now we're goin' to have to work on your romance skills," she told him.

"Up to par? Did you just say *up to par*? Woman, you really are askin' for trouble. *Superior* skills in that department." He danced her off the dance floor and right around the corner of the building, across the sprawling lawn down to the grove of trees. "We're getting the hell out of here so I can do a little provin' of my point."

"We can't just run away from our own wedding celebration," she protested, but she didn't stop moving.

Remy tugged at her hand. "I know you're especially good at undressin', Blue. Try doin' it on the run."

His jacket and tie went floating behind him.

"Oh my God, you're serious," Bijou exclaimed, caught somewhere between laughter and shock. "I'm in a wedding dress."

His hand tore at the pins in her hair even as he dragged her through the trees toward the swamp. "And it's damned beautiful, but I personally like you with no clothes on. And so do our leopards. Come on, Blue, let's be bad."

"There're like a million buttons."

He stopped running. "Is that a no?"

"Are you kiddin' me? Undo them right now, Remy. And hurry up about it."

"I'm madly, crazy in love with you," he admitted, his hands eagerly slipping small pearly buttons out of their loops.

"I know," she said, and waited for her wedding gown to fall to the ground.